Aman ... ver
fifty novels, including the modern crime series The
Graveyard Queen. Her be...
... atmospheric, and a new take ...
... in the rural ...
... on, Texas, where she enjoys b...
watching, bike riding and the occasional margarita.

Tyler Anne Snell genuinely loves all genres of the written
word. However, she's realised that she loves books filled
with sexual tension and mysteries a little more than the
rest. Her stories have a good dose of both. Tyler lives in
Alabama with her same-named husband and their mini
"lions." When she isn't reading or writing, she's playing
video games and working on her blog, Almost There.
To follow her shenanigans, visit tylerannesnell.com

SOMEONE IS WATCHING

AMANDA STEVENS

IDENTICAL THREAT

TYLER ANNE SNELL

MIX
Paper from
responsible sources

FSC
FSC C007454

This book is produced from independently certified FSC
paper to ensure responsible forest management.

For more information visit: www.harpercollins.co.uk/green

Printed and bound in Spain
by CPI, Barcelona

MILLS & BOON

First Published in Great Britain 2020
by Mills & Boon, an imprint of HarperCollins*Publishers*
1 London Bridge Street, London, SE1 9GF

Someone is Watching © 2020 Marilyn Medlock Amann
Identical Threat © 2020 Tyler Anne Snell

ISBN: 978-0-263-28042-5

SOMEONE IS WATCHING

AMANDA STEVENS

Chapter One

For the past three nights, Ellie Brannon had been receiving staticky messages from an unknown caller on the open-line portion of her radio program. The reception was so poor she could barely make out the anonymous caller's voice, let alone the broken message. But there was something disturbing about the timing of the calls. Something unsettling about the frenetic undertone that sputtered through the white noise.

Cocooned as she was in her soundproof studio, Ellie could normally lose herself to the weird and unusual stories brought to her via her most avid listeners.

The subject matter she covered ran the gamut from paranormal activity to political conspiracies to unsolved mysteries. Unlike most talk radio hosts, Ellie refused to use a screener despite the fact that *Midnight on Echo Lake* was now broadcast on sixty stations around the country, as well as live-streamed on the popular internet radio network where she'd gotten her first big break

Adjusting the microphone arm, she glanced at the clock on the wall, noting the time as she pushed the blinking button and greeted the caller.

Static once again crackled in her headphones.

"Go ahead, Caller. You're on the air with Ellie Brannon."

The reception cleared for a moment, allowing the

woman's urgent whisper to come through loud and clear. "He's coming…"

Ellie ignored the shivers down her back as she kept her tone even. "I'm getting a lot of noise in my ear, Caller. Can you move the phone away from the radio?"

The voice faded as the interference rose to a deafening crescendo. Ellie fiddled with the slider on the audio console as she tried to filter out the annoying clatter. "Caller, are you still there?"

Nothing now but chilling silence.

Ellie's hands trembled as she adjusted the controls. She didn't know why. Strange calls were her raison d'être, but something about the persistence of this particular caller unnerved her.

Probably a prankster.

Ellie was accustomed to a fair amount of prank calls, though not as many as one might expect given the premise of her show. Most people who took the time to call in just wanted a chance to tell their story in a forum that didn't openly ridicule or pass judgment. But from time to time, some of the local teenagers dared each other to call in with outlandish stories about alien abductions just as they'd once goaded their classmates to spend the night in the Ruins, an abandoned psychiatric hospital not far from Ellie's studio. On a clear night, she could see the smokestack rising up through the pine trees as she trekked the short distance from her studio to her back deck. Sometimes, if she was feeling brave, she would walk down to the dock and sit with her feet dangling in the water as she traced the crumbling roofline and remembered.

On most nights, though, she hurried inside her house and locked the doors. Still. After all these years.

He's coming…

With a start, she realized she'd broken the golden rule

of radio—no dead air. Shrugging off the final caller, she queued up the closing music. "You've been listening to open-line Wednesday on the After Dark Network. I'm your host, Ellie Brannon, signing off from the banks of eerie Echo Lake…"

Wrapping up her callout, she turned off the mic and removed her headphones as the on-air lights winked off on her console and over the studio door.

What now?

She tried reversing the call using star-sixty-nine but nothing went through. Should she contact her brother? Tom was the Nance County sheriff. If someone was in trouble, he needed to know. But the call could have come from any part of the country. Or even out of the country. It was probably nothing more than a prank call, anyway. If someone were really in trouble, why not notify the authorities instead of calling in every night to a syndicated radio show?

Go home. Have a glass of wine, listen to some music and relax. Maybe take a long bath to unwind.

Sound advice, yet she lingered, checking the log to match the time the call had come in to the previous two nights. A screener would have required a name and location before putting the call through to Ellie, but she had nothing more to go on than *Unknown Caller*.

Locking everything down for the night, she left the studio and hurried along the path to her house. The moon hung low over the lake, silvering the water and casting long shadows along the bank. The eerie wail of a loon sent another tingle down her spine. At least it wasn't the scream of a peacock, though she was used to that screech by now. Her nearest neighbor had died some time back, leaving Ellie to care for the peafowl that roosted on her property.

She was only a few feet away from her back steps when

the wail segued into a tremolo, the maniacal laughing sound of a loon sensing danger. Ellie turned to sweep the water. The surface was calm and the air still, but she imagined she could hear the low grumble of an outboard motor somewhere in the distance. The bullfrogs and crickets had long since gone silent. The predators owned the night.

What a creepy thought.

She'd allowed herself to get caught up in the spookiness of her surroundings and those staticky phone calls and now she felt the *thump, thump, thump* of an accelerated heartbeat, the cold sweat and tightened chest of paralyzing fear. She hadn't suffered a panic attack in years, but she recognized the signs. The old defensive exercises came back to her automatically. *Take deep breaths. Find a focal point. Picture your happy place.*

The techniques worked if she allowed them to, but her instinct at the moment was to rush headlong for the house. She knew better. A full-blown episode could debilitate her for hours. Or she might stumble and fall on the uneven terrain in her freak-out. Better that she take the time to ward off that dark visitor.

Drawing in slow measured breaths, she found a distant spot on the lake where moonlight gleamed down through the cypress branches, creating delicate twinkles on the surface, like the dance of a thousand fairies. Ellie pictured herself in a boat, trailing her fingers through that cool shimmering water. Drifting, just drifting…

After a few moments, her heartbeat slowed and she turned back to the path, forcing herself to take her time. There was nothing to be afraid of in the woods. How long had she lived out here alone? Five years? Or was it six now? Despite the recent spike in violent crime in Nance County, she'd been perfectly safe in her bungalow. Nothing truly scary had happened to her since—

A twig snapped behind her and she whirled, peering into the woods even as she chided herself for an overactive imagination. Had a few prank calls really put her this much on edge?

He's coming...

Thump, thump, thump went her heart.

Focus on the shimmers...

Taking another deep breath, she turned back to the house, using the solar lights that lined the pathway to guide her to the deck steps. She went up quickly and didn't linger outside to enjoy the night air. Letting herself in the back door, she turned the deadbolt and quickly reached for the light switch, leaning against the wall in relief as illumination flooded her tidy kitchen. She concentrated on her breathing for several more minutes until the tightness in her chest eased and she felt steady on her feet.

Opening a bottle of wine, she took a glass with her upstairs where she settled for a hot shower rather than a long bath. Shrugging into her favorite robe, she went back downstairs to replenish her drink, carrying both stemware and bottle into her cozy den where she curled up on the sectional to watch late-night TV.

She dozed. Sometime later a loud noise awakened her. She thought she was dreaming at first. Even lying with her eyes wide open, she wasn't certain the banging on her front door was real.

Her movements were sluggish as she sat up and glanced around the room, eerily illuminated by the flickering TV. She switched off the flat screen with the remote, wondering if the sound had come from the infomercial that had taken over the airwaves since she fell asleep. Reaching for her phone, she checked the time. Then she got up, still lethargic, still mostly unconcerned until the doorbell rang in quick staccato bursts that startled her fully awake.

She bolted upright on a gasp, realizing that the pounding on her door, the flickering TV and the infomercial had all been incorporated into her dream.

She wasn't dreaming now.

Rising for real this time, she pulled her robe around her as she moved to the front window to glance out. The moon was still up, unnaturally brilliant as its light glowed over the pine forest. She could see all the way down her driveway to the main road. No parked cars. No lurking shadows. She checked the back door, letting her gaze move across the deck and slowly down the steps to the dock. Despite the full moon, the shadows were deep along the bank. A mild breeze stirred the Spanish moss that hung in heavy layers at the water's edge.

Retracing her steps through the house, Ellie removed a key from a carved box on the console table in the foyer. She held it in her palm for a moment before unlocking the drawer and removing the small pistol she kept there for protection. She had another like it in her nightstand drawer upstairs.

Her late father had been the Nance County sheriff for nearly thirty years. He'd made certain that she and her brother knew how to respect and handle weapons from an early age, and after the disappearances, he'd insisted that Ellie learn how to protect herself.

If she'd settled down in a more populated area, she doubted she would have wanted a gun in the house. Living alone on Echo Lake was a different matter. Out here, she was miles from town, miles from help. A stone's throw from the place where her friends had been taken and where she'd been left for dead. Her location was by design, of course. The result of a promise she'd long ago made to herself. *Stare down the monster or you'll never be free of him.*

Keeping the pistol at her side, she peered through the

sidelight. The motion detector flood on her front porch had come on. She had a clear view of the steps and the yard. No one was out there now, but the light had recently been activated. Raccoons, possums and stray cats were the usual culprits, but an animal hadn't rung her doorbell.

Another prank? A harmless game of Ring and Run?

It wouldn't be the first time. The subject matter of her radio program invited mockery. Some of the local teenagers had started hanging out at the Ruins again. She'd seen the bobble of their flashlights along the bank lately, had heard the whoops of their laughter as she sat out on the dock. She tried not to think harshly of their mischief. She'd been a teenager once, susceptible to peer pressure and the tug of her own curiosity.

There'd been a blood moon on the night she and her friends had ventured into the Ruins, but she wouldn't think about that right now. She wouldn't dwell on the creaking floorboards that should have been a warning or the gleam of eyes that had watched from the shadows. She wouldn't dwell on the lost memories of that night, the survivor's guilt that still dogged her after all these years or the violent images that came to her in dreams from time to time.

She wouldn't dwell on any of that, even though all of it had brought her back to Echo Lake.

She kept watch at the window for the longest time. Nothing seemed amiss. Whoever had been at her front door was either long gone or watched from the bushes to see how she reacted. Maybe if she went outside and waved her gun about, they'd turn tail and run. Might think twice about their next little game of Ring and Run.

Of course, she would never behave in such a reckless manner. She would never knowingly terrorize anyone over a silly prank.

Locking the gun back in the drawer, she returned the

key to the box and told herself to turn in. Forget about pranks. Forget about those disturbing calls. *Just get some rest. Everything will be fine in the morning.*

The good news was, she'd managed to fend off a panic attack and she could take comfort in knowing she was stronger for it.

Even so, sleep was a long time coming. When she finally dozed off, images of a demonic face flickered across her subconscious like the strobe of an unwatched TV.

SAM REECE COULDN'T sleep. He sat out on the balcony of his Dallas townhome and watched the shimmer of moonlight on the surface of the landscaped pond that curved around the gated community. The streets were empty at this hour, the neighborhood almost preternaturally silent. Earlier, he'd spotted a young couple out walking their dog, but they'd long since scurried home.

An odd restiveness plagued him, though he had no idea why. He liked it here well enough, having settled in a quaint area of town halfway between the hustle and bustle of downtown and One Justice Way where he worked. Maybe the neighborhood was a little too laid-back at times, but at thirty-seven, he no longer felt the need to be in the mix. The proximity of bars and restaurants had become less important to him than quiet neighbors.

There'd been a time not so long ago when he never would have imagined himself in such a place. Never would have considered a voluntary reassignment to any field office—let alone Dallas—after spending so many years in DC. Maybe he was going through some sort of pre-midlife crisis, feeling the pull of his roots more strongly than the soar of his wings. He'd grown up in northeast Texas and had cut his teeth in the Tyler satellite office after Quantico. Eventually, he'd been transferred to the Dallas field office and from there to FBI headquarters where he'd spent the past ten years as a member and then leader of one of the first Child Abduction Rapid Deployment teams in the country.

It had been an exciting, fast-paced life, grueling in some ways, but Sam had always thrived on chaos and clutter. He lived for new challenges and liked nothing more than the exhilaration of a complicated case. Yet here he was back on his old stomping grounds.

He reminded himself that Dallas was hardly a demotion. The field office was one of the busiest in the country with no shortage of stimulating cases. But in all honesty, he hadn't come back because of boredom or even to be close to his family. He'd come back because his first case still haunted him.

On the night of a blood moon, three teenagers in Belle Pointe, Texas, had entered the ruins of an abandoned psychiatric hospital. One of the girls had been found unconscious the next morning at the edge of the lake. Another girl had been spotted a few weeks later wandering along the side of a country road in a fugue state. The third girl, Riley Cavanaugh, had never been seen or heard from again.

In the days and weeks following her disappearance, the local authorities had combed the countryside and interviewed dozens if not hundreds of witnesses. In desperation, they'd finally requested help from the Bureau. Sam, fresh out of Quantico with a savior complex the size of Texas, had been sent in to offer assistance. He'd used all the federal resources at his disposal, but Riley Cavanaugh had never been found and her kidnapper remained elusive to this day.

Sam had done everything by the book. Everything in his power to find and bring that girl home. He had no regrets as to his conduct, but if he'd had more experience or a deeper insight into the criminal mind, things might have worked out differently.

The two survivors—Ellie Brannon and Jenna Malloy—hadn't been forthcoming. Jenna had been deeply traumatized by her captivity. Her reticence was understandable. Ellie Brannon was another story. Sam had suspected all along that she was hiding something, maybe even from herself. To this day, he wondered if the key to solving Riley Cavanaugh's disappearance was still tucked away somewhere in Ellie Brannon's subconscious.

Which was why, for the past few years, he'd been tuning in to her radio show every chance he got. *Midnight on Echo Lake.* An evocative name for a strange broadcast patterned, he supposed, after the more famous *Coast to Coast AM.* At first he'd listened to try to pick up on subtle clues and gain some insight into the host. Ellie's calm demeanor and soothing voice kept him coming back. He wondered what she was like these days in real life. She'd been a frightened kid when he'd last seen her, wary, defensive and perhaps a little intimidated by the presence of an FBI agent, even one still wet behind the ears.

Jenna Malloy had been the opposite. She'd taken to Sam when she'd refused to see anyone else, including her family and, for a time, Ellie Brannon. After he'd been transferred to DC, he'd still managed to touch base with her now and then. Maybe that had been a mistake. She had a tendency to fixate and he'd been forced to set some boundaries.

Strange how he hadn't heard from her in a couple of years and then all of a sudden in the past few weeks, he'd gotten a spate of phone calls and letters. It was almost as if she'd somehow intuited his return to Dallas before he'd known himself he was coming back.

Now that they were in the same city, he'd have to be

careful how he handled their interaction. He didn't want to turn his back on her, but neither could he allow her to think of him as a friend. He needed to maintain professional distance, but that wasn't always easy when he remembered the shape she'd been in after her rescue. She'd spent the first two years after her captivity in one mental health facility after another. Sam could still picture her sitting in front of the large window at the Penn Shepherd Hospital in Dallas staring absentmindedly out at the grounds until she would turn, blue eyes shimmering with quiet excitement as the fog lifted and she recognized his features.

Special Agent Reece! How nice of you to come and see me.

How are you feeling today, Jenna?

Better, I think.

That's good to hear.

Can I ask a favor of you, Agent Reece?

Of course. What is it?

I would like it very much if you called me Jenny, the way Riley used to.

All right... Jenny.

You have no idea how happy that makes me. Will you say it again?

Let's focus on something else, shall we? I'd like to ask you some questions if that's okay.

I guess so. But I hope you haven't come to talk about her again.

You mean Riley?

You know that's not who I mean.

Why don't you want to talk about Ellie Brannon?

She left me there. She left us both. We were her best friends. Like sisters, she used to call us. I don't understand how she could have done such a thing.

I don't think she had a choice. She was found uncon-

scious at the edge of the lake the next morning. If her brother hadn't acted as quickly as he had, she would have died.

There are worse things than dying, Agent Reece.

I'm well aware, Jenny.

The ringtone on Sam's cell phone crashed the memory. He checked the screen, startled to see Jenna's name on the caller ID. How could she possibly have known he was sitting out here in the dark, thinking about her? Sometimes her intuition seemed downright uncanny.

He considered letting the call go to voice mail, but his conscience wouldn't let him. "Hello, Jenna."

"It's Jenny, remember?" She sounded peeved.

He kept his voice moderate but firm. "Do you have any idea what time it is?"

"I know it's late, but you're still up, aren't you?"

He scanned his surroundings, peering between buildings and down each street. Was she out there somewhere watching him? He didn't think that likely and yet he felt an inexplicable apprehension. "You couldn't have known that, though. We agreed you would only call during the workday at a preset time, remember?"

"This couldn't wait."

"Even until morning?"

She sighed. "You're angry with me."

"I'm not angry. I just want to make sure you understand our agreement."

"Of course I understand. I'm not a child. But sometimes there are extenuating circumstances."

"What are the circumstances?"

She didn't say anything for the longest moment.

"Jenny? Are you still there?"

"Yes, I'm here."

He searched the darkness. "Tell me what's on your mind tonight."

"A lot of things, actually. Did you know that I have a new job?"

He tried to temper his impatience. "That's great, but you didn't call me at one o'clock in the morning to talk about a new job, did you?"

"I also have a new place. I'm not far from you now."

He rubbed the back of his neck where the hair at his nape suddenly stood on end. "How do you know where I live?"

Another long silence.

Sam got up and paced to the end of the balcony. The moon was up and the grounds were well lit, but the shadows on the other side of the pond were impenetrable. He told himself that even if she'd somehow managed to ferret out his address, she wouldn't be able to get through the gate without a code. But as he knew only too well, there were ways of breaching any space if one wanted in badly enough. Jenna Malloy was nothing if not resourceful.

"Don't worry, Agent Reece. The location is just a coincidence."

Was it?

"My roommate had already rented the house when she invited me to move in with her. Her name is Hazel. Don't you love that name? So dreamy and old-fashioned, although there's nothing traditional about Hazel Lamont. She's unlike anyone I've ever known."

Sam wasn't in the mood for chitchat, but he also knew better than to allow annoyance to creep into his voice. His relationship with Jenna Malloy was unorthodox and not without risk, but he always had the hope that something would come back to her during one of their conversations. That something would still break in the Riley Cavanaugh case.

"How did the two of you meet?" he asked.

"Oh, we've known each other for quite some time. I guess you could say we met through a mutual acquaintance. We have a lot in common."

"That's great. I'm happy for you," Sam said. "But you also didn't call to talk to me about your new roommate."

"No, I didn't. I'm just making small talk to try to calm my nerves. It's an exercise one of my therapists taught me a long time ago."

"Why are you nervous?"

Her voice lowered to a near whisper. "I'm not just nervous. I'm scared, Agent Reece."

Suddenly she sounded young and vulnerable, and Sam remembered why he always tried to hold back his irritation even when she crossed an uncomfortable line. He'd never been able to shake the image of her on that lonely country road, eyes haunted as she clutched a dirty blanket around her frail shoulders. He'd never been able to forget the photographs and medical reports that had graphically documented her abuse.

"What are you afraid of?" he asked gently.

"Weren't you listening tonight?"

He knew what she meant, but he asked anyway. "You mean to Ellie Brannon's radio program? I missed it tonight. I didn't get home until late."

"She called again, Agent Reece."

"Who called?"

"Riley."

"You know that's not possible."

Jenna's voice rose in agitation. "I don't know anything of the sort and neither do you. Her body was never found. She could still be alive for all we know."

"That's highly unlikely after all this time."

"Well, *someone* has been calling into Ellie's show for the past three nights. She's been calling me, too, Agent Reece."

"What?" Sam leaned against the railing as he tried to quell his unease. The night was still quiet. The brick wall that surrounded the community muted the traffic noises, and yet the darkness suddenly seemed alive with prying eyes and creeping shadows. His imagination, of course. No one was about this time of night. Not here. Not inside his protected haven. Outside the gates, where Jenna Malloy dwelled, was another matter.

"Why are you only mentioning this now?" he asked.

"Because I wanted to make sure it was Riley. She always calls at night. Maybe that's the only time she can get away. Sometimes the phone goes dead as soon as I answer, but sometimes I can hear her breathing."

"How do you know it's Riley?"

"She started to cry once. Tiny little sobs that reminded me of a lost kitten. It made me cry, too, Agent Reece. I felt so helpless, not knowing where she was or how I could help her."

"Have you told anyone else about these calls?"

"Like my therapist, you mean? She wouldn't believe me."

He chose his words carefully. "The caller says nothing, but you're convinced she's Riley?"

"Yes."

"How long has this been going on?"

"A few days, I guess. You know how I sometimes lose track of time."

"What did she say tonight when she called the radio show?"

"She said he's coming."

"That's it?"

"Isn't that enough, Agent Reece? What more would you want her to say?"

"This isn't the first time you've heard Riley's voice," he reminded her. "You were once convinced she was living down the street from you. You said you spotted her at the bus stop, remember?"

"This is different," she insisted. "I was confused in the past. I know that now. I sometimes couldn't tell the difference between fantasy and reality. I blame that on all the medication they were giving me in that awful place. But I'm better now." Her voice dropped again. "She doesn't just call, Agent Reece. She was at my house tonight. That's why I *had* to call you. I didn't think I should wait until morning to tell you."

"You saw her?"

"No, but she left something on my front porch. A gift that has meaning only to me."

"Can you be more specific?"

"Since we were little girls, Riley and I both loved peacocks. It was our thing. A local woman used to raise them and we would ride our bikes out to the lake to watch them. Sometimes we'd find their feathers on the ground and Riley collected them. She left a peacock feather on my front porch as a message. She's trying to let me know that she's alive and in trouble."

"If that were the case, why wouldn't she go to the police?" Sam reasoned. "Why take the time to leave a feather on your porch, much less to call in to Ellie Brannon's radio show?"

Jenna once again fell silent. When she finally spoke, her voice was still low but surprisingly determined despite an underlying tremor. "I was held against my will for nearly three weeks. Nineteen days of unspeakable horror. When I was found wandering down the side of that road, I had no idea where I was or where I'd been. I could barely speak. I didn't know enough to flag down a car for help, let alone call the police. Riley has been with that monster for fifteen years. *Fifteen years*, Agent Reece. Can you even imagine such a thing? Can we really expect her to behave in a rational manner? She's found a window and she's reaching out in the only way she knows how."

Her argument was so compelling that Sam found himself buying into the possibility before he mentally shook himself. Riley Cavanaugh had disappeared without a trace fifteen years ago. The chances she could still be alive were miniscule. Hallucinations or a cruel hoax was the more logical explanation.

But if there was even the slightest chance…

"Maybe we should set a time to meet so we can discuss this further," Sam said.

Jenna said eagerly, "Yes, of course. We have to figure out what to do next, don't we? If she's somehow managed to get away, he'll come for her again. He's probably out there looking for her at this very minute."

Sam tried to reel her back in. "Let's not get ahead of ourselves, okay?"

"But we've wasted too much time as it is!"

"Jenna—"

"Promise me you'll find her. Promise me you won't give up like you did last time."

The accusation stung like the point of a white-hot dagger. "I never gave up," Sam said quietly.

"Then go find her, Agent Reece. Go find her before *he* does."

Chapter Two

Ellie awakened again before dawn. Not from a knock on her front door this time, but from a vivid dream that left her trembling with dread. The funny thing was she couldn't remember much about it, only that she'd been running down a dark corridor, trying to flee a nameless, faceless assailant. Or had she been running from her past?

She got up and reached for the water bottle on her nightstand, carrying it with her to the bedroom window. From her vantage, she could see all the way across the lake where a fishing cabin perched on stilts at the edge of the piney woods. The owner had recently died and now the cabin sat dark and forlorn against a backdrop of feathery bowers.

A few stars twinkled out, dimmed by the light of the approaching dawn. As Ellie stood there, sipping tepid water, she had the strangest sensation of floating in time, of being suspended in a haze of lost memories. Once, she would have tried to piece together the fragments that came back to her now and then, but she'd long ago learned that some things were best left alone.

Her brother used to ask her if she'd moved out to the lake hoping the proximity to the Ruins would prod her memory. Maybe in the beginning, but mostly she hadn't wanted to live in fear for the rest of her life. She hadn't wanted to spend her time worrying about a monster in her closet or a depraved psycho watching from the shadows. If she could live so near to where her best friends had been taken, then she could face anything. She could take on the monster without flinching. Or at least without cowering under the covers in sheer terror.

She'd worked very hard for a very long time to get to this point. In some ways, her fear had been easier to conquer than her guilt, but she'd managed to come to terms with what had happened. She would probably never know why she'd been spared—if one could call being left for dead spared. Maybe because she'd been the sheriff's daughter and the kidnapper had feared a more intense search. Or maybe he'd only wanted two captives and Ellie hadn't fit a certain criteria in looks or personality. She'd learned years ago that it was pointless to speculate about the unknowable. It was better to focus on the things in her life she could control.

Smothering a yawn, she stretched her arms over her head to work out the kinks. She had a long day ahead of her. People had the notion that her job entailed nothing more than showing up in her studio to chat with callers and guests, but being on the air for three hours a night, five days a week required a lot of preparation. Her workday started no later than nine in the morning and ended at midnight when she signed off. Long hours required adequate rest, but she knew she wouldn't be able to get back to sleep. Might as well go down and make coffee.

She started to turn away from the window when a movement at the edge of the lake caught her attention. Ellie's heart thudded even as she told herself it was nothing more than a shadow or a tree limb waving in the breeze. But the longer she stared, the more defined the silhouette became until she was certain the intruder was female.

Ellie couldn't make out her features. She was too far

away and the shadows were too deep along the bank. But as she stood there, watching, the woman whirled as if startled by a noise in the woods. Then slowly she turned and lifted her head toward Ellie's window.

Their gazes connected for the longest moment. Ellie could have sworn the woman mouthed something up to her. That had to be her imagination. She couldn't even see the woman's features. Maybe this wasn't real, just another waking dream.

The woman glanced over her shoulder. Then she shot one last glance up at Ellie's window before she plunged deeper into the shadows and disappeared into the woods.

Ellie put her hand on the glass as she leaned in, trying to catch another glance. Clearly, someone was playing a cruel joke on her. Whoever the woman was, she knew Ellie's house well enough to look up at her bedroom window.

The ringtone of her cell phone shattered the loaded silence, leaving Ellie trembling as she moved back to her nightstand to glance at the screen. *Unknown Caller.* She told herself to let the call go to voice mail. Someone was messing with her big time. Someone wanted her scared and on edge, but why?

She snatched up the phone and lifted it to her ear. "Hello?"

Nothing but static.

"Hello? Hello?"

"He's coming," a whispery voice warned through the crackles.

Ellie's fingers curled around the plastic case. "Who is this?"

Silence.

"What do you want?"

Silence.

Ellie closed her eyes. "Why are you doing this?"

"He's coming, Elle."

She stifled a gasp at the nickname. No one had called her that in a very long time. "Who's coming?"

"Preacher," said the whispery voice.

"Preacher is dead," Ellie said fiercely.

"He's not dead, Elle. He's coming back for you."

Cold sweat beaded across her brow as she clutched the phone. "Even if he were alive, why would he risk coming back here after all this time?"

A wrenching pause. "Because you're the one that got away."

ELLIE TRACKED HER brother's flashlight beam as he walked the bank and then disappeared into the woods. He was gone for a good thirty minutes before she heard his footsteps on the deck. She went outside to join him and they sat drinking coffee as the sun climbed over the horizon and the sky turned a flaming pink. Streamers of mist hung like wet cotton from the treetops. The day was already warm and still, the early morning silence broken only by the melodic whistle of an overeager wood thrush.

When Tom had first arrived, Ellie had played him the recording of the call that had come in during the previous night's broadcast and now she reluctantly admitted to her near-panic attack on the way home.

"This has really got you wound up," Tom said as he stretched his long legs in front of him.

"The calls that came in on Monday and Tuesday night were so staticky. I could barely make out a voice. As you heard for yourself, last night was different."

"Last night's call came in at the same time as the others?"

"Yes. They seem timed to be the last call of the show."

"After you signed off, you came straight home?"

"Except for the brief panic attack on the trail. I took a shower, drank some wine and fell asleep on the couch."

"How much wine?"

"Not enough that I hallucinated the doorbell or the woman staring up at my window."

"Did you happen to notice the time when the doorbell woke you up?"

"It was a little after one."

"What did you do after that?"

"I went up to bed, but it took me awhile to fall asleep. Just before dawn, I woke up again and that's when I saw the woman down by the lake."

"What woke you up?"

"A nightmare, I think."

He frowned. "You're having nightmares again? Why didn't you tell me?"

She tried to shrug off his concern. "Everybody has nightmares now and then. I'm not going to bother you every time I have a bad dream."

He looked as if he wanted to argue, but asked instead, "What happened then?"

"That's when I got the next call." Ellie raked fingers through her tangled hair. "I know how all this sounds, but it wasn't a dream or a hallucination. I'm not making any of this up."

"I never thought you were."

"Obviously, it's someone's idea of a sick joke. I probably shouldn't have bothered you with any of this."

He gave her a stern scrutiny. "You're not bothering me. You know you can always call me about anything. That's what brothers are for."

"You're not just my brother, though. You're also the county sheriff. I don't like wasting your time."

"Listen to me. You call whenever you need me. I'll let you know when and if I think you're wasting my time. Agreed?"

Ellie nodded, wrapping her hands around the warm mug. "You didn't find anything down by the lake?" she asked reluctantly.

"I saw some footprints along the bank. A broken twig or two at the edge of the woods." He sipped slowly. "When was the last time you walked down that way?"

"Late yesterday afternoon when I went over to the Thayer house to feed the peacocks."

"Some of those prints are probably yours then. Now that it's daylight, we can go down and have a look around together. But I think you're right. Someone is having a go at you. Ever since Sophie's disappearance and all that business with Jackson, Riley's kidnapping has been in the news again," he said, referring to a recent kidnapping incident involving yet another Cavanaugh.

Ellie let her head fall back against the rocker as she stared out over the water. Such a peaceful scene and yet her thoughts were increasingly chaotic. "The caller said Preacher is coming back for me."

"You know that's not possible."

She turned to study her brother's profile. "Do I? For all any of us knows, he's still out there somewhere."

"Silas Creed would be an old man by now. If he isn't dead, he's likely incarcerated for another crime. He's not coming back."

"She called me Elle."

Tom shrugged. "I sometimes call you Elle. That doesn't prove anything."

She gave him a reproachful look. "You rarely call me Elle. Riley was the only one who used that name on a regular basis."

"She's not coming back, either, sis."

"I know. It's just…" She shot him an anxious look. "You believe that I saw someone down there, don't you? I didn't dream her up. I didn't imagine those phone calls or someone ringing my doorbell."

"You certainly didn't imagine the caller who phoned into your radio program last night. I heard the recording myself," Tom reminded her.

Doubt still niggled, but Ellie hated giving voice to her old worries. She folded her arms defensively as she searched the lake.

"What is it?" Tom coaxed.

"What if that phone call somehow set everything else into motion?"

"What do you mean?"

"It triggered a panic attack. Maybe it also awakened old memories. Old fears. Maybe everything else that came afterward really was a dream. Or maybe I'm losing it," she said. "It wouldn't be the first time."

"A minute ago, you were certain it wasn't a dream."

"Maybe I was trying to convince myself."

He placed his cup on the floor beside his rocker and turned to face her. "It's not surprising you're on edge. Anyone would be rattled. That doesn't mean you're losing it. It just means you're human."

"You're a good brother, Tom. Don't let anyone tell you otherwise."

"I'll remind you of that next time you're on my case." He picked up his cup and turned back to the sunrise.

They sat in companionable silence while they drank their coffee. Ellie could tell that Tom had dressed in a hurry after her call. Later, he'd take more care with his appearance, discarding the sneakers for his signature polished boots. As the Nance County sheriff, he had a certain image to uphold. Ellie had no such restrictions. Shorts, tank top and canvas slip-ons were her everyday summer uniform.

She bent and swatted a mosquito at her ankle. "If you believe the woman I saw by the lake was real, then why don't you have more questions about her?"

"Is there something else I need to know? I assumed you'd told me everything."

"I told you everything I remember, but maybe the right question will jog my memory. Don't be afraid to challenge me. Don't treat me any different than you would anyone else who'd called you out at the crack of dawn."

Tom nodded. "All right, then. You say you didn't get a look at her face, but you saw her silhouette. What about height, weight?"

"She was about my size, but taller, I think."

"What about her hair? Long, short, curly, straight?"

Ellie closed her eyes, summoning an image. "I had the impression she was blond." Like Riley. Like Ellie herself. "I remember the way moonlight gleamed off the strands when she whirled toward the woods."

"What about her clothes?"

"A white dress, I think. Or a nightgown."

"You said she looked up at your window and mouthed something to you. Yet it was too dark to make out her features."

Ellie pounced. "See? I knew you didn't believe me."

"I never said that. If you're asking whether or not I think Riley Cavanaugh called tonight to warn you about Preacher or that she came to your house to stare up at your bedroom window, then the answer is no. I don't believe that. But I do believe someone is messing with you. Probably some bored kids egging each other on, but whoever it is and whatever their motivation, I don't like it. Maybe

you should come stay in town for a few days until all this
blows over."

"I have to prepare for tonight's show and besides, you
and Rae don't need me underfoot while you're trying to
plan a wedding."

"She wouldn't mind."

"*I* mind. You two deserve this time together."

Tom and Rae Cavanaugh had gotten engaged at the
start of the summer. Funny how things sometimes worked
out, Ellie reflected. For most of their adult lives, Rae had
blamed Tom for her sister's disappearance. They'd barely
spoken to one another in the fifteen years since Riley had
gone missing and now here they were planning to spend
the rest of their lives together.

Ellie was happy for her brother, but their bliss sometimes served to magnify her loneliness. She would never
want Tom to know that, of course. He was still the protective big brother. He didn't need another reason to worry
about her.

He gave her a look.

"What?" she asked.

"There's something you need to know. I probably should
have brought it up when I first got here."

Ellie straightened. She didn't like his tone. "What is it?"

"Do you remember that reporter named Melanie Kent?
The one that wrote the series of articles about Riley's disappearance?"

Icy fingers curled around the base of Ellie's spine. "I'm
not likely to forget her. She made our lives a living hell
until you finally exposed her. Why are you bringing her
up now?"

Tom paused. "She may be back in town."

Ellie shot forward, clutching the arms of her chair.
"What? What do you mean *may* be back in town?"

He could hardly meet her gaze. "I haven't seen her myself, but Rae said one of her cousins at the newspaper told her Melanie had applied for a job there."

"When was this?"

"Recently. In the last week or two."

"And you're just now telling me?" Ellie's voice rose in agitation. "You didn't think this was something I needed to know?"

"She didn't get the job," Tom said. "I'd hoped she'd leave town as quietly as she came in."

"But she didn't."

"I don't know. I haven't been able to locate her."

"Tom." Ellie stared daggers at her brother. "I can't believe you didn't tell me."

He shrugged helplessly. "I knew it would upset you. I was trying to protect you."

"By allowing me to be blindsided by a woman who tried to destroy me?"

"When you put it like that." He winced. "You're right. I should have told you."

Ellie tried to quell her anger as she settled back in her chair. Taking out her frustration on Tom wasn't going to help anything. If Melanie Kent was back in town, they needed to stick together.

Melanie had first entered their lives when Ellie was a junior in college. A few weeks into a new assignment as host for a call-in show at the university radio station, Ellie had started receiving calls from a troubled young woman named Marie Nightingale, an obvious alias. Marie claimed to have been kidnapped and held prisoner for years before her daring escape. Night after night, she captivated Ellie and her audience with her harrowing tales. Once a connection had been established based on their histories, Marie started showing up on campus, insinuating herself into

Ellie's circle of friends in order to ferret out information about her personal life and Riley's disappearance.

Tom had eventually uncovered the woman's real identity and her true motivation. By then, however, she'd already published a sensational, mostly fictional book on the kidnapping, calling into question Ellie's innocence and tainting Tom's reputation in the process. Why had Ellie been the only one of the three friends to escape Preacher's clutches that night? And how convenient that her brother had been able to save her but not the other two girls.

Melanie Kent wasn't the only one who'd harbored those dark suspicions. When Tom had discovered that Ellie and her friends had snuck out of the house that night, he'd rushed out to the Ruins to find them, only to be ambushed and also left for dead on the banks of Echo Lake. Regaining consciousness, he'd had to make the tragic choice of searching for the missing girls or rushing his sister to the ER. His actions had likely saved Ellie's life, but there were still doubters in town that held to the notion both Tom and Ellie had abandoned Riley and Jenna in order to save themselves.

It had taken a lot of years and a very thick skin to live down the ugly innuendoes. Which was why Ellie had been reluctant to call Tom earlier, why she hated dragging him into a situation that might stir bad memories and bitter feelings. The Cavanaughs weren't the only family that had been put through the wringer by Riley's disappearance.

"I've made some inquiries," Tom said. "Melanie was recently fired from the publication she worked for in Tyler and before that she was let go from the *Dallas Herald*. I'm guessing that's why she's sniffing around Belle Pointe again."

"You think she's behind these calls?"

"I wouldn't put anything past her, especially if she's desperate. She was always a ruthless and ambitious reporter. It wouldn't be the first time she cooked up an outlandish scheme to get a story or a book deal."

"I wish you'd told me sooner," Ellie said again worriedly.

"Yeah, me, too. I should have told you the minute I heard she was back in town. That was my mistake."

"Don't keep something like that from me again."

"I won't." He paused, looking discomforted.

"What?" Ellie pressed. "What else aren't you telling me?"

"Nothing about Melanie, I swear. But if it's all the same to you, I'd rather Rae not know about the phone calls or the woman you saw by the lake. At least not yet."

"You think it's a good idea to keep secrets? She's bound to find out sooner or later," Ellie warned.

"I know, but after everything she and her family have been through, I want her to enjoy all the wedding preparations without having the specter of her sister's kidnapping hanging over her. I say we keep a close eye on things and see if we can put a stop to this nonsense quietly."

"Fine by me," Ellie said.

"Meanwhile, I'll keep digging and see if I can find out what Melanie Kent is really up to."

"You do that, Tom."

His gaze deepened. "I don't think there's anything to worry about, but promise me you'll take precautions. Lock the studio door when you're on the air. Secure the house when you get home. And call me night or day if you hear or see anything suspicious or troublesome."

"I will. Let's hope whoever is behind this has had their fun and nothing else will happen. But, Tom…" She closed her eyes on a breath. "What if it isn't someone playing a cruel joke or a sleazy reporter after a story? I'm not saying I think Riley is still alive or anything, but what if that caller really is in trouble?"

"Then why wouldn't she go to the police?"

"Maybe she can't for some reason. I don't know," Ellie said helplessly. "I just need to make sure for my own peace of mind that I've done all I can."

"I understand. We'll get it all sorted out, I promise."

Ellie nodded, but she couldn't shake a lingering unease that something darker than a prank may have motivated those phone calls.

THEY SPENT AN hour examining footprints and tramping through the woods, searching for additional evidence left by the predawn visitor. Coming up empty-handed, Tom reluctantly headed back into town and Ellie set out for the Thayer place to feed the peacocks.

She told herself she wouldn't dwell on the motivation behind those phone calls or the reason some strange woman had been staring up at her bedroom window. Maybe she really had imagined the whole episode. She recalled vividly the disturbing phone conversation that had come after the sighting, but already the figure at the water's edge seemed hazy and surreal.

It wouldn't be the first time she'd seen or heard something that wasn't really there. She'd been plagued by nightmares and hypnagogic visions for years. In some ways a figment of her imagination might be the preferable explanation. A flesh-and-blood intruder was a whole different worry. The notion that she might be the target of a stalker or even a malicious prankster chilled her more deeply than she wanted to admit.

A strutting peacock greeted her with an eerie scream. The peahens were less noisy as they gobbled up the grain and seeds she tossed out to supplement their diet of insects and berries. As always, the male wanted her to know that she had intruded upon his domain. He fanned his magnificent tail feathers before picking his way to the edge of the embankment where he turned to watch her with avid curiosity.

She sat down on the porch steps and let her mind wander for a few minutes. She needed to get home and start her workday, yet she lingered, as if that swaggering peacock could somehow protect her from what was coming. A smaller male joined the peahens pecking in the dirt. He was only too happy to strut his stuff until the older and larger male made his way back into the circle. Then the younger one retreated to the perimeter to nibble on wild grapes.

Ellie didn't know how long she'd been sitting there, lost in thought, when a prickling at the back of her neck brought her head up to search her surroundings. She didn't see anything amiss, but the peafowl scattered. Someone was coming through the woods.

Her first thought was that Adam Thayer, the owner of the property, might have returned from Dallas. Or maybe his girlfriend, Nikki Dresden, had come over to check on the place in his absence. But Ellie hadn't heard a car. She kept her gaze fixed on the overgrown driveway, hoping to see a familiar figure appear through the lush vegetation.

All was still. Even the mild breeze had died away. Yet she knew with dreaded certainty that she was no longer alone.

She rose, clutching the banister as she scanned the woods and then glanced down toward the lake. A boat bobbed alongside the dock. Had the small vessel been there when she arrived? She would have heard an outboard motor, but she'd been so lost in thought, she might have missed someone paddling up. They could have tied off quietly and slipped through the woods to watch her.

As many times as Ellie told herself she had no reason to worry, the whispery warning came back to haunt her. The unknown caller had tapped into her greatest fear. Buried deep down in her subconscious was the gnawing terror that Preacher would someday return for her. Rationally, she knew her brother was right. That particular monster was long dead or imprisoned. Even if he still roamed free, he was an old man now. Why would he risk coming back here to torment her?

Because you're the one that got away.

But she hadn't gotten away. Not really. She and the other two girls had separated that night in the Ruins. Riley had been terrified from the start. She'd clutched Jenna's arm as the two stood at the bottom of the stairs and watched Ellie ascend to the second floor. Halfway up, she'd regretted her bravado, but she was too proud to turn back even when Riley had pleaded with her to come down.

If we're going to do this, we need to stick together, Elle.

Don't be such a worrywart, Riles. It's just an old building. Nothing to be afraid of. Why don't you come up here with me?

Not a chance.

Fraidy-cat.

Leave her alone, Ellie. We should never have brought her out here in the first place.

You wanted to come, didn't you, Riles?

I...guess so.

See there, Jen? Now you're the worrywart.

No, I'm just being a good friend. Unlike you, who never thinks about anyone but herself.

Stop it, both of you! Let's just get this over wi— What was that?

What was what, Riles?
I heard something.
Probably just a floorboard settling.
No, she's right, Ellie. Someone's here...

The memory floated away as Ellie came down the porch steps slowly. Sunlight shimmered on the surface of the lake, but the thick canopy of pine trees in the yard blocked all but a few anemic rays. A moment ago, the air had been still, but now a breeze riffled through the leaves, stirring the pungent scent of the evergreens and something that might have been cigarette smoke.

Ellie started to call out, but the paralyzing fear of her dreams held her back. For a moment, she stood rooted to the spot, unable to scream, unable to flee, unable to do anything but imagine the demonic face of her nemesis peering at her through the shadows.

Panic gripped her. She tried to focus on the sparkle of sunlight on the water. So pretty. Like diamonds. *Focus on the diamonds...*

She concentrated on taking slow deep breaths until the paralysis lifted and she could put one foot in front of the other. It seemed to take an eternity to cross the yard to the embankment, but then she descended too quickly, turning an ankle on the wooden steps and scraping her knees when she fell.

Scrambling to her feet, she hurried the rest of the way down and paused at the edge of the dock to study the small fishing boat. She didn't see any oars, couldn't tell if the boat had been there all along or not. Adam Thayer owned one very much like it. She'd seen him tooling across the lake on several occasions. He'd probably removed the small outboard to store in a safe place while he was away.

See? A logical explanation. Nothing to be afraid of. You've come here dozens of times to feed the peacocks—

Her thoughts scattered on a gasp when she saw some-one at the top of the embankment.

A man stood in shade so deep that Ellie had only an impression of a human form. She told herself it was nothing. Just a shadow. A tree or a bush. *No one is there.*

He moved up to the edge of the ridge. Slowly. Stepping into thinner shade but not venturing out into full sunlight. He was dressed in a black suit and he wore an old-fashioned parson's hat pulled low over his face. Someone had painted a mural of Preacher on the ceiling of the Ruins, distorting his features into a demonic grimace beneath the brim of a similar hat.

It was that evil face that had terrorized Ellie's sleep for years, whereas she could barely remember Silas Creed, a former mental patient who had once worked odd jobs in town. He'd disappeared on the night of the kidnapping. No one had seen or heard from him since. No one knew what had happened to him, though there'd been claims of sightings from time to time. Some swore he was still hiding out nearby, foraging and stealing to get by. Some insisted he'd died a long time ago and his ghost now haunted the Ruins. Ellie tried not to think about him at all, but there he stood…there *someone* stood…

He's not real. He's not real. He's not real.

Sunlight glimmered down through the pine bowers, bathing his dark-clad form in a soft glow that made her wonder for a moment if she really was seeing a ghost.

He didn't glance her way. Didn't once make eye contact. He merely stood there with his head bowed as if in deep prayer or contemplation.

Something splashed in the water and Ellie whirled toward the dock. The noise distracted her for only a split second, but when she turned back around, the figure had vanished.

The pungent smell of smoke grew stronger. Ellie scanned the embankment, worried that he might have somehow descended without her seeing him. Then she turned back to search along the tree line as she tried to calculate the fastest way home. The road would be quicker, but she'd have to go back up the steps, across the yard and down the tree-shrouded drive to the gravel lane. Maybe she should climb into the boat and push off so that she could drift out into the middle of the lake where she could see in every direction—

Just go!

Heart pounding, she rushed headlong down the trail toward home. A flock of snowy egrets took flight, startling her so badly she almost went down a second time. She righted her balance and kept moving. Rounding the final bend, she finally glanced over her shoulder to make sure the coast was clear.

That was a mistake. When she whirled back around, he stood on the path, blocking her escape.

Chapter Three

Ellie threw up her arms and braced herself, prepared to go down fighting if she had to. Her law enforcement dad had also taught her self-defense. However, no action was needed in this case. The man on the path stepped out of the way at once, but the adrenaline still pumped so furiously through Ellie's veins that she had the primal urge to lash out. He must have glimpsed something in her eyes that startled him because he took another step back. "Whoa, there. You okay?"

He wasn't the man she'd seen on the embankment. He wasn't dressed in black, didn't wear a hat and he was too young to be Preacher. Ellie tried to calm herself enough to reassess the situation as she glanced over her shoulder. The trail behind her was clear, thank goodness.

She took a moment to catch her breath as she turned back to the newcomer. He was tall, fit, late thirties maybe. Dark hair. Dark eyes. Charcoal trousers, white shirt open at the neck and rolled up at the sleeves.

"You shouldn't sneak up on someone like that," she admonished, as the adrenaline rush subsided.

"I generally don't make a habit of it." He sounded the tiniest bit defensive. "You came around that bend in such a hurry I didn't have time to get out of your way."

Ellie threaded her hair behind her ears as her heart rate gradually returned to normal. Had she really seen someone at the top of the embankment or had the black-clad figure been another figment of her imagination?

Now that she was out of danger, self-doubt crept in and she wasn't sure why. It was broad daylight and she was wide-awake. She hadn't dreamed up that shadowy form in the hat any more than she'd imagined the woman by the lake. Both were real, which meant someone was deliberately tormenting her. But why?

"Are you sure you're okay?" the stranger asked.

She snapped back to the present, lifting her gaze to meet his. His eyes were dark and piercing. Unnerving under the circumstances.

"I'll be a lot better when you tell me who you are and what you're doing out here." She took in his casual business attire once more. Not a sight she often saw on the banks of Echo Lake. Her gaze narrowed. "Wait a minute. I know you."

He held up a hand as if to reassure her of his benevolence, then slowly reached back with the other hand to retrieve his credentials from his pocket. "Agent Sam Reece."

The name hit Ellie like a sledgehammer blow. Another person from her past. Another face from her nightmares.

Oh, did she ever know Agent Samuel Reece. She remembered only too well his endless questions after Riley had gone missing. The flashes of skepticism and impatience when Ellie hadn't been able to give him the answers he wanted. She'd thought him arrogant and aggressive back then. Ruthless in his quest to uncover the truth no matter who got in his way. Under most circumstances, his resolve would have been appreciated, but he'd made no bones about his concern that the county sheriff might be covering for his daughter.

"What do you want?" The question came out far terser than she'd intended, but instead of offering an apology, she lifted her chin in defiance.

"I'd like to ask you a few questions if that's okay." Those fathomless eyes observed her with open curiosity. He was an attractive man. She remembered that about him, too. The years had only enhanced his good looks with an air of quiet confidence that wore more easily than the previous sharp edges. Fifteen years was a long time. People did change, but it was too risky to give him the benefit of the doubt.

Ellie said coolly, "Do you think my answers will be any different than they were fifteen years ago?"

He shrugged. "Probably not. This isn't about fifteen years ago. I'm here about the call that came into your radio show last night."

She stared at him in astonishment. "How do you know about that?"

"I listen to your program from time to time."

She didn't know which revelation disturbed her the most—that he'd come about the call or that he listened to her show. The notion that he'd kept tabs on her all these years unsettled her.

"I find the subject matter fascinating," he added.

"Which subject matter in particular?" she shot back.

"I enjoy all the shows, but I'm partial to the ones on unsolved mysteries."

"Yes, I can see how that topic would interest you." Ellie brushed past him as she moved toward the steps. "Maybe you should come on the program sometime. I could interview you for a change."

"Name the night."

She turned. "You're serious?"

A smile flickered as he shrugged. "Why not? I should probably warn you, though, that I'm hardly a polished speaker."

"Somehow I doubt that," she muttered, scouring the shadowy trail once more. If anyone had followed her from the Thayer place, that person was either long gone or in hiding. Maybe she had Agent Reece to thank for that. She let her gaze roam along the tree line before she glanced back.

"Are you sure you're okay?" he pressed. "You seem nervous. Just now when you came along the bank, you looked frightened. Did something happen?"

Who better to confess her fears to than an FBI agent? But this particular agent had once accused her of hiding something. The last thing she wanted was to trigger a new round of suspicions, so she decided to say nothing until she learned the real reason for his unexpected visit.

"I'm fine," she said briskly. "If you're here to interrogate me, we may as well go up to the house where we can be comfortable. But I've work to do so I don't have a lot of time."

Something flashed in his eyes, an emotion she found hard to define. If she didn't know better, she might have thought it remorse.

"No interrogation, just a few simple questions," he said. "I'll try to be brief."

He followed her up the steps to the shady deck. Instead of inviting him into the house, she motioned to one of the chairs that faced the water. "Have a seat. I'll bring out some coffee. Or would you prefer iced tea?" The sun was already hot and she was still perspiring from her mad dash back home, but it was comfortable and breezy in the shade. She wished she had nothing more pressing than a leisurely morning on the deck, wished she had the nerve to send Agent Reece packing. But curiosity niggled. Why was he really here?

"Coffee is fine, thanks." Ignoring the chair, he went over to the edge of the deck and stared out across the water. His dark hair was cut short, though it seemed a little longer than she remembered. When he turned his head just right, she could see the barest glimmer of frost at his temples.

She tore her gaze away from his profile.

"This is nice," he said. "Peaceful. I'd forgotten how beautiful Echo Lake is."

"By day, yes. When the sun goes down, it gets really dark with all the trees. Some people find it spooky."

"Yet you live out here anyway."

"I'm used to the dark. And as you said, it's a beautiful place." If one didn't look too hard for the monsters.

He turned at that. "It's good to see you again, Ellie."

The familiar way he used her first name unnerved her. She felt the flutter of something halfway between fear and attraction in the pit of her stomach.

His gaze swept her house and the wooded landscape. "It seems you've done well for yourself."

"I've done okay."

He seemed at a loss for a moment. "I know I came on strong back then. It was my first big case. I was inexperienced, obsessive and we were up against a ticking clock. Every second that went by counted. So I pushed you to remember details. Probably harder than I should have, considering what you'd been through. But it was never personal."

"It felt personal."

"Then I apologize. I've wanted to tell you that for a long time."

Ellie didn't know whether to believe him or not. She

wanted to. He looked and sounded sincere, but she told herself not to let down her guard. Not yet. She'd been taken in one too many times by consummate actors. People looking for a story, looking for an angle, looking to trip her up. She liked to think she'd learned from her mistakes.

"All I ever wanted was for Riley to come home," she said.

"That's what we all wanted."

She started to say something else, then turned and went inside the house. Her view of the deck from the kitchen window allowed her to discreetly study Agent Reece as she prepared a fresh pot of coffee. Whenever she'd thought about him over the years, she'd always remembered his eyes. In her mind, they were cold, black and fathomless, but in reality they were a deep, intense blue, almost navy. Earlier, she'd noticed the addition of worry lines at the corners and something indefinable lurking beneath the surface that made her wonder about his past.

He must have seen some pretty terrible things in the fifteen years since they'd last met. He hunted missing children and the monsters that took them. A job like his could change a person in ways most people could barely comprehend, but that didn't mean he got a pass from her. That didn't mean she ever had to trust him again.

She ran a hand through her messy hair, wondering if she should take the time to brush out the tangles. Maybe even change from shorts into jeans so that she didn't feel quite so exposed. Then she shrugged and thought, *To hell with that*. She wasn't a frightened, traumatized kid anymore. She could handle a few questions without needing to don armor.

He heard her footsteps and strode over to open the door. Waving aside his offer of help, she handed him a steaming mug and once again motioned to the chairs.

Across the lake, a family of white-tailed deer drank at the water's edge, but the idyllic setting did little to calm Ellie's trepidation. Why was he here?

Reluctantly she returned her focus to the man beside her. "So you were listening to my program last night," she prompted.

"That surprises you?" He took a tentative sip.

"Astounds me, actually. How did you even know about my show? I occupy a very small niche on the airwaves."

"Not as small as you might think. You have a devout following. Word gets around."

"All the way to DC?"

"I'm not in DC anymore. I'm back in Dallas."

She tried not to show her alarm. He was that close? "Since when?"

"Recently."

Ellie set aside her cup and folded her arms protectively. "Let's quit beating around the bush. Why don't you just tell me why you're really here? Why now, after all this time? Surely there's more to your visit than a few prank phone calls. Has something new turned up? You haven't…" She trailed off.

"Haven't what?"

She could barely bring herself to say it. "Found remains."

"No, nothing like that." He set aside his cup, as well. "Before we go any further, I should make one thing clear. I didn't personally hear your show last night. Someone told me about the caller. And you're right. That's not the only reason I'm here."

"Who told you about the caller—" Ellie broke off as something occurred to her. She felt a surge of anger as she studied his features. "You've been in touch with Melanie Kent, haven't you? That's why you're here. Both of you coming back to Belle Pointe at the same time can't be a coincidence. What has she told you?"

He said in confusion, "I'm sorry. I don't know what you're talking about. I don't know anyone named Melanie Kent."

"Of course you do. She interviewed you for a book she wrote about Riley's disappearance. *I always thought the Brannon girl was hiding something.* Your exact words, I believe. That quote was picked up by all the local news outlets. You have no idea how long it took me to live it down."

He had the grace to look discomfited. "She took that quote out of context."

"So you do remember her."

"Vaguely."

Ellie nodded. "Now it's all starting to make sense. Melanie Kent turns up back in town after all these years and I start getting strange phone calls. And here you are. If I didn't know better, I might think she'd orchestrated everything."

"I can assure you I haven't talked to Melanie Kent or any other reporter about the Cavanaugh case in years. If I recall correctly, what I really said was—"

"I don't care what you said," Ellie cut in. "I'm only interested in why you're here."

"I'm here because Jenna Malloy is convinced the person calling into your radio program is Riley."

Ellie stared at him in shock. "You've talked to Jen? When?"

"Last night after she heard your broadcast."

Ellie hardly knew what to make of this new information. Jenna had notified the FBI about the mysterious caller? And Agent Reece had taken her seriously enough to drive out to Echo Lake? "You can't possibly think Riley is still alive."

"The chances are slim," he admitted. "But it seems

Jenna has also been getting phone calls. Last night, someone left a peacock feather on her front porch. She thinks Riley is trying to send her a message."

A *peacock* feather? "Why would she think that?"

"She said peacocks were their thing. Hers and Riley's."

"No, peacocks are my thing," Ellie said. "Riley was afraid of them. She didn't like the sound they made at night. She said the screams gave her nightmares. Why would Jenna tell you that peacocks were their thing?"

"She seems to think the feather has meaning only to her."

Ellie said carefully, "I've kept in touch with Jenna over the years. Not as often as I should, but I know she still has a lot of issues. Understandable after everything she went through."

He nodded, his gaze somber. "I'm aware of those issues. We've kept in touch over the years, as well."

They'd kept in touch. He and Jenna.

Ellie didn't know what to make of any of this. She suddenly felt disconnected, as if she'd awakened from a long, deep sleep only to find that a lot of troubling things had occurred while she slumbered.

That's what you get when you hide out for too long. You lose track of time and people.

She gave him a doubtful glance. "I find that strange since I've never heard her mention your name."

His gaze on her remained steady. "How often do the two of you talk?"

"Often enough to know this isn't the first time she's imagined Riley reaching out to her."

"Yes, but something seems different this time."

"Different how?"

He hesitated. "Nothing I can define at the moment. I

haven't talked to her in person. Maybe once we meet, I'll have a better handle on the situation."

Ellie found herself gripping the arms of her chair. She flexed her fingers, forcing her muscles to relax. "I still don't understand why you've come to see me."

He got up and went back over to the edge of the deck, leaning against the railing as he faced her. He was even taller than she remembered. Still intimidating, though she didn't like to admit it. She took a few steadying breaths, careful not to inhale so deeply that he'd notice.

"I wanted to get your take on the phone conversation before I talked to Jenna," he said.

"It wasn't much of a conversation. The connection was poor and I kept getting a lot of interference in my ear."

"You didn't recognize the voice?"

Now Ellie was the one who hesitated. "It was a very brief staticky call."

"What did the caller say?"

"'He's coming.'"

"Nothing else?"

"Nothing that I could make out. I assume you explained to Jenna that if by some miracle Riley is still alive and has somehow managed to get away from her captor, she'd go to the police or her family instead of taking the time to call into a talk radio show."

"I did. And Jenna reminded me that after fifteen years in captivity, Riley might not be able to think rationally."

Ellie glanced away, shivering in the heat as dark images floated through her head. She closed her eyes, trying to block out the bits and pieces of horror. "You *can't* believe she's still alive."

"As I said, the chances are slim."

"Yet you came all this way because of a phone call."

"The case has never been closed. We continue to follow leads as they come in."

"How often is that?"

"Rarely these days." He planted his hands on the railing and leaned back. He appeared infuriatingly at ease as Ellie's heart continued to thud. She turned to scan the lake, keeping Agent Reece in her periphery. Fifteen years ago he'd been fresh out of Quantico, an ambitious young agent out to make a name for himself at her expense. And now? She couldn't get a good read on him. Did he really believe Riley could still be alive or was he here because he remained suspicious of Ellie?

She needed to keep him talking for a bit, find out what he was really after before she sent him away. But she had to tread carefully with Special Agent Reece. He was older, wiser and despite his calm demeanor, probably a lot more cynical.

"I suppose Jenna also told you about the other calls that came into my program on two previous nights. They came in at roughly the same time, but the reception was so poor I couldn't make out the caller's voice until last night."

"What do you think is going on with these calls?" he asked.

"The truth? I think they're part of an elaborate hoax. A sick prank. Ever since Sophie Cavanaugh's kidnapping several weeks ago, Riley's disappearance has been all over the news. The rehashing always provokes calls from people claiming to have seen her. Or claiming to be her."

"How often has that happened?"

"A few times over the years. The Cavanaughs are important people around here. Whenever one of them makes the news, the kidnapping is invariably brought up."

He nodded thoughtfully. "I assume you have a recording of last night's broadcast? I'd like to listen to the portion with the phone call, if you don't mind."

"I don't mind, but you won't learn much."

"I'd still like to hear it. I'd also like for you to walk me through the rest of your night."

She frowned. "Why?"

"I'm trying to fill in the blanks," he said. "I'd like to get a sense of your routine. You don't have to tell me anything you'd rather I not know."

What did he mean by *that*? Was he still implying she had something to hide?

"I signed off the air, locked up the studio and came home."

He nodded behind her to the long row of windows. "The studio isn't in your house?"

"It's just down that path." She pointed toward the bottom of the steps.

"Convenient to have it so close," he remarked.

"The beauty of modern technology."

His tone and expression remained impassive despite a dark glimmer in his eyes. He was still looking to her for answers, but nothing good came from pawing around in all those fractured memories. Silas Creed was long gone, long dead. Nothing else mattered.

She lifted her chin, giving him an answering scrutiny and took a measure of petty satisfaction when he looked away first.

He glanced down the deck steps toward the path. "So after the call came in, you locked up the studio and came home. What then?"

"I took a shower and got ready for bed."

He gave a vague nod as if his mind had gone elsewhere. Then he turned to face her. "I'm curious about something.

Why would you label a few staticky phone calls an elaborate hoax? Elaborate implies multiple layers and accomplices."

She should have been more circumspect with her wording, Ellie realized. But did it really matter in the long run? She remembered only too well Agent Reece's perception and doggedness. If he sensed she was holding something back, he'd keep poking and prodding at her defenses until weariness finally let him in.

"After my shower, I went downstairs to watch TV," she said. "I fell asleep on the couch. The doorbell woke me sometime later, but no one was there. Then just before dawn, I got up again and saw a woman at the edge of the lake. She seemed to be staring up at my bedroom window. She disappeared into the woods and a few minutes later, I received another call on my cell from someone claiming that Preacher was coming back for me. Just now? Just before I ran into you on the path? I saw someone dressed in black wearing a parson's hat. You know what that is, right? It's the same style depicted in the ceiling mural at the Ruins. Is all that elaborate enough for you, Agent Reece? And that's not even taking into account everything going on with Jenna."

He straightened from the railing as he gazed down at her. "Is there a reason you didn't tell me any of this earlier?"

"You took me by surprise. I wasn't expecting to bump into you on the trail."

He looked as if he wanted to press her with more questions about the *hoax*, but then relented. "Fair enough. Do you think the calls are coming from the same person?"

"I assume so, but I can't be sure." She glanced down where her fingers were once again clutching the arms of her chair.

"Can you describe the woman you saw by the lake?"

"Light hair, slender, about my height or a little taller. I really didn't get a good look at her. She was too far away and the shadows were too deep along the bank."

"What about the man in the parson's hat?"

"I never saw his face."

"Is it possible they could be the same person?"

The notion took Ellie by surprise. "I suppose so. Come to think of it, the build was similar." She paused. "What are you getting at, Agent Reece?"

"Nothing specific. I'm still trying to figure some things out."

"That makes two of us," Ellie said. "The only thing I can tell you for certain is that neither of them was Riley Cavanaugh."

Chapter Four

Sam watched the flicker of emotions across Ellie's face as she queued the recording. He knew her voice so well from her radio show that he had to remind himself she was a virtual stranger. He hadn't seen her in years and she looked a lot different than he remembered. That was to be expected, of course. She was an accomplished woman now rather than a traumatized teenager. An attractive woman, if he were honest, but still defensive and evasive. Still holding onto her secrets.

She glanced up reluctantly. "Take as much time as you need. I've work to do back at the house. Just lock up when you're finished."

"Thanks."

She nodded and looked as if she wanted to say more, but instead turned and left the studio. He could see her through the large picture window that looked out on the wooded trail. He followed her progress along the path until she disappeared into the lush vegetation near her deck. Even then he stared after her for a moment longer before returning his attention to the task at hand. Slipping on the headphones, he pressed Start and adjusted the volume. Then he played the recording all the way through her sign-off and hit Repeat.

He'd heard Riley Cavanaugh's voice from videos supplied by her friends and family at the time of her disappearance. Could the caller really be her? Nearly impossible to fathom after all this time and yet Sam couldn't deny a vague familiarity that may or may not have been his imagination. Had he heard this voice before?

After a few more listens, he removed the headphones, turned off the equipment and exited the studio.

Shading his eyes, he gazed across the shimmering water. Spanish moss rippled in the mild breeze as yellow water lilies unfurled in the heat. It was a beautiful clear morning now that the mist had burned off. He took a moment to appreciate the primal beauty of the landscape before lifting his head to trace the old smokestack that rose up through the treetops.

He hadn't been to the Ruins in years, but during those first few weeks of the investigation, he'd spent a lot of time going from room to room, searching through the rubble, sometimes just standing quietly in the shadows as he tried to visualize what had happened. He thought about heading over there now, but he wasn't quite finished with Ellie Brannon.

She was seated at a table on the deck with her laptop. When she heard him on the steps, she closed the lid and glanced up expectantly. Her eyes were a beautiful light blue, almost crystalline even in the shade. She'd brushed her hair while he was gone, pulling the blond strands back into a smooth ponytail that glistened in the morning light. She wore a white T-shirt over jean shorts, and Sam's gaze dropped to her tanned legs for a split second before he caught himself. *Don't even think about it.*

Those shimmering eyes seemed to note his attention as she lifted her chin. "Well?"

He strode across the deck and took a seat across from her at the table. "I'd like to have the recording analyzed if you've no objection. If we can filter out enough of the noise, we may be able to pick up something in the background."

She pushed aside the laptop and folded her arms on the table. "You can do with it what you want, but why waste time and resources? Surely you've more pressing cases."

He said carefully, "I doubt Riley's family would consider it a waste of time and resources."

Her voice sharpened. "I hope you're not planning to talk to them about any of this. At least not yet. It seems unnecessarily cruel to get their hopes up."

"Don't you think they have a right to know?"

"Know what?" she demanded. "That some awful person has come out of the woodwork to torment Jenna and me?"

"The incidents you've both described take planning and coordination. I think we can safely say this has gone beyond the prank stage."

"Then what do you think is going on?" Fear shadowed her eyes as her fingers curled around the chair arms. She was a lot more anxious than she wanted to let on, Sam thought.

He tried to remain cool. The last thing he wanted to do was worry her, but if his hunch was correct, she needed to be on guard. "Do you have any enemies or professional rivals? Someone who would want to damage your credibility? Drive you off the air, maybe?"

"Radio is as cutthroat as any other entertainment medium, but in the scheme of things, my show is small potatoes. I keep my head down and do my best not to offend any listeners or tick off the suits. I'm comfortable in my niche with no ambition to move out of it. Besides, if the phone calls and visits are professionally motivated, why go after Jenna? That's rhetorical, by the way, as I suspect you've already made the same deduction."

He watched her closely. "Yes, but sometimes it's helpful to talk through various scenarios. Process of elimination."

She didn't look convinced. He could hardly blame her. He'd given her no reason to trust him in the past. Finesse and tact had been late additions to his investigative arsenal.

"Tell me more about this Melanie Kent," he said.

"There isn't much I can tell you. My brother said she'd been let go from the publication she worked for in Tyler, and before that, the *Dallas Herald*. He said she'd applied for a job with the local paper, but they turned her down."

"Sounds like she may be getting a little desperate."

Those crystalline eyes had taken on a peculiar glitter at the mention of Melanie Kent. "As unscrupulous as that woman was on her way up the ladder? I hate to think what she'd be willing to do for a story on her way down. I haven't personally spoken with her, but I do find it curious that all these incidents coincide with her return to Belle Pointe. Maybe she's trying to convince both Jenna and me that Riley is still alive so that she can finally write her sequel."

"I'll see if I can find out what she's up to," Sam offered.

"No need. My brother will take care of it."

"I can tap into resources that are unavailable to a county sheriff."

Ellie looked both annoyed and skeptical. "Is that really the job of the FBI?"

"Melanie Kent's name has come up in the course of my investigation. That makes her fair game in my book."

"Investigation? So I'm to take this as an official visit?" She seemed unduly disturbed by the prospect. Sam couldn't help wondering why.

"As I said, the case has never been closed."

"And you follow every lead as they come in. I know. I heard you." She held his gaze for a moment before glancing away. "You should probably talk to my brother anyway if you're planning on being in town for a while. Things will go a lot smoother for you here in Nance County if you alert him of your intentions."

"I'll do that," Sam said with a nod. "I learned the hard way it's not a good idea to get crossways with the Nance County sheriff." He'd had his differences with the first Sheriff Brannon. He'd just as soon not get off on the wrong foot with the current one. "I was sorry to hear about your dad," he added.

Ellie's head came up. "How did you know about my dad?"

"We kept in touch."

Her eyes widened at the revelation. "Why?"

"Mostly to share information. We both made it a point to keep apprised of anyone connected to the Cavanaugh case. If anything relevant came to either of our attention, we passed it on."

She was silent for a moment. "Is that why you listen to my show? To keep apprised of my whereabouts and activities?"

"It may have started out that way. Now I tune in because I enjoy your program."

"Somehow I find that hard to believe."

"Okay. Maybe I am still trying to learn something from your broadcasts," he admitted. "I don't think you're hiding anything, but I do believe it's possible something may come back to you."

She frowned. "After all this time?"

He didn't answer right away, but instead examined a bank of white clouds hovering over the pine forest before bringing his gaze back to her. Her eyes seemed too knowing, as if she could peer into his soul. He found her intensity strangely enticing. "Right after it happened, you said you didn't notice anything out of the ordinary until you heard one of the girls scream. Then you were grabbed from behind. You never got a look at your assailant. Never heard him speak."

"That's right."

"I believe that's what you think, but dissociative amnesia can be a tricky thing. Traumatic memories can be buried so deep it's like the event never happened. Then years later something can trigger a flashback. A nightmare maybe or a photograph. Even the sound of a voice."

"Or maybe I really didn't see or hear anything out of the ordinary that night," she said. "A possibility you never wanted to accept."

He waited another beat. "Have you ever considered hypnosis?"

"I've done more than consider it. I tried it once."

"When was this?" he asked in surprise.

"In college. I couldn't be put under."

"Do you know why?"

She shrugged but it almost seemed more like a shudder to Sam. "A natural resistance to losing control, I suppose. The reason really doesn't matter because the experts will tell you that hypnotic regression is unreliable. The subject's perception of events may or may not be accurate. Which is why forensic hypnosis is still highly controversial."

"That's all true," he agreed. "But under the guidance of a trained therapist, regressive hypnosis can be helpful. I've seen it work."

She sat back in her chair, physically withdrawing from the conversation. "That's great, but as I said, it didn't work for me. What would be the point now, anyway? Nothing will ever bring Riley back. Nothing will ever make Jenna whole again. It might only make things worse for her. And as for their captor..." She closed her eyes briefly. "I have to believe Silas Creed is dead. He's not coming back and I doubt his remains will ever be found."

"You're that certain Creed took Riley? Even though you never got a look at your assailant?"

"Yes. I'm that certain."

Sam sat back, too, contemplating her expression as he tried to tread softly. "There was very little physical evidence tying him to the kidnappings other than a few fingerprints and fibers that could have been left in the Ruins at any time prior to the night in question. No DNA. No eye witness accounts placing him at the scene."

She tried to hide her reaction, but he saw her breath quicken. "So? That doesn't prove anything. Fifteen years ago, the CSI shows on television had already educated the public about DNA and trace evidence. He knew to be careful."

"Do you really think Silas Creed was that sophisticated?"

"He was educated. People seem to forget that about him because of the way he lived after he left the psychiatric facility."

"All right. But do you think he was *physically* capable of following you and your friends to the Ruins and rendering you unconscious with chloroform, which, incidentally, takes a lot longer than movies make it seem. You would have struggled with him. Then when your brother comes looking for you, Creed knocks him on the head, rolls both your bodies down the embankment and flees with presumably an unconscious Jenna and Riley, all without leaving much of a trail."

Fear and dismay glimmered in her eyes, but not surprise. The thought had crossed her mind, too, at some point but she still didn't want to believe it. She dug down deep. "If he wasn't guilty, why did he run? He disappeared without a trace after that night. No one ever saw or heard from him again."

"Maybe he knew that given his mental health history and proclivity for hanging out at the Ruins, he'd be a likely suspect. Every law enforcement officer in the state would be looking for him. Creed had family in the area. Your dad once told me that he'd always wondered if a friend or relative had helped Creed leave town because they were afraid he'd be blamed for something he hadn't done. After all, he would have been an easy patsy. A loner and former psychiatric patient who delivered fire and brimstone sermons to an invisible congregation at the Ruins. He was familiar with the property. Knew every way in and every way out. Think about it. Even the nickname Preacher helped demonize him."

"You sound as if you want him to be innocent." There was an edge of accusation in her tone.

"I only want the truth."

"Still, it would be a fairly substantial boost to your career if you were to solve the case after all this time. Not to mention all the accompanying publicity. You might even score a book deal yourself."

He tried not to take the insinuation personally. "Don't you want the case solved?"

"In my mind, it is solved."

"I get it," Sam said. "It's a scary proposition to think that the real kidnapper could still be out there somewhere. Even if he were still alive, Silas Creed would be getting on in years. A non-threat. But I'm not convinced he was capable of pulling off those kidnappings alone and neither was Sheriff Brannon. We both had to live with the very real possibility that he had an accomplice. Or that a lone unsub may have been right under our noses, someone also familiar with the Ruins and the ritualized practice of local teens daring each other to spend time out there. Someone a lot more devious and clever than Silas Creed." He paused. "Someone who may still reside in this area."

Her face went ashen despite her tan. He heard a tremor in her voice when she spoke. "And you think this person has suddenly decided to come after Jenna and me? *Why?* It's been fifteen years. Why torment us now?"

"You said yourself Riley's disappearance has been all over the local news this summer. Maybe it's awakened something inside him, a need that he's managed to subdue all these years. Or maybe he wants you off balance, wants you to appear unstable and your memory unreliable in case something does come back to you. I don't have the answers right now. That's why I'm here. That's why I needed to come back after all these years."

"No matter how many painful memories you have to dredge up? No matter who gets hurt in the process?"

He hardened his resolve at the raw emotion she tried to blink away. "If that's what it takes to get justice for Riley and closure for her family, yes. Don't you want that, too?"

"Of course I do!"

"Then work with me. Help me find the truth."

"How?"

"If hypnosis is out, we can try returning to the scene. Maybe something will come back to you if we retrace your steps."

The suggestion seemed to render her speechless.

"It'll be okay," he offered lamely.

She shot him a dark look. "That's exactly what I told Riley before we entered the Ruins that night."

Chapter Five

The rest of the day passed quietly for Ellie. No anonymous phone calls, no strange sightings, no visits from the FBI. She tried not to obsess on any of those things, especially her conversation with Sam Reece, as she prepared for the evening's broadcast.

Normally, she was good at compartmentalization, but Agent Reece's visit had opened a door, allowing old fears to creep back in. What if the perpetrator really was someone she knew, perhaps even someone she spoke to on a regular basis? What if he'd watched her from afar for fifteen years, hiding behind a familiar face until those dark urges had lured the monster inside him back into her orbit?

She tried to push the disturbing images back into their cages as she settled down in her office to work. Turning her chair so that she couldn't stare out the window, she opened her laptop and went over her notes. She had an interesting guest lined up for the evening's broadcast. They would be speaking remotely about his latest book on collective consciousness. Ellie knew the author's work so well that it was easy to jot down several bullet points to keep the conversation flowing.

If she wasn't on her game or the interview didn't go as expected, she could opt for opening the phone lines. Her listeners relished the interaction portion of the show. Ellie had always enjoyed their questions and contributions until she started hearing from the unknown caller. Now dread niggled as she left the house late that afternoon to walk the short distance to her studio.

The sun was just sinking beneath the pine trees, casting long shadows across the water. The woods seemed to close in on her. She peered anxiously through the trees before turning to scan the opposite bank.

The August air was hot and steamy, but Ellie shivered as she contemplated her isolated surroundings. The monster from her past was dead and gone, and the shadowy creatures from her nightmares couldn't hurt her. She could stand on the bank of Echo Lake, lift her gaze to the old smokestack that loomed up through the pine trees and not cower in dread. It was just an old artifact. Just an abandoned structure.

Then why haven't you gone back there?

She had, once or twice. In broad daylight. She'd stood in the arched entrance, visualizing the mural on the ceiling from photographs that had run in the local newspaper. The painting had been done sometime after Riley's disappearance, but the demonized depiction with a wide-brimmed hat pulled low over the red eyes was the way Ellie now pictured Silas Creed. It was the way most people in Belle Pointe thought of him, too.

Yet in reality, he'd been a slight, nondescript man, ordinary in appearance except for the hard glitter of madness in his eyes. The fiery orations he delivered from the tumbledown psychiatric hospital had become legendary, but Ellie had never known anyone who had actually seen him at the Ruins, let alone heard any of his apocalyptic preaching.

Had he been falsely accused? Was Silas Creed a tragic

and disturbed individual who had become an easy target for the town's rage? A convenient face for Ellie's fear?

She closed her eyes for a moment, searching her memories and sifting through remnants of her nightmares. She must have seen something that night, heard a sound other than the pounding of her own heartbeat. Had there been footfalls on the stairway? Creaking floorboards? A face peering down at her a split second before everything went black?

Someone had screamed, but she'd never known if it was Jenna or Riley. Ellie had raced back along the second-story corridor to peer over the banister, down into all those shadows.

Riles? Jen? Is everything okay?

When no one answered, she'd started down the stairs, quickly at first and then more slowly as fear dragged at her feet like quicksand.

Something was wrong. Something terrible. It was all Ellie could do not to run away, but she had to find her friends and make sure they were okay. She couldn't leave them here.

A scent came to her as she reached the bottom of the steps. Acrid and smoky, like a smoldering cigarette. She couldn't tell where the scent came from, only that it burned her eyes and made her cough.

Lifting a hand to her throat, she forced herself to move forward, one step at a time...

Jenna? Riley? Where are you? Please answer me. If this is a joke...

Where were they? Where were they? If something had happened to them, she would never forgive herself. This was all her fault...her idea to come out here. Riley hadn't wanted to come...she'd been so scared. Don't be a baby,

*Ellie had taunted. Of course, we're going. We've been
dared. We have to go...*

Riles? You okay? Jenna?

*Something lay crumpled on the floor in front of her.
She thought at first it was a pile of old rags. But the rags
moved...*

*Footsteps sounded behind her as the smell of smoke
grew stronger...an arm came around her waist...something
was pressed against her mouth and nose...she couldn't
breathe...couldn't breathe...the room spun, her knees
buckled...it happened so fast...*

And then darkness...nothing but darkness...

Ellie let go of the memory with a gasp and the black-
ness gave way to the gilded colors of an East Texas sunset.
She hadn't realized that she'd been standing with her eyes
squeezed shut. Now she drank in the sights and scents of
the piney forest, allowing her surroundings to ground her
in the present. That terrible night at the Ruins was fifteen
years behind her, yet her heart continued to pound as a
dark cloud of panic loomed. *Breathe. Slowly in, slowly
out. Now focus.*

She picked a spot on the opposite bank where sunlight
glimmered down through the pine trees.

In... Out...

Already the water lilies were closing for the day. The
cicadas came out, along with swarms of mosquitoes. The
pink horizon deepened to scarlet and then softened to lavender as the sun dropped beneath the horizon.

In... Out...

Ellie's gaze was still focused like a laser on the opposite bank. She could have sworn she saw a boat tucked up
behind the heavy curtains of Spanish moss that skimmed
the surface of the lake. She put up a hand to shade her
eyes as she peered across the water. A human shape took

form through the silvery strands. A man was seated in a boat, head bowed, facial features obscured by the wide brim of his hat.

Her chest tightened. She felt lightheaded with fear. *Breathe!*

A mirage. That's all it was. A figment of her imagination summoned by the deepening shadows. Preacher had been so much on her mind that she'd conjured his ghost. He wasn't real. No one was there.

In. Out.

If one stared at the same place for too long, the light played tricks. Like the explosion of color behind the lids before one drifted off to sleep. Not real.

She said the affirmation aloud. "Not real." Again. "Not real!"

The sound of her voice bolstered her courage. "Hey! What are you doing over there?" The question echoed back to her across the water. She laughed shakily and kept right on talking to the shadows. "Yeah, you!"

No answer. No movement. Nothing but an illusion.

She held her position, even though she had the strongest urge to turn and dash back to the house, lock herself inside and call her brother. Or she might even call Agent Reece. Desperate times called for desperate measures.

Drawing another breath, she walked all the way down to the water's edge, daring the mirage to paddle out into the fading light.

"Who are you?" she shouted across the lake. "What do you want?" Emboldened by the silence, she waved her arms. "Hey, you!"

You're losing it, Elle. Yelling at shadows. Seeing things that aren't there.

The countryside had gone silent at the sound of her voice. She heard nothing now but the lap of water against the bank. The light faded and the sky deepened as she stood there. The lake took on a mysterious shimmer.

"I'm not afraid of you!" she called out. "Know why? Because you're not real!"

Something plopped in the water just beyond the mossy curtain. Ellie told herself it was just a frog or a fish or a turtle. Nothing human. Nothing monstrous.

Another tiny splash, followed by another and another as if someone beyond her view had skimmed a stone across the surface of the lake.

A memory nudged its way out of the fringes.

Not like that, Riles. Skim. Don't throw. It's all in the wrist. Here. Let me show you.

Plop, plop, plop.

Not a frog, not a fish, not a turtle. Someone was over there.

Ellie didn't call out now, but instead stood frozen in silence. Fear lifted the hair at her nape, and she wanted nothing so much as to glance over her shoulder, make sure nothing or no one had come up behind her on the trail. But she was afraid to take her gaze off that silvery curtain in case Preacher could somehow materialize at the water's edge and come for her.

She stared at the spot for another few minutes before bracing her shoulders and deliberately turning her back to the water. What had she hoped to accomplish by yelling across the lake like that? Did she really think Preacher—or Agent Reece's unsub—was sitting in a boat, watching her?

Ignoring the icy prickles up and down her spine, she forced herself to walk unhurried to her studio. Once inside, she calmly locked the door and moved around her console to the picture window that looked out on the lake.

Still nothing moved. *Because no one is there.*

The clattering of her ringtone shattered the hush of her

soundproof studio. She glanced down in dread, expecting to see *Unknown Caller* on the screen, but instead her brother's name appeared. She answered at once.

"That was fast," Tom said. "Everything okay?"

"Yes, I'm in the studio getting ready for the show."

"This early? It's barely even sundown."

"Which goes to show how little you understand about what I do. I don't just show up at airtime and start talking, you know." How perfectly normal she sounded. She was glad Tom couldn't see her at that moment. She must still look a bit wild-eyed. Holding her hand out in front of her, she confirmed a slight tremor.

"I won't keep you," Tom said. "I'm just calling to check in."

"Thanks." She gripped the phone as she peered out the window. She could still see all the way across the lake even as twilight eased in from the woods, blending with the shadows to hide the predators. A mild breeze parted the Spanish moss, but she couldn't see anything or anyone inside the cocoon.

"I need to tell you something before I go," Tom said hesitantly.

His tone jerked her back from the water. "What?"

"It's not a big deal," he rushed to assure her. "But I promised not to keep anything from you. I had a visitor this afternoon. I understand he came to see you, too."

She let out a breath, "You mean Agent Reece. Yes, I saw him this morning. What did he have to say to you?"

"It was mostly a courtesy call, but he did ask if he could take a look at the Cavanaugh case files. He seemed particularly interested in Dad's notes. Apparently, he's decided to look into Riley's kidnapping again."

Ellie shivered. "I know."

"He told me about Jenna. He said she's been getting

anonymous calls, too. And someone left a peacock feather on her front porch." Tom paused. "He also told me about the man in the hat you saw earlier at the Thayer place. Why didn't you call me?"

She tried to keep her tone relaxed. "Because I didn't want you rushing back out to the lake when you've more pressing duties to attend to. Nothing happened. It was just more of the same. Someone playing a prank. Or maybe I imagined the whole thing."

"You didn't imagine anything and you should have called me."

Her brother had a tendency to be overprotective and Ellie usually pushed back, but not today. "You're right. I'm sorry. I didn't think it necessary because I wasn't alone. I ran into Agent Reece on the way home. That's when he told me about Jenna. It seems she's convinced Riley is trying to reach out to us."

"We both know that's not possible," Tom said.

"Yet here Agent Reece is back in Belle Pointe." It was all she could do to suppress another shiver. "I'd like to say that I admire his dedication, but his presence is going to dredge up a lot of bad memories. A lot of bad feelings, too. He wasn't the most tactful interrogator."

"If he crosses a line, you let me know," Tom said.

"I can handle his questions. I just hate that Rae is going to be put through this again." Ellie moved away from the window and took a seat behind her console. "Tom, Agent Reece said something I can't get out of my head. He told me Dad had never been convinced that Silas Creed acted alone. Or that he was even guilty. Did you know they'd stayed in touch? He said they'd both kept apprised of everyone connected to the case and had shared information over the years. I had no idea. Dad never said a word."

"He didn't like bringing that stuff home," Tom said with

a note of caution. "Especially anything pertaining to the Cavanaugh case. He didn't want to upset you."

Ellie tucked a loose strand of hair behind her ear. "I know. He wanted to protect me just like you do, but I hate being kept in the dark. I'm not as fragile as you seem to think."

"I don't think you're at all fragile," Tom protested. "I do think you're too damn hardheaded for your own good at times. But you're right about keeping things from you. That's why I called you as soon as Reece left my office."

"Thanks." Ellie got up and paced restlessly, avoiding the window that looked out on the woods and lake. The deepening shadows unnerved her. "He said Dad had considered the possibility that a friend or relative may have helped Silas Creed disappear because they were afraid he'd be blamed for the kidnapping. He was worried the real kidnapper might be someone local and that the person may even still live in the area. Tom…" She couldn't help glancing out the window. "Did you know about any of this?"

"I knew a lot of people were questioned back then and various theories were considered. That's standard procedure. Or should be. A good investigator does his best to avoid focusing in too early on any one suspect, especially when the evidence is circumstantial. It's too easy to get tunnel vision."

Ellie gripped the phone. "And yet neither of you thought I needed to know about these other possibilities?"

"We didn't want to scare you. You were in a bad way after it happened. You almost died and your best friends were missing. We did what we could to protect you, and as time went on, we made sure you knew how to protect yourself. The last thing Dad wanted was for you to spend the rest of your life hiding behind locked doors or always looking over your shoulder. He wanted you to have a normal life."

"But what about you, Tom?"

"What about me?"

"Is that why you've always hovered?" Ellie asked. "Because you're afraid the kidnapper is still nearby?"

"I don't consider it hovering. I've looked out for you because I'm your brother."

"You didn't answer my question. Tell me the truth. Do you think Silas Creed was innocent?"

"I don't know, Ellie. That's the God's honest truth." She could picture him running his fingers through his hair as the crinkles around his eyes deepened. "I've been over that night in my head a million times and as much as I want to believe he's guilty and that he acted alone…who can say for certain? He did have relatives in the area. It's possible one or more of them helped him get out of town quietly."

"Do they still live around here?"

"His half sister died a few years back. Her son came back home and took over the family farm. I haven't seen or talked to him in years, though I understand he's added greenhouses and a nursery to the vegetable gardens. His property is located about ten miles south of here on Route 27, near Carlisle. His mother always avoided Belle Pointe after what happened. I guess Cory does, too."

"What's his last name?"

"Small."

Cory Small. The name rang a faint bell. "Does Agent Reece know about these relatives?"

"I'm sure he does. The half sister was questioned any number of times after Creed disappeared. Dad always felt sorry for her. She was a widow, trying to make a living in a physically demanding business. She had her hands full. As I understand it, Creed was in his twenties when the family had him committed. They couldn't handle him anymore. He remained in the hospital until the facility closed down in the eighties. By that time, his parents had died. His sister was his closest living relative. She helped him find jobs and a place to live, but she had Cory to look out for. She cooperated with the authorities to a certain extent, but family is family."

"Do you think she helped her brother leave town?"

"It's possible, although her resources were limited. It takes a lot of money and connections to make someone disappear without a trace. The truth is we may never know what happened to Silas Creed. Sometimes I think that might be for the best."

SAM LET HIMSELF into his darkened townhome and flipped on the light as he tossed his keys on the console table in the foyer. He was bone-deep tired and he wasn't sure why. Maybe revisiting the Cavanaugh case wore more heavily on him than he'd anticipated.

Every missing child case haunted him, especially the ones that went unsolved. He'd long ago had to face the grim reality that some families would never find closure, much less peace. The Riley Cavanaugh case was different, not because it had been his first, but because of the nagging fear that he'd missed something. That his arrogance and inexperience had allowed a psychopath to go free all these years, one that may have kidnapped and murdered again.

He tried to shake off a creeping gloom. His office was on the ground floor and he thought about putting in a little extra time at his desk before calling it a night. There was always a case that needed more attention. Never enough manpower or hours in the day to get everything done.

Instead, he went straight upstairs to the kitchen and poured himself a drink. Then loosening his tie and shedding his jacket, he carried the whiskey out to the balcony and leaned a hip against the railing as he gazed off into the night.

His trip to Belle Pointe had stirred a lot of memories. He hadn't been back since he was pulled off the case three months into the investigation. On the surface, the place hadn't changed much, but the rose gardens and picturesque town square hid a lingering darkness. Sam had felt a strange oppression the moment he'd crossed the city limits. Fifteen years after her disappearance, the ghost of Riley Cavanaugh still haunted the shady streets.

He let his mind wander back to his conversation with Ellie Brannon. He couldn't seem to get her out of his head. He'd thought about her on the long drive back to Dallas and for the rest of the afternoon as he'd worked his way through a mountain of paperwork. Even now, hours later, the combination of exhaustion and good whiskey did little to dull his preoccupation.

He believed as he always had that Ellie held the key to solving the Cavanaugh case. Jenna Malloy's memories of her abduction and captivity were locked away forever. Her very survival depended on burying those memories deep. Ellie's experience was different. She hadn't been taken with the other two girls and that, too, remained a mystery. Sam didn't think she was deliberately holding anything back, but there was a chance she'd seen or heard something before she lost consciousness. Something long forgotten. Under the right circumstances, even seemingly innocuous details could still come back. The situation would have to be handled carefully, of course. He would need to slowly gain her trust.

He'd taken the first step today. Planted a seed. Under normal circumstances, she wouldn't be inclined to cooperate, but the sightings had her rattled. No matter how hard she tried to downplay everything that had happened she'd been terrified when he saw her on the trail that morning. Her fear would eventually demand answers, and Sam had long since learned the virtue of patience.

Meanwhile, he would clear his desk and head back to Belle Pointe as soon as his schedule allowed. Something was definitely going on down there. Something more than a prank or a vicious practical joke. Ellie Brannon was being targeted, and even though she had her brother to look out for her, Sam was surprised at how anxious he was to see her again.

Something stirred in the pit of his stomach and he took another sip, using the fire of the whiskey to avoid the inevitable. But the truth was right there, poking and prodding his resolve, demanding his acknowledgment.

The attraction had caught him by surprise. Who would have ever thought? Ellie had been a frightened kid when he'd last seen her. Wounded and lost and yet still defensive when he'd pushed her hard to remember. Now she was a grown woman. Tall, slim, blond with the clearest blue eyes he'd ever looked into. Deceptively clear, because like the town of Belle Pointe, the shadows of her past still lurked beneath the surface.

He couldn't help wondering what her life had been like for the past fifteen years. He knew the basics. An RTF major at the University of North Texas. A talk radio host in a niche market. Single. Never married. Lived alone on the lake.

His life hadn't turned out so different. He lived alone, lived for work. When he moved from DC to Dallas, he'd left behind a string of failed relationships with strong, attractive, successful women. Patient women who'd soon tired of his travel and long hours. Good women who'd eventually been repelled by the darkness that clung like a bad odor after every missing child case.

Ellie Brannon knew all about that darkness. She'd lived it.

That stirring again. A longing that made Sam shift uncomfortably at the railing. That made him peer harder than usual into the night, searching for monsters to quell his human needs.

Ellie was off-limits. Had to be off-limits. Even if she offered encouragement—which she wouldn't—he'd never make that move. After everything she'd been through, she deserved better. Not that he was a bad man. He wasn't. But he lived in the world of her nightmares. He was a good enough man to know that he was a bad match for someone like her.

Why was he even thinking about this?

Maybe he needed to get out of the house. Go out to a bar. Have a few drinks. Make a connection. Forget about the monsters and all those missing kids who paraded through his sleep at night, some he'd found and some he hadn't. Forget about Belle Pointe, Texas, and a missing girl named Riley Cavanaugh and her best friends, Jenna Malloy and Ellie Brannon.

He definitely needed a distraction. It was still early even for a weeknight and Dallas was a vibrant city. *Go have a drink and talk to some people. Remember what it's like out there in the real world.*

He went inside and put his glass on the counter before going back downstairs to grab his jacket. Driving alone at night, he kept his eyes peeled. The predators he hunted were out there even now, lurking around malls and movie theaters, watching from the shadows, watching through windows. Scoping out the easy victims. Sam had learned to live with the bleak realities of his job, but even wide-awake, he'd never found a way to keep the nightmares at bay.

A few minutes later, he found a parking place and walked down the street to one of the few bars he'd visited since his return to Dallas. A lot had changed in fifteen years. The city sprawled in every direction and the traffic seemed endless. He glanced at faces on the street as he walked along, made eye contact now and then, murmured a greeting once or twice. It was good to be out and about. Or so he told himself.

The place was crowded and noisy. The beat of the music vibrated across his nerve endings as he took a seat at the bar and ordered another whiskey, sipping slowly as he observed the crowd in the mirror. He wasn't looking to hook up. Just needed to escape the darkness for a while. Needed to feel normal.

The crowd cleared after a while and a blonde seated alone at a table caught his eye. Slim, attractive. She reminded him of Ellie. He glanced away quickly before she got the wrong impression. Not tonight.

He sipped his drink and wondered if he should order another. He could always take a cab home and pick up his car in the morning. Or he could stop now and go get something to eat. He motioned to the bartender.

His phone rang and Jenna Malloy's name appeared on the screen. As always, he thought about letting the call go to voice mail, but he wouldn't. He never did. He took another sip of his drink, then pressed the phone to his ear in order to hear over the music.

"Hello?"

No answer.

"Jenna? Are you there?"

Someone was there. He could hear music and voices in the background. Then the call abruptly dropped.

He got up and walked outside, leaving his fresh drink on the bar. The evening was warm and clear. He leaned a shoulder against the building as he turned his face to the breeze, still fighting that odd restiveness.

His ringtone pealed again and he answered immediately.

"Jenna?"

"Hello, Agent Reece."

Apprehension prickled across his scalp. He didn't recognize the voice, yet it seemed uncannily familiar. "Who is this?"

A soft laugh.

He could still hear the pounding bass of the music but the sound was muted now. A horn blared on the street and in his ear. Sam's head came up as he glanced around, his senses heightened. He peered at passersby, looking for anyone on a cell phone, which seemed to be almost everyone.

"Who is this?" he repeated. "Why do you have Jenna's phone?"

"I wasn't sure you'd answer if I used mine."

He took a stab in the dark. "Hazel?"

"Very good, Agent Reece."

Jenna's new roommate. The prickling intensified. "Where's Jenna?"

"Oh…she's around."

"Put her on the phone. I'd like to talk to her."

"That's probably not a good idea right now."

"Why not?"

A pause. "She's not herself tonight."

Sam started walking, forcing a slow, easy gait as he searched for the caller. "What's that supposed to mean? Is she okay?"

"Don't worry about Jenny. She'll be back to her old self in no time. Our girl is nothing if not resilient, but I don't have to tell you that. You know exactly what she's been through, don't you, Agent Reece?"

"Why are you calling, Hazel?"

"I thought it a good opportunity for the two of us to talk."

"What do you and I have to talk about?"

"Aren't you curious about who Jenna is living with now? I'm certainly curious about you. She talks about you all the time. She's got quite a thing for you. I'm beginning to see why."

"Where are you, Hazel?"

Another soft laugh.

"Please have Jenna call me. I need to know she's okay."

"I told you, Jenna's fine. I'm more worried about you at the moment."

He paused and glanced around. "Why are you worried about me?"

"You look so lonely tonight."

Reflected headlights in a store window caught Sam in the face. After the vehicle passed by, he glimpsed someone standing on the curb across the street. A blonde with a phone to her ear.

He could have sworn the woman was Jenna Malloy, but when he turned, no one was there.

Chapter Six

Ellie didn't hear from the unknown caller on her show that night. The broadcast ended without a hitch and after she signed off the air, she removed her headphones and let out a breath of relief. Maybe whoever had been responsible for the calls had gotten bored with the prank and moved on.

But the anonymous calls were the least of her worries now. As much as she hated to admit it, Agent Reece was right. Everything that had happened took planning and coordination. Someone had gone to the trouble of finding out where she lived and memorized her daily routine. One hundred and sixty miles away, a peacock feather had been left on Jenna's front porch.

Was it possible the message behind the feather had been meant for Ellie? She was the one who had always loved peacocks. Not Jenna. Not Riley. The feather was symbolic, but of what?

The questions churned endlessly as she finished her nightly tasks. Pausing at the window, she peered out across the water, searching for a hidden boat, searching for shadows and monsters. No one was there. No one that she could see. Still, the notion of leaving the safe haven of her studio to walk the short distance to her deck filled her with dread.

Don't be ridiculous. If Tom thought you were in the

slightest bit of danger, he would never have left you alone. You're fine. Go home, grab a shower and get some rest.

Maybe she'd make a cup of tea, something soothing and aromatic. A few days ago, she would have carried her drink out to the deck so that she could enjoy the night air, but now she anticipated sipping from the comfort of her bedroom with the downstairs doors locked tight and her weapon within easy reach.

She turned off all the lights and stood in darkness for a moment. Then hardening her resolve, she left the studio, locked the door and headed for home. An owl hooted from one of the pine trees as she hurried along the trail. The moon was up, casting a silver radiance over the path and wooded landscape, but the lake looked dark and forbidding.

Glancing over her shoulder, Ellie scanned the trees behind her. A breeze whispered through the leaves and feathered along her bare arms, raising goose bumps. She could smell something pungent on the wind, like the smoke from a distant campfire. Or a smoldering cigarette.

A thrill of fear shot through her. Someone was in the woods. She didn't see anything, didn't hear anything and yet she could feel someone watching her.

He's coming...

The warning echoed in her ears. She almost expected to hear the peal of her ringtone at any moment from the same anonymous caller, but all was silent except for the excited thud of her heartbeat and the drone of a mosquito in her ear. She whirled and darted up the path, tripping in her haste to get home and scolding herself for her carelessness.

As she rounded the bend in the trail, she halted abruptly. What if instead of fleeing from someone behind her, she was running headlong into danger?

She turned her ear to the woods and then to the lake.

Was that the hum of a distant outboard? The lap of water against a fiberglass hull? She swept the water. Why hadn't she brought one of the pistols with her when she left the house earlier? Why hadn't she stayed locked inside the studio until morning?

The darkness closed in on her from every direction as panic hovered.

She took a deep, calming breath and started forward. Her house was just footsteps away. She lifted her gaze to the bedroom window. She could have sworn someone stared down at her, but in the next instant, she realized the movement was just moonlight glinting off glass.

Fishing the key from her pocket, she hurried up the steps. The security lights illuminated the deck and grounds, but still the shadows encroached. She moved to the door, inserted the key and then froze yet again.

Someone had been on the deck while she was sequestered in the studio. The intruder had left a gift, something from Ellie's past that would only have significance to her and to Jenna... And to Riley.

Draped over the doorknob was a length of braided red yarn similar to the friendship bracelets that had been popular for a brief time when Ellie, Jenna and Riley were in middle school. They'd made their bracelets together, weaving strands of each of their favorite colors into the plaits. Ellie's had been blue with intertwining single threads of yellow and red, Jenna's yellow with blue and red threads, and Riley's red with blue and yellow strands.

Ellie touched the faded yarn and an icy tingle shot up her arm. She snatched her hand away as another memory prodded. She tried to push the image away as she glanced frantically over her shoulder.

She wanted to leave the bracelet on the doorknob and pretend she'd never seen it, but when had burying her head in the sand ever been helpful? If someone was coming for her, she needed to be prepared.

Grabbing the braid, she hurried inside and locked the deadbolt behind her. She turned on the kitchen light and scurried down the hallway to check the front door. Satisfied the house was still secure, she went back into the kitchen, put the kettle on and only then did she uncurl her fingers to examine the bracelet under the light.

She told herself it was just a bit of faded yarn. It could have come from anywhere. But that wasn't really true. Even though the bracelet was worn and badly stained, she could still make out the single yellow and blue strands that had been woven into the red braid.

Gently, she placed the bracelet on the counter as memories swamped her.

Riley had worn her bracelet on the night they'd gone out to the Ruins. Ellie and Jenna had teased her about it, but she hadn't cared. She swore the braided band would protect her. The girls had agreed to stop wearing the bracelets when they left middle school. The crude jewelry had seemed too childish for high school. Ellie had tossed hers in the trash one night and then fished it back out the next morning. She couldn't bear to part with it. The interwoven threads signified the bond the girls had shared since kindergarten.

She'd kept that bracelet all these years in a secret compartment of her jewelry box, but she never looked at it anymore. The memories were too painful, the guilt still too strong.

The kettle whistled, startling her. She went through the motions of pouring the hot water over the tea bag, hoping the mundane chore would calm her. But her gaze kept darting back to the bracelet. She wondered where it had come from and where it had been all these years. She wondered about those dark stains.

Should she call Tom? He'd want to know about her latest discovery and yet she hesitated to reach out. She didn't want to worry him, but even more, she hated the notion of dragging Riley's sister back into this nightmare. The Cavanaughs had been through so much. Rae deserved a little peace. She and Tom deserved to be happy.

But was concern for her future sister-in-law the only reason for her hesitation? Maybe she didn't want to acknowledge even to herself that the bracelet might really be Riley's. Who besides the kidnapper could have had it all these years?

Despite her reservations, Ellie knew she needed to tell someone. This wasn't the kind of discovery that could be swept under the rug. The bracelet could very well be evidence.

Plucking a baggie from underneath the sink, she carefully zipped the braid inside. The stains would need to be examined and tested, but nothing could be done at this late hour. Maybe she'd bypass her brother and go directly to Sam Reece. He had a broader reach and a lot more resources at his disposal. If nothing turned up in the tests, Rae would never have to know about the bracelet and Tom wouldn't be put in the uncomfortable and ill-advised position of keeping something from his fiancée.

So far nothing dangerous had happened to her, Ellie reasoned. The calls, the sightings and now the bracelet seemed dark and malicious, but she hadn't been physically threatened. Until that time, there was little her brother could do in an official capacity, and she certainly wasn't going to move into town with him and Rae. She wouldn't be chased from her home or her studio. She wouldn't have her life upended for...what? A prank? A hoax? Someone trying to get under her skin? If someone truly meant her harm, why broadcast his or her intentions?

Turning out the lights, she carried her tea upstairs, along with the bagged bracelet. Placing the cup on the nightstand, she went over to the dresser and opened the lid of her jewelry box. One of the trays concealed the compartment where she stored her most treasured keepsakes.

Removing her friendship bracelet from the box, she placed it on the dresser and smoothed the braid with her fingertip. The blue yarn was unfaded, unstained and not frayed.

Pristine compared to the red bracelet.

SAM'S CELL PHONE woke him up. Usually a call came in the middle of the night when another child had gone missing and his team had been activated. Lately, however, he'd been hearing from Jenna Malloy at all hours. He braced himself as he fought his way up out of the haze.

He still wondered if he'd seen her on the street earlier. Wondered if she'd called from her own phone, pretending to be her roommate. He'd picked up on something in Hazel's voice that niggled. Maybe there was no Hazel Lamont. Why Jenna would pull such a childish prank, Sam had no idea, but he suspected she'd called at least once before pretending to be someone else. When he'd questioned the disguised voice, the caller had hung up and Jenna hadn't contacted him for months.

He lifted himself on his elbow and squinted at the clock he kept on his bedside table, along with his phone and watch. Overkill, he supposed, but old habits die hard. The digital display read a little past one o'clock. Approximately the same time Jenna had called the night before. However, when he picked up his cell phone, he was shocked to see Ellie Brannon's name on the screen.

He came wide-awake as he rolled over in bed and lifted the phone to his ear. "Agent Reece." She didn't say anything for so long that he wondered if his number had been called by mistake. "Hello?"

She cleared her throat. "It's Ellie Brannon."

"Is everything okay?" Sam asked.

Another pause. "I'm not sure. I'm fine physically. But something's happened."

He pushed himself up against the headboard. The illumination filtering in from the streetlights cast an eerie glow inside his bedroom. Fitting, he supposed, since Ellie Brannon's voice in his ear was like hearing from a ghost. "What's going on? Are you sure you're all right?"

"Yes, I'm fine." He heard her take a breath. "Look, this was a bad idea. An impulse. I'm sorry for disturbing you so late."

"Don't worry about that. You said something happened?"

"It's not an emergency. I can explain it all to you in the morning. Right now I should let you get back to sleep."

"No, don't hang up. Tell me what happened."

He put the phone on speaker, allowing her voice to fill his bedroom. Sam felt a shiver down his back as he swung his legs over the side of the bed and reached for his pants.

"When I came back from the studio tonight, I found a friendship bracelet looped over the handle of my back door," she said.

He stood and zipped up. "A friendship bracelet?"

"You've seen them. Yarn or embroidery floss braided together and tied around the wrist. A lot of kids used to wear them. They made a comeback when I was in middle school."

"I know the kind you mean. I remember my kid sister and her friends wearing them." He picked up his watch from the nightstand and buckled it in place. "The bracelet obviously means something to you or you wouldn't have called. What's the significance?"

"Jenna, Riley and I made ours together. It was a huge production, picking out coordinating colors of yarn and so forth. Mine was blue, Jenna's yellow and Riley's red. But we each wove a strand of the other two colors in our braids to symbolize our friendship." She paused again. "I don't know if I'm explaining this well."

"No, I get the picture," Sam said. "Go on."

"The bracelet I found tonight is red. Like Riley's. With blue and yellow threads woven in."

"And you think the bracelet is hers?"

"I know that seems impossible. After all these years? After what she must have gone through?" He heard her take another breath and imagined her sitting in the dark, clutching the bracelet in her fist. Or maybe standing at the window, peering out at the moonlight. "Riley disappeared without a trace. Not so much as a scrap of torn clothing or a broken fingernail was found in the Ruins. Now fifteen years later her red friendship bracelet turns up at my back door. Except... I don't know if it's hers. I don't know what to think about any of the things that have happened recently."

He heard a tremor in her voice and took the phone off speaker. He wasn't sure why. The sound of her vulnerability in his quiet bedroom somehow seemed a little too intimate. He lifted the phone to his ear as he walked over to the window. "Tell me more about these bracelets."

"There's not a lot to tell. They've gone in and out of fashion over the years. When we were in middle school, everybody had one. They were cheap and easy to make. The one I found tonight looks old. It *could* be Riley's. The yarn is faded and frayed, and I noticed some dark stains that might be blood."

That got Sam's attention, though he tried to keep his voice neutral as he peered out into the night. "Maybe that's what someone wants you to think. Anyone could have made that bracelet and dirtied it up to make it look old."

"How would anyone know about those blue and yellow threads, though?"

"You said the three of you wore them in middle school. Someone could have noticed."

"And remembered all these years later? I don't think so. The threads are subtle."

"Where is the bracelet now?"

"Right here on the nightstand beside me. I put it in a plastic bag for safekeeping. If the stains are blood, you could order a DNA test and run the results through some kind of database, right? You could at least prove whether or not the DNA is Riley's."

"It's an interesting possibility." He tracked the headlights of a car pulling into the parking lot. Someone was out late. "Does Sheriff Brannon know about the bracelet?"

"No and I have my reasons for not calling him tonight. I would appreciate it if you wouldn't say anything until I have a chance to talk to him."

"Okay." Sam drawled the word as he considered this turn of events. Curious that she would reach out to him instead of her brother. "I have to say, I'm surprised you decided to call me. You seemed reluctant to speak with me earlier."

"I know. I'm a little surprised myself," she admitted. "I suppose I owe you an explanation."

Sam's gaze was still on the car. The driver had killed the lights but no one got out. "You don't need to explain yourself to me," he said. "I'm just glad you told me about the bracelet."

"No, I think I need to get this out."

She seemed to want to talk and Sam was more than willing to listen. He closed his eyes briefly as her velvety voice seeped into him.

"Earlier after I found the bracelet, I sat for a while in the dark. The house was so quiet I could hear my own heartbeat. I kept thinking about Riley and Jenna…about the horrible things that were done to them. God, the images that went through my head…"

Sam knew all about those images.

"Most of the time, I try not to dwell on the past, but with everything that's happened recently… I don't know. I guess I just needed to hear a familiar voice. To connect with someone who understands what happened back then. Your number was on my nightstand so I called. I really am sorry for disturbing you so late."

Sam took a moment before he answered. He was a little more affected by her explanation than he wanted to admit. Images were also storming through his head. "I gave you my number so you could call whenever you needed to. The why doesn't matter."

"Doesn't it?"

"Only if you want it to." He squinted down at the parked car. He could see a silhouette behind the wheel. The driver was probably waiting for someone, but Sam's job had made him perpetually wary. It was too dark to see a license plate number. He committed a description of the vehicle to memory just in case. "I'm a little concerned about your brother, though. I'd hate to get off on the wrong foot with Sheriff Brannon as I reboot my investigation and I can't imagine he'll be too thrilled with either one of us if we leave him out of the loop. I think you should let him know about the bracelet. He can be at your house in fifteen minutes. It'll take me two hours to drive down."

"You don't need to drive down here tonight." She sounded taken aback by the mere suggestion. "Anyway, you'd have to break every speed limit between here and Dallas to make it in two hours even at this time of night."

"Wouldn't be the first time," he said.

"No, please don't come. That's not why I called. The bracelet seemed like a significant development, and as I said earlier, your number was handy. There's no need to come down here in person. Not tonight."

"Where are you now?" he asked.

She sounded surprised by the question. "I'm upstairs in my bedroom."

"Is the house secure?"

"The doors are locked and the security lights are on. There's a pistol in my nightstand and I know how to use it."

"Good."

"I'm not afraid, Agent Reece."

"It doesn't hurt to be a little afraid," he said. "Let's talk this through for a minute. You say Riley had on the bracelet the night she disappeared?"

"Yes. We teased her about it, but she didn't care. She was always good-natured about our ribbing. That night, though…"

"What about it?"

A long pause on Ellie's end. "She didn't want to go to the Ruins. She said she had a bad feeling about that place. I thought she was just scared by all the stories we'd heard, but looking back, it was almost as if she had some kind of premonition."

"Do you believe in premonitions?"

"I believe we all have internal warning systems and I believe those instincts are more finely tuned in some than in others. Riley felt strongly enough about the Ruins that she wore something that night she thought would protect her."

Sam leaned a shoulder against the window frame. His gaze remained fixed on the parked car. "Let's go back over that night. Everything you said, everything you did. The preparations you made before going out to the Ruins. Tell me anything at all that you can remember."

The old defensiveness crept back in. "I told you everything I remembered fifteen years ago. It's all in the files."

"Then tell me about Riley and Jenna. What were they like back then?"

She didn't say anything for the longest time and Sam thought at first she might not answer. Then he heard a soft sigh. "We were as close as sisters. We even looked alike. Same hair color, same size. Jenna was the smart one. Always so driven and intense, whether it was grades or sports or whatever. I wish you could have known her back then, Agent Reece. We all thought she would one day conquer the world. I've often wondered what she would have done with her life…the things she might have accomplished if I'd been taken instead of her."

"What about Riley?" Sam asked softly.

"She was the sweet one. Always smiling. Always so upbeat and warm. People naturally gravitated to her, but she didn't care about being popular. She came from money, but she was down to earth and humble. Everyone who knew her loved her."

"And you?"

She fell silent again. Sam watched the car below as he waited.

"As hard as it is to admit, there was a time when I cared too much about being popular."

"There's no shame in that," he said. "Teenagers are by nature shallow and self-centered."

"Oh, I was all that and more," she said with remorse. "Not that it's an excuse, but it wasn't always easy being the sheriff's kid. Just ask my brother. The other kids thought they had to watch their every move around us, especially in high school when our social lives became such a big deal. That was why I pushed Jenna and Riley to go out to the Ruins that night. Not just because we'd been dared, though that was important, too—it meant we'd been noticed. I wanted to prove that I wasn't above breaking a few rules now and then. If I'd been even slightly less selfish and immature, things would have turned out very differently that night."

"What happened wasn't your fault," Sam said.

"I know that rationally. But it doesn't change the fact that it was my idea to sneak out of the house and ride our bikes out to the lake. I knew Riley was afraid. I could have backed off at any time, but I just kept pushing and pushing until she finally gave in. Once we were inside, I had to prove how brave I was. That's how we got separated. I went upstairs and left Jenna and Riley alone."

"You had no way of knowing what would happen. If you'd stayed with them, you might have been taken, too."

"I don't think that's true. I was attacked when I came back downstairs. He must have already subdued Jenna and Riley. Drugged them, knocked them unconscious. I don't know how he did it. But I do know that if he'd wanted to take me, too, he would have."

"Why do you think you were left behind?" Sam asked.

"I've asked myself that question a thousand times. The only thing that makes any sense is that I was the sheriff's daughter. Ironic, isn't it, since that's the reason I went out to the Ruins in the first place."

"Who else knew you would be there that night?"

"It wasn't a secret. All our friends were aware that some of the older kids had dared us."

"Anyone specific dare you?"

He heard a shrug in her voice. "Word got around. That's the way it worked back then. Someone told someone who told someone else who told us. But you already know all this. You asked these same questions fifteen years ago. I don't know what good it does to go through it again."

"You've refreshed my memory on some of the details," Sam said. "That's always helpful."

"I guess. But I think I've done enough talking for one night. It's late and you probably have to be at work in a few hours."

"I don't require much sleep." He turned away from the window, reluctant to let Ellie hang up.

"Why do you think all this is happening?" she asked. "What do you really think is going on?"

Now it was Sam who paused. "I don't know. But I promise you one thing. I'm going to find out."

"It's never a good idea to make promises you can't keep, Agent Reece."

Chapter Seven

Ellie was startled to find Sam sitting on her deck steps the next morning when she came downstairs. Despite their late-night phone conversation, she'd risen at her usual time, showered, dressed and dried her hair. Adhering to a routine gave her the illusion of being in control, but the startled thump of her heart at the sight of the FBI agent disabused her of that notion.

She paused at the kitchen window to study his silhouette. He had a strong profile, though his nose was slightly crooked. She wondered if he'd been injured in the line of duty. She didn't recall any physical imperfections from fifteen years ago. She only remembered how intimidated she'd been by the abrasive federal agent who had interviewed her. Intimidated and in awe, if she were truthful. If the circumstances had been different, she might have developed a crush on Agent Reece, but she would never have admitted it in a million years. Instead, she'd cultivated an intense dislike and distrust of the man for pushing her to remember details of a night she desperately wanted to forget. He'd seemed so much older than her back then, more worldly and sophisticated, but here they were fifteen years later, both in their thirties and both looking for answers. Funny how time had a way of narrowing divides.

He sat in the shade but a tiny shaft of sunlight filtered

down through the leaves, shimmering off the silver that was nearly invisible at his temples. He was dressed in his usual attire of suit trousers and dress shirt. Leaving his coat and tie in the car was undoubtedly his idea of dressing down. Ellie wondered if he even owned a pair of jeans, much less a T-shirt and sneakers. His adherence to a strict dress code once again gave her second thoughts about her shorts and sandals, but then she shrugged. She lived and worked in the boonies. No reason to dress up for Agent Reece or anyone else. She was who she was.

Instead of going outside to join him right away, she toasted bagels while the coffee brewed and then assembled cups on a tray, along with cream cheese, jam and fresh fruit. He rose when he heard the back door and strode over to offer his assistance.

"Good morning, Agent Reece," she greeted. "You do know you're trespassing on private property, don't you?"

"I would have knocked, but I thought you might be sleeping in this morning. I didn't think you'd mind if I waited." He nodded toward the loaded tray. "That's quite a spread. I hope you didn't go to all that trouble on my account."

"I didn't," Ellie replied bluntly. "I always have breakfast on the deck when the weather is nice." His unwavering regard disconcerted her, and she avoided his gaze as she set the table and poured the coffee. "What are you doing here so early, anyway? You must have left Dallas at the crack of dawn."

"I wanted to beat the traffic."

"Well, as long as you're here, you may as well sit and have a bite to eat." She waved him to a chair and handed him a cup of coffee.

"Thank you." He accepted the coffee with gratitude, but

waited until she sat before taking his place across from her. "This is a real treat. I usually grab something on the run."

"It's just bagels and fruit. Took all of five minutes to put together." She sounded defensive and made an effort to soften her tone. Giving him a quick smile, she unfolded her napkin and tried to act normal. She didn't want to contemplate why she felt so nervous in Agent Reece's company. Yesterday she'd been defensive because of their past and because she'd been certain he still thought she was hiding something. This was a different kind of tension. In the space of one phone call, something had changed between them and she didn't know why.

Or maybe she did. It was simple, really. She'd let down her guard with Sam Reece. She'd allowed him a glimpse of her vulnerability and now the familiarity between them made her uncomfortable. Strange that the more awkward she became in his presence, the more at ease he seemed, as if he found it perfectly natural to be seated across from her at the breakfast table. Maybe he was used to sharing meals, but Ellie was a loner and had always told herself she preferred it that way.

He eyed her over the rim of his cup. "Everything okay this morning? You seem a little subdued. No more discoveries or phone calls?"

"I've got a lot on my mind these days. But no, nothing since the bracelet." She scooted back her chair. "Should I go get it for you? I assume that's why you're here."

"No hurry. Finish your breakfast."

She nodded reluctantly and settled back down. "What will you do with it? What's the protocol?"

"I'll log it into evidence and send it to the lab for analysis. I have to warn you, these things take time. A case this old won't be considered a priority. It could take weeks to get back the results."

"You can't call in a favor to speed things up?" she asked hopefully. Their gazes connected for a moment before she glanced away.

"I'll do what I can."

She picked up her cup and then set it back down. "This is awkward. I feel I need to clear the air before we go any further."

"About?"

"I want to apologize again for calling you in the middle of the night. I don't know what I was thinking."

"I told you, I gave you my number for precisely that reason. You did the right thing."

He spoke so matter-of-factly Ellie found herself relaxing, but she didn't know if that was a good thing or not. She wanted to believe Agent Reece's charm and goodwill were genuine, but he seemed so different from the intense young agent she remembered. Had he really changed that much or was he playing her? If so, to what end?

"What is it?" he asked.

"I'm sorry?" she asked in confusion.

"You were staring at me now with a pained look on your face." He put down his cup and returned her stare across the table. "I get it. You still don't trust me. But you can. I'm not your enemy."

"There was a time when it seemed like you were my enemy."

"For that, *I* apologize. I had a lot to learn back in those days. But my only objective then and now is to find out what happened to Riley. If possible, to bring her kidnapper to justice. I could still use your help."

She drew a deep breath and slowly released it as if she could somehow let go of the past. Something came to her as the morning breeze drifted across her deck. Fifteen years ago, Agent Reece had conducted himself poorly in his zeal to uncover the truth, but Ellie had clung to her resentment mostly out of fear. Fear that he might be right about her buried memories. What if she had glimpsed the kidnapper's face that night? What if she could have identified him years ago if only she'd had the courage to explore her subconscious?

"I can't be hypnotized," she blurted.

A brow rose at her adamant tone, but his voice remained calmly encouraging. "I'm not talking about hypnosis. I need you to stay alert. Make sure you keep the doors locked and your guard up. Call me if you see or hear anything the slightest bit suspicious. Night or day. I mean that."

Her gaze burned into his. "What else?"

He waited a long beat before he answered. "Return to the scene of the crime with me."

Her heart skipped a beat at the prospect. "Go out to the Ruins, you mean? Do you know what you're asking of me?"

"It's been fifteen years. Don't you think it's time you went back?"

"I've been back."

He cocked his head slightly. "When?"

"A few years ago. I got as far as the doorway."

"You didn't go inside?"

"I couldn't." A panic attack had frozen her at the doorway. She likened the episode to being trapped in her worst nightmare for what had seemed an eternity. When the paralysis finally subsided, she'd turned and headed for home as fast as she could run and hadn't dared go back.

"I think you should try again," he said.

"Easy for you to say."

His voice softened. "There's nothing to be afraid of. I'll be with you every step of the way."

That note in his voice…the way he looked at her…

She had *everything* to be afraid of.

Ellie lifted her gaze. "Surely you don't mean right now. Today."

He sat back in his chair, his posture loose, but his gaze still deeply intense. "We should wait until dark. If we're going to retrace your steps, I'd like to see everything the way you saw it."

She couldn't seem to get rid of the icy needles at the base of her spine. "I'm on the air tonight until midnight. It was just after ten when we went out there that night. Besides, you can't recreate something that happened fifteen years ago. The landscape has changed and there isn't a blood moon."

"Then we'll have to make do with ordinary moonlight. I don't expect you to decide right now. Just give it some thought. I plan to be in town for a couple of days. Maybe we can set something up for tomorrow night. You're off the air on weekends, right?"

"Yes." She told herself not to give him a definitive answer. She needed time to think this through. But what if a trip to the Ruins could trigger a memory? What if returning to the scene of the crime could help lay old ghosts to rest? She wouldn't be alone. Sam would be with her every step of the way. Even so, her pulse quickened as she closed her eyes and saw herself standing in the arched doorway, peering through layers of cobwebs and shadows in search of the monster that lay hidden in her memories.

She turned to the lake, sweeping her gaze over the shimmering water. If she went down to the dock, she'd be able to see the smokestack of the old boiler room rising up through the pine trees.

"You okay?"

The deep timber of his voice drew her back to the deck. Ellie stood abruptly and began clearing the table. "I'll think

about it and let you know. Right now, though, I have a lot
of work to do to prepare for tonight's show. Books to skim,
blogs to read…"

He reached over and put his hand over hers to still her.
"If you could spare another minute…"

A tremor shot through her. She pulled her hand away
and sat back down. "What is it?"

"You mentioned a reporter named Melanie Kent yesterday. I told you I would look into her."

Ellie said anxiously, "What did you find out?"

"Your brother was right about her employment history.
She's lost several positions in the past five years and is
apparently in between jobs at the moment. You were also
right about her aspirations. It seems she's writing another
book."

"How do you know that?"

"I've scanned her blog and social media accounts."

Ellie sat forward. "She has a blog?"

"I'll text you a link. She writes mainly about cold cases
in the tristate area. That seems to be her area of interest."

"That doesn't surprise me. I met her years after Riley's
kidnapping and she was still obsessed with the case."

"Her obsession doesn't appear to have abated," Sam
said. "She has a lot of material on her blog about the investigation—inside stuff. At one time, she must have had
sources within the Nance County sheriff's office."

Ellie nodded. "My dad worried about that. Some of the
information that turned up in the papers could only have
come from inside his department, but he could never root
out the leaker." She paused. "This new book she's writing.
Is it about the kidnapping?"

"Apparently, it deals more with the aftermath. The time
frame is a week or two after the kidnapping until present
day. It seems she's working on a whatever-happened-to

angle." He searched her face as if anticipating her reaction. "She's calling it *The Girl That Got Away*."

A thrill shot down Ellie's spine. "Meaning Jenna or me?"

"Could be both, I guess."

"The caller told me the other night that Preacher is coming for me because I'm the one that got away. Now Melanie Kent is back in Belle Pointe and all these weird things start happening. This can't be a coincidence."

"I'm inclined to agree, but I don't want to jump to any conclusions until I've had a chance to talk with her."

"You haven't been able to find her, either?"

"She gave up her apartment in Dallas a few weeks ago and didn't leave a forwarding address. She isn't registered at any of the area hotels and motels as far as I can determine."

"She's been known to use an alias," Ellie said. "Try Marie Nightingale."

Sam's gaze turned curious. "I'm guessing there's a story behind that name."

"When she was writing her first book, she called a few times under her real name trying to get an interview with me. I wouldn't agree to talk to her so she started calling into the college radio show I hosted using the alias Marie Nightingale. She pretended to be the survivor of a brutal kidnapping. Each time she called, she recounted the most harrowing and horrifying details about her time in captivity."

"Given your background, you were naturally sympathetic to her story," Sam said.

"I hung on her every word and so did my listeners. She was that good. After we'd established a rapport, she asked to meet for coffee and I agreed. I knew it wasn't a good idea, but I felt sorry for her and she was an expert at using my survivor's guilt against me. I couldn't help Riley, but maybe I could somehow help Marie."

"What happened?"

"The next thing I knew she'd wormed her way into every aspect of my life, trolling for dirt to include in her book. One of my friends became alarmed by her obsessive behavior. She told my brother about Marie and he dug around until he uncovered her real identity."

"You haven't had any contact with her since then?"

"Right after the book came out, I took a couple of calls on my show from someone pretending to be a fan. She asked a lot of probing questions and I wondered at the time if the caller might be Marie... Melanie."

"You didn't recognize her voice?"

Ellie met his dark gaze and shivered. "Like I said, she was that good."

AFTER LEAVING ELLIE'S place that morning, Sam made the two-and-a-half-hour drive back to Dallas to fill out the necessary paperwork that would accompany the friendship bracelet to the crime lab in Virginia. He made a few phone calls, hoping to rush things along, but he doubted even under the best of circumstances that he'd hear anything for a few weeks. He worked at his desk until after lunch and then by late afternoon, he was back in Nance County. Instead of driving to the lake or into Belle Pointe, he took the scenic route out to Cory Small's farm.

The lush countryside hadn't changed much in fifteen years. The paved road was shaded by a deep pine forest and scented with honeysuckle that grew in thick hedges along the ditches. Sam lowered his window, letting the fragrant country air wash through his car.

He knew the way despite the passage of time. After the local authorities had requested FBI assistance, Sam had driven out a couple of times with the first Sheriff Brannon and once by himself to talk to Silas Creed's sister. He remembered Ellen Small as a thin, harried woman with a sad smile and a careworn expression. The son, Cory, had been a senior in high school at the time of the kidnapping. Both Sam and Sheriff Brannon had taken a hard look at the boy, but he'd had an alibi for the night in question and nothing so much as a speeding ticket on his record. By all accounts, he was a good kid and model student, courteous, cooperative and protective of his mother.

As Sam neared his destination, professionally painted signs advertising the farm cropped up on the side of the road. He'd done a little research before leaving Dallas. Cory Small had expanded the business after his mother died, adding a nursery and landscaping service to the vegetable gardens. The farm also offered hayrides, picnics and seasonal berry picking to elementary schools in the area. If parents and school officials remembered Cory Small's relationship to Silas Creed, they didn't seem to hold it against him.

A young woman wearing a green logo T-shirt waved from behind one of the fresh produce stands as he turned off the main road. The gates were still open so he drove right through, his tires crunching on loose gravel as he pulled into the parking lot.

He got out and glanced around at his surroundings. The property was beautifully landscaped with lush shrubs and trees and wooden tubs overflowing with flowers. Sam adjusted his tie and put on his suit coat despite the heat. People tended to respond more cooperatively to a professional presentation.

A man watering the hanging baskets gave him a brief nod as he took in the business attire.

"Can I help you?"

"I'm looking for Cory Small."

"He was in the greenhouse last I saw him. Straight back. You can't miss it."

"Thanks."

Sam made his way through the maze of plant beds and displays of ceramic planters toward the greenhouse. The doors were open and two women milled about inside, admiring the orchids. Sam spotted a man at the back unloading more plants. He was in his early thirties, average height, lean build, deeply tanned. He smiled and nodded pleasantly as Sam approached.

"I'm looking for Cory Small," Sam said. "I was told I could find him in the greenhouse."

"And so you have. What can I do for you today? If you're looking for an orchid, the cymbidiums just arrived this morning. They're about as fresh as you can get in these parts. We also have a few exotics, but they'll cost you," he warned.

"I'm not here to buy a plant." Sam took out his credentials. "Agent Sam Reece with the FBI. Do you have a moment to talk?"

The man's guard went up. The smile disappeared as he straightened, casting a wary glance toward the entrance where customers still lingered over the orchids. Then he scanned Sam's identification and glanced up with a frown. "Don't I know you? Yeah, I remember you now. You and Sheriff Brannon came out here to talk to my mother about my uncle after those girls disappeared. You came back the next day by yourself. You asked a lot of questions, as I recall. What's this about, anyway?" His voice dropped as he tugged off his work gloves. "Have you found my uncle?"

"Silas Creed remains a person of interest and is still at large so far as we know. But there has been a new development in the case," Sam said.

The man's expression grew even more guarded. "What would that be?"

"I'm not at liberty to say. Is there somewhere more private where we can speak?"

Cory Small looked as if he wanted to refuse, but then nodded and motioned for Sam to follow him out the back door of the greenhouse. Sam paused as his gaze lit on a black hat hanging from a wooden peg inside the door.

"Is that your hat?" he asked.

Cory glanced back, startled. "I'm sorry, what?" His gaze went to the wall and he frowned. "Oh, the hat. It was my mother's. I can't remember a time she didn't have that thing on when she was working out in the sun. I keep it around because she's still so much a part of this place." He paused reverently. "I've kept all her favorite tools, too. Didn't seem right to get rid of them." He nodded to the crowded pegs beside the hat.

Sam took in the memorial as he expressed his condolences. Silas Creed had been depicted with a similar hat on the ceiling of the Ruins. Sam thought about the description Ellie had given of the person she'd seen the day before— average height, slim build. Wide-brim hat pulled down low to hide his features. His gaze went back to Cory Small.

"She's been gone nearly five years and I still miss her every day," he said. "Always will, I guess."

"It's hard losing a parent no matter your age."

Cory nodded. "My mother's life wasn't easy. I comfort myself that she's at peace now."

He stared at the hat for a moment longer, still with a contemplative frown, before he turned to the back exit and stepped outside. Sam followed him out. They walked several yards away from the greenhouse before Cory turned. "Why don't you tell me the real reason you're here, Agent

Reece? If you haven't found my uncle, what is it you want to talk to me about?"

"As I said, there's been a new development. Since the case has never been closed, we follow up on every lead."

Cory ran fingers through his hair as he glanced out over his property. "I'd like to help you. I really would. But I don't know what more I can do. My mother and I told you everything we could about my uncle after he left town."

"A lot can happen in fifteen years," Sam said. "You or your mother never had any contact with Silas Creed after he disappeared? No phone calls or letters?"

A shadow drifted over the man's features. Something that might have been anger glinted in his eyes. "All these years later and you people are still trying to drag her into that nightmare."

"I don't mean any disrespect," Sam said. "I'm just trying to get at the facts."

"The facts? How many times do we have to tell you? We never saw or heard from my uncle after that night nor did we help him leave town. If you want to know the truth, we were both glad he was gone. We felt terrible about what happened to those girls—"

"Riley Cavanaugh and Jenna Malloy," Sam supplied.

The shadow deepened. "Yes. Riley and Jenna. I went to school with them. My mother knew their families. We would have done anything to change what happened. You can't imagine what it was like for her, knowing her brother had done such a terrible thing. It took years off her life. So, no. I wouldn't have lifted a finger to help him."

"But you can understand why we'd wonder if you had," Sam said. "It's not easy to disappear without a trace."

"That may be true, but my uncle was a lot more resourceful than most people gave him credit for. He was smart and educated. Brilliant in some ways. Read everything he could get his hands on. Highly functional when he took his meds."

"And when he didn't take his medication?"

Cory winced. "He could be volatile. At times, violent. Which was why my mother didn't want him living under the same roof with us. I think her childhood must have been pretty traumatic before her parents sent him away. The stories I've heard?" He shook his head. "After the hospital closed down and they turned out all the patients, she got him a place in town, helped him find work. Saw to it that he had enough money for food and bills. She did what she could and hoped for the best. Then all those stories started getting back to her about how he would stare in people's windows at night and how he would sometimes stand outside the fence at the elementary school, watching the children play. I don't know if any of that was true. You know how cruel people can be, especially when someone is different. But the locals didn't like having him around and that wore on my mother."

"Was he ever violent with either of you?" Sam asked.

"He never hit us or anything, but he could be scary as all get out when he lost control. He'd get this look in his eyes? I remember once when I was about twelve or thirteen, he tried to chop down our front door with an ax. My mother and I hid in a closet until Sheriff Brannon arrived. Who knows what would have happened if he'd gotten inside? I kept my distance after that night."

"How do you suppose he was able to take Riley and Jenna from the Ruins all by himself without any signs of a struggle? He wasn't a big man and yet somehow he subdued three teenage girls and knocked Tom Brannon out cold."

Cory nodded. "I've thought about that. He wasn't big but he was tough as nails. All that physical labor kept him in shape. He had a truck, too, don't forget. He could have loaded those girls in the back and driven across the state line before anyone knew they were missing."

"And then he drove Jenna back to the area nearly three weeks later and let her go?"

"You're the FBI agent. You tell me how he did it."

"It's possible he had help," Sam said. "It's also possible Jenna and Riley were held somewhere nearby. This area is rural with dozens of abandoned farmhouses and barns, not to mention basements and storm cellars. We're talking miles and miles of dense forest. No way to cover every inch of it."

"Yes, but if they were still in the area, wouldn't the bloodhounds have picked up the trail?"

"If your uncle was as smart as you say, he would have known how to mask their scent. But that's a lot for one person to accomplish in a short amount of time. Did your uncle have any close friends or buddies?"

"Buddies? Are you serious?"

"You never saw him hanging out with anyone?"

"People around here thought my uncle a weirdo at best and a psycho at worst. I guess they were right on both counts."

"He was able to get work so he must have had some interaction with the locals."

"People gave him work as a favor to my mother." Cory shoved his hands in his pockets and glanced back at the greenhouse. "Look, this is just a rehash of what we discussed fifteen years ago. I don't have anything new to add to the conversation so if you'll excuse me, I really need to get back to work."

"Just a couple more questions," Sam said. "You mentioned stories about your uncle that got back to your mother. Is that the reason she brought him to the farm to live?"

"She didn't exactly bring him here to live. Sometimes he just needed a place to crash when he took a bad turn. She'd let him stay in the garden shed at the back of the property until things leveled out. He had a kitchenette he could use, a bathroom with a shower, everything he needed, and she made sure he had a warm bed and plenty to eat. He'd sometimes spend weeks holed up out there and never talk to another living soul except for my mother. When he got better, he'd go back to his place in town."

"Is the garden shed still standing?" Sam asked.

"Yeah, it's in pretty good shape. I recently repaired the roof and added a fresh coat of paint. Sometimes one of my seasonal workers needs a place to stay so I try to keep the place livable."

"Is anyone staying there now? I'd like to take a look around before I leave."

Cory frowned. "Why? If you didn't find anything out there fifteen years ago, what makes you think you'll find something now?"

"I don't expect to find anything. Like I said, I just want to take a look around." Sam gave him a pointed look. "Is there a reason you don't want me to go out there?"

He shrugged. "Normally, no, but I've got the place rented out. I don't let strangers stay there as a rule but she was pretty persuasive. One of the stipulations of our agreement is that she be allowed to work without interruption."

"She?"

"Someone from the city. A writer named Melanie Kent."

Chapter Eight

Sam glanced over his shoulder as he strode along the dirt path. Cory Small had returned to the greenhouse and Sam didn't see anyone else about. He'd pretended to go back to his car after their talk, but instead had doubled back once Cory was out of sight.

No wonder he and Tom Brannon had had so much difficulty locating Melanie Kent. The reporter had purposefully dropped off the grid while she wrote another book about the kidnapping. What better inspiration than Silas Creed's former retreat, the place where he'd been holed up when he abducted Jenna and Riley and left Ellie and her brother for dead?

As the structure came into view, Sam paused once more to search his surroundings. Nestled at the tree line, the garden-shed-turned-cottage was quiet and secluded. The charcoal color blended with the deep shade of the woods. Two small windows flanked the entrance and a metal awning over the front door provided protection from inclement weather.

Sam could almost imagine Silas Creed peering out one of the windows, tracking his approach. The hair lifted at the back of his nape. He didn't believe in ghosts or demons, but in his experience, evil had a tendency to linger in physical places. He tried to shake off a dark foreboding as he walked the perimeter, noting the placement of windows and the rear exit before he came back around to knock. He rapped firmly and the door creaked open. Melanie Kent hadn't felt the need to lock up, which likely meant she was either inside or somewhere nearby. He toed the crack wider.

"Federal Agent! I'm here to see Melanie Kent. Anyone home?"

He glanced over his shoulder. The path behind him remained clear. He turned back to the door and called out again. "This is Agent Sam Reece with the FBI. I need to speak with Melanie Kent."

Still no response.

He pushed the door inward and stepped over the threshold. The late afternoon sun shone through the open windows, creating shafts of warm light in the shadowy interior. His gaze swept the room. No red glowing eyes peering around furniture. No lurking silhouettes in darkened doorways.

No Melanie Kent, either.

On first glance, the place seemed almost pleasant in its utilitarian design. The rough-hewn walls had been painted white, but the floor and ceiling beams had been left natural. It was only on deeper scrutiny that one noticed the gloom creeping in from the corners.

Sam took a moment to scope out the place. The kitchenette was located to his immediate left and the living space to his right consisted of a worn chair, a neatly made daybed and a small desk, which doubled as a nightstand. A ceiling fan stirred pages in a yellow legal pad that had been tossed on the bed and the dozens of images that had been tacked to the wall above the desk.

Sam took a quick glance out one of the front windows before he strode across the room to browse the photo-

graphs. Melanie Kent had divided the images into two cat-
egories—people and places. Sam started with the Ruins.
The reporter had shot the crumbling hospital from every
angle at various times of the day. The place looked to be
in a lot worse shape than he remembered. Most of the
front windows were broken and boarded and the roof had
collapsed in places. An old wheelchair lay upended in the
weeds. Sam studied the exterior shots before following
the photographic trail inside where graffiti covered the
walls and Preacher peered down from the ceiling. The red
glowing eyes beneath the brim of the black hat seemed to
pierce right through the camera lens.

Upstairs, the reporter had meticulously documented the
shadowy rooms where gurneys and rat-infested mattresses
had been piled to the ceiling, and on the third floor, where
sunlight glimmered down through the holes in the roof and
vines snaked in through jagged windows.

She'd photographed the lake, the Cavanaugh ranch and
various locations in Belle Pointe, including the sheriff's
office and the houses where Jenna Malloy and Ellie Brannon had grown up.

Then there were the people pictures—old photographs
of Ellie, Riley and Jenna intermixed with recent snapshots
of Jenna and Ellie. Neither woman appeared to know she
was being surveilled, much less photographed. Melanie
had taken only a few candid shots of Jenna, but dozens of
Ellie relaxing on her deck, exiting her studio and standing on the dock, peering down into the water. Apparently
she'd been watching Ellie for weeks. Sam took his time
with those images, but eventually his attention drifted back
to Jenna.

He removed one of the photographs for a closer scrutiny.
Jenna was sitting on the porch steps of a white house—
presumably her place in Dallas—gazing out at the street.

It was an arresting shot, quiet and pensive, and yet Sam found something unsettling about her facial expression and body language.

His pulse jumped as he plucked one of the older photographs of Riley from the wall, his focus going back and forth between the photographs. The same tilt of the head, the same dreamy half smile...

Why would Jenna emulate Riley's mannerisms so closely? Or had it been the other way around?

He moved over to the window to examine the photographs in better lighting. The similarities to Riley were troubling enough, but now he saw something in the shot of Jenna that he hadn't noticed before.

A woman stood at a window peering out at Jenna. The porch lay in deep shadows, rendering the silhouette nearly invisible. Sam wondered if Melanie Kent even realized she'd captured a second person in the photo. Who might this mystery person be? Hazel Lamont, perhaps? Maybe Jenna's new roommate existed, after all.

He told himself there was nothing strange or unusual about someone gazing out a window. Yet his uneasiness deepened as he remembered his conversation with the roommate and his initial impression that he might have been speaking to Jenna. Had Hazel Lamont deliberately manipulated him into doubting her identity?

Taking out his phone, he clicked off a few frames and returned the photographs to the wall. Then he picked up the legal pad and thumbed through the handwritten draft, pausing here and there to skim a passage.

The girls were similar in appearance— indeed, they were often mistaken for sisters—but as different as night and day in personality and upbringing.

Riley came from money. That alone set her apart. Before the start of each school year, her sister, Rae, would

*plan a weekend excursion to Dallas for the two of them.
Booking a suite at the Ritz, they'd pamper themselves with
expensive lunches, spa treatments and lavish shopping
sprees.*

*Her two best friends could hardly imagine such luxury,
though Jenna's family was comfortably middle class and
she was a coddled only child. The Malloys lived in a beautifully restored Victorian house on King Street with lush
front and back gardens and a maid who came every two
weeks to clean the house and do the laundry. Independent
and assertive, Jenna was the first of the trio to go away
to summer camp, the first to get her own cell phone and
later, the first to earn her learner's permit.*

*Ellie Brannon's family lived in a modest two-story home
on Oak Street. Her father was the county sheriff and her
mother a homemaker who sometimes worked as a substi-
tute teacher to bring in extra income. From an early age,
the kids were expected to pull their weight. Ellie babysat
to earn spending money and her brother, Tom, mowed
lawns. Rather than extravagant shopping trips to Dallas for school clothes, Ellie had to settle for outlet malls
and thrift stores. She once bought a pale blue cashmere
sweater from a church rummage sale only to discover that
it was one of Riley Cavanaugh's castaways. The humilia-
tion dogged Ellie for months and fed into the jealousy that
had already put a strain on the friendship.*

Jealousy? That was the first Sam had heard of any trouble between Ellie and Riley. He took the revelation with a
grain of salt. He'd learned the hard way that Melanie Kent
relied heavily on artistic license to create drama.

Sam scanned a few more pages and then tossed the note-
book back on the bed. Taking another quick glance around
the room, he left through the same door he'd entered.

The sun had dipped beneath the treetops by this time,

casting long shadows across the path. He stepped to the edge of the woods, keeping a sharp eye out as he checked his voice mail. He didn't have to wait long. A woman dressed in jeans, sneakers and a striped T-shirt came hurrying along the trail. Her sunglasses and the brim of her floppy hat disguised her features, but Sam had no doubt as to *her* identity. Who else but Melanie Kent would be headed for the garden shed at this time of day?

Using bushes for concealment, he pressed deeper into the shadows as someone called out her name. She glanced over her shoulder and then turned as Cory Small came into view. Removing her sunglasses, she dropped them into the tote slung over her shoulder and moved beneath the awning to wait.

"I'm in a hurry," she said as he approached. "Whatever this is about, can it wait?"

"No, it can't," he said bluntly. "You've been dodging me for days and I'm sick and tired of your runaround. We agreed on a weekly rental, remember? That means you pay up every Friday, but I haven't seen a dime since you moved in."

She folded her arms. "We also agreed I wouldn't be disturbed while I work, but here you are."

His voice hardened. "You're giving *me* attitude? Get over yourself. I'm not running a charity here. I only agreed to let you use this place because I needed the extra cash."

She gestured toward the nursery and gardens in the background. "Looks like you're doing all right to me."

"This is a slow time of year so I need every buck I can get my hands on just to make payroll. If you can't afford to pay what you owe, then pack up and get out."

"Or what? You'll throw me out? I told you I'd have your money by the weekend and I will so ease up, Bubba."

He caught her by the arm. "Don't call me that."

"Let go of me," she said in a deadly quiet voice.

"You think you can just blow me off? This is still my property."

"I *said* let go of me." She yanked her arm free, but they still stood toe to toe, face-to-face.

For a moment, Sam thought he might have to step out of his hiding place and intervene. This was a side of Cory Small he'd never witnessed before.

"Careful," Melanie taunted. "You just might reveal your true colors."

"What's that supposed to mean?"

She threw her head back. "I know your type. Good ol' boy on the surface with all kinds of nasty resentment festering beneath."

"You don't know anything about me."

"I know *everything* about you. I've researched every aspect of your uncle's life and how closely it intersected with yours and your mother's. I even found out something the cops don't know."

Sam stood stone still, riveted by the argument as he peered through the leaves.

"Oh, yeah? Like what?" Cory demanded.

"You'll have to read my book to find out."

He gave a derisive snort. "That's what I thought. You don't know anything."

"I guess we'll see, won't we?"

He seemed amused now. He folded his arms and leaned a shoulder against the wall. "Instead of keeping all these little secrets to yourself, maybe you should talk to the FBI agent that came by a little while ago. He sure seemed interested in you. He even wanted to come out here and take a look around."

Melanie stared at him for a moment. Then she glanced

down the trail uneasily as she clutched the strap of her tote. "What FBI agent? You better not be lying to me."

"Now, why would I lie to you?" Cory drawled. "Fiction is your specialty, not mine."

"I don't write fiction."

"That's your opinion."

Sam saw her draw a deep breath, as if she were hanging onto her temper by a thread.

"Did you get his name?" she asked.

"Agent Sam Reece. He's not exactly a stranger in these parts."

"I know who he is. Did he say what he wanted?"

"What's it worth to you?"

"For God's sakes, just tell me!"

Cory looked as if he were thoroughly enjoying himself now that he thought he had the upper hand. "Maybe I'll write a book so you can find out."

"Don't be an ass. Tell me what he said."

"Apparently, there's been a new development in the Riley Cavanaugh case. He was pretty tight-lipped, but I'm starting to wonder if it has something to do with you. Strange how you turned up out of the blue the way you did."

"What's so strange about it?"

"You're up to something. I can feel it."

"I'm writing a book, moron. That's what I'm up to."

He let the insult roll off his back this time, but Sam saw the glitter of something unpleasant in the man's eyes. "Moron, huh? I'm smart enough to recognize bad news when I see it. See, I know you took something from the greenhouse the other night. I just can't figure out why."

"What are you talking about?"

"My mother's hat. The one that hangs on the wall? It

was missing when I went to lock up night before last. Today it was back in its normal place."

She shrugged. "Maybe one of your workers borrowed it."

"They know better. Taking something without asking permission seems more like something you'd do."

"I have my own hat, thank you. I wouldn't dream of desecrating that little shrine you've erected to your mother. But keep telling yourself Agent Reece was here because of me. Denial is not just a river as they say."

"You really are a smug little—"

"Watch it, Bubba. Your misogyny is showing."

As Sam exited the nursery, he noticed a beige sedan parked in the shade of a large oak tree. The sun glinted off the windshield so that he could make out little more than a female silhouette behind the wheel. She ducked her head when she saw him staring. Then she started the engine and peeled out, showering gravel in her wake.

Sam wondered if the vehicle was the same one he'd seen the night before outside his townhome in Dallas. He had a dark hunch that Hazel Lamont was the driver. He hadn't been sure she existed until now, but the snapshot he'd found in the garden shed had convinced him otherwise. There was something intriguing about that figure at the window. Something a little disturbing about the way she watched Jenna from behind the glass. Sam got out his phone and enlarged the image. The shadows hid her features, but he had the impression of malice. His imagination or gut instinct?

Sam pocketed his phone and strode to his car. He had no idea why Jenna Malloy's roommate would be following him, but he intended to find out.

He left the farm and headed toward Belle Pointe. The

road behind him remained clear until he reached the city limits and then he caught a glimpse of the beige sedan in his rearview mirror. He slowed and the vehicle quickly gained on him until the driver seemed to realize her mistake and backed off the gas. Sam drove through town, stopping for every yellow light to allow his pursuer time to catch up.

He pulled into the Belle Pointe Inn, removed his bag and checked in. Then he rode the elevator up to his third-floor room and after a quick perusal of his accommodations, he went over to the window and parted the curtains. The beige sedan was parked across the street facing the inn.

Sam strode out of the room and took the stairs two at a time down to the lobby. By the time he exited the building, the vehicle had disappeared.

ELLIE WAITED UNTIL she was safely home that night to check her messages. Sam had left a voice mail just after nine o'clock when her broadcast had barely begun. Maybe he'd lost track of the time or had forgotten when her program started. Or maybe his message was so important that he hadn't wanted to wait until she was off the air, much less until morning. However, he didn't sound urgent nor did he give her a clue as to why he was calling. He merely asked that she return his call when she got the chance.

Ellie tapped her fingers against the counter in deep contemplation. Maybe the reason for the call was to try to arrange a time for a trip to the Ruins. In which case, she needn't call back until morning because she hadn't yet made up her mind. Retracing her steps on the night of the kidnapping might seem a reasonable thing to do, but the very thought filled her with dread. She'd visited that place too many times in her nightmares. If she closed her eyes, she could imagine a dark-clad figure in a parson's hat skulking through the shadowy corridors, waiting until she had her back turned to grab her.

She'd researched the effects of chloroform, knew that even with a saturated rag pressed to the nose and mouth, it could take five minutes or longer to subdue a victim. Yet she couldn't remember much of a struggle. Surely she'd fought her assailant until she'd succumbed to the fumes, but all she remembered was a hand clamped to her mouth and then darkness. Had she glimpsed the kidnapper's face before she'd gone under?

How could a single attacker overcome three teenage girls without one of them managing to break free? Maybe someone really had helped Silas Creed that night and now the accomplice had once again turned his attention to the girl that got away.

Ellie replayed Sam's message. His tone was calm and measured. Almost soothing in a way. No need to be alarmed. She was letting her imagination anticipate the worst. She would call him tomorrow. Meanwhile, a little space was a good thing, especially since she still regretted her impulse the night before. The intimacy of that call troubled her. She could acknowledge and deal with the glimmer of attraction she'd felt upon his return. But letting down her guard and inviting him into her innermost thoughts was a complication she didn't need at the moment.

Despite her resolve, his message continued to niggle as she put on the kettle and waited for the water to boil. The results of the DNA testing on the bracelet wouldn't be back for weeks so that couldn't be the reason for his call. She let her mind skip ahead to the possible outcome of those tests. If the blood embedded in the yarn belonged to Riley, then someone, possibly an accomplice, had held onto her bracelet all this time. If the blood belonged to Silas Creed, then maybe the Cavanaughs could finally have some sort of closure. Assuming, of course, the DNA could be matched. Silas Creed had at least one relative in the area. Surely he could be persuaded to provide a sample.

On and on her mind churned while she fixed the tea, made sure the house was locked up and then carried her cup upstairs to get ready for bed. Nestled under the covers, she sipped the chamomile and watched a mindless TV program on her tablet until she grew drowsy. Sam didn't call again. That was a good thing, she decided.

Finishing her drink, she unplugged and got up to brush her teeth. She stood at the window for a few minutes, watching the glint of moonlight on water. A breeze animated the shadows along the bank, causing her heart to thud with each movement. She stared hard into the night, but if anyone watched from afar, she didn't notice.

Climbing back into bed, she turned off the lamp and pulled up the covers. Despite the chamomile, she felt tense and out of sorts. Why couldn't things just go back to the way they'd been before the Unknown Caller had reached out to her? Before someone in a black parson's hat had appeared at the top of the embankment. Before the bracelet, before the peacock feather, before Sam Reece had come back into her life.

The monsters had been there all along, nipping at her heels, but somehow she'd managed to keep them at bay. Now they'd come slithering through her defenses, coiling and hissing at the fringes of her memory until she once again began to doubt herself. What had she seen that night?

She lay on her back and watched the shifting patterns on the ceiling until she finally dozed off. Her cell phone awakened her sometime later. She bolted upright in bed, still groggy and unsure of what she'd heard until the ringtone pealed again. She picked up the phone and peered at the screen. *Unknown Caller.*

Don't answer. Let it go to voice mail.

But she couldn't ignore the call any more than she could pretend everything had gone back to normal while she slept. She hit the accept button and lifted the phone to her ear.

"Hello?"

"Ellie?"

Riley? She almost said the name aloud before she caught herself. "Who is this?"

"Don't you recognize my voice?"

Ellie came wide-awake with another start. "Jenna?"

The ensuing silence went on for so long that Ellie thought the call might have dropped.

"Jenna? Are you there? Hello?"

"I'm here—"

Her voice cut out. Ellie pushed herself up against the headboard as she gripped the phone to her ear. "Hello? Hello?"

The voice sputtered to life. "Can you talk?"

By this time Ellie was thoroughly distressed. Jenna sounded strangely muffled, as if she were speaking from underneath the covers or inside a closet. As if she didn't want someone nearby to overhear. Strange that such a thought would even occur to her. A weak signal was the logical explanation.

She cleared her throat as she tried to clear her head. "Yes, of course I can talk. But you're breaking up a bit."

"Hold on." Another long pause. Then, "Is this better?"

"Yes, I can hear you now. But you're calling awfully late. Is everything okay?"

"It's late?" Jenna sounded confused. "I'm sorry. I sometimes lose track of time when I get like this."

Apprehension tingled along Ellie's spine. "Like what? What's wrong, Jen?"

Ellie heard a shuffling noise as if Jenna were moving around while they talked. Then she heard what sounded like another voice in the background.

"Jenna? Are you alone? Is someone there with you?"

"It's…no one."

Ellie was starting to get a very bad feeling about this phone call. She tried to remember the last time she'd spoken to Jenna. Must have been months ago. Had she been like this then? It wasn't unusual for her to sound vague and distracted, but this seemed different somehow, though Ellie couldn't put her finger on exactly what it was that bothered her. Maybe the late hour was cause enough to worry.

"Ellie?"

"I'm here, Jenna."

"I'm sorry I woke you up. You're not mad at me, are you?"

The uncertainty in her voice made her seem young and vulnerable. Ellie swallowed past a sudden lump in her throat as memories stirred. "I'm not at all mad. I just want to make sure you're okay."

"Can I ask you a question?"

"Of course. Anything."

Her voice dropped to a near whisper. "Do you ever think about that night?"

Ellie closed her eyes. "Yes. Every day of my life."

"Do you ever wonder…?" Jenna's words trailed away.

"What, Jen?"

"Why you weren't taken?"

The question was so softly spoken Ellie might have thought she'd dreamed it. She drew a breath and released it. "Every day of my life."

"Why me and not you?" There was a harder edge in Jenna's voice now.

Ellie gripped the phone. "I don't know. I've asked myself that same question a million times over. Maybe because my dad was the sheriff or because my brother came looking for me. We'll likely never know."

"Don't you think it strange that you and Tom were both spared? That you were the *only* ones spared?"

She asked the same question that any number of people in Belle Pointe had asked behind closed doors for the past fifteen years. Why had only Sheriff Brannon's kids been saved?

Ellie gave her friend the same answer that Tom had always given to her. "I don't think we were spared. I think we were both left for dead. Tom was hit in the back of the head so hard it took nearly thirty stitches to sew him up. When he came to, he found me lying facedown in the water. It's a miracle I didn't drown."

"But you didn't drown, did you? You lived."

"So did you, Jen."

"Did I? Sometimes I wonder. Maybe I'm not really here at all. Maybe I'm just a ghost lost in all this mist." Her voice was still soft and wistful but that underlying darkness worried Ellie.

"You're not a ghost. You're a survivor and you're stronger than you know," she said fiercely.

"I don't feel very strong tonight."

"What's wrong?" Ellie drew up her legs and huddled beneath the covers. "Has something happened?" When Jenna didn't answer, she started to panic. "Where are you calling from?"

"Why does that matter?" Jenna asked.

"I just want to make sure you're somewhere safe."

"I'm safe…for now."

"What does that mean, for now?"

"Nothing. It just means the future is always uncertain.

Who would know that better than me? Can I ask you something else?"

Ellie braced herself. "What is it?"

"What do you remember about that night?"

She thought about how to respond. "We've talked about this before. I'm not sure it's a good idea to go over it now. It's very late."

"Please, Ellie. I've been having so many dreams lately. Just tell me what you remember once we got to the Ruins."

Ellie didn't want to talk about that night. She'd long ago come to the conclusion that it did no one any good to dwell on the past. But she could hardly deny Jenna's tremulous request. Maybe going over the details would somehow be cathartic this time. "We split up once we were inside. I went upstairs while you stayed below with Riley. I walked down the hallway, glancing in rooms until I heard a scream. I couldn't have been gone that long. It seemed like only minutes. I ran back downstairs to make sure you and Riley were okay. That's when I was grabbed from behind. I don't remember anything else until I woke up in the hospital."

"Are you sure you didn't see anyone there that night? Even just a glimpse?"

"Not that I can recall." Ellie paused. "Did you see someone?"

"Maybe. I'm not sure. I have all these images in my head, but I can't make sense of them. Everything seems so blurry and distant. Like I'm trying to peer through clouds."

"Yes. That's exactly the way it seems to me, too," Ellie said. "Tell me about these dreams you're having."

"I'm inside the Ruins. The moon looks blood red through the broken windows. I stand there, listening to the creaks and moans in that old place and I think about all the patients that once lived there. All the misery that must still be trapped there."

Ellie shivered. "Go on."

"I can hear the wind in the trees outside and the scream of a peacock down by the water. Cobwebs stick to my hair as I move across the room. *Shush.* Riley said she heard something." Her voice changed as she shifted verb tenses. Ellie wondered if she even noticed. "We thought she'd imagined the sound at first. She was so nervous about being there. You told her not to be a baby and then you left us and went upstairs."

She was no longer recounting a dream, but a memory. When she paused, Ellie could hear whispering somewhere nearby. She tensed.

"Jenna? Who's with you?"

"I told you. No one."

"I can hear someone whispering to you."

Another pause. "How do you know she's not whispering to you?"

Goose bumps popped along Ellie's arms. "She?"

"I don't hear anything," Jenna insisted. "It must be your imagination."

Was that a taunt? Ellie wondered.

"Where was I?" Jenna asked. "Oh, yes. Riley heard something. She was right, of course. Someone *was* there. After you went upstairs, she and I heard footsteps in one of the other rooms. Then we heard a door open and close. Riley said she saw someone staring at us from down the hallway. I figured it was just one of the older kids trying to scare us so I went to check it out. I told Riley to wait for me."

She and Riley had separated? This was new information to Ellie. "What else do you remember?"

"I don't remember anything. I'm telling you about my dream."

"What else do you remember about your dream?"

Another silence stretched before she said softly, "The floor is cold."

"The floor in the Ruins?"

Jenna ignored the question. "The floor is cold, but Riley's skin is burning up, like she's on fire from the inside."

Ellie's heart skipped a beat. Jenna was no longer inside the Ruins. She'd fast-forwarded to her and Riley's captivity. Ellie had never heard her talk about it before. As far as she knew, Jenna's memory of that time was a complete blank. Something must have been unleashed in her dreams. The images she'd conjured were so disturbing Ellie wasn't sure how to proceed. She didn't want to push, but neither did she want Jenna to retreat.

"Where are you in your dream?" she asked softly.

"I don't know. It's pitch black in here. I feel my way around the room over and over, but I can't find a door or window. Just bars. I think we're in a cell or a cage. No bed, no chairs. There's a bucket in the corner. You know. For when we need to go. After a few days, the smell gets really bad."

Ellie took several breaths. "What about food and water?"

"A little now and then. Not enough for Riley to get better. I've tried giving her my share, but she won't take it. She just gets weaker and weaker. She hasn't eaten anything in days and she no longer talks to me."

"Is she...?"

Jenna's voice hardened. "I don't want to talk about that."

"You don't have to talk about anything you don't want to," Ellie soothed.

"Don't hang up, okay?"

"I won't. I'm here for as long as you want me."

"Ellie?" The voice grew soft again.

"Yes?"

"I'm scared."

"In your dream?"

"No, in real life. I don't want to fall asleep. If I close my eyes, he'll come for me."

"Who, Jen?"

"Preacher." The word was spoken in a reverent whisper.

A wave of panic washed up through Ellie's chest and clogged her throat. For a moment, she allowed herself to be drawn into Jenna's delusion. What if Silas Creed really was alive? What if he'd been watching her, too? How else would he have known she would be at the Thayer house feeding the peacocks that morning?

With an effort, she reined in her paranoid thoughts. She needed to stay calm for Jenna's sake. "That's not possible. Silas Creed is dead. He can't hurt you anymore. He can't hurt anyone."

Jenna's voice rose. "You don't know that! No one can know that for sure. Except maybe Riley."

"Riley isn't coming back, either, Jen."

"Then why is she calling me? Why is she leaving clues on my front porch?"

"You mean the peacock feather?" Ellie swung her legs over the side of the bed and got up to pad over to the window. The moon was so bright she could see all the way across the lake. She trailed her gaze along the bank, searching through the shadows.

Jenna said sharply, "How did you know about the feather?"

"Agent Reece told me."

"When did you talk to Sam?"

Sam? "He came down to see me after you told him about the call that came into my live broadcast."

"Then he believed me?"

"About the call? Of course he did. I played him the recording."

"I don't mean that. Did he believe me about everything else? He must have. Why else would he have made the trip to Belle Pointe if he didn't think Riley was still alive?"

"I wouldn't read too much into that," Ellie cautioned. "It's his job to follow every lead, no matter how remote. I know you want to believe Riley is still alive. I do, too. But we have to be realistic. It's been fifteen years."

"I am being realistic," Jenna said stubbornly. "She's alive and she left that feather on my porch to prove it. Somehow she's managed to get away and she's trying to warn us about Preacher."

"Jenna—" Ellie broke off abruptly as she moved closer to the window. She could see the dock of the empty fishing cabin across the moonlit lake. Two women sat on the edge, dangling their feet in the water. At least, Ellie had the impression they were female. She could make out the soft curves of their silhouettes and the outline of long hair down their backs. They sat very close, heads together, shoulders touching. As she watched, one of them got to her feet, quickly undressed and dove into the water. Ellie was so riveted by the scene that for a moment she could have sworn she heard the splash.

She pressed the phone against her ear. *Had* she heard the splash?

Jenna's voice broke into her reverie. "We have to find her, Ellie. Sam will do what he can, but you and I both know we're the only ones who can save her."

The woman in the water swam back to the dock and

hitched herself up beside the other figure. Ellie watched from afar as her nerve endings bristled.

"Maybe we should meet and talk this through. Where are you, Jenna?"

Her voice grew petulant. "Why do you keep asking me that?"

"I told you. I want to make sure you're safe."

"And I told you, I'm safe for now. When do you want to meet?"

"Tomorrow is my day off. I can drive to Dallas first thing."

"No, don't do that."

"Why?"

The swimmer scooted closer so that their heads were together once again.

Ellie cradled her phone against her shoulder as she opened the window. Voices carried at night and over water. She leaned out, letting the night air stir her tangled hair. She listened closely, but the only sound that came to her was the breeze whispering through the leaves.

"Why don't you want me to drive to Dallas?" she asked.

"I'll come there," Jenna said. "Let's meet in town. I've been meaning to get back to Belle Pointe anyway. I'll text you later and we can figure out a time and place."

"Jenna?"

"Yes?"

"Are you sure you're alone?"

"I'm alone and never alone all at the same time. But I don't expect you to understand that."

"Jen—"

"Good night, Ellie."

She remained at the window as both figures rose. One of them started up the steps that led to the cabin. The other grabbed her clothes from the dock and glanced over her shoulder as she dressed. Ellie was too far away to know for certain, but she could have sworn the woman's gaze lifted to her bedroom window.

Chapter Nine

Ellie couldn't fall back asleep after her conversation with Jenna. So many disturbing things had come to light during the course of that call, not the least of which was the possibility that Jenna may have been sitting across the lake the whole time they'd spoken. But why?

Everyone in town knew the fishing cabin had been empty since the owner's death earlier in the summer. Anyone could have driven out to use the dock for a midnight swim. It made little sense that Jenna and her companion had come all the way from Dallas to go out to the cabin in the middle of the night.

But Ellie couldn't shake the suspicion that Jenna had been hiding something. Nor could she forget Jenna's *dream* revelations that seemed to have merged with her forgotten memories. Those dark images kept Ellie tossing and turning until dawn broke and she finally threw back the covers and got up. She worked around the house and in her office until midmorning when she received a text from Jenna. They agreed on a time and place to meet and then Ellie went back upstairs to shower and dress.

A little while later, she drove into town and found a parking place down the block from the restaurant. Located across the street from the Belle Pointe Inn, the Lantern Grill had been a staple in town for as long as Ellie could remember. The elegant eatery enjoyed a brisk dinner business, especially on weekends, but most people sought out the less expensive and more family-friendly atmosphere of the Corner Diner for lunch. Ellie had suggested the Lantern Grill for that very reason. She and Jenna could sit at a quiet table without being disturbed.

Jenna was already seated at the back of the restaurant by the time Ellie walked in. She looked lovely in a soft blue top that matched her eyes and complemented her blond hair. A stranger seeing her in passing would never have suspected the trauma she'd been through in her lifetime, but Ellie immediately noted the faint shadows beneath the blue eyes and the hollows in her pale cheeks. She'd lost weight since they'd last met.

Another young woman was seated beside her at the table. She was also blond, but with strawberry highlights and eyes more green than blue. Despite the summer heat, she was chicly dressed in black with large gold hoops in her earlobes. As Ellie approached the table, the woman leaned over to whisper something in Jenna's ear, reminding Ellie of the two silhouettes she'd spotted across the lake the night before.

She paused briefly beside the table to smile down at Jenna. They made no move to embrace. A tacit agreement had kept a formal distance between them for years.

"Hello, Jenna."

"Ellie! There you are!"

"I hope you haven't been waiting long." She slid into the chair directly across from Jenna. "You look lovely as always. What a beautiful top."

Jenna smoothed a hand across the silky fabric. "Hazel picked it out."

Ellie's gaze moved to the stranger.

"I'm sorry," Jenna said quickly. "You two haven't met

yet, have you? Jenna, this is my roommate, Hazel Lamont. Hazel, this is—"

"You don't have to tell me who she is. I would know Ellie Brannon anywhere." She gave Ellie a long appraisal as she thrust her hand across the table. "You look just as I imagined."

Ellie wasn't quite sure what to make of the woman's gregarious greeting. Or the hint of slyness glinting in the green-blue eyes.

They shook hands. "This is quite a surprise. Jenna didn't mention that you would be driving down with her," Ellie said.

"I hope you don't mind my crashing your little party. I've been dying to meet you in person for a long, long time. Of course, I feel like I already know you. Jenna has told me *so* much about you."

Ellie wondered if the emphasis was meant to provoke a reaction. They'd only just met so any assessment on her part would be tainted by her suspicion that Hazel had been with Jenna on the dock of the fishing cabin last night. In the light of day, Ellie was less certain of what she'd seen— or whom she'd seen—but she couldn't shake the feeling that Hazel Lamont was more than she seemed.

A coy smile tugged at the corners of her lips as if she'd correctly interpreted Ellie's misgivings.

Ellie slung the strap of her bag over the back of the chair and did her best to relax. "When did you drive down? You must have gotten an early start."

"Oh, yes. We're both morning people, which makes for a harmonious living arrangement," Hazel said. "Wouldn't you agree, Jenna?"

Jenna nodded as she locked gazes with Ellie. "I would. There aren't many people I could live with these days, especially since I've come to realize how rare true friendship really is."

"Well said," Hazel murmured, her gaze also on Ellie.

Why do I feel ambushed? Ellie wondered. The vibe at the table was odd to say the least. But then the conversation with Jenna the night before hadn't exactly been normal.

"Hazel isn't just my roommate, she's my hero," Jenna added. "She's saved my life on more than one occasion."

"And you mine." They exchanged a glance and a smile. The intimacy between them didn't seem at all romantic, but certainly more than a casual friendship. They seemed to want Ellie to be aware of their closeness.

She took it all in from across the table, trying to keep her demeanor pleasant and her tone mildly curious. "How long have you known each other?"

Jenna unfolded her napkin. "Not as long as you and I, but long enough. We lost contact for several years. A mutual friend who knew that I was looking for a roommate put us back in touch."

"It was fate," Hazel declared as she propped her elbows on the table and rested her chin on folded hands. "But enough about us. Let's talk about you, Ellie. I've listened to your radio show with Jenna. You have some strange people calling in, but what a fascinating way to make a living."

"It has its moments. Other than my job, though, I'm a pretty boring subject."

"Just a simple, small-town girl," Hazel said, still with that hint of guile.

"Yes, pretty much. What do you do, Hazel?"

"Oh, look how you managed to turn the conversation back on me so quickly."

"You'll have to forgive my curiosity," Ellie said. "It isn't every day I get to meet Jenna's roommate."

"Then ask me whatever you like. I'm an open book.

Mostly." She winked. "As for what I do, I'm between jobs at the moment. Luckily, I don't have to worry about finances."

"That is lucky," Ellie said. "Where did you two meet?"

Hazel turned to Jenna. "Should I tell her the story or should we keep her guessing?"

"Now I think you have to tell me," Ellie said.

Hazel seemed to consider. "Maybe later."

The server appeared with glasses of water and menus. Hazel said briskly, "We'll need some time. We're still catching up."

"Let me know when you're ready." The young woman discreetly faded away.

Hazel fiddled with one of her earrings, drawing Ellie's attention to the large moonstone on her right hand. Recognition stirred and for a moment the milky iridescence seemed to mesmerize her. Riley had once had a ring very similar to the one on Hazel Lamont's finger. She'd stopped wearing it one day and claimed she'd lost it. When Ellie had offered to help her search, she'd mumbled something about the ring bringing her bad luck anyway. For someone so young, Riley had been awfully superstitious.

"She recognizes it."

Hazel's voice drew Ellie back with a start. "What?"

A smug smile flashed before Hazel glanced at Jenna. "See? I told you she'd remember."

Ellie felt an irrational urge to snatch the ring off the woman's finger. She tamped down the compulsion as she studied Jenna's expression. "That can't be Riley's ring. She told me she lost it."

Jenna's smile was a fleeting imitation of Hazel's. "She didn't lose it. She gave it to me."

Ellie frowned. "Then why would she tell me she lost it?"

Jenna's eyes glittered with something dark and unpleasant. "She didn't want you to know. You always loved her things so much. Her clothes, her shoes. Especially her jewelry. She was afraid if she told you she'd given the ring to me, you'd be angry."

"Why would I be angry?"

"Come on, Ellie. You were always jealous of my relationship with Riley."

Ellie felt blindsided by the accusation. "That's not true. I loved you both like sisters. I'm stunned that you would think otherwise."

Jenna merely shrugged. "I guess we remember things differently."

"I guess we do."

"It *is* a beautiful ring." Hazel waggled her fingers. The moonstone shimmered mockingly at Ellie. "I don't blame you for coveting it."

"I never—" Ellie broke off, turning her attention back to Jenna. "Maybe this wasn't such a good idea after all. I think another day might be better for our discussion."

"Oh, I'm sorry. Am I in the way?" Hazel asked innocently, but Ellie had the feeling she wasn't sorry at all. The uncomfortable vibe she'd detected earlier had turned into an antagonistic undercurrent.

"I just think it might be better for Jenna and me to discuss certain things in private."

Jenna bristled. "We can talk in front of Hazel. I trust her with my life."

All well and good, Ellie thought. But she wasn't sure she trusted Hazel Lamont with hers.

She was wondering how to gracefully exit the table when she spotted Sam Reece at the front of the restaurant. Their gazes connected and he nodded briefly before he started toward their table. Ellie didn't say anything until he was almost upon them and then she looked up in relief, happier to see him than the situation warranted. She noted his suit and tie, and decided he must still be on the FBI clock even though it was Saturday.

Across the table, Jenna visibly started when she saw him. Her hand flew to her heart as her gaze lifted. "Agent Reece! What a surprise to see you here."

"I'm a little taken aback myself." He glanced around the table, his gaze lingering on Ellie before he shifted his focus back to Jenna. "I was across the street at the inn when I saw Ellie come inside. I decided to try to catch up with her."

"Is everything okay?" Ellie asked anxiously.

"Yes. Just a matter or two I wanted to talk over with you." He searched her face, his eyes smoldering with mystery. She couldn't deny the impact he had on her and wondered if anyone else had noticed. She took a quick survey. Jenna stared back at her, frowning.

"You two are on a first-name basis?" she demanded.

"No," Ellie said a little too quickly. "That is, I'm not." Why did she feel so defensive, all of a sudden? So intensely aware of Sam Reece staring down at her?

Hazel loudly cleared her throat. "I don't think we've met. At least not in person."

Before Jenna could make the introductions, Sam said, "You must be Hazel."

She extended her hand, gazing up at him through long, thick lashes. "And you're the famous Agent Reece. Jenna has spoken of you often. How wonderful to finally put a face with that deep voice." She leaned over and whispered something in Jenna's ear, causing her roommate to nod as her frown deepened.

Ellie couldn't help noticing that Sam kept his contact with Hazel brief. He dropped his hand to his side as he said to Jenna, "You didn't mention you were planning a trip to Belle Pointe the last time we spoke."

"It was sudden. Ellie suggested we meet." She made it sound like an accusation.

Ellie tried to shrug off her qualms as she addressed Jenna's claim. "After you called last night, I thought it a good idea that we talk in person."

"And here we all are," Hazel said cheerfully.

Sam's gaze was on Ellie again. She glanced away, more rattled by his attention than she wanted to admit.

"Won't you join us, Agent Reece?" Hazel invited. "Or do you prefer Sam?"

"Agent Reece is fine."

Hazel's tone shifted imperceptibly. "In any case, you'd be a welcome distraction. The conversation had taken an awkward turn when you came up. Sit down and I'll tell you all about it."

He lifted a brow at Ellie. She scooted over to the next chair, allowing him to sit across from Jenna. Ellie was now seated across from Hazel. The roommate gave her a knowing look, which Ellie had no idea how to interpret.

"Jenna and Hazel were just about to tell me how and where they met," Ellie said, before Hazel could mention the ring.

"Why is that awkward?" he asked.

"I guess it all depends on your perspective," Hazel replied. "We met at the Penn Shepherd Hospital in Dallas. I believe you're familiar with the facility, Agent Reece?"

"I am, yes."

"The Penn Shepherd Hospital," Ellie murmured. "Isn't that where—"

"They lock away the crazy people? Again, depends on your perspective." Hazel was still smiling but her gaze on Ellie had darkened. "I was a patient there when Jenna was admitted."

Jenna put her hand on Hazel's arm, but she gently brushed it away. "It's all right, Jenny. We're among friends." Her gaze slid back to Sam. "Maybe Agent Reece would be interested in knowing why I was there."

"Only if you feel like talking about it," he said.

"Yes, I think I do." Her eyes glittered dangerously. "When I was sixteen, my parents were brutally murdered by an intruder as they lay sleeping in their bed one night. For a while, the FBI agent assigned to the case considered me a suspect."

"Why was the FBI involved in a homicide investigation?" Sam asked.

"I'm sure it had something to do with my father's business affiliations, if you get my drift."

"When and where did this happen?"

Ellie marveled at Sam's calm response. She felt stunned by the revelation and was almost certain her eyes, if not her entire body, reflected the shock.

"Sixteen years ago at our home in Westlake."

"Ritzy neighborhood," Sam noted.

"You can look it up. Ken and Cynthia Lamont. Anyway, my uncle, who had been appointed my guardian, decided that I was having trouble coping with the loss. Acting out, as he called it. He thought a nice long stay in a psychiatric hospital might help me deal with my emotions. My incarceration also gave him ample time and opportunity to steal a sizable portion of my inheritance."

Sam remained unfazed. "That's quite a story."

"I thought you might enjoy it."

Ellie wondered if even a word of it was true.

"As luck would have it, when Jenny came to the hospital, the only available bed was in my room." Hazel's gaze moved back to Ellie. She looked quite pleased with herself. "We became fast friends. *Sisters*. We told each other *everything*."

"How long were you roommates?" Sam asked.

She sat back in her chair, somehow managing to look bored and amused at the same time. "A few months. At some point, the staff decided we needed to be separated. They claimed I was a bad influence, if you can imagine such a thing."

I can, Ellie thought. With very little effort.

"But you weren't," Jenna said fervently. "You were my only friend in that awful place. I couldn't stand being there after they moved me."

"We're together now," Hazel soothed. "That's all that matters. And no one will ever separate us again. *No one*."

Ellie and Sam exchanged a worried glance, which seemed to agitate Jenna. She sat forward suddenly. "I'd like to know what you're doing to find Riley, Agent Reece. I have a right to know about your investigation."

He answered cautiously. "I've made some inquiries."

"What kind of inquiries?"

He sat back as he studied the table. "Has either of you been contacted by a woman named Melanie Kent?"

Ellie started. "You found her?"

"Who's Melanie Kent?" Hazel leaned in, mimicking Jenna's posture. It was disconcerting to see the two of them together. Hazel seemed overbearing and protective, her larger-than-life persona completely overshadowing the reserved Jenna. Yet Ellie had the strangest notion that the real power in the friendship belonged to Jenna.

"Melanie Kent published a book about the kidnapping several years ago," Sam explained. "Apparently she's writing a sequel." He got out his phone and scrolled through the camera roll. Then he turned his phone so that Jenna could see the screen. "Do you recognize this photograph?"

Jenna stared at the image for the longest time. "When did you take that?"

"I didn't. I found it tacked to the wall of a converted garden shed where Melanie Kent has been staying." He rotated the phone toward Ellie. "She has several candid shots of you on that wall, as well."

Ellie frowned. "She's been taking pictures of us without our knowing? Why?"

Sam shrugged. "I'm sure she'd call it research. My guess is she's been at it for weeks."

Hazel reached over and snatched the phone, using her fingertips to enlarge the image. "I remember that day. You'd just moved in, Jenny. Your parents had come to help unload all the boxes. You walked them outside and sat down on the porch to watch them leave."

"When was this?" Sam asked.

"A couple of weeks ago at least. Sometimes it's hard to keep track. Days tend to run together even out in the real world."

"You said she's staying in a converted garden shed?" Ellie asked. "That seems a little strange."

"Not as strange as you might think." Sam placed his phone on the table. "Which brings me to my next question. How well do you remember Cory Small?"

"He was a student at Belle Pointe High School at the time of the kidnapping," Ellie said. "He would have been going into his senior year at the end of that summer."

"What else?" Sam asked.

"He's Silas Creed's nephew. I barely knew who he was before the kidnapping, but afterward, he and his mother were all anyone in town could talk about. I came to feel very sorry for them. All those ugly accusations and gossip must have taken a toll. He transferred to another school before the start of his senior year. I didn't keep up with him after that."

"He runs the family farm and a landscape nursery south of Belle Pointe," Sam said. "I drove out there yesterday to have a chat with him."

Jenna's eyes widened. "Why did you want to talk to him? Do you think he knows something about Riley?"

"Not necessarily. There's always been the question of whether or not someone helped Silas Creed leave town. Small still denies that either he or his mother was involved."

"Of course he would deny it," Hazel muttered.

Ellie's father had thoroughly investigated the Smalls after Silas Creed disappeared. He'd found no evidence that either had been in any way complicit, but there were those in town who had already passed judgment. People needed someone to blame and Silas Creed's family became an easy target. Ellie could only imagine the bad memories stirred by Sam's visit.

"I've no reason to believe he's done anything wrong," Sam said. "But I'm curious if either of you remember anything out of the ordinary."

Jenna shrugged. "I'm sorry. Nothing comes back to me."

"Are you sure? Think hard." Hazel placed her hand over Jenna's. "Didn't you once tell me there was an older boy in high school who had a thing for Riley?"

Jenna grew nervous and snatched her hand away. "How could I tell you about something I don't even remember?"

Hazel's voice dropped to a soothing monotone. "No worries. I must be mistaken. The name sounds a little familiar to me, too, but maybe I heard it from someone else."

Sam's gaze narrowed in puzzlement. "Who besides

Jenna would have talked to you about Cory Small? Or about Riley, for that matter?"

"Maybe it was the reporter you mentioned earlier," Hazel suggested. "Melanie something-or-other."

"I didn't say she's a reporter."

Her gaze faltered. "Well, whatever she is, maybe she mentioned this Cory Small person."

"Then you have talked to her?" Sam pressed.

"It's possible," Hazel said with an ambiguous shrug. "She's obviously been hanging around our house."

"But you don't remember speaking with her?"

Hazel sighed. "I'm bored now. I don't want to talk about this anymore."

Sam's phone beeped. He glanced at Ellie, silently communicating the weirdness of the conversation before he picked up his cell. He read the text message, then pocketed his phone. "Would you excuse me? I need to make a quick call."

Ellie nodded. "Of course."

"Hurry back," Hazel drawled.

Jenna seemed hardly to notice his absence. Her gaze was on Ellie. She still looked upset, but there was something hard glittering beneath the faraway gaze.

Ellie wanted to find out more about an older boy's crush on Riley, but she hesitated to distress Jenna. She seemed to hover on a dangerous precipice, anxious and reticent one moment, hardened and resentful the next. Maybe it would be better to let Sam handle the questioning.

She pushed back her chair. "This seems like a good time to visit the ladies' room. Would you excuse me, too?"

Hazel gave a lethargic wave. "Take your time."

Ellie glanced back as she moved away from the table. The two heads were together again as Hazel spoke animatedly in Jenna's ear. Then she slowly turned and winked, as if she'd known all along that Ellie would be watching. As if the two of them shared some deep, dark secret. A chill shot through Ellie as she whirled and started toward the front of the restaurant.

She glimpsed Sam through the large plate glass window. His expression was intense as he stood in the shade, phone to his ear. Ellie wondered about the text message that had prompted what appeared to be an urgent call. She wondered a lot of things about Sam Reece. Why hadn't he told her earlier about his conversation with Cory Small?

Which brought her back to Hazel's disturbing claim. If Jenna had been aware of an older boy's interest in Riley, why hadn't Ellie known about it? The three friends had always confided in each other about boys, parents and everything else. Cory Small had been a rising senior that summer. Getting hit on by an older guy wasn't something a fifteen-year-old girl would have kept from one of her best friends. Or so Ellie wanted to believe.

But it seemed Riley and Jenna had kept other things from her, as well. She'd certainly been clueless about the moonstone ring. Had she really been the type of person in whom neither of her closest friends thought they could confide?

Inside the ladies' room, she stood at the sink, going through the motions of washing her hands, tightening her ponytail and reapplying her lipstick. She didn't want to go back out to the table. Jenna's erratic behavior was more than a little troubling. *And don't get me started on Hazel.*

After applying a second coat of lipstick, she took her time putting everything back in her bag. The door opened as she stood contemplating her reflection. Hazel sauntered in, looking as sleek as a cat in expensive black jeans and a fitted tank top. Ellie watched her suspiciously in the mirror. The enigmatic woman moved toward the stalls but didn't go inside one. Instead she stood behind Ellie so that their reflected gazes met. Ellie felt a tingle of apprehension but she tried not to show it. Tried not to worry that she was alone in the bathroom with a woman who may or may not have murdered her parents.

"Barely There," Hazel said.

Ellie stared at her in confusion. "I'm sorry?"

"The name of your lipstick. Barely There. Am I right?"

Ellie fished the lipstick from her bag and glanced at the bottom of the tube. "How did you know that?"

"Jenna has worn that same neutral shade for years, even though I tell her it's too bland for someone with her looks. She's attractive enough to go for a much bolder color. The shade suits you, though."

The dig might have amused Ellie if she hadn't found the woman's performance so unnerving. And it was a performance, Ellie was almost certain.

Hazel cocked her head, still watching her in the mirror. "You don't wear much makeup, do you? Don't fuss with your hair or bother with your clothes." Her gaze took in Ellie's simple sleeveless dress and sandals. "Just a simple small-town girl."

"We've already established I'm a boring subject." Ellie looped her bag over her shoulder as she turned from the mirror. "Do you have a problem with me?" she asked bluntly.

Hazel shrugged. "Why would I have a problem with you? I know exactly who and what you are. You seem to have Agent Reece fooled, though."

"I'm sorry, what?"

Hazel tossed back her hair. "I saw the way he looked at you just now. Jenny saw it, too. You must know how she feels about him. Why would you flaunt your relationship in front of her?"

Ellie stared at her in stunned disbelief. "I have no idea what you're talking about. I don't have a relationship with Agent Reece. I hardly know him."

"So you say. But I happen to know the two of you have been spending a lot of time together lately."

The revelation made Ellie uneasy and borderline frightened, but she tried not to show it. "How would you know that? Have you been watching my house?"

Hazel's eyes flared. "So you admit Sam Reece has been out to your place recently."

"Didn't Jenna tell you? He came to see me because she was worried about the phone call that came into my radio broadcast."

"Of course she told me. She tells me everything." Hazel moved up to one of the mirrors, running fingers through her strawberry tresses. "If anyone were to ever hurt her again, I just don't know what I would do."

Ellie hated confrontations, especially an unfair attack from a woman she'd only just met. Her first instinct was to walk away, but instead she leaned back against the counter as she met Hazel's gaze straight on. "Why on earth would you think I'd ever hurt Jenna? She's my friend, too."

"A true friend would never have left her that night."

The accusation stung no matter the accuser. "I didn't leave her."

"Oh, right. You were rendered unconscious. Tossed down a hill and left for dead. Or so you say. But, conveniently, your brother was the only one who could corroborate your story."

"It wasn't a story. It was the truth."

Hazel's voice rose menacingly. "You have no idea what she went through. You may think you do, but you don't." She turned on the faucet and vigorously scrubbed her hands, as if trying to wash away something tainted. "It was storming the night they brought her into my ward. I remember the flashes of lightning through the windows and how the thunder helped to drown out her screams."

Dear God, her screams?

Ellie suppressed a shudder as she studied Hazel's reflection. The enigmatic woman wasn't so much beautiful as striking, the reddish-blond mane framing a long, narrow face dominated by those aqua eyes. Like Jenna, she was thin almost to the point of gauntness, but her arms looked toned, her hips and thighs sinewy beneath the fitted jeans. The image of a jungle cat once again came to mind. Fast, sleek and deadly.

Their gazes met once more and Hazel's smile sent a fresh chill rippling along Ellie's nerve endings.

"Jenny was like a wild thing that night, like something had come completely unleashed inside her. The orderlies had to hold her down to sedate her. Then they had to strap her to the bed because when the drugs wore off, she tried to pull out her hair and claw off her skin. They left her in my room even when another bed opened up because I was the only one who could calm her. I sat with her night and day. I held her hand for hours. I was there for her when no one else wanted to come near her, including her own parents. Including *you*."

Ellie's blood ran cold with shock. Every word Hazel spoke was like a knife thrust into her heart. "I came to the hospital to see her. At first, they wouldn't let anyone in, and then later, she…didn't want visitors. Not for months. But I'm glad she had you. You were a good friend to her."

"We were so much more than friends. I don't expect someone like you to understand, but Jenny became a part of me. When they took her away, it was like they'd cut out a piece of me."

"Why did they take her away?" Ellie couldn't help asking.

"I told you. They thought I was a bad influence. They put her in another wing and wouldn't let me see her because one of her doctors decided I was feeding her delusions. I wasn't feeding her anything." She dried her hands just as forcefully. "She wanted desperately to believe that Riley was still alive and so I gave her hope. I still do."

Ellie frowned. "By convincing her Riley is still alive? What happens when she finds out otherwise?"

"She won't because Riley isn't dead."

"How can you possibly know that?"

Hazel paused, cocking her head as she searched her reflection. "You really don't understand, do you?"

For a moment, Ellie wasn't sure if Hazel had addressed her or an invisible third party that only she could see. "Understand what?"

Hazel peered more closely into the mirror, turning her head first one way and then the other. She seemed fascinated by her own image. "Do you know Jenny's parents?"

Ellie checked the door, wishing someone else would walk through. The more time she spent alone in Hazel's company, the more unsettled she became. Yet she couldn't seem to tear herself away from a conversation that both fascinated and repelled her. "I used to. They moved to Fort Worth after the kidnapping to be closer to Jenna's doctor."

"Is that what they told you? That's funny. Jenna said they moved away because of you."

Was that true? Ellie wondered. The Malloys had sold their beautiful home and left town because of her? Because they blamed her for what happened?

A wave of nausea washed over her, even though she told herself to take anything Hazel Lamont revealed with a grain of salt. Hazel was obviously the one who had a bone to pick with Ellie, not the Malloys.

"They've never accepted the fact that their daughter is

all grown up. They still forbid her to associate with the *wrong* people." Hazel air-quoted in disgust. "It seems we have more in common than you think."

Ellie really hoped that wasn't true. Hazel Lamont seemed unstable and vindictive, a treacherous combination.

She was still watching Ellie in the mirror. "Her parents took her away from Penn Shepherd without letting us say goodbye. Jenny was there one day and poof...gone the next." Her eyes took on the same faraway look Ellie had noted in Jenna's. "They wouldn't even let her write to me. No visits, no phone calls. There's always a way, though. I didn't forget Jenny and she never forgot me. When I was able, I used some of my inheritance to buy a house in a nice, quiet neighborhood. Then I went to rescue Jenny."

"Rescue her?"

Hazel turned with that disturbing smile. "Yes, rescue. Her parents now know there isn't anything they can do to keep us apart. You should probably know that, too." She moved in closer, forcing Ellie to take a reluctant step back. "I'll let you in on a little secret."

Ellie swallowed. "What's that?"

"You may know how to deal with the freaks and weirdos that call into your radio show, but you've never dealt with anyone like me."

Chapter Ten

Sam was alone at the table when Ellie came back. He rose as she approached. She looked around, perplexed. "Where's Jenna?"

"She got a text message and rushed out of here. She said to tell you she'd call you later." He paused. "Everything okay? You look upset."

"I just had a run-in with Hazel Lamont in the bathroom. I'm sure the text message Jenna received was from her."

Sam touched her elbow briefly. "What happened? What did she say to you?"

"I'll tell you outside." She threw some bills on the table, even though they hadn't yet ordered. "Let's get out of here. I've lost my appetite."

They wound their way through the maze of tables, pausing outside the door while Sam scanned the street.

"Are you expecting someone?" Ellie asked anxiously as she moved into the shade of the building. The late summer sun beat down on the concrete walkway and she was still feeling a little queasy from the confrontation with Hazel.

Sam lifted a hand to shade his eyes briefly before he stepped back beside her. "You didn't happen to see what kind of car Jenna and Hazel were in, did you?"

"No, they were already inside the restaurant when I got here. Why?"

He looked uneasy. "A beige sedan has been tailing me for the past two days. I'm trying to figure out who the vehicle belongs to."

Ellie stared at him in confusion. "You think the car belongs to either Jenna or Hazel?"

"It's just a hunch." His attention was still riveted on the street. "I haven't been able to get a good look at the driver or the plate number."

Ellie glanced over her shoulder. She couldn't seem to help herself. It was the middle of the day. People were out and about. No reason to feel afraid and yet she couldn't shake the chill that had deepened with every word Hazel Lamont had uttered.

"You must have a reason for your hunch," she said.

He answered reluctantly. "Nothing specific, but their behavior has been troubling lately."

"*Their* behavior? I thought today was the first time you'd met Hazel."

"In person, yes. She called two nights ago from Jenna's phone. I was downtown at the time. When I asked to speak to Jenna, she wouldn't put her on. She said Jenna wasn't feeling herself. Before the call ended, I could have sworn I saw Jenna's reflection in a building window. She stood across the street with a phone to her ear. By the time the traffic cleared, she'd disappeared."

Ellie flashed back to the silhouettes on the dock across the lake. Had they been following her, too? "Are you sure it was Jenna?"

"Call it a strong suspicion."

"Was that night the first time you'd spoken to Hazel on the phone?"

"As far as I know."

Ellie frowned. "As far as you know?"

"This may also sound odd, but I wasn't sure Hazel

Lamont was a real person until today. Jenna has called and pretended to be someone else before."

Ellie stared at him in shock. "Who does she pretend to be?"

"She's never given me a name. Sometimes she pretends she's called a wrong number."

"Doesn't her name and number show up on your caller ID?"

"I'm guessing she uses a burner."

"Then how do you know it's her?"

"Call it another strong suspicion."

Ellie leaned back against the wall. "Why would she go to all that trouble? Buy another phone, call you and pretend to be someone else?"

"Only Jenna can answer that question."

Had Jenna ever called her under an assumed name? Ellie wondered. Melanie Kent had easily duped her years ago by adopting a fake persona. Ellie liked to think she was more savvy and insightful after a decade on the airwaves, but could she really know the true identities of her callers? How could she really know what Jenna had been up to since her parents had removed her from the Penn Shepherd Psychiatric Hospital years ago?

"Can I ask you a personal question?"

Sam glanced at her warily. "What is it?"

"Do you think Jenna has romantic feelings for you?"

He tried to shrug off the possibility, but Ellie saw his mouth tighten imperceptibly. "She certainly has boundary issues and she can become too dependent too quickly, which is why I had to set rules regarding when and where she can contact me."

"Maybe that's why she sometimes pretends to be someone else. To get around those boundaries." Ellie paused. "I can see why the hospital wanted to keep her away from

Hazel. That woman strikes me as someone who knows how to exploit a person's weaknesses. I don't trust her. She seems the very definition of a loose cannon."

"I have my concerns, as well," Sam said. "I'll make some calls and find out what I can about her background."

"Thank you." Ellie kept going over that conversation with Hazel Lamont. The more she thought about it, the more convinced she became that Jenna's roommate was dangerously unstable and obsessively possessive. Ellie shuddered to think what might happen if Jenna had once again fallen under Hazel's influence.

She tucked loose strands of hair behind her ears as she watched the traffic in front of the restaurant. "About that beige sedan. Can't you check to see if a vehicle matching that description is registered to Hazel or Jenna?"

"I can, but if the car is a rental, it'll take longer to track down without a license plate number."

Something occurred to Ellie as he responded. "Wait a minute," she said slowly. "If you saw the beige sedan in Belle Pointe yesterday, then Jenna could already have been in town when she called. Maybe I really did see her and Hazel on the dock last night, although I have no idea why they would have gone out to the fishing cabin at that hour."

Sam leaned a shoulder against the wall. "You've lost me. What dock? What fishing cabin?"

"Oh, right. You don't know about that yet. There's an empty fishing cabin across the lake from me. I think I saw Jenna and Hazel on the dock last night while she was on the phone with me. I'd like to drive out there and see if they left anything behind. If you feel like riding along, I'll tell you about my conversation with Hazel on the way."

He nodded. "Sure. But let's take my car instead. I'll drive, you talk."

"What about my car?"

"I'll bring you back later to pick it up."

Ellie hesitated, a little disconcerted by the notion of being alone in the close confines of a vehicle with Sam Reece. Then she chided herself for having such a ridiculous and immature reaction. "We'll need to take the bridge across the lake. I'll give you directions as we go."

"Just give me a minute to change my clothes and bring the car around. Unless you'd like to wait for me in the inn."

"No, that's okay." She nodded down the street toward the town square. "I'll find a bench in the shade and wait for you there."

"Are you sure? It's awfully hot out here."

"I won't melt."

She waited until he'd crossed the street and disappeared inside the inn and then hitching her bag over her shoulder, she strolled along the sidewalk until she came to the town square. The stores were crowded with weekend shoppers. She found a bench in the shade where she could sit and people watch.

Directly across the street was the shadowy entrance to Ghost Alley, so named for the stories that cropped up from time to time about phantom lights and eerie whispers. In middle school, she, Jenna and Riley used to meet in the tiny cemetery located between the buildings and read ghost stories aloud. How quaint and innocent it all seemed now, sitting in the grass beside the old graves, goose bumps prickling their napes. No inkling of the real horror coming their way.

Ellie had fallen so deeply into her reverie that the ping of a text message startled her. Thinking Sam was probably ready to go, she hauled out her phone and glanced at the screen. There was a number but no name. The message read, Do you want to know what really happened to Riley? Call me.

Ellie shivered in the heat as she glanced both ways down the street. She told herself the message was just more of the same. An anonymous prankster was messing with her. But she couldn't ignore the possibility, no matter how remote, that the person who had sent the text might really know something about Riley's disappearance.

She tapped the number and lifted the phone to her ear. After two rings, a female voice answered. "Ellie Brannon?"

"Yes. Who is this?"

"You don't recognize my voice?"

Ellie frowned as she shifted the phone to her other ear. "Should I?"

"We've spoken before on numerous occasions. I'm surprised you don't remember me."

Jenna? Hazel? The voice did sound vaguely familiar, but how could she be sure of anyone anymore? "I don't like games. Why won't you just tell me your name?"

"All in good time. Are you alone?"

Apprehension niggled. "Why does that matter?"

"I don't want any cops or FBI agents hanging around when we meet in person."

Ellie clutched the phone. "What makes you think I'll agree to meet you?"

"Do you want to know what happened to Riley or don't you?"

She tried to keep her voice neutral as she searched the street. "How can you possibly know what happened to Riley?"

"I've been investigating Riley Cavanaugh's disappearance for the past fifteen years. I've made solving her case my life's work. You'd be surprised how much I know." The voice went silent for a moment, allowing Ellie time to digest the disturbing claim. "When I end this call, put your phone back in your bag and get up from the bench. Casually. Don't call attention to yourself."

Ellie squinted across the sunny street, wondering if someone watched her from behind a store window. "Where are you? Who are you?"

The caller ignored her questions. "After you put the phone away, enter the alley and go all the way back to the cemetery. Wait for me inside the gate."

"You must think I'm crazy," Ellie said. "Why would I do that?"

"You live alone on Echo Lake. Twice a day, you walk to an abandoned house to feed a dead woman's peacocks. You leave your studio at midnight with nothing but woods and water surrounding you. If I wanted to hurt you, I could have done so long before now. I just want to talk."

"Then tell me your name."

"Marie," she said softly. "My name is Marie Nightingale."

A wave of anger and panic washed over Ellie as she glanced around the square, frantically searching for Melanie Kent. A few passersby caught her eye and nodded. She told herself to calm down. Nothing was going to happen to her in the middle of town in broad daylight. Melanie Kent might be a ruthless, ambitious reporter who thought nothing of manufacturing evidence or a new identity to get a story, but she wasn't lethal. She posed no physical harm.

"Hello?" Ellie said into the phone. "Are you still there? Hello?"

The call had ended. Ellie rose from the bench and took a moment to contemplate her next move before she crossed the street and entered the alley. She'd waited years for the opportunity to tell Melanie Kent what she thought of her. But more important than airing past grievances was the need to know what the woman was up to in the here and now. What had brought her back to Belle Pointe at precisely this moment in time and why was she skulking about, taking pictures of Ellie and Jenna?

And what did she really know about Riley?

Ellie paused inside the alley to send a brief text to Sam, letting him know where to meet her. Then glancing over her shoulder, she put away the phone and headed toward the cemetery.

It was cool and dim in the shade of the buildings. Ellie was anxious but not afraid. People often used the alley as a shortcut over to the next street. This time of day, she was likely to encounter any number of people. Nothing was going to happen. She would be on guard the whole time. If she didn't like what Melanie Kent had to say or if her behavior seemed suspect, Ellie would leave at once.

A latticework gate opened into the tiny cemetery. The dozen or so graves had been left from a larger burial ground that was excavated and moved to the edge of town when Belle Pointe began to expand at the turn of the last century.

Ellie hesitated with her hand on the latch and then, taking a breath, she opened the gate and stepped through. She didn't see anyone at first. The park-like setting was shady and cool and she could hear the tinkle of a water feature nearby. She moved inside and glanced around. A woman sat on one of the benches with her back to the entrance. When she heard the latch click, she rose and turned to face Ellie.

A decade had passed since Ellie had last seen Melanie Kent. The years hadn't been particularly kind to the woman. Or maybe it was just the situation. She looked nervous and flighty, her feverish gaze darting from Ellie to the gate and then back. She wiped her hands down the sides of her jeans as she regarded Ellie from across the graves.

She wore a floppy white hat that shaded her face and an oversize shirt that hid the thin contours of her body. As Ellie took a step toward her, Melanie's hand slipped to the backpack that rested beside her on the bench.

"It's been a long time," she said and then cleared her throat awkwardly as if she were having trouble coming up with the proper response. "How have you been, Ellie?"

"Are we really going to do this?" Ellie demanded. "Try to make small talk as if meeting in a cemetery after all these years is perfectly normal behavior?"

"Brass tacks, then." Melanie looked relieved. She pulled off her hat and tossed it on the bench, then ran fingers through her flattened hair to fluff it. "I'm a little surprised you agreed to see me."

"I'm a little surprised myself," Ellie said as she moved into the cemetery. A stray breeze ruffled tendrils at her temples and she tucked back the strands impatiently. "Don't make the mistake of thinking all is forgiven. I haven't forgotten what you did or how you played me. All those lies you told. The fake tears." She shook herself before anger toppled her defenses. "But that's not why I'm here. At least, it's not the main reason I'm here. You said you know what happened to Riley."

"It still haunts you, doesn't it? The not knowing." The subtle taunt seemed more like the old Melanie.

"Of course it does. Unlike you, I have real emotions." Ellie struggled at that moment to curtail those said emotions.

"Including regret?"

Ellie closed her eyes and counted to five. "Just tell me what you know about Riley."

Melanie moved to the side of the bench and perched a hip against the armrest. Reaching behind her, she pulled the backpack closer, as if afraid a ghost might make off with the contents. "You have to promise that nothing of what you learn here will leave these gates."

Ellie frowned. "I can't make that promise. If you know something about Riley's disappearance, then the authorities will need to be notified."

"Even if telling them would put my life in danger?"

"From whom?"

Her gaze darted again to the gate. "I'm not ready to name names. I need to put some protections in place first. Do you know what a dead man's switch is?"

"Yes, of course. That's a little dramatic, don't you think? But then, drama has always been your specialty."

Something flickered in the woman's fierce eyes. She took another glance around the cemetery as if to make certain they were still alone. Ellie wanted to believe her wariness was just an act. Melanie Kent was every bit the performer that Hazel Lamont was. Yet the woman's cautious behavior was contagious. Ellie found herself fighting the urge to glance over her shoulder.

"As you well know, I've been working on Riley's case for most of my adult life. I've conducted hundreds of interviews and amassed digital mountains of research." Melanie held up her thumb and forefinger, leaving a miniscule gap. "I'm this close to putting it all together."

"Then you don't really know what happened to Riley, do you? You're only guessing."

"It's more than guesswork. I know what happened that night. I can't prove it beyond a shadow of a doubt. Not yet. But I *know*." Her voice dropped. "I may even know where to find the remains."

Ellie gasped. "What?"

The reporter's gaze softened unexpectedly. "You didn't really think she'd still be alive after all this time, did you?"

"No, of course not." But the idea of fifteen-year-old

Riley hidden and alone for so many years tore at Ellie's heart. She tried to dispel the heartbreaking images, warning herself again to be wary of Melanie's machinations. "Tell me what you actually know. No theories, no guesswork, just facts."

The reporter nodded. "All right, then. We'll start slow and work our way to the finish. If I blurt everything out at once, you may have trouble absorbing the truth. It's… disturbing to say the least."

Ellie rubbed her bare arms and nodded.

Melanie rose but made no move to breach the distance between them. "If you want to know more after today, we can schedule another meeting. Discreetly, of course. Right now, I'm prepared to give you only a small taste of what I've uncovered. Do you understand and agree to my conditions?"

"I understand you only too well," Ellie said. "Can we just get on with it?"

"Did you know that Riley and Jenna had a falling out before you went to the Ruins that night?"

Ellie didn't know whether to be relieved or angry. She'd mentally braced herself for a horrifying revelation. Instead Melanie was presenting her with nothing more than a new fabrication. "That's not a fact, that's an outright lie. There was no falling out. We were all getting along fine. I should know. I was there."

"Jenna was there, too. If you don't believe me, maybe you'll believe her."

"You've talked to Jenna about this?"

"I've done better than that." She reached around to unzip the backpack and remove a cell phone. "I've got it all queued up, in Jenna's own words. Would you like to take a listen?"

"Listen to what?"

"It's a recorded session with one of her doctors at the Penn Shepherd Psychiatric Hospital in Dallas."

Ellie gaped at her. "That's private information. There's no legal way you could have obtained such a recording."

"It's one of half a dozen I now have in my possession. How I obtained them is beside the point. Do you want to hear this one or don't you?"

"Why are you doing this?" Ellie asked helplessly. "Why come to me? If you have information relevant to the kidnapping, then why not go to the local police or to the FBI?"

"Aside from the legalities of the recordings and the need to protect myself, I'm not giving my story away to the cops. Not when I'm so close to solving the case on my own. As for why I'm telling you…" She shrugged. "Believe it or not, I do have a conscience and you need to know what you're up against. Your life could be in danger, too."

Ellie wasn't convinced. "Even if that were true, you don't do anything out of the goodness of your heart."

Melanie smiled. "Maybe you're right. How about an exclusive interview in exchange for what I know?"

"And have you twist my words to justify whatever story you've decided to manufacture? No, thanks. I won't talk to you today or ever. I won't listen to a private recording between Jenna and her doctor. This is a waste of my time."

"And yet you're still here." Melanie held up the phone. "Tell you what. I'll press Play. You can listen or not. Up to you."

Ellie told herself to turn around, march through the gate and not look back. Aside from the fact that Melanie Kent was obviously up to her usual tricks, neither of them had any right to listen to a recorded session between Jenna and her therapist. Ellie could hardly imagine a worse violation of privacy. Yet the moment the recording started to play, she stood paralyzed by something in Jenna's young voice. It was the same subtle quality she'd heard in Hazel Lamont's voice earlier. An icy breath blew down her collar as she met Melanie Kent's knowing gaze.

How are you feeling today, Jenna?

I'm okay. Tired. I haven't been sleeping well lately. I've been having bad dreams again.

Would you like to talk about them?

I guess.

Whenever you're ready.

(A slight pause.) *It's dark. I'm at the Ruins with Ellie and Riley. I don't want to be there.*

Are you frightened?

No. I don't want to be there because Riley's so mad at me and I have to pretend everything is okay so that Ellie won't get suspicious. What happened is none of her business.

What did happen?

(A longer pause.) *Riley thinks I took something that doesn't belong to me. She came over to my house while I was gone and the housekeeper let her go up to my room.*

She found something of hers in your room?

Some jewelry. I tried to explain that I only wanted to borrow those things, but she wouldn't listen. She started yelling all sorts of hateful accusations at me. I'd never seen her like that. She said she didn't care about most of that stuff, but she wanted her locket back. It belonged to her mother.

You took her mother's locket?

(Defensively.) *In my dream, I took it, but not in real life. I would never do such a thing. You believe me, don't you?*

I believe you, Jenna.

It was such an awful dream. The things she screamed at me. She said if I didn't give her back the locket, she'd tell Ellie's dad that I'd been stealing from her. He'd throw me in jail with all the other criminals.

Ellie's father is the county sheriff, right? In real life and in your dream?

Yes. I've always been a little afraid of him. Most everyone in town is. I knew that if he found out what I'd done, he'd come to my house and arrest me in front of my mom and dad. They'd be so upset. So disappointed in me. I probably wouldn't even be able to finish high school, much less go to college. My whole life would be ruined because of that stupid locket.

Did you give it back to Riley?

Yes. But it didn't change anything. She was still mad at me. She said she didn't want to be my friend anymore. (Resentfully.) *All that fuss over a stupid necklace.*

Why did Riley agree to go out to the Ruins if she was so angry with you?

She didn't want to disappoint Ellie. It was always Ellie this, Ellie that. Honestly, I used to get so tired of the way Riley looked up to her. It wasn't like Ellie was especially nice or even pretty. Sometimes I wanted it to be just the two of us, like it used to be when we were younger. Back in middle school, we did things all the time without Ellie having to horn in.

Is that why you took Riley's things? To get her attention?

(Another long pause.) *You mean in my dream, right?*

(The therapist paused.) *What happened at the Ruins?*

We split up. Ellie went upstairs. She didn't seem to notice the tension between Riley and me. She never noticed anything that didn't involve her. Riley said she heard a noise. I didn't hear anything but I pretended to go check.

You left Riley alone?

I said I pretended to go check.

What happened then, Jenna?

Riley screamed.

Why?

I...don't know.

You don't know why Riley screamed?

Why does it matter? It was just a dream.

A dream that upset you.

Did I say I was upset?

You said you hadn't been sleeping well.

Not because of the dream.

Then what's keeping you awake?

I don't want to talk about this anymore. I'd like to go back to my room now.

In a minute. When you took Riley's locket, did you know that it had belonged to her dead mother?

I knew.

Then you must have also known how much it meant to her. Why did you take it?

Why did I take it in my dream?

Of course.

Because I could.

Chapter Eleven

Sam spotted Ellie on the sidewalk and pulled to the curb, reaching over to push the door open so that she could climb in. She'd put on sunglasses, even though she waited for him in the shade. He couldn't see her eyes, but there was tension around her mouth and in the slight slump of her shoulders.

She closed the door and snapped on her seat belt as he pulled away from the curb. For a moment, neither of them said anything. She stared straight ahead as if her attention were riveted on some distant point. As for Sam, he kept a keen eye on the rearview mirror as he maneuvered through the slow crawl of vehicles around the town square. If a beige sedan lurked somewhere behind him in traffic, he couldn't spot it.

He gave Ellie a sidelong glance. "You okay?"

"I just had an impromptu meeting with Melanie Kent. It's my day for confrontations, it seems."

He glanced at her again, this time in surprise. "Where did this happen?"

"Back in the alley. I think she must have followed me from the restaurant. She texted, I called her back and we met."

"You met her in an alley?"

"It's smack in the middle of the town square. As she

pointed out, I live alone on the lake. If she wanted to hurt me, she could have chosen a much more remote location."

"She said that?" He scowled at the road. "What did she want?"

Ellie turned and met his gaze through the dark glasses. "She claimed to know what really happened to Riley. She said she might even know the location of the remains."

Sam said in astonishment, "Why hasn't she shared that information with the local authorities or the FBI?"

"She said she wants to be the one to solve the case." Her mouth thinned in disgust. "I don't think she has any actual evidence or proof. But she has managed to get her hands on some compelling information for her book."

"What kind of information?"

"Recordings of Jenna's old therapy sessions. She played one for me. She said it was recorded while Jenna was still at Penn Shepherd."

"Are you sure it was the real thing?" Sam asked.

"It sounded authentic. I'd swear it was Jenna's voice. Maybe Melanie paid off an employee of the hospital to duplicate the recordings or hired someone to break into the therapist's office. I don't know. What I do know is that Jenna will be devastated if a transcript of the recording I heard ends up in Melanie's book."

"What was on it?"

"She talked about a disturbing dream she'd had. In this dream, she and Riley were fighting over some missing jewelry. Riley accused Jenna of stealing her mother's locket. She threatened to tell my dad if Jenna didn't return it."

Sam's scowl deepened. "Seems pretty specific for a dream."

"I know. That's why I don't think it was a dream at all. She used the same tactic when she called me last night.

I've thought about it a lot. I think pretending she dreamed these things is her way of coping with bad memories."

"You never knew anything about an argument between Riley and Jenna?"

She shook her head. "Maybe Jenna was right. Maybe I was oblivious back then to anything that didn't involve me."

"She said that?"

Ellie shrugged. "She wasn't wrong."

Sam shot her a glance. "Try not to be so hard on yourself. You were fifteen years old."

Ellie sighed. "Seems hard to believe I was ever that young."

Sam observed her out of the corner of his eye. She looked more attractive than usual today in a simple sleeveless dress that complemented her slender waist and subtle curves. Her blond hair was pulled back into a thick straight ponytail and her bare arms and legs against the white dress looked tanned and toned. Her toenails were painted the same pale shade of light pink as her lips. There was nothing provocative or unusual about her clothing or demeanor, and yet Sam found himself thinking that she was one of the most alluring women he'd ever met.

He tapped his fingers impatiently on the steering wheel as he tried to corral his thoughts toward a more neutral direction. "Tell me about Jenna's phone call."

"The one last night?" She nodded. "She talked about the terrible place she and Riley had been taken to. She called it a cell or a cage. It was pitch black. She couldn't locate any windows or doors, just metal bars. She said the floor was cold."

"Did she say anything about the person who had taken them there?"

"No, but she said Riley was really sick. So sick she hadn't eaten or spoken in days."

They exchanged a glance.

"She related all of this as if it were a dream," Ellie said.

While he watched the road, Ellie recounted as much as she could remember of the conversation and how she'd spotted two silhouettes on the dock across the lake that may or may not have been Jenna and Hazel. Then she'd filled him in on the threatening altercation with Hazel at the restaurant.

The phone conversation with Jenna, the confrontation with Hazel and the meeting with Melanie Kent had obviously taken a toll. Ellie seemed more apprehensive and guarded than he'd ever seen her. Her disquiet brought out Sam's protective instincts, though he told himself Ellie Brannon was more than capable of taking care of herself. However, she was right to be cautious. Things had taken a disturbing turn at the restaurant. Sam knew nothing about Hazel Lamont, but the kind of possessiveness she'd displayed toward Jenna could sometimes spell disaster.

As if reading his mind, Ellie said, "Do you think I should call Jenna's parents? I'm really worried what Hazel might do if she considers them a threat. I'm worried about Jenna, too. If she's fallen under that woman's influence, I shudder to think what might happen."

"You still have their contact information?"

"Yes. I haven't seen or talked to either of them in years and I'm not at all sure they'd even want to hear from me. But I can't sit back and do nothing. Then again, maybe I'm overreacting."

Sam felt her gaze on him. "I still have their information. Why don't I give them a call? Or better yet, maybe I'll go see them in person. Maybe they can shed some light on what's going on with Jenna and Hazel."

Ellie nodded and sat back in her seat. "I really hope I am overreacting but you should have seen the look in her eyes. Her behavior seemed increasingly aggressive. That story she told about an intruder killing her parents and the FBI agent who considered her a suspect…" She hugged her arms around her middle. "I figured she'd made the whole thing up, but now I'm starting to wonder."

"I'll check into it," Sam said. "I know a nurse who used to work at the Penn Shepherd Psychiatric Hospital. We got on pretty well during that time. She was always helpful about getting me in to see Jenna. If she still remembers me, maybe I can get her to open up about Hazel Lamont."

"Ask her about Melanie Kent, too. Maybe she'll have some idea how Melanie got her hands on those recordings." Ellie took off her sunglasses and brushed a hand across her eyes. "You know what else I keep thinking about? Hazel's claim that an older boy had a crush on Riley and the implication that it could have been Cory Small. Riley never said a word to me about an older guy and now it seems unlikely that she would have confided in Jenna. But someone had to have put the notion in Hazel's head."

"Jenna denied she knew anything about a crush."

Ellie seemed to consider the possibilities as she toyed with her sunglasses. "I'm beginning to wonder if I knew either Jenna or Riley as well as I thought I did. Maybe Cory really did have a crush on Riley and, for whatever reason, she felt she couldn't tell me. Sam—" She caught herself and offered a quick apology. "Sorry. Agent Reece."

He said easily, "Sam is fine."

She gave him a reluctant glance. "I don't know that I'm ready to be on a first-name basis with you. Maybe we should keep things a little more formal."

Her eyes looked translucent in the sunlight shining in through the windshield, her lips lush and glistening.

He wondered what it would be like to kiss those lips and abruptly turned his attention back to the road. "I don't see a problem. We've known each other for a long time."

"That's not really true. You know everything there is to know about me, but I know hardly anything about you. Maybe that's for the best."

Sam lifted a hand and rubbed the back of his neck. "Whatever makes you more comfortable." He felt unaccountably disappointed, which only served to prove her point. "Let's talk a little more about Cory Small."

She said in relief, "Okay, but I've already told you everything I remember about him. I never really knew him, even though our school was fairly small. He was older so we didn't run in the same circles. I'm not even sure I would recognize him if I met him on the street." She paused. "You don't think he had anything to do with the kidnapping, do you? My dad looked into him because of his relationship to Silas Creed. If Dad had thought there was anything suspicious about him or his mother, he would have come down hard on both of them."

"I checked him out, too," Sam said. "He had an alibi for the night in question and we never found any physical evidence that linked him or his mother to the kidnapping. When I talked to him yesterday, he swore neither of them had heard from Creed since he left town fifteen years ago."

"Of course he'd say that."

"True." Sam turned onto the highway and headed toward the lake. The road behind them remained clear. "Something interesting happened while I was out at that farm." He shot another glance in the rearview before glancing at Ellie. "I mentioned earlier that Melanie Kent is staying in a converted garden shed to write her book. That shed is at the back of Cory Small's property. It's the same one Silas Creed used to hole up in when things got tense for him in town."

Ellie had been gazing out the window but now she whirled to face him. "Is that where you found the pictures of Jenna and me?"

"Yes. Did you ask Melanie about those photographs?"

"I didn't even think about it," Ellie admitted. "Maybe that's a good thing because I'm guessing she doesn't know you went through her things. But it does make my blood run cold, the idea of her skulking around, taking pictures of us without our knowing. At least I know now to keep an eye out for her."

"There's something else you need to know," Sam said. "I saw a hat hanging on the wall in the nursery. Black. Wide-brimmed." He glanced at Ellie. She sat rapt.

"Cory said the hat had belonged to his mother. Apparently, it went missing a couple of days ago. Then it reappeared in the greenhouse yesterday, which means it would have been gone from its usual place at the same time you spotted someone in a black hat by the lake. Cory seemed to think Melanie took it."

"I wish I could say that I'm surprised, but I'm not," Ellie said. "I suspected even before we talked today that Melanie Kent was somehow involved in everything that's happened. But what could she hope to accomplish by pretending to be Preacher? I have no doubt she'd do anything for a story, but what's she really after?"

"Maybe it's something as simple as her wanting to get a rise out of you. Force you into making a statement she can quote in her book. Or maybe it's some kind of publicity stunt. I'll drive back out there later and see if I can get her to talk to me. She's one cool cookie, but an FBI badge has a way of shaking people up."

Ellie nodded. "Do you think she planted the idea in Hazel's head about Riley and Cory Small? Maybe she heard something on one of the tapes."

"It's possible, but I'm inclined to think it was the other way around. Maybe Hazel planted that seed in Melanie's head."

"Why would she do that?"

"I can think of one reason." He turned to meet her gaze. "Maybe she's setting Cory up as a scapegoat."

"For what?"

"You and Jenna and Riley were best friends. Closer than sisters, you said. Riley's gone, but you're still here. Maybe Hazel thinks of you as a rival."

"But Jenna and I hardly ever see each other anymore."

"You're still an important part of her life. She thinks about you, talks about you. In Hazel's mind, you're someone who could take Jenna away from her."

Ellie's eyes widened as the implication sank in. "My God. Are you saying she might try to harm me?"

"It's a theory," he said. "It explains everything that's happened—the anonymous calls from someone pretending to be Riley. Maybe she was the one in that black hat pretending to be Preacher. What better way to keep you frightened and off balance?"

"How does Melanie Kent figure into all this?"

"I suspect Hazel is using her in some way. I haven't put it all together yet, but I'm starting to see how some of the pieces may fit. I need to get back to Dallas as soon as possible."

"Should we go back for my car, then?"

"I don't mean today, but soon." He resisted the urge to put his hand over Ellie's to reassure her. "I'm not trying to scare you, but until we know more about Hazel Lamont, it's best to keep your distance. Probably a good idea to stay away from Melanie Kent, too, while you're at it."

I'M NOT TRYING to scare you...

Too late, Ellie thought as she folded her arms and shivered. Aloud she said, "You need to take the next left and then a hard right. The bridge is only a quarter of a mile or so from the turnoff."

Sam followed her directions without comment. He'd gone silent after his warning about Hazel and Melanie. Maybe he regretted his candid speculation. It all seemed so farfetched when spoken aloud, but then, Hazel was right. Ellie had never dealt with anyone like her. The woman seemed clever and cunning and she'd all but threatened Ellie back at the restaurant. What if she really did view Ellie as a rival for Jenna's friendship and affection? Was she using Melanie Kent's ruthless ambition to set up Cory Small to be the fall guy for Ellie's elimination?

Ellie stared out the window, but the beauty of the countryside barely registered. Fifteen years after the kidnapping, she found herself once again drowning in fear and uncertainty. Would she ever be free of this nightmare?

"You okay?"

She answered without turning. "Sometimes I wonder if it will ever be over."

"I wonder that, too, at times."

"It always comes back to that night. The decisions we made. How different so many lives would be today if we hadn't gone out to the Ruins."

"It does no good to look back," Sam said. "All any of us can do is try to navigate the here and now."

She pointed to the turnoff. "Speaking of which...that way."

He pulled onto the narrow lane and the shade from the encroaching woods stretched over the car. Ellie lowered her window and the fecund scent of the swamp drifted in, conjuring images of dark water and deep secrets. They rounded the final bend and the cabin came into view, a modest A-frame perched on stilts with wide decks and sweeping views of the lake.

The tires crunched on the gravel drive as Sam pulled to a stop. He sat for a moment, taking in their surroundings before turning to Ellie. "Who owns this place?"

"His name was Charles Nance. He was murdered earlier in the summer. It was in all the local papers. If you've kept tabs on the community, I'm sure you heard about it."

"The doctor, right? That was a big case for the county sheriff's office."

"I doubt Tom looks at it that way. Dr. Nance's death was a blow to all of us. The cabin has sat empty since his passing."

"Maybe we should knock on the door anyway just in case."

They got out of the car together and walked up the porch steps. Sam glanced at Ellie as he knocked. When no one answered, he peered through the sidelights. "Place looks deserted. Let's check around back."

They took a quick perusal of the back deck and then descended the wooden steps to the dock. Ellie stood at the very edge, letting her gaze drift along the opposite bank. She couldn't help catching glimpses of Sam out of the corner of her eye. He'd changed into jeans and a plain gray T-shirt back at the inn. He looked the same and yet completely different without his formal FBI attire. The slight shimmer at his temples mesmerized her before she forced her attention back to the distant bank.

"The Thayer house is directly across the lake," she said.

"That's where you feed the peacocks?"

"Peafowl. Male and female. And yes, that's also where I saw someone in a black hat. He stood at the top of that embankment. I assumed it was a man at the time, but now you've made me think the person may have been Melanie or Hazel. I never got a look at the face." She pointed out her house and studio. "You can see the broadcast tower through the pine trees. That's my bedroom window. I was looking out at the lake when I saw Jenna and Hazel here on this dock. I still can't figure out why they'd come out here in the middle of the night. Hazel, sure, if she's behind everything. But Jenna? I don't want to believe she has anything to do with this."

"She may not be the person you've always thought her to be," Sam said.

"I know. And I can't discount Hazel's influence, either. It's possible she's convinced Jenna I'm to blame for what happened to her. Jenna seemed so bitter and resentful at lunch."

"Try to keep it in perspective. Whatever else is going on with Jenna, she's lived through a horror that few people can imagine. Good or bad, she'll never be the person she was before the kidnapping."

They stood in deep shade at the end of the dock. Sam took off his sunglasses and slipped them in his pocket. His eyes were dark and intense as he stared down at her. "We'll figure this out together."

"You sound so sure, but it's been fifteen years since Riley went missing."

"Something's changed," Sam said.

Between them, too. It wasn't just the fact that his given name had slipped through her lips so easily or the way his eyes darkened to navy when he stared down at her. Ellie didn't want to contemplate her attraction on any deep level, but all of a sudden her awareness of Sam Reece was all she could think about.

"It's strange, isn't it?" she said.

"What is?"

"When we first met, I found you intimidating. You seemed so cold and single-minded and I resented all your questions. I hated you for making me relive that terrible night over and over."

"And now?"

"Here we are fifteen years later working together to figure things out." She glanced up at him. "I'll do whatever I can to help you."

"You'll go back to the Ruins with me?"

"Yes. I doubt my memory will be jolted after all this time, but I suppose we have to try." Her gaze lifted reluctantly to the smokestack rising up through the treetops. "Did you know that you can see it from here?"

He turned, following her gaze. "The smokestack? I'm surprised it's even still standing. It's a wonder someone hasn't bulldozed that whole place to the ground by now."

"I've thought about that hospital so often. Dreamed about it hundreds of times. I still go over everything in my mind, trying to figure out what I might have seen, what I might have missed that night."

"You were attacked from behind. Maybe you really didn't see anything," Sam said.

"I remember the rag over my face and the fumes. I wouldn't have gone under immediately. We must have struggled. I must have fought him. Yet I never caught a glimpse of his face."

"He was careful," Sam said. "It's possible he wore a mask. We know he must have had everything planned out in advance."

"Does that sound like something Silas Creed could do?"

"You said yourself, he was an educated man. He could have gotten his hands on chloroform from any number of sources or he could have made his own with bleach and acetone. As to the timing, he was known to hang out around local schools and playgrounds. He spied on people through their windows. He could have overheard some of your classmates talking about the dare."

"Do you really believe that?"

Sam hesitated. "I've always had my doubts he acted alone, but it's possible." He moved to the other side of the dock and stared out over the water. "We'll go after dark."

Ellie's heart lurched. "Tonight?"

"Better to get it over with. I'll drive back to Dallas first thing in the morning."

Uncertainty crept over her. "What if I don't remember anything? What if we go through that awful place and nothing comes back to me?"

"Then you'll have at least proved to yourself that you can stare down the monsters."

Chapter Twelve

After Ellie picked up her car in town, Sam followed her back out to the lake. She fixed sandwiches and iced tea for a late lunch and they ate on the deck with a soft breeze drifting off the water. Later, they walked over to the Thayer house to feed the peafowl and then they returned to the deck to watch the sunset. The breeze cooled as the light faded. Ellie went inside to change into shorts and sneakers and grab a flashlight.

Sam waited for her on the dock. He stood at the railing, peering into the water as she approached. The platform rocked slightly as she moved up beside him. With the coming darkness, her dread had blossomed. She tried not to think about what lay ahead. Tried not to panic when she contemplated the moment she stepped through that crumbling doorway.

"If you lean far enough over the water, you can see the smokestack from here, as well," she said. "Urban legend had it that the boiler room was also used as a crematorium. I doubt that's true. But there is a tunnel that leads from the basement out to the boiler room. I never learned the purpose of that tunnel."

"I've been through it," Sam said. "We searched every inch of that building after the kidnapping. I went out there a couple of times by myself. Creepy place even in daylight."

"Did you ever find anything?"

"Nothing useful."

"I've never been particularly superstitious, but that place…" She trailed off on a shiver. "Looking back, I'm not sure how we mustered the courage to go inside."

"Kids do all sorts of things on a dare," Sam said.

She turned back to the water. "When should we go?"

"Let's wait for the moon to rise. As I said, I'd like to see the place from your perspective that night."

"Sam—" She didn't correct herself this time.

He straightened and turned, his eyes glinting in the dark. He looked tall and fit and steady. Reassuring.

His gaze on her intensified. "What is it?"

"Do you really think this is a good idea?"

"Yes. Don't you?"

"I thought so earlier when the sun was shining. Now I don't know." She glanced down into those obsidian depths. The water lilies had closed for the night and the bullfrogs were just tuning up. It was a beautiful setting, lonely and primal. Ellie suppressed another shiver as she leaned over the railing and traced the smokestack silhouetted against the rising moon. "We should probably go before I change my mind."

But they waited until the moon soared over the treetops and then they left the dock to follow the trail along the bank. As they neared the bridge, Ellie paused and angled her flashlight beam up under the braces.

"We left our bikes here that night. We covered them with leaves and branches so they couldn't be spotted from the bridge."

"You rode all the way out here from town?"

"It's only a few miles." She shrugged. "We were young. I remember we barely spoke the whole way. After we'd hidden the bikes, we used our flashlights to find the trail. By that time, the eclipse was almost over, but the moon still had a bloody hue. Riley said it was a sign that we shouldn't go on, but I told her we'd come too far to turn back. I suggested she wait for us at the bridge if she was too afraid, but Jenna said we should all stick together. It was safer in numbers." Ellie thought back to Jenna's voice on the tape. *I don't want to be there because Riley's so mad at me and I have to pretend everything is okay so that Ellie won't get suspicious.*

She moved back to the path and Sam fell in beside her.

"People say this lake is haunted. On a clear night when the moon is up and the wind is still, you can hear the echo of screams across the water. Screams from the lost souls trapped in the Ruins and from the Native Americans that were forced from their land by settlers. That's why they call it Echo Lake."

"Have you ever heard the screams?" he asked.

"Yes, from the peacocks."

As if on cue, a staccato cry echoed out over the water. *Uhhhhh. Uhhhhh. Uhhhhh. Uhhhhh.*

The sound undulated down through the trees, stopping Sam dead in his tracks. "Good Lord. *That* was a peacock?"

"You've never heard one before?"

"I think I would have remembered that scream. It's inhuman and yet uncannily human at the same time. Like a child in terrible pain."

"The stuff of nightmares and legends," Ellie said.

Sam swore as he glanced out over the water. Then he turned back to the path. "Let's keep going."

But something had changed during that interlude. They both grew tense as they neared the Ruins. Ellie lingered on the path to run her flashlight beam up the steep embankment.

"Doesn't look too bad," Sam said.

They used vines and tree roots to pull themselves toward the summit where they paused yet again as the Ruins loomed before them, a three-story mausoleum with arched windows and doors that must once have been beautiful. Moonlight glinted off jagged glass, creating the illusion of watchful eyes. Ivy and trumpet vines crept up the side of the building, snaking through broken windows and over the caved-in roof.

The place seemed alive, as if decades of memories and misery had somehow been personified in those crumbling walls. Ellie was almost afraid to speak, so powerful was the spell. A breeze drifted through the trees, sounding for the world like the whispers of all those trapped souls.

She closed her eyes on a shudder. "This is as far as I've come since that night."

Sam's gaze raked over the walls. "I'd forgotten how imposing this place is, especially in the dark. And yet there's something almost stately about the remains."

The remains. What an apt choice of words, Ellie thought. "Should we go inside now?"

"Tell me what you did fifteen years ago."

"We huddled outside for a bit. As you said, it's an imposing sight. I remember the way Riley clutched my arm as we gazed up at all those broken windows."

"What about Jenna?"

"She stood on the other side of Riley. A little away from us now that I think about it, but maybe that recording has colored my memory. I remember she was very protective of Riley. She kept asking if she wanted to turn back. Eventually, we walked through the weeds to the front steps. I remember thinking about snakes. It was summer and the copperheads and moccasins were out."

Sam shone his flashlight beam across the overgrown

grounds to the front steps. "I'll lead the way—scare off any reptiles in our path."

"No, let me. I went first that night."

Sam stepped aside and she moved past him on the path, her insides tingling with fear and excitement as she brushed against his arm. He felt warm and stable, a sentient reassurance in that withering place.

Her sneakers whispered against the concrete as she climbed the steps and hovered at the threshold. She said over her shoulder, "I went in first, then Riley and Jenna. I remember thinking as I stepped through the door that maybe our coming out here hadn't been such a good idea after all. The place felt cold to me. Haunted. I didn't believe in ghosts. I still don't. And yet…" She glanced back to make sure Sam was behind her.

"I felt it the first time I came here," he said. "I've felt it in other places, too, where children have gone missing. Like a lingering evil."

Ellie's voice dropped to a whisper. "Did you have to say that?"

He flicked the beam past her into the interior. "Watch your step."

They made their way through the lobby, the floorboards creaking beneath their shoes. The dueling beams of their flashlights arced over the walls, into the shadowy corners and finally up to the ceiling where Preacher's red eyes gleamed beneath the brim of his black hat.

Ellie gasped. "My God. I had no idea the painting was so large."

"This is the first time I've seen it, too," Sam said.

"The local paper did a story on it years ago. They ran photographs. I thought I knew what to expect…" Those red eyes seemed to mesmerize Ellie so that she had to tear her gaze away. "No one knows who painted it. It just seemed to appear one day. People trekked out here for months to stare up at it and take pictures."

"But not you."

"No, not me. I tell myself it's just graffiti painted on the ceiling of an old building."

"Where to now?" Sam asked.

They were at the bottom of the stairs. "This is where we separated. I went up to the second floor and Jenna stayed here with Riley. She begged me not to go and Jenna insisted again that we should all stick together. I wanted to prove how brave I was. I told Riley not to be a baby. That was the last thing I ever said to her."

"You couldn't have known what would happen."

"Maybe I should have known. There must have been some clue we weren't alone. A closing door, a creaking floorboard. Something. But I don't remember anything out of the ordinary."

"Let's go up to the second floor and take a look."

"I need to go up there alone," Ellie said.

"I don't think that's necessary. Just being here in the dark is enough to trigger a memory. Besides, we've no way of knowing the condition of the floors up there, let alone the staircase."

"I'll be careful. I need to do this alone."

Sam ran his beam up the curving staircase, trailing it along the wrought iron banister that hung loose in places. "I don't like this. That's a steep staircase. If you fall through, you could break a leg or worse."

"This was your idea, remember? I'll be fine. If I need you, I'll call out. Otherwise, I'll do exactly as I did that night."

She went up the stairs slowly, chasing away shadows with her flashlight. She paused at the top to glance back down at Sam. He stood in almost the exact same spot where she'd last seen Riley. Ellie had hesitated on the landing that night, staring down at her friends as she secretly bolstered her courage.

Willing the memories to come, she eased across the landing and started down the corridor. The old elevator shaft was somewhere ahead, a gaping hole that dropped all the way to the basement.

"Everything okay?"

Sam's voice echoed up the stairwell. Ellie had the strongest urge to rush back down the steps, straight into his arms, but instead she cleared her throat and called back to him. "I'm fine. I'd only been up here a few minutes that night when I heard a scream."

"Which one of the girls screamed?"

"I was never certain." She closed her eyes, remembering Jenna's voice on the recording. "I think it was Riley."

"Is that a memory?"

"I don't know."

"Pretend you just heard the scream. What did you do then?"

"I turned and rushed back to the landing. I peered over the banister before I started down the stairs."

"Do that now."

She turned back, the flashlight beam arching over the walls and down into the empty corridor. For a moment, Ellie could have sworn she saw someone lurking in the shadows. A black-clad figure with a hat pulled low over his eyes.

Her imagination. She was merely projecting into the shadows what she had glimpsed on the ceiling. Preacher was dead. *Dead.*

The shadow moved. For a moment, Ellie stood frozen, unable to call out, unable to breathe.

"Ellie? You okay?"

"Sam—Sam!"

The shadow rushed toward her. Ellie screamed and whirled, dashing headlong toward the stairs, forgetting about rotting floorboards and dangerous stairwells. She was nearly at the landing when the phantom caught up with her. He grabbed her from behind and pushed her hard against the banister. Rusted bolts snapped and a section of the wrought iron swung away from the wall, carrying Ellie with it. She dangled in midair as she imagined herself falling through the floorboards below all the way down into the basement.

Dimly, she heard Sam call her name and the sound of his footsteps clamoring up the stairs. Another bolt snapped and the railing dropped several inches. Ellie's fingers slipped as the jagged metal ate into her flesh.

Sam was on the landing by this time. He placed the flashlight on the floor and reached for Ellie, but the railing had swung just out of his grasp.

He thrust his hand toward her. "Grab hold of my fingers. I'll pull you toward me."

"I can't."

"It's okay. I won't let you fall."

She flailed, missed his hand, and the railing creaked and shuddered as she swayed.

"Again," he said.

She tried to inch closer, but with every movement, the banister gave a little more. Sam was on his stomach now, hanging over the edge of the landing as he reached for the banister, swinging her toward him, grabbing her wrist, pulling her to safety just as the last bolt gave way and the heavy wrought iron crashed to the floor.

Ellie lay shaking for a moment before she scrambled away from the edge. Sam followed her. She pulled her legs up and hugged her knees as she pressed her back against the wall.

"Someone was up here," she said. "Did you see him?"

He shook his head slowly. "I saw you go through the banister. I thought you must have tripped."

"I didn't trip. I was pushed."

"Did you see who it was?"

"Yes." She clutched Sam's hand as her voice lowered to a whisper. "It was Preacher."

SAM HUNKERED BESIDE her on the landing. "What?"

Her grasp tightened. "You have to go after him! Don't let him get away!"

"Hold on. What did you actually see?"

"Someone in a black hat. I think he had a mask over his face."

"You're sure it was a man?"

"I don't know!" She tried to scramble to her feet, but he held her in place.

"Did he have a weapon?"

"Not that I saw—"

She broke off as Sam's head came up. He put a fingertip to his lips to silence her. Then he drew his weapon and swiveled toward the corridor. He peered through the shadows before lifting his gaze to the ceiling. Someone was on the third floor directly above them.

He pressed his finger to his lips again and then pointed skyward. Ellie tipped her head, tracking the soft footsteps. "He's up there," she whispered.

Sam put his lips close to her ear. "He's trying to find a way out. Wait here."

When he would have stood, she pulled him back down. "Be careful. This isn't a hoax."

He nodded and rose, then moved quickly and quietly

down the corridor, flashlight positioned over his weapon. He swept the beam through the empty rooms as he went, making sure an accomplice didn't still lurk on the second floor.

Every now and then, he stopped to listen. The footsteps had gone silent. He didn't think the suspect had had time to climb out a window, much less scale down a wall. More likely he'd found a hiding place—

Sam froze, one foot poised over nothing but air. He hovered on the brink of the old elevator shaft for a heart-stopping moment before he managed to regain his balance. Then he trained the beam down into the pitch-black chute, almost expecting to see gleaming eyes staring back up at him.

Sidestepping the shaft, he eased down the corridor until the sound of breaking glass halted him at the bottom of another stairwell. He turned off the flashlight and tucked it into the back of his jeans. Using both hands to steady his weapon, he went up the steps and flattened himself against the wall of the landing.

Moonlight filtered in through the long windows at the end of the corridor and through the gaping holes in the roof. A rat scurried across his shoe as he stood listening. Weapon at the ready, he started down the corridor, moving past one room after another before he backtracked to a doorway where shards of glass glittered on the floor. Most of the windows in the building were either broken out or boarded up. The unsub must have knocked out the jagged glass so that he could safely crawl through.

Sam tried to step quietly, but his boots crunched on the shards as he moved to the window and leaned out. The night wind blew across his face as he trailed his gaze down the wall.

Out of the corner of his eye, he caught a quick movement on the narrow ledge that ran the length of the building just beneath the windows. Someone in a black hoodie stood flattened against the wall. He seemed to be searching for a way down. When he saw Sam, he sprinted around the corner.

Putting away his weapon, Sam crawled out the window and paused to get his footing as he glanced down three stories to the ground. He pressed his back to the wall and closed his eyes briefly. He'd never much cared for heights.

Inching sideways, he kept his back to the wall, pausing to peer around the corner where the assailant had disappeared. The ledge was empty.

Sam glanced downward. He saw nothing, heard nothing. It was as if the unsub had disappeared into thin air.

Then he spotted an old metal ladder bolted to the wall that went up to the roof. It must have been once used for maintenance. Sam went up quickly, pretending a three-story fall wouldn't break every bone in his body. Hitching himself up over the eaves, he scrambled crab-like up to the peak and cautiously straightened to survey his surroundings. From this vantage, the building looked much larger than from the inside. Many of the shingles had long since crumbled away, exposing large sections of rotted wood.

Halfway along the peak, a black-clad figure stood silhouetted against the full moon.

Sam called out to the suspect. "Federal agent! Stop where you are!"

The figure glanced over his shoulder as he moved erratically along the peak, seemingly driven by panic. Sam lunged after him, gaining confidence as he picked up speed.

"Federal Agent! I said stop!"

Cornered, the figure glanced around frantically and then half scrambling, half sliding, he went back down the slope, positioning himself at the very edge as he contemplated his predicament.

Sam pulled his weapon. "Hands up!"

The suspect teetered at the edge before he went over. For a dizzying second, Sam thought he had jumped. He scrambled down the slope and peered over the edge. The suspect had somehow managed to cling to an old drainpipe. He shimmied down to the ledge and then used the tangle of vines to rappel to the ground.

As Sam stood watching, the suspect landed with a thud and sprinted for the woods.

Chapter Thirteen

A little while later, Sam sat on a barstool in Ellie's kitchen and watched as she rummaged frantically through her cabinets. Neither of them had said much on the way home, but it was obvious the adrenaline was still pumping.

"What are you looking for?" he finally asked.

"I know I've got a bottle of whiskey around here somewhere. Aha!" She produced a nearly full bottle and got down two shot glasses, filling both to the rim.

Sam picked up his glass. "You sure you want to do this?"

"Yes. My nerves are still a mess." She eyed him over the rim before she downed the contents. "I still say you should have shot him. Her. Whoever."

"The Bureau frowns on shooting unarmed suspects in the back."

"He tried to kill me."

"I know," Sam said grimly. He chugged the whiskey.

Ellie tried to replenish his glass but he held up a hand blocking her. "That's it for me. Best to keep a clear head for the rest of the night."

"Fine." She poured herself another drink and tossed it back. The fire seemed to momentarily take her breath away. She took a deep breath and shuddered. "Okay. I'm done."

"Should we call your brother?"

She scowled. "Why? Whoever was behind that mask is long gone. There's nothing Tom or anyone else can do tonight."

"You're going to have to tell him at some point. He needs to know what's going on in his county, much less with his sister."

"I know that. Of course, I'll eventually tell him, but it's your case, right? The FBI is in charge."

"I doubt he would agree with that assessment. Is there some reason you don't want him to know?"

"Aside from the fact that he worries too much? It's not so much Tom I'm keeping in the dark as it is his fiancée, Rae. Rae Cavanaugh. Riley's sister."

"You mentioned they were engaged."

Her eyes glittered from the whiskey. "Since you've kept abreast of everything going on in Bell Pointe I assume you know about Rae's niece."

"She was kidnapped and held for ransom," he said.

Ellie nodded. "You can't imagine all the bad memories that were stirred for that family, especially Rae. She had to relive her worst nightmare. And then to find out about her brother…" Ellie trailed away. "She finally has something good in her life. Something to celebrate. I don't want to be the one to take that away from her."

"You've done nothing wrong," he said reasonably.

"I know, but can't we just give them a little more time? At least until morning. There really isn't anything Tom can do tonight except worry." She eyed the whiskey bottle for a moment and then returned it to the cabinet. "You know what I can't figure out? How that person knew you and I would be at the Ruins tonight. The attack can't have been random nor could we have been followed. That person was already hiding out on the second floor when we arrived."

"I've been thinking about that, too," Sam said. "Come outside with me."

"No, thank you. I'd rather stay right here behind locked doors if you don't mind."

"This will only take a minute."

They went out to the deck. The moon was still up, casting an eerie glow over the preternatural landscape. Ellie's face looked pale and drawn. She was putting up a good front, but the attack at the Ruins had left her shaken. It had left Sam rattled, too. He didn't want to think what would have happened if he hadn't been able to pull her up in time. Maybe she would have walked away from a one-story fall. Then again, people had died from tumbling off ladders.

"What are we doing out here?" Ellie asked with a shiver.

"Wait here." Sam went down the steps and angled his beam under the deck where Ellie stored lawn equipment and old patio furniture. Then he shined the light up through floorboards.

Ellie called down to him. "What are you doing down there?"

He came back up the steps. "Someone could have hidden under your deck and listened to every word we said earlier. All they had to do was slip away, hide in the Ruins and wait for us to come."

Ellie shivered. "Hazel did threaten me earlier."

"It may have been Hazel, but anyone could have followed us out here from town." He shined the light down through the floorboards.

Ellie cast a wary glance toward the lake. "She could still be around, sitting in a boat somewhere, watching us. The shadows on the other side of the bank are so thick, we'd never see her."

"Let's not get ahead of ourselves. We don't know that it was Hazel."

"We don't really know anything." She turned to go back inside, waiting for Sam to follow so that she could close and lock the door. "What do we do now?"

"I don't want to leave you alone tonight. I'll bunk down here on the couch."

"I appreciate that, but you don't need to sleep on the couch. I have a spare room down the hallway. The bathroom is stocked with whatever you need. Sometimes a guest will stay over after a live interview so I make sure to keep a fresh toothbrush around."

"Thanks. I'll be fine."

She hesitated at the bottom of the stairs. "This is getting stranger and stranger. Even for my world."

"And for mine," he said. "But we will figure it out."

"So you keep saying."

After Ellie had gone upstairs, Sam walked from room to room, familiarizing himself with the layout of the house. He checked all the doors and then stood guard at the windows overlooking the deck. The night was still. Almost too still. He could hear Ellie moving around upstairs and desire stirred as his imagination kicked in.

He told himself it was just the residual adrenaline, but deep down he knew better. He'd allowed Ellie Brannon to get under his skin. Not a good time for distractions when a fifteen-year-old investigation was just starting to heat up.

ELLIE LAY ON her back and stared up at the ceiling, hoping the shifting patterns would eventually lull her to sleep. No such luck. Even the whiskey had failed to settle her nerves. She went back over everything that had happened at the Ruins, getting herself so worked up that she tossed the covers aside and rose, padding over to the window to stare out at the moonlit lake.

She felt anxious and wired and braced herself for that

paralyzing moment when panic engulfed her. It didn't come. Maybe that was a sign. Maybe something good had come out of that trip to the Ruins. After fifteen years of nightmares, maybe she'd finally faced down her monsters.

Or maybe they'd just gone into hiding.

She searched the shadows for a moment and then moved her gaze back to the lake. The water shimmered like fine silk in the moonlight. She pushed up the window and leaned into the night.

Footsteps sounded on the stairs. She turned as Sam appeared in the doorway. He'd taken off his shirt and shoes. His jeans hung low on his hips. Ellie's breath caught. She'd never seen anything so startlingly sexy as Sam Reece standing in her bedroom doorway.

"You okay? I heard a noise," he said.

His deep voice tripped along her nerve endings. "I opened the window," she said. "I needed some fresh air."

He glanced toward the rumpled bed. "Couldn't sleep?"

"I'm still too keyed up." She turned back to the window. "Come take a look at the view."

He moved up beside her.

"My brother hates that I live out here alone, but this is why I stay." She breathed in the fragrant air. "Have you ever seen anything so beautiful?"

She felt his gaze on her. "No," he said. "I don't think I have."

They weren't touching and yet Ellie's skin tingled as if he'd run his fingers down her arm. She glanced up at him. His eyes were as dark and shimmery as the moonlit lake. Tension crackled for the longest moment and then she leaned into him, cupping his face as she stood on tiptoes to kiss him.

He leaned back slightly. "Are you sure about this?"

She responded by bringing his lips down to hers. He

wrapped his arms around her, lifting her off the floor as he kissed her back. He lowered her slowly and then they silently undressed in the moonlight. Ellie crawled back into bed and he slid in beside her. Arms and legs entwined, their kisses grew more heated until Ellie gently pushed him away.

He rolled to his side and propped himself up on his elbow. "Should I go back downstairs?"

"I don't want you to leave. I just want to slow things down a bit."

"Okay."

"Tell me something about yourself. Something personal so that I feel I know you."

He wound a strand of her hair around his fingertip. "What do you want to know?"

"Where did you grow up? Where did you go to school?"

"Longview. My parents and sister still live there. I went to school at UT Austin. The FBI recruited during my senior year." He rolled to his back and stared up at the ceiling. "I was near the top of my class at Quantico so I expected an assignment at headquarters, or possibly a field office in New York or LA. Instead, I was sent to the satellite office in Tyler, Texas. The kiss of death before my career had ever gotten off the ground."

"Why?"

"Who knows? Maybe I pissed off someone important or maybe I impressed myself more than I did the powers-that-be. Looking back, it was probably a deserved comeuppance. I was a little too full of myself. I can see that now, but at the time, I was devastated. Which is why I pushed so hard when I was assigned to Riley's kidnapping. I should have concentrated more on solving the case than on proving my brilliance."

"You did all you could. My father was an excellent law-man. He couldn't solve the case, either."

"Eventually I was sent back to DC where I was assigned to one of the Child Abduction Rapid Deployment teams. I had a lot to learn."

"You've hunted monsters ever since," she said. "It's a noble job but it must take a toll."

"You find ways to cope."

"Never been married?"

"No."

"Engaged?"

"No. Relationships are hard in my profession."

"I can only imagine."

"What about you?" He turned, lifting himself on his elbow again as he stared down at her.

"No husbands, no fiancés, no boyfriend at the moment. Relationships are hard for me, too. Trust is an issue."

"I can only imagine."

"I like sex, though."

He bent and kissed her neck. "Good to know."

She slid her hand under the covers. Sam's breath sharpened. He fell back against the pillows, succumbing to the cleverness of her fingers before he rolled on top of her. Bracing his hands on either side of her, he stared deep into her eyes. A smile tugged as he brought his lips to hers, tasting her with his tongue and then sliding slowly downward. He touched and teased until Ellie clutched the covers and twisted her fingers in his hair. When he finally came up for air, she was breathing hard and tingling all over.

She reached inside the nightstand drawer. Her gaze raked over the pistol, but that wasn't the protection she sought. She found the packet, tore it open and dealt efficiently with the contents.

Sam shuddered as she touched him. She climbed on top

of him, pushing back her hair as she positioned her hips. Moonlight pooled over their naked bodies as she moved, slowly at first and then with feverish abandon. Maybe it was the adrenaline, maybe it was the whiskey, more than likely it was Sam Reece himself. His dark eyes drew her in as his deep whispers egged her on until she collapsed, shuddering against his chest.

Chapter Fourteen

Sam left for Dallas at midmorning, but not before he'd surprised Ellie with breakfast on the deck and extracted a promise that she would call Tom sometime that day to fill him in on recent events. She walked him out to the car and they kissed goodbye, a perfectly natural and affectionate gesture without any of the awkwardness Ellie had been dreading.

She watched until his car disappeared down the road and then she went back inside to work. Settling down in her office with a fresh cup of coffee, she went over the previous notes she'd made for a remote interview she would be recording later that afternoon for a future broadcast. She was thankful to have a pressing assignment to keep her thoughts occupied.

Breaking for a late lunch, she texted Sam to make sure he'd arrived safely in Dallas, to which he promptly responded, and then she decided to give her brother a call.

To her surprise, a woman answered Tom's cell phone.

"Rae? Did I call the wrong number?"

"Not if you're trying to reach Tom," her future sister-in-law responded. "Is everything okay?"

"I was about to ask you the same thing."

Rae sighed. "Everything's fine, but your brother is being as stubborn as always. He refuses to accept the fact that he's not yet one hundred percent. His doctor and I have both warned him about overdoing it. A gunshot wound doesn't heal overnight, or even over the course of a few months. I insisted he take the day off. He's only allowed to respond to emergencies." She paused. "Do I sound as much like a nag as I think I do?"

"You sound like you're looking out for my brother. He is okay, isn't he?" Ellie asked anxiously.

"He's fine. To be honest, I mostly wanted a day to ourselves so we can go over our wedding plans together. But if you need him, I can go get him."

"No," Ellie said quickly. "It's nothing that can't wait. I'll call him back in a day or two. Don't even bother telling him that I called."

They spoke for a minute or two longer and then Ellie went back to work. Just before four that afternoon, she gathered up her notes and a copy of her guest's latest book and headed over to the studio. Sunlight shimmered down through the pine bowers, but on the opposite bank, shadows had already started to lengthen. She peered through the trees, wondering if someone watched from across the water. Or from somewhere even closer.

Maybe she should have asked Tom to send a patrol car by now and then. She hated asking for special favors. It put her brother in an awkward position. Besides, Sam would be back soon and she'd equipped the studio with strong locks to protect her expensive equipment. She'd be fine.

Once inside, she bolted the door and seated herself behind her console, positioning her chair so that she could see out the large window. She was safer here in her soundproof studio than almost anywhere else in the world.

Or so she wanted to believe.

SAM GLANCED AT his watch. Ellie would be in the studio by now. She'd likely turned off her cell for the interview so he had no way of getting in touch with her. He sent a text anyway, alerting her that he would be returning later than he'd originally planned. Jenna's parents had agreed to meet with him, but not until after church and a potluck luncheon that had been on their schedule for months.

He located the address and pulled to the curb in front of the one-story ranch, a much more modest home than the stately Victorian he remembered from his previous time in Belle Pointe. Jenna's treatments in expensive facilities like the Penn Shepherd Psychiatric Hospital had undoubtedly taken a toll on their finances.

Glancing over his shoulder, he walked up the porch steps and rang the bell. Both of the Malloys greeted him at the door. They'd been in their mid-forties when Jenna had been taken and then later found wandering along a country road. They would be approaching sixty now and the passing years of despair and heartache were deeply etched into their faces. They were both tall and slender, still an attractive couple despite their solemn expressions.

They invited him into a den comfortably furnished with a leather sofa and two overstuffed armchairs. He took one of the chairs and the Malloys sat side by side on the couch.

"We were surprised to get your phone call," Jim Malloy said anxiously. "It's been a few years since we last spoke."

Donna Malloy slipped her arm through her husband's. "Is there news…" she faltered and started over. "Have you found remains?"

"Nothing like that," Sam said. "I'd just like to ask you a few questions."

"After all these years? Why?" Jim demanded. "Something must have happened. Why else would you be here?"

Sam was careful in his approach. "Has Jenna mentioned anything about Riley to you lately?"

They exchanged a glance. "We haven't seen much of

Jenna since she moved out a few weeks ago," her mother said. "She's okay, isn't she? Nothing has happened to her?"

"I saw her yesterday," Sam assured them. "She seemed fine."

Jim Malloy's voice hardened suspiciously. "You talked to our daughter? Why? What aren't you telling us?"

"It seems that both Jenna and Ellie Brannon have been receiving anonymous calls from someone pretending to be Riley."

Donna Malloy gasped. "Ellie, too, this time?"

Sam lifted a brow. "Jenna has received these calls before?"

"Yes, years ago. She swore Riley was still alive and was trying to reach out to her. She even claimed to see her from time to time."

Sam remembered Jenna's bus stop story. "When was this?" he asked.

"Right after she left the hospital for the first time."

"Mr. and Mrs. Malloy, why did you take your daughter out of Penn Shepherd?"

"It's an expensive place," Jim Malloy said with a scowl. "And she didn't seem to be getting any better. If anything, she got worse."

"Did you remove her because of a patient named Hazel Lamont?"

Mrs. Malloy folded her arms around her middle and shivered as her husband leaned forward, eyes glittering like glass. "You know Hazel?"

"I've met her. She and Jenna seem extremely close."

"Abnormally close. Her doctor's words, not mine. Have you ever heard of a mental condition called folie à deux? It's where two people share a delusion. That's how the therapist described Jenna and Hazel's relationship, but I never really bought it. Hazel knew exactly what she was doing when she encouraged Jenna to believe that Riley was still alive. There was no delusion about it. She also convinced Jenna that Preacher was coming back for her."

"We think it was Hazel's way of making Jenna dependent on her," Mrs. Malloy said. "She convinced Jenna that she was the only one who would believe her and the only one who could protect her."

"It was nothing more than a sick and twisted game to that young woman," Jim Malloy said bluntly. "She never cared about our daughter."

"So her relationship with Hazel is why you took Jenna out of the hospital?"

"We tried having her moved to a different wing. That didn't work. Hazel knew how to manipulate the staff to get what she wanted. We had no choice but to separate them permanently."

"Did you know that Jenna has moved in with Hazel?"

"We know," Jim Malloy said gruffly. "Jenna is a grown woman. There's nothing we can do legally to interfere." He paused for a moment. "You say Jenna and Ellie have both been receiving these phone calls? Why is the FBI involved?"

"The case has never been closed," Sam said. "I've never given up on finding the person or persons responsible for abducting Riley and Jenna from the Ruins that night. I follow every lead no matter how remote."

Jim Malloy looked skeptical. "I still have to believe there's something you're not telling us. You say you're here to follow a lead, but Hazel Lamont wasn't around back then. Yet all your questions have been about her. What's really going on, Agent Reece?"

Mrs. Malloy leaned forward worriedly. "Is our daughter in any danger?"

"I don't know," Sam answered candidly. "Hazel Lamont

accosted Ellie Brannon in a restaurant yesterday. She made a few veiled threats about anyone who would try to keep her and Jenna apart. She mentioned the two of you. Ellie was sufficiently concerned to believe you should be warned."

Jim Malloy gave Sam another one of those hard stares. "You think we don't already know to take precautions around that woman? Why do you think we changed the locks on all our doors after Jenna moved out? Why do you think I keep a loaded gun on my nightstand?" His eyes glittered dangerously. "You know what I'm really afraid of, Agent Reece? That Hazel Lamont may somehow convince our own daughter to come into our home and murder us in our sleep."

TWILIGHT HOVERED AROUND the edges of the lake when Ellie left the studio. Sam had left a couple of texts during the interview. He was on his way back from Dallas, but would arrive a little later than he'd intended. He'd met with the Malloys and would fill her in on the conversation as soon as he saw her. He'd yet to touch base with the nurse who had worked at Penn Shepherd, but he hoped she'd get in touch just as soon as she received his message.

Ellie glanced at the time on her phone, contemplating whether or not to text him back. An hour had passed since his last message. He'd be arriving soon despite his late start. She wouldn't bother him while he was driving since she had nothing new to report.

Clutching her phone in one hand and her keys in the other, she hurried along the trail. The pistol she kept downstairs was tucked in the back of her jeans. She needed to go over and feed the peacocks, but until Sam arrived, they'd have to fend for themselves—

She halted in her tracks as she spotted someone sitting

on her deck. She put the phone away and reached behind her for her weapon just as Jenna caught sight of her and rose. She came down the steps and waited for Ellie at the bottom. Her hair was tangled, her clothing askew. She looked as if she'd been running for her life.

"Ellie, thank God! I've been waiting for you for the longest time."

Ellie's hand dropped from the pistol. "I've been in the studio. What's wrong?" She caught sight of a jagged scratch down Jenna's arm and gasped. "What happened?"

Jenna grabbed her hand. "He's coming, Elle. He's coming back for us."

SAM'S RINGTONE PEALED as he exited the interstate and turned down the state highway toward Belle Pointe. He tapped his earpiece and greeted the caller.

"Special Agent Reece."

"This is Dianne Collier. You left a voice mail for me earlier?"

The name clicked and Sam said anxiously, "Yes, Ms. Collier. Thank you for calling me back. We used to speak occasionally when you worked at Penn Shepherd. This would have been about fifteen years ago. I came to the hospital on several occasions to interview a young patient named Jenna Malloy."

"I remember you well, Agent Reece. And, of course, I remember Jenna." She paused. "She's been one of the harder patients to forget. Has something happened to her? Is that why you're calling?"

Sam briefly explained the situation. After he finished, she said nothing.

"Did I lose you?" he asked.

"No, I'm still here. You say Hazel Lamont is back in Jenna's life?"

"I gather it's a recent development," Sam said. "What can you tell me about their relationship at Penn Shepherd?"

"They were roommates for a time. They grew quite close as I recall." Her tone was guarded.

"So close the doctors thought they were sharing delusions," Sam said.

"Hazel was clever and manipulative. Jenna was more subtle."

"That's an interesting observation."

"Jenna was an interesting patient. She spoke of the girl who'd gone missing as if she were still alive."

"Riley Cavanaugh."

"Yes, Riley. Jenna claimed Riley could reach out to her even in the hospital. She claimed their abductor was able to communicate with her, too. Her doctors thought at first that Jenna exhibited characteristics of dissociative identity disorder. Split personalities. To Jenna, her friend, Riley, was very much alive and forever on the run from the monster she called Preacher."

"You said *at first* her doctors thought she exhibited these characteristics."

"Jenna could be very convincing. She was also quite the actress."

"Are you saying she faked these characteristics?"

"A diagnosis of DID is rare and still somewhat controversial. It garnered Jenna a great deal of attention for a while." Another long pause. "I don't know if she was faking. What I do know is that the Preacher persona gave her an excuse to act out. I always believed it was this personality, real or not, that Hazel Lamont was most attracted to. And most susceptible to, too."

"What do you mean?"

"Everyone, including Jenna's doctors and her parents, thought that Hazel was a bad influence on Jenna. I was around those two girls more than anyone. I never saw it that way. I always believed it was the opposite, in fact."

JENNA SAT AT the kitchen table while Ellie cleaned the scratch on her arm and applied antiseptic. Neither of them said much during this time. Jenna seemed unwilling or unable to explain how she'd gotten injured or even how she'd ended up at Ellie's place. The driveway was empty. No car in sight. No sign of Hazel, either.

Ellie closed the first-aid kit and stood to wash her hands at the sink. Twilight had fallen by this time, but the horizon still glowed from the last of the sunset. Behind her, Jenna stirred.

"I left her there," she said in a voice that didn't sound like her own. "I left her in that awful place."

"You mean Riley?"

Jenna looked up through haunted eyes. "She got so sick toward the end he didn't take her away anymore. That was a relief, even though it meant he came for me more often. But at least I didn't have to lie in the dark and listen to Riley's screams."

Ellie's heart jolted. "I'm so sorry, Jenna."

She nodded vaguely. "When he came for me, I'd close my eyes and pretend to be someone else until he was done. It wasn't me he touched. It wasn't me he hurt."

Ellie came back over to the table and sat down.

Jenna went on as if Ellie's presence didn't really register. "He told us that only one of us would ever leave that awful place. Survival of the fittest, he called it. In order to be free, one would have to die by the hand of the other."

Ellie gasped as icy fingers slid down her spine. "Did you ever see his face?"

A frown flickered, as if the question confused her. "You

mean Preacher? He was careful. It was always so dark and sometimes he wore a mask."

"You remember his voice, though?"

"Yes. Sometimes he whispers to me when I sleep."

Ellie closed her eyes briefly. "What happened to Riley?"

"She got weaker and weaker. She told me that I would have to be the one. She didn't have the strength. It had to be me. But I couldn't do it." Jenna grabbed Ellie's hand and squeezed. "I couldn't do it. I couldn't do it."

"Shush," Ellie soothed. "It's all over. You're safe now."

"It'll never be over," Jenna said. "Not as long as he's still out there. Not as long as he knows what I did."

Ellie shivered. "What did you do?"

"She was so hot. Her skin was on fire. I used what little water we had to try to cool her forehead with my shirt. She grabbed my hand and placed it over her nose and mouth. I knew what she was trying to do. She was trying to help me. But I couldn't do it. Not at first. Not for a long time. She just kept pleading with me to end it. She was going to die in that awful place no matter what I did. If I ended her suffering, maybe I could at least go free. She begged and begged until I finally placed my shirt over her face and pressed. After a while, she went limp but I kept the shirt to her face. I kept on pressing until her skin cooled and then I lay down beside her and waited."

Ellie could hardly speak. "What happened then?"

"He came for me one day. He blindfolded me, tied my hands behind my back and took me away. I don't know how long we drove before he stopped the car and made me get out. He untied my hands but he told me not to take off the blindfold until I counted to one hundred. I heard his car drive off, but I kept on counting. Ninety-eight, ninety-nine, one hundred. I removed the blindfold, but I still couldn't see. The sun was so bright. I had no idea where I was or even who I was by that time. But I knew what I had done."

Ellie clutched her hand. "What happened wasn't your fault. None of it was your fault."

She drew her hand away and closed her eyes. "He's coming."

Ellie sat frozen in dread. "Who?"

Jenna's voice altered subtly. Deepened. Hardened. "You know who."

Ellie rose slowly and backed away from the table. "Jenna?"

Her eyes flew open. "He's here."

Chapter Fifteen

Ellie's gaze remained riveted on Jenna. She was so taken by the look of dread in Jenna's eyes that she failed to glimpse the dark figure slipping across the deck until he—she—stood outside the door. Before Ellie had time to reach for her weapon, he kicked the door open, shattering the frame.

Someone screamed. Ellie wasn't sure if it was her or Jenna. She lunged across the kitchen floor, placing herself between Jenna and the door.

"Jenna, run!"

The command seemed to awaken her from a deep trance. She bolted from her chair and dashed for the dining room. Ellie drew her weapon, but the intruder was on her in a flash, slinging her against the counter where she crumpled like a rag doll. The gun flew from her hand and slid under the table. She scrambled toward it, but Preacher grabbed her legs and pulled her back. Then he straddled her, pinning her down as his hand closed around her throat.

Ellie tore at the knit mask while she reached frantically for her weapon. The fabric gave way, revealing the monster's face.

Cory Small swore. Jenna screamed.

Ellie fought him with every ounce of her strength, but the hand only squeezed tighter. Panic set in. Her energy waned. Still she frantically felt for the gun, her fingers finally closing around the cool metal. Shoving the pistol between them, she pulled the trigger.

He clutched his side in stunned disbelief. Ellie tried to fire off another round, but he slammed her hand against the floor again and again until she released the weapon. Then he wrapped both his hands around her throat.

A voice said from the doorway, "Federal agent! Stand down or I'll drop you on the spot."

Three shots rang out and it was over.

When Ellie was able to breathe, she scrambled across the floor where Jenna sat huddled with her knees tightly drawn to her chest.

"It's okay. It's okay. He'll never hurt you again."

Sam kicked away the weapon and checked Cory Small's pulse. Then he took out his phone and called for an ambulance and backup.

"Everyone okay here?" he asked as he hunkered beside Ellie and Jenna.

"I hope so," Ellie whispered.

Sam put his arms around both of them and held on tight.

Chapter Sixteen

Two days later...

Ellie stood on her deck at sunset, staring out at the gilded water as she reflected on everything that had happened. In between surgeries and before he'd lawyered up, Cory Small had told the authorities where to find Riley's remains, along with those of his uncle, Silas Creed. With his confession and certain evidence that had been recovered from his farm, a grim story had unfolded.

Cory had had a fascination for Riley for a long time, perhaps even years, before he'd taken her. He'd spoken to her a few times, once or twice in the presence of her friend, Jenna Malloy, who may or may not have begun to get suspicious. Cory couldn't take that chance so he backed off, covertly encouraging some of his classmates to dare the girls to go out to the Ruins. He even arranged for Tom Brannon to be lured away from the house that night, allowing the girls to slip away undetected.

Whether willingly or unwittingly, Silas Creed had become his nephew's accomplice. He had helped Cory subdue the girls and roll their bodies in plastic, using chemicals from the farm to disguise their scent from the bloodhounds. They had taken Jenna and Riley deep into the woods, to an old storm cellar that Cory had worked on for months, installing bars and padlocks.

Afterward, he killed his uncle, disposed of the body down a well and drove his truck into the river. Silas's timely disappearance had made him the main suspect, as Cory had known it would.

Ellie felt bone-deep weary from all the questions and discoveries, but strangely at peace, as if a weight had finally been lifted from her shoulders. Sam stood beside her, a calm and steady presence.

"Why didn't he just kill Jenna, too, I wonder. He took an awfully big risk letting her go."

Sam gazed out at the water. "By that time, he probably felt omnipotent. It gave him a thrill to watch Jenna out in the open and know that he could take her again at any time."

"That level of depravity doesn't manifest overnight," Ellie said. "How could his mother not have known? How could we not have known?"

"The same way serial killers fool their families and neighbors for years. Monsters aren't always quiet loners," Sam said. "But they are almost always clever and cunning. We don't know that Riley was his only victim. We'll comb the farm and woods for remains and we'll go back through the cold case files and see if we can connect him to any unsolved disappearances. But it's possible he was one and done. He might have lived forever on the crumbs of his secret if Melanie Kent hadn't turned back up, asking questions. He let her stay in Creed's shed so that he could find out what she knew. Then he must have started to worry about what you and Jenna might remember."

"Melanie went to see Jenna, too?"

Sam nodded. "Melanie's questions and Hazel Lamont's reappearance in Jenna's life created the perfect storm.

Riley and Preacher started to battle inside her again. She made those anonymous phone calls to your radio show, trying to warn you. It was Jenna you saw by the lake and probably Jenna you saw in the black hat."

"The friendship bracelet, the peacock feather…all of it was Jenna. She even tried to push me over the banister at the Ruins. Preacher came back for the girl that got away, just like the Unknown Caller warned me that he would."

"After she scaled down from the roof, she probably hid out in the woods all night, trying to elude Preacher when he was there inside her all along. She came to your house to try to warn you."

Ellie shivered. "She gave me a glimpse of what she and Riley went through. He made her kill her best friend. You don't come back from something like that."

"No," Sam said grimly. "But she can get better. Riley and Preacher went away for a long time until Melanie's questions and Hazel's encouragement brought them back."

Ellie glanced at him. "What happens now? For you, I mean."

"I go back to Dallas. Back to my other cases."

"Back to chasing monsters."

His gaze narrowed as he scanned the opposite bank. "They're out there, watching from the shadows."

Ellie turned back to the water. "I'll miss seeing you every day."

He turned at that, his deep gaze taking her in. "Dallas isn't that far away. My commute in DC was almost as long. You can see as much or as little of me as you like. I'm only ever a phone call away."

"I'm counting on that." She moved closer and his arm came around her. She laid her head against his shoulder as she stared out at her beloved Echo Lake. "After all these years, it's finally over."

He pulled her close. "I prefer to think of it as just the beginning."

* * * * *

IDENTICAL
THREAT

TYLER ANNE SNELL

This book is for Alaina D. You let me talk about twins before, during and after this book was written like it was normal…and never once complained. Thank you for being a supportive friend during a very frustrating time in my life. I couldn't have asked for better.

Chapter One

The unmistakable truth was that the woman who had just entered the party wasn't a local. The very mistakable truth, however, had to do with her intentions for being there in the first place.

Was she a prospective donor for one of the nonprofits they worked alongside?

Was she there to ask how the Second Wind Foundation would operate now that it was moving its official headquarters to the town of Overlook, Tennessee?

Was she a Wildman County reporter?

Was she there as someone's date?

Desmond Nash tried to keep his attention on the small group of guests who had crowded around him like he was some kind of animal on display at the zoo, but it was hard not to keep track of the woman as she split through the party with practiced ease. The descriptor of *siren* lodged itself in Desmond's head at the sight of her.

Long tangles of dark red curls flowed across her shoulders and back, water infused with the very concept of mystery. Her brows matched, thick and sculpted, hooding dark eyes that, even from the distance between her and Desmond, pulled at him. Without the tall heels she wore pushing her height up a few inches, he supposed he would have to tilt his chin down to see into those dark eyes.

The interest certainly didn't stop there. The way she carried herself spoke of confidence and grace. Like the rest of the outdoor gala attendees, she was wrapped in a dress meant only for special occasions. Black silk contrasted against her pale and freckled skin, dipping low at the chest and clinging to the curves of her hips.

Whoever the woman was, she was commanding the outdoor gala just by existing.

"We're just so glad you decided to come home, Desmond."

His name was what finally broke the trance he'd fallen into looking at the newest guest. Desmond turned to the deep voice of Garfield Taylor, one of the town council members and once a very good friend of Desmond's father, Michael.

"You've been going nonstop since you started Second Wind," Garfield continued. "Maybe now since you're back it's time you finally slowed down?"

It was said with a twinkle in his eye and a slight tease in his tone. The older man cut his gaze to where Desmond had just been staring. He grinned. Desmond had been caught gawking at the new arrival. Now he'd given Garfield the perfect excuse to ask what his mother had already been asking without actually saying the exact words.

When are you going to settle down?

If Desmond had been one of his brothers—their tact was all but absent when it came to someone trying to pry into their personal lives—he would have responded in a saltier manner.

I'll slow down when you show me that book of yours you've been working on for ten years, he wanted to say.

Instead Desmond chose a more diplomatic response.

"Second Wind is just as much a part of my life as this ranch," he said, pulling up an easy smile. "As long as there are people out there I can help, I don't think slowing down is an option for me."

The group around them started smiling; some laughed; most everyone had a drink in hand. Garfield was grinning but didn't press the issue. Instead another Overlook local took the floor and, thankfully, kept it to the topic of work. Desmond was prepared to go over Second Wind's construction schedule for the umpteenth time that night but a slight tug at his elbow gave him an excuse to switch gears. A pair of blue eyes that matched his to a *T* stared up through long lashes at him.

"Sorry to interrupt but can I pull you away for a second, Des?"

Madi knew she could do just that without apologizing. Whereas he was the star of this particular party, Madeline Nash was just as infamous as he was. Being a local was synonymous with knowing every detail about the Nash family.

Specifically, Desmond, Madi and Caleb.

It was a fame none had asked for and yet one they couldn't escape. Even if they moved off the ranch and married into a new last name as Madi had.

"Sure," Desmond said. He tipped his Stetson to the group. "Excuse me, folks."

Madi led him a few feet away before she spoke, waving at him to follow her as she did. Desmond didn't need a triplet connection with Madi to know she was headed toward the sweet tea bar. Most of the guests had champagne flutes. Madi Nash was about to have a mason jar of Milo's.

"I didn't really need anything," she said, eyes on target. "I just felt like you needed a break from that particular crowd. I saw the way Garfield was looking at you. Not to mention Missy. I'm pretty sure she was two seconds from drooling on you."

Desmond chuckled.

"I didn't notice Missy but I do thank you for the save

from Garfield. And talking about the construction again. It's been the most-asked question of the night other than *What's next for Desmond Nash?*"

It was Madi's turn to laugh. She slowed as she neared the bar and Desmond couldn't help but take the atmosphere all in again.

The outdoor gala had been set up by an event company out of Kilwin, the city next to Overlook. They'd erected giant and, dare he think it, classy tents across the field between the main house on the ranch and the horse stable. They'd taken a field of grass and dirt and somehow made it into a high-class event. Set against the backdrop of mountains, forests and stars and everyone's tuxes and dresses, it all just seemed to work.

Desmond was definitely impressed, even more so with the catering staff.

They were local and they kept up casual conversation with most of the guests as they bustled in and out of the designated food-prep area. Matthew Jenkins bebopped past them with another tray of drinks. He nodded to Desmond and tipped his hat to Madi. It was an interesting contrast to the image Desmond had of the same man but years younger, drunk as a skunk and trying to tip Mr. Elroy's cow because he saw it in a movie once.

"Overlook isn't used to a good kind of excitement," Madi said, smiling at the attendant in charge of filling the jars with tea. "You, not only coming home, but literally building a three-story structure for Second Wind right here in town is a big deal. If you think you're going to be able to smile away that type of hype, you're foolin' yourself there, cowboy."

Madi wasn't wrong. Overlook was a small town. They got by, sure, but there hadn't been a new business that had set up shop on the same scale as Second Wind. Construction had roughly two months left, and every time he'd been to the site to see the progress, he'd seen at least two or three bystanders checking it out too.

Madi also wasn't wrong about the excitement part either. Overlook had had one heck of a streak of chaos in the last few years. The fact that it had all revolved around the Nash family only threw more fuel on the gossip-and-talk fire.

"I know, I know," he conceded. "But it would be nice if they at least shook up the conversation. Dressing up in a suit makes my skin crawl—dodging personal questions only makes matters worse."

Madi took her sweet tea with a smile. Desmond once again followed her.

"You can't get all hot and bothered about those kinds of questions," she said, keeping her voice low as they navigated around a pocket of guests next to one of the buffet tables. "They're all just wondering why the most charming and sweet-talkingist Nash doesn't have a plus-one dangling on his arm."

Desmond sighed. It earned another laugh. "You better find yourself a better answer than annoyance," Madi continued. "Now that you're living full-time in Overlook, every single one of Ma's friends are going to start parading their unattached daughters up Winding Road and right to your front door. And they won't take any sighs for answers."

Desmond thought of the siren. He almost asked if Madi had seen her too when her path led them right to Julian Mercer.

He was often described by Madi as "a mountain of a man" and the description was apt. Desmond was a tall man and yet he had to tilt his chin up a fraction to stare his brother-in-law in the eyes.

"Extraction successful," Madi said, conspiratorially.

"No casualties?" Julian played along.

"Other than Missy's pride? None."

Julian looped his arm around Madi and pulled her into

his side. He was smiling, just as he always was when Madi was near.

An ache of loneliness reminded Desmond that he hadn't had that kind of closeness, or any kind really, in a long time. Second Wind wasn't just his livelihood, it had become his entire life in the last few years. His late nights were spent with facts and figures, his dinner dates with potential investors and his holidays with ideas of what to do next.

Moving back to Overlook hadn't originally been his idea. In fact, it had been the family's.

"You need a connection to something outside Second Wind," his mother had said. "Trees can't grow without roots. You need to attach somewhere. Why not in Overlook?"

Now here he was, trying to keep his eye on the professional ball while letting invisible tree roots dig into the ranch ground.

"You two are a hoot," Desmond deadpanned. It only made the couple smile wider.

"We'll be here all night," Madi teased. "Available for dinners too."

They devolved into playful bickering followed by the appearance of Overlook's sheriff, the eldest Nash sibling.

Declan Nash looked even more uncomfortable wearing a suit than Desmond did. He gave them a gruff greeting. He wasn't one of the triplets but that didn't mean they weren't just as close with him as each other. Madi's brow creased in concern just as Desmond voiced what she was thinking.

"What's wrong?"

Julian, not as well-versed in all of the subtleties of the family yet, tensed. Desmond angled his body so they were in a huddle-like circle.

Declan sighed. It was his trademark move.

"It's nothing but it's something."

Something happened but it wasn't a big deal. Desmond felt his brow raise.

"Be more specific and I can agree with you," Desmond prodded.

Declan sighed again.

"I just got back from the construction site. There's been some vandalism on one of the first-floor exterior walls."

Desmond clenched his jaw. Declan continued. "It's nothing that a little gray paint can't fix but it's also nothing you want showing out to the road. Caleb and I were on the way here when the call came in so we went over and covered it with a tarp. That's why we're late."

"What was it?"

Declan shook his head.

"Just some idiots being idiots. Nothing you need to deal with right now."

"You have security cameras, right?" Julian asked.

"Interior cameras, but the law office across the street has one pointed at the building. Marty McLinnon works there. He's actually here at the party. I can go ask him if we can get the footage?"

Declan took off his cowboy hat and shook his head.

"Let me go see if I can't find him. If not, this can wait until tomorrow. Don't worry."

He clapped Desmond on the shoulder and headed off to the tent that housed the most people mingling. Before he could penetrate the main group he was called this way and that by his constituents. Desmond might have been dubbed the "most charming" Nash but as sheriff Declan had his own claim to fame.

"He didn't tell me what was put on the wall," Desmond realized.

Madi's gaze went over his shoulder. Her cell phone started to ring as she spoke.

"There's Caleb… And this is the babysitter with an update since I'm a neurotic parent." Madi and Julian moved farther away from the party to take the call as Desmond turned to the last Nash sibling.

Caleb was half Declan, half Desmond. He was a detective at the sheriff's department and smart as a whip. Like Declan, his love of law enforcement was ingrained in him. However, like Desmond, he was more inclined to lean on humor and lightheartedness when managing the rest of his life. That separation had become more pronounced after he'd met his wife, Nina. As he scanned the crowed, Desmond knew she was who he was looking for.

Too bad Desmond was about to bombard him with questions that led straight back to the work side.

The live band in the main tent started up a slow song that leaned into a piece of piano music. It didn't pair well with the tension now lining his shoulders. Desmond didn't care. He had Caleb in his sights, tunnel visioned in.

Second Wind meant more to him than people seemed to realize. It was a lifeline for some. It was a lifeline for him.

After everything his family had been through…

After the abduction.

After his father's death.

After years of therapy, physical and mental.

After realizing the fallout of what had happened might never stop coming.

Second Wind might have been a foundation that helped nonprofits who in turn helped others with precision and expertise, but it was so much more for Desmond.

It might have seemed idiotic that something as small as vandalism that could be covered with a little paint had completely derailed his entire focus, especially at a party, yet it had.

So much so that he nearly ran into a guest who found her way into the path between him and Caleb. She'd been staring up at the tent's ceiling.

"Oh, excuse me," Desmond said, stopping so suddenly he had to put a hand on her arm to keep them from colliding farther. The woman reached a hand out to his chest to keep the same collision from happening, clearly startled.

It was the siren.

Her face flushed. Her dark eyes widened.

"No, excuse me," she said with a nervous laugh. "I'm the one walking around in here staring at these tents without looking where I'm going!" Recognition flared behind her eyes. Her cheeks turned an even darker shade of crimson. She dropped her hand and took a step away from him like she'd been bitten. "And you're Desmond Nash, the host. Wow. Talk about an embarrassing first impression."

"I'm actually happy someone else is in awe of these," he said, pointing up. "I'm not about to be upset at someone else for doing what I was ten minutes ago."

She still looked nervous but she smiled all the same.

"Well, I might as well introduce myself now." She extended her hand. "I'm Jenna Stone."

The name was familiar.

Yet, Desmond couldn't place it.

A look that seemed to reach way past worried flashed across her expression. She dropped his hand quickly and took another step backward. Desmond almost turned around to see if it was someone else who had caused the almost scared reaction.

"I'll let you get on your way," she hurried. "I think it's time I checked out the band now."

Desmond opened his mouth to say something— he wasn't sure what—but Jenna was fast.

One second she was there.

The next he was standing alone.

Chapter Two

It was a lie.

She was *not* Jenna Stone but, boy oh boy, had she said it. Out loud.

To another human.

To *him*.

No. She was Riley Stone, Jenna's sister. Her twin to be exact. Identical in every physical aspect—well except for the tattoo she'd gotten her first spring break in college that her parents *still* didn't know about—the Stone sisters were nearly indistinguishable.

Which was why Riley was at the Nash family ranch, attending an extremely fancy gala wearing an extremely tight dress and trying to limit the amount of lies she was telling.

To help her sister she had to *be* her sister. At least for the night.

But then she'd gotten swept up in the atmosphere and literally run into the man who had made the party possible.

Desmond Nash looked nothing like he did on the foundation's website. The professional portrait had shown a commanding man with gelled dark hair, cold blue eyes and a smile that said he knew exactly how much he was worth. His bio, with its lists of every successful business venture he'd run before starting Second Wind, only backed up the image of a businessman who never bit off more than he could chew. In person, however, the intimidating image Riley had held since that morning's briefing by her sister had slightly skewed.

He wore a suit but his cowboy hat threw off the uptight business ensemble, just as his messy hair and carefree laughter had tipped the scale from consummate professional to normal, well-dressed man with a smile that had done something to Riley's stomach when she'd seen it. His eyes had crinkled at the corners and those baby blues had seemed a lot warmer when she had been close enough to touch him.

Desmond Nash was not what she had expected.

All you have to do is be present, Jenna had coached earlier that day. *Go in, eat and drink, mingle, smile and make small talk. That's it.*

Riley wanted to bean her sister on the head. She wasn't a fan of deception, even if it was for a good cause. Lying, well lately it had taken on a new face for Riley. It meant something else. It hurt more. It angered her more. Now she was moving through a party filled with guests who didn't even suspect she was effectively a walking and talking lie.

It's not that big of a deal, Riley tried to assure herself. *Jenna couldn't come so we did a weird version of* The Parent Trap. *It's not like we're trying to grift or anything.*

The inner pep talk didn't completely land but Riley raised her chin and moved on to the next tent, following a beautiful piano medley.

Overlook was much like the Nash family ranch which was *also* much like Desmond. Riley hadn't expected to be surprised and impressed with any one of them.

A small, small town in mostly rural Tennessee, Overlook was a far cry from Riley's last home of Atlanta, Georgia. There was no constant hustle or bustle, no tall buildings of metal and glass, no concrete jungle, no excitement at every turn. Yet, it was beautiful.

Just like the ranch at the end of Winding Road.

The copy online about the family-owned-and-run establishment gave the bare-bones facts: over a hundred acres of land, residential housing on the property as well as a horse stable, barns and the Wild Iris Retreat, also owned and run by Nashes. Riley had done as much homework as she could to dig a little deeper, using Google Earth to zoom in on the land and get a general feel for it.

Trees, fields, mountains. The usual.

Yet, before Winding Road had even ended, Riley had been stunned at the beauty surrounding them.

Rolling fields of green dipped and straightened around, between and at the edges of a forest that went across the ranch and seemingly all the way into town. Ranch buildings, including a red barn that looked like it belonged on a postcard, were interspersed in between, looking as natural as the scenery around them. Overlook was a shock of flora. Just as the mountains in the distance were. Riley had seen the curved outlines against the darkening blue sky when she'd first driven up to the party. She had had the strongest urge to reach out and pretend to touch them, tracing their dips and peaks like a child enthralled in a moment of wonder.

Now, at the very least, she understood some of her sister's reasoning for settling in Overlook.

It was a far cry from lives that had crumbled in the last year.

It was a cozy and beautiful respite.

But that didn't mean Riley was any more comfortable lying to everyone who reached out to say hello. One major drawback of the small town? Everyone seemed to know everyone else. She stuck out like a sore thumb. Even more so after her impromptu, and embarrassing, run-in with Desmond.

No sooner had she made it to the end of the tent, ready to

glide over into the next one, did a man catch her attention. He was short, stocky and had hair that was messy but not in the charming way. His blazer hung a little too loosely on his frame and the shirt beneath it was somewhat wrinkled. His brown eyes jumped to her and then the area around them.

Riley might be nervous about pretending to be her sister but she had a feeling the man in front of her was a lot more nervous about something else.

"Pretty nice party, huh?" he greeted. "Desmond Nash sure is something, isn't he?"

Riley felt her sister's customer-service smile move across her lips.

Play the part.

"Yes! To both! I'm definitely impressed and having a great time."

The man's brows pulled in together for the briefest of moments. Riley didn't know how to classify the emotion that did it but then he was smiling again.

"You aren't the only one. I'm Brett." Riley expected him to offer his hand but he didn't move an inch.

"Jenna Stone."

"So how long have you been living in Overlook? I don't think I've seen you around."

Brett took a small step forward as if he was trying to physically engage with the conversation. It put him close enough that Riley could smell a hint of cologne. It wasn't altogether pleasant.

"Not long enough to know everyone yet," she hedged. While Riley had been in Overlook for a little over a month, Jenna had made the move six months before that. Very few locals knew her by sight, let alone name. If Brett didn't recognize her then Riley wasn't about to give out information on her sister. "How about you?"

The man shrugged.

"Not that long either."

He didn't offer anything else. A silence moved between them. The piano medley faded out and was replaced by an acoustic guitar.

"Well," she finally broke in. "This party sure is great. Just like Second Wind. Desmond Nash really has a knack for knowing how to help people, doesn't he?"

Brett actually snorted.

"People like him always think they have the answers—I'll give you that."

Riley was starting to feel uncomfortable outside her lying. She didn't know this man—okay, *anyone* at the party—but she didn't think her sister would want to make a connection with him. Jenna was trying to grow her business in Overlook and Riley couldn't imagine Brett was into graphic design.

"This music is lovely, though, isn't it?" she asked lamely. The man wasn't taking any normal social cues in the conversation. He just kept staring. Eyes never straying from hers.

I've never felt more awkward in my life, Riley had the time to think.

She took an unintentional step backward. That, at least, he seemed to register. His smile widened. He nodded.

"It's sure something." He angled his body as if to leave. Instead he held out his arm. "Maybe we can dance to it?"

Riley felt like she was getting whiplash from the very brief and exceptionally strange conversation. She understood that not everyone could wear charm with ease—heck, her ex-husband Davies used to say she could burn through a good conversation with just one heated opinion in a flash—but there was something about the man that slunk under her skin and went to itching. Still, Riley tried to be gracious as she let him down.

She *was* pretending to be Jenna after all.

"I would but there's a few people I was hoping to talk to before I started in on the fun. Rain check?"

Brett shrugged. He dropped his arm, seemingly nonplussed.

"Suit yourself."

Then he walked off.

Just like that.

Riley stared after him a moment, dumbfounded. Even though she wanted to go to the main tent, she decided to turn around. She was almost disappointed when Desmond Nash was nowhere to be seen.

SECOND WIND FOUNDATION had spent its career finding and funding nonprofits that all seemed to focus on helping people after tragedy. That's what Jenna had surmised when she was stepping Riley through small talk all day, yet that wasn't what any of the guests were discussing when Riley infiltrated each of their groups.

Instead the conversations ran the gamut of brief facts and heavy gossip. Not all of it Riley could follow, but still, she nodded along with everyone else. While Jenna had taught her everything she knew about Overlook, Second Wind and Desmond Nash, there was apparently a lot she hadn't.

"I hope that Second Wind building isn't an eyesore. I already don't like how many trees they cut to clear the lot to build."

"How much money did they spend on this party? Where does it come from? Don't you think it's suspicious?"

"Did you hear about what happened to Madi last year? And what about Caleb a few years before? Talk about bad luck. This family is lousy with it."

"I heard Desmond only came back because he couldn't handle being away from his mom."

"Did you see his limp? Remember when he was a kid? It's gotten a lot better. Do you think he had surgery on it?"

"Is Desmond here alone? Maybe I can change that."

The last conversation was from a woman who appeared to be a few years younger than Riley's thirty. She was done up in a short cocktail dress made entirely of sequins. When she spotted the cowboy across the main tent—which Riley was excited to say she'd finally made it to without running into Brett—the woman had actually readjusted her dress, pushing her breasts higher. That woman was one of three around Riley. The only one she had focused on meeting was Claire, the owner of the same-named coffee shop in town. She had been kind and inviting as Riley introduced herself as Jenna. She had even asked for a business card once Riley was done with her memorized spiel.

The woman now openly ogling the businessman hadn't been as accommodating. She'd barely met Riley's eye when the introductions started. There was even a bit of a sneer when Claire asked if Riley had talked to the host already and she admitted she had.

The party might have been celebrating Second Wind and the man behind it, but Riley was finding a lot of focus had found its way to Desmond's dating life. Riley couldn't deny she was just a bit curious about it too.

She was about to finally cave and ask a few questions herself when Desmond seemingly disappeared. The next half hour brought in a new wave of conversational topics about other citizens of Overlook. Riley was starting to feel a touch uncomfortable with getting the 411 on relative strangers when a text vibrated her phone. It was from Jenna.

You've been there over an hour. Officially shutting down Twin Trickery. Come on home. Made snickerdoodles.

"Well, it's been wonderful to meet you all," Riley said, stifling a chuckle. She discreetly put her phone back into her clutch and fished for her keys. "But I think I'm going to call it a night."

Jenna and Riley were emotional bakers through and through, just like their mother. Every problem had a baked-good answer. Stressed? Gooey brownies. Angry? Chocolate-chip cookies with sea salt. Feeling guilty? Snickerdoodles. The list went on and changed with their moods but it had always made their father laugh.

"No matter what happens, the house always smells wonderful," he'd said.

Riley was more than ready to benefit from her sister's most recent bout of emotion. It was just kismet that it synced up with the fact that Riley's feet were starting to get sore.

Claire and the rest said their goodbyes and Riley strutted out into the night air with more pep in her step than before. When Jenna had begged Riley to pretend to be her for just one night, Riley had thought she was crazy. They were identical, sure, but their personalities varied widely, love for baking excluded.

Yet, as Riley followed the lit garden path to the make-shift parking area, she felt an unfurling of pride in her chest.

She'd helped her sister, and after the year Jenna had, it felt good to get a win for her.

Riley held on to the good feeling and got into her Jeep with a little excited hop. Her mind went to the snickerdoodles and she flung her high heels into the passenger's seat with vigor. She gave the party in the distance one more long look. The tents were lit up and glowing, the music was soft yet far-reaching and the stars and moon were nothing but ethereal above it all.

The Nash family ranch was a fairy tale.

One Riley was surprised to already miss.

But this wasn't her life. She wasn't like her sister. Overlook was a pit stop on the way to *something* else.

She'd hang around long enough to get her feet back on the ground and help her sister do the same. Then she'd be gone.

Riley drove out of the parking area and onto the road that went through the heart of the ranch. She was curious about the other paths that branched off it going this way and that but kept on straight to Winding Road. Once she was through the ranch's main gate and on the two-lane road, she pressed Play on the CD player and started to rock out to the *Greatest Hits of the 80s*. Moonlit scenery flashed by on either side of the Jeep until the open fields turned to forests and the darkness between the road's shoulders thickened.

Riley bobbed her head to the music, tapped her foot against the floorboard to the beat and was fully prepared to belt out the opening to "Take on Me" by a-ha. She slowed her speed since streetlights were far apart and few in number.

However, as she opened her mouth to start singing, she realized the headlights that had been somewhat behind her belonged to a car that was in no way adhering to caution. In fact, it was gaining speed.

Riley gripped the steering wheel, the words to her song forgotten. Her stomach tightened but her mind tried to reassure her she was just imaging that the car had not only sped up, but was nearing her bumper.

But then the car went into the middle of the road. The relief made her shoulders relax. The idiot was going to pass her. Impatience, that was all.

Riley glanced over as the red Buick drew even with her. The lights were on inside the car.

That relief vanished.

It was Brett.

He was smiling as he jerked his wheel toward her. Riley didn't have any time to react.

The song's chorus started to build.

It didn't have a chance to finish before Riley was screaming.

Chapter Three

The Jeep was sky blue and always carried a faint scent of cinnamon within its cab. Riley had owned and driven it for ten years and, in all of that time, never figured out why that was. It had driven her ex-husband mad trying to solve the mystery, just as it frustrated him that no matter what air freshener or spray he used, the scent of cinnamon never went away. Riley had oddly come to love the smell. It was synonymous with the feeling of home, if she was being honest with herself. It put her at ease.

However, not even the faintest trace of cinnamon could stop the horror that shot through Riley the second Brett's car connected with hers.

"What are you doing?"

An awful scraping of metal against metal combined with Riley's scream. She struggled to keep the Jeep on the road. Dirt and rocks kicked up from the shoulder. Brett didn't seem to care. He maneuvered his car back to the middle of the road while Riley tried for the brakes.

If it had been an accident before, it surely wasn't now.

Brett was relentless as he swerved right back at her. This time Riley tried to avoid him. She hit the brakes but not before the back of his car collided with her driver's-side door with a sickening crunch and undeniable force.

Riley wasn't sure what happened next.

One second she had a death grip on the steering wheel. The next the world was chaos.

Awful sounds surrounded her. Glass shattered, metal warped. Something hit Riley's face. The feeling of gravity tugging her in the wrong direction was tangled in a burning sensation across her chest. On reflex she tried to touch the pain when the world around her stopped moving. Once her hand was off the steering wheel, though, her entire body shifted.

Riley yelled.

She realized then that she was upside down.

Her red curls were reaching for the crumpled roof of the Jeep. One of Jenna's dangling earrings slipped out of its place and *plink*ed against something that sounded like glass below her. Something mechanical whined in the distance. The *Greatest Hits of the 80s* had gone silent but the lights from the dash sent a faint glow out around her.

Riley had a moment of total confusion. It left her frozen.

But then she heard it. A car door shutting.

Then Riley remembered why she was upside down in the first place.

Brett.

"Oh my God."

She fumbled for the seat-belt buckle and hit the release without any more hesitation. The distance between her seat and the roof of the Jeep was a short journey. And a painful one. Her palms hit glass and twisted metal but saved her face. Her knees didn't fare as well. Neither did her side. Pain radiated across her and settled in the injuries she had no time to investigate.

The driver's-side door was twisted and broken. Riley didn't need the full light of day to see she wasn't getting out that way. Instead she rolled over to the passenger's-side door. It was already hanging open.

Riley crawled for it like her life depended on it.

And, didn't it? All she could picture was Brett smiling.

He'd done this on purpose and that thought terrified Riley to the point of shaking as she pushed through the door and tumbled out of the Jeep and onto the grass.

She was on the shoulder where it dipped and disappeared into the start of the tree line.

It was that tree line she was scrambling for when Brett appeared next to the Jeep.

He was still smiling.

And he was holding a baseball bat.

Riley's heartbeat was in her ears. Her bare feet complained as she ran full tilt into the darkness of the woods. That run turned into a fast limp. She slapped tree trunks as she tried to navigate around them. Roots she couldn't see twisted the ground. Her feet caught them and the ground caught her body after. The beautiful dress she'd worried about getting dirty earlier that night was slowly becoming ribbons the farther into the trees she went.

The beauty of the moonlight and stars meant nothing. All she could think about was how no one knew where she was, how she'd not even looked for her phone before running and how that running was about to end. Her body couldn't keep it up. Not anymore.

So when she tripped over a fallen log, instead of getting up and keeping forward, Riley crawled along its length, kept low and hurried to a neighboring tree. She flattened herself against its trunk and prayed that Brett hadn't followed her.

"Here, kitty, kitty!"

Riley's stomach dropped somewhere near her feet. Brett's baritone carried with ease to where she was hiding. He *had* followed her. What's more, he'd kept up.

"You're fast. I'll give you that," he continued. There was a laboring effort to his words. He seemed, at least, tired by their jaunt through the woods so far. "But I'm guessing you're sitting still now. It's gonna be hard to get back up."

Riley was absolutely trembling but she was also weighing her options. She could keep hiding and hope he just left or she could try to make it back to the Jeep. There was no telling where the woods ended. She didn't want to find out by running all night into the darkness that the trees kept going for miles and miles.

"I just want to talk," Brett said after a moment. Riley almost sang in relief. He sounded farther away from her. "Come on out!"

Riley took a deep breath. She thought about her sister. She thought about Hartley. She thought about her parents, and she hated to realize, she thought about her ex-husband Davies.

If he hadn't lied, I wouldn't be here right now.

But, the fact was, she *was* there and if she wanted to see her sister and nephew again, she was going to have to move like Hell was on her tail.

Riley didn't waste any more time. She hiked up her dress, pushed off the ground and prayed Brett wouldn't hear her.

If she could get back to the road she could—

Two arms wrapped around her no more than a foot from her hiding place.

They were strong and unmoving, a vise keeping her against him, pinning her arms to her sides. When a hand slapped over her mouth, Riley had every intention of biting through the bone if she had to.

"Quiet or he'll hear us."

The smooth, deep voice most certainly didn't belong to Brett. Riley craned her neck around to see who had her back against his chest.

Riley didn't have enough emotion left in her to be surprised that it was Desmond Nash. Wearing his cowboy hat to boot.

"DON'T MAKE A SOUND," Desmond whispered at Jenna's ear. She nodded. He felt the movement across his body. Just as he felt her trembling.

He knew he wasn't faring much better. He'd been running after the man and her since he saw them take off into the woods. Even without his limp it had been in no way an easy trek.

Slowly he took his hand from her mouth. He loosened his arms around her but didn't fully disengage. Instead he lowered his lips so close to her ear that she jumped when he spoke.

"Does he have a gun?"

Her shrug moved his arms.

"All I saw was a baseball bat."

Desmond's blood would have been boiling at that if he hadn't been trying to stay focused. He let go of her and reached into the pocket of his slacks. He yanked his cell phone out, careful to hide the light of his screen. He'd pulled them behind a tree but he didn't know exactly where the man was.

Desmond turned Jenna around and handed her the phone. He leaned in again so close that their foreheads touched.

"My brother is on the phone," he said, barely above a whisper. "Talk to him while I talk to that man. Do you know who he is?"

The screen's glow showed Desmond the dark eyes he'd admired over an hour ago. They widened. Desmond wanted to give her more comfort but he could hear her pursuer stomping around, crunching through the underbrush. He was starting to swear.

He was losing patience.

Desperate men did desperate things and Desmond wasn't going to wait to see if this man had any last-ditch efforts he was ready to employ to get Jenna.

Her voice wavered but she managed an answer.

"He was at the party. His name is Brett."

Desmond scrolled through the list of people he knew named Brett as he nodded to her. When he stepped around the tree, he was sure he hadn't talked to anyone with that name during the party. A troubling fact but one of many that had and was taking place.

The moonlight barely scratched the darkness's surface but Desmond's vision had adjusted enough to see the outline of the man. He was a few yards away, slinking between standing and downed trees. The bat was propped up on his shoulder.

He was looking for Jenna.

He was about to find Desmond instead.

Desmond had moved around in a semicircle so that Jenna wasn't behind him. He didn't want to chance her getting hurt if there was cross fire. Desmond also wasn't going to let her attacker get away. Brett might have pulled up after the wreck and looked like a man wanting to help but him chasing Jenna into the woods when Desmond arrived had painted a damning picture of intentions. The woods they were in stretched back for miles, ultimately leading to a neighboring property. Through that you could get back to the Nash family ranch

Another chance Desmond wasn't going to take.

If he could just keep the man occupied while he waited for Declan and Caleb to arrive…

"I have a gun. You move—I shoot."

Desmond's voice echoed around them.

Brett stopped.

For a moment no one spoke.

Desmond wasn't bluffing about the gun. He had one. Just not with him. He hadn't brought it to the gala, and when he sneaked out of the gala to go to the construction site, he hadn't thought to go by the house and get it. Still, Brett didn't have a light. They were both dealing in outlines and shadows. He wouldn't be able to see that Desmond wasn't holding a gun.

Then again, the same could be said for Desmond. The man might have been wielding a bat but that didn't mean he wasn't also carrying something else.

"There was a car accident," Brett said. There was concern clear in his voice. Along with surprise. "I tried to help the woman who was in it but she ran in here. I think something's wrong with her."

"Did you call the police?" Desmond stalled.

There was no response.

Desmond narrowed his eyes, locking in on the outline in the distance.

"Why do you have a bat?" he added.

The outline shifted. Desmond balled his fists.

"You've gone quiet, friend," Desmond said after another tense silence. "Why don't you tell me why you're really out here?"

A flurry of motion streaked straight toward him. Desmond stood his ground, careful not to blink. The man was coming right at him, bat raised and growling like a deranged animal.

It wasn't the time, it wasn't the place and it certainly wasn't the same Desmond but just like that he was back in a memory. The worst memory.

He was eight. The smell of summer was dancing along the heat and humidity and creating the need for the Nash triplets to do something other than hang around the ranch, and when the park called their name, they answered.

Desmond remembered their laughter as they played hide-and-seek. He also remembered Madi's screams.

The man, one he still saw in his dreams from time to time, had been a walking nightmare then. Yet, after he'd hurt Madi and after he'd hurt Caleb, all he had been to the Desmond of then was a target.

A target for his anger. For his fear. For his confusion.

Without a second thought Desmond had gone at a man twice his size. A man who had a gun. A man who had a plan he didn't understand.

Just as the man with the bat was doing now.

The dull pain in Desmond's leg reminded him of how raw emotions could irrevocably change the outcome for the worst.

Brett was acting on instinct.

Desmond was acting on patience.

Brett let out a wild war cry as the space between them disappeared. He wound the bat and his arm up, pulling it back over his shoulder, and prepared to swing. Desmond didn't need lights surrounding them to know where to hit first.

He waited until the last possible second and lunged at the man.

They exchanged grunts as Desmond's shoulder made contact with Brett's chest. The attack wasn't meant to put the man out of commission. It was meant to stun him.

And boy did it work.

His momentum redirected to the ground. Desmond fell with him.

As soon as they hit, Desmond made fast work of grabbing for the bat.

Brett growled, once again sounding more animal than human. He didn't relinquish the bat without a fight. The man punched out with his left fist. It connected, but so did Desmond's flurry of hits in return.

Their scuffle turned into a rolling match as each tried to get the upper hand.

Desmond held on to the bat just as Brett did, neither relinquishing control.

It wasn't until a light appeared a few feet from them that Brett's attention broke. Desmond leaned into the oversight. He pulled the bat free, delivered a hard blow with his fist against the man's jaw and watched with deep satisfaction as the body he'd been fighting went slack. Brett thumped back to the ground. Desmond took a deep breath and pushed up and away from him, brandishing the bat over his shoulder.

With a heaving chest, bruised jaw and a layer of dirt and sweat galore, he turned to the light expecting to see his brothers.

What he saw instead were two dark eyes and wild red hair.

"I didn't want to leave you," Jenna said. She motioned to something in her other hand. It was a stick. "I was going to try to hit him." She gave a weak laugh.

Then her face fell.

Now that they weren't trying to hide the cell phone's light, Desmond could see more of the woman.

Including the tears starting to run down her cheeks.

Desmond closed the space between them just in time for the woman to fall into his arms.

They were still standing like that when the sheriff arrived.

Chapter Four

Lights danced between the trees as the woods filled with men and women dressed to the nines. The sheriff was still in his suit from the gala, same as Detective Nash who ran into the woods alongside his brother. A woman wearing a beautiful velvet green gown that shimmered in the glow of the cell phones and flashlights brought up the rear with a look as severe as the other two.

All three had their guns drawn.

When they saw Desmond standing there and Brett unconscious on the ground, Riley could nearly feel their relief.

"I'm okay. He just got a few lucky hits in is all," Desmond assured the sheriff before he could ask it. Then everyone's gaze fell to Riley. She was still against Desmond's chest, head turned like a terrified child peeking out around the skirt of her mother. Though the warmth of Desmond's embrace in no way reminded her of her mother.

Riley opened her mouth to say *something* but the words got caught in her throat. Her body had already devolved into a shaking mess. She didn't say it but she had a sneaking suspicion that Desmond's hold on her was the only thing keeping her upright. Thankfully, he also spoke for her.

"We need to get her to the hospital."

"EMTs are on the way," the woman said. She followed Desmond's brother to Brett. He pulled out a set of cuffs from his jacket pocket and she covered him while he tugged Brett's arms behind his back and closed the metal around his wrists. The sheriff holstered his gun. His expression softened as he looked at Riley.

"I'm Declan. I was the one on the phone," he said, tapping the badge on his hip that said Sheriff. Claire had already pointed out the sheriff and the detective at the gala, but even if Riley hadn't known about the man, she would have guessed it right away. Declan Nash was giving off pure authority just by standing still. "What's your name?"

Despite everything that had just happened, despite the fact that she was talking to the sheriff, Riley felt the irrational urge to stick to the lie she'd been telling all night. To protect her sister from scrutiny. It was weirdly easy to keep it going now.

"Jenna. Jenna Stone."

No recognition flashed across the sheriff's expression. Neither did suspicion. He simply nodded.

"Well, Jenna, how do you want to do this? Would you like to wait for the EMTs to come in or do you think you're up for walking back to the road?" He motioned to the woman. "Detective Santiago *and* Desmond will be with you every step of the way while Detective Nash and I wait here for backup."

"I can carry you, if you need," Desmond offered. His words rumbled through his chest and against her body. It was encouraging in a way. She took a deep breath, steadying her nerves.

She was safe now.

They both were.

"I can walk," she decided. "I don't want to be out here anymore."

The sheriff nodded.

"I don't blame you one bit on that. I'll come talk to you

after we get everything handled here." He shared a look with Desmond. "And you're okay to walk too?"

"Yeah. The leg has been through a lot worse."

Slowly he released his hold on Riley, as if afraid she'd fall to pieces once he wasn't keeping her together anymore. Riley hated to admit it but she was worried about the same thing.

But then the warmth of him was gone, replaced by an ominous chill in the night air. Detective Santiago walked up to her side. Her gun was lowered but she didn't put it away.

Riley didn't look back at Brett, lying motionless on the ground.

She also didn't dare look down at the baseball bat discarded at Desmond's feet.

The EMTs were already at the road by the time they came out of the tree line. So was a growing crowd. It was as if every gala attendee had decided to ditch their vehicles for a better view. Uniformed deputies were arriving and trying to block off the road. Brett had left his car on the shoulder opposite the Jeep.

The poor Jeep.

It was upside down and resembled a crushed Coke can.

Riley sniffled back tears again as she walked past it to the back of the waiting ambulance.

The EMT was a woman who looked around Riley's age and obviously knew Desmond. She gave him a once-over and told him she was glad he was okay before turning her attention to Riley. The once-over came with a look of acute concern, followed by a recommendation that they go to the hospital. It created a new surge of panic. She must have read it in Riley's face. Her expression softened.

"Everything looks like superficial wounds but it's better to be safe than sorry." She pointed to the Jeep. "You were in that when it flipped, I'm assuming?"

"I was."

The EMT gave an apologetic smile.

"Then I think we should get you checked out. Just to make sure you're alright. Okay?"

Riley conceded and soon she was sitting on the gurney. Detective Santiago joined her, taking the side seat and producing a notepad out of her purse. The shoulder holster she had on was quite the contrast to her gown. She asked questions and Riley answered them the best she could while being caught up in the bustle of the EMT and the driver. So much so that she didn't notice when Desmond slipped away. He didn't come back and soon they were on the road and pointed to Overlook Hospital.

Riley tried not to look for the cowboy who had saved her. Or feel the sting that he had disappeared without a word.

THE HOSPITAL FLUORESCENTS were in no way flattering. Not that Riley had a chance of looking anything other than *rough*. She stood in front of the bathroom mirror and tried to decide what looked the worst.

Was it the darkening bruise across her cheek from, she assumed, the airbag deploying? Or maybe the small cuts along her forehead from glass? Maybe it was the fact that all of her makeup had streaked down her face when she lost it and sobbed into a relative stranger's shirt.

It would have been the state of Jenna's dress had she still been wearing it. A once beautiful and daring piece had been torn in several places, including a thick tear over her hip. She'd seen her lacy black underwear through it the moment she'd stepped into the ER lobby. Now she was in a hospital gown, wearing safety socks that were hiding bandages for her poor feet. Like her purse and phone, she'd forgotten her shoes in the Jeep. There were other little cuts and bruises across her body that would probably make onlookers do a double take, but thankfully, no injuries extended past minor aches and pains.

Still, she had been glad for Detective Santiago's presence as she waited for the nurse to take her to get X-rays. Once everything had calmed down, Riley realized her neck was throbbing—because her nerves were officially shot. It didn't help that she spent the time between recounting what had happened on Winding Road and at the gala with Brett. Neither woman could think of a reason for his actions but the detective promised they'd get to the bottom of it.

Now, alone in the bathroom attached to the small room she'd been assigned, Riley decided to stop dwelling on her appearance. After the night she'd had, she was just thankful to be alive.

A knock sounded against the room door. Riley gave herself a nod of reassurance in the mirror and went out of the bathroom and back to the bed. The movements made her wince. Her feet were still tender from running through the woods.

"Come in," she called once she was back in bed. She positioned the blanket over her lap, self-conscious about her mostly bare legs.

Desmond Nash appeared around the door, sans cowboy hat. He did, however, have a purse in his hands and a smile on his face.

"Sorry I didn't get this here sooner," he greeted. "My truck got blocked in and then Declan got blocked in and, well, let's just say Winding Road wasn't made to handle fifty-plus gawkers, their cars and an active investigation."

What had been long strides at the gala had now become a noticeable limp as Desmond brought her purse over. Riley had assumed the limp she'd witnessed in the woods was due to an injury from the fight but now she wondered if it was from an older one instead.

Either way, she wasn't about to pry. Not when she was filled with equal amounts gratitude and guilt. She addressed the first feeling with her own smile and open arms for her bag.

"Thank you so much for getting this," she said, sincere. "I forgot about even trying to find my phone or purse until I was in here already. Thank you!"

Riley could have cried for joy. She hadn't remembered where her phone was before the crash. Now she found it within the folds of faux leather.

There were five missed calls. All were from Jenna.

Riley felt that second emotion bubbling to the surface. Guilt.

She had convinced herself to wait until the doctor officially said Riley could leave before calling Jenna. But really it had been more about keeping herself sane. She knew the moment she saw Jenna, the emotional dam would break again. Just like it had in the woods with Desmond.

Now, though, Riley knew she had to face the music. She didn't want her sister to worry more than she had to, but first, Riley had to address the other well of guilt within her.

Desmond was studying her, his brows drawn together in thought.

"Are you okay?" he asked, simply.

"Yeah. It all looks much worse than it is."

"I heard you got some X-rays done?"

She nodded.

"My neck was hurting but they said it was just the whiplash." Riley felt the heat of a blush before she continued. "Now I'm just waiting to make sure I don't have a bad reaction to the pain meds they gave me. It was a, uh, shot."

Right in the butt cheek, she thought but definitely didn't say out loud.

"I already feel a lot better," she added. "I'm just tired now."

"Good," Desmond said. "That's good."

"What about you?" She traced the mark across his jawline. She hadn't been able to see the punches being thrown in the woods but she'd heard the hits landing.

Desmond shrugged.

"Nothing a bag of frozen peas can't help. It coulda been worse."

"I know the feeling. If you hadn't been driving by when you did—" Riley didn't need to finish the thought. She knew later she'd cycle through the several what-if situations and go back into panic mode. She didn't want that now. "What I mean to say is thank you. And not just for grabbing my purse."

Desmond Nash sure could smile. Even the small stretch was quite the sight. So, when it snuffed out so suddenly, Riley felt a different kind of panic.

"I'm sorry that it even happened in the first place," he said with startling venom. "The gala was meant to be a happy occasion and yet you were stalked by a guest. I'm sorry, Jenna. I really am."

Riley felt the burn in her cheeks. Time to address the other reason for her guilt.

"I in no way blame you for Brett," she started. "*But* I do need to apologize to *you*."

Desmond's eyebrow rose.

"I'm not *actually* Jenna Stone."

DESMOND HADN'T SEEN that one coming.

Jenna—or, well, maybe not—let her gaze hit the floor before she dragged it back up to his. Her cheeks had tinted crimson. When she continued her voice had lowered.

"I'm Riley Stone, her sister."

Desmond liked to think he was a fair guy. After what his family had been through, he had made a life out of striving to do what was right by his loved ones and the people he met through his philanthropy. Those goals had always gone hand in hand with being a straight shooter. There wasn't room for lies or deceit in his life.

Not after that day in the park when he was eight.

Not after the three days in that basement.

Not after the repercussions of it spread out and consumed his father years later.

The truth, *honesty*, was important to him.

Important to living a life he hoped to never get as complicated as it had before, a goal all of his family had been trying to attain with varying degrees of success.

So, despite the trauma that had just happened to the woman, Desmond's default response went from confusion to deep suspicion to, quite frankly, disappointment.

Also it highlighted one concrete fact Desmond had somehow managed to ignore until that moment given what they'd been through.

He knew nothing about the woman sitting in front of him.

It was a rare occurrence in Overlook, one he should have looked into before rushing over to the hospital to make sure she was okay.

"I can explain," Riley hurried to tack on, her cheeks turning an even deeper shade of crimson. It contrasted against her pale skin, making her freckles stand out even more. "See, my sister, Jenna, started her own business a while back and really put herself out there to do it, and tonight was supposed to be her chance to finally connect with the local businesses and leaders of the community. *But* then Hartley, her son, wasn't feeling good and she panicked and decided to stay home. She was so worried that if she didn't go people would judge her for being a single mom and not give her a chance to prove herself and so I decided to go in her place." She let out a long breath, deflating.

"But you told Declan, the sheriff, you were Jenna," he pointed out.

She gave him an apologetic shrug.

"There was so much going on and I—I don't know, in my mind I was protecting her image still."

Desmond understood loyalty but it didn't take away from the fact that she'd lied to *his* family, law enforcement.

"This could change the entire investigation. If the attack wasn't random or because of opportunity, then Brett clearly knew he was targeting you, not your sister. How did you not think this was going to change everything? How irresponsible can you be?"

Desmond started to get hot under the collar. And not because Riley was as beautiful out of her makeup as she was glammed up. He'd nicknamed her the siren at the party and here she was, admitting she'd led him and law enforcement astray.

All at once Desmond couldn't help but think of anything other than his father. He'd run his life into the ground trying to solve the mystery of what had happened to the Nash triplets and eventually died because of it. Among the stress that had done him in? People lying and hindering his investigation.

Logically, Desmond knew it wasn't the same situation, yet a wounded heart doesn't always accept logic.

"How did you even think this was going to pan out? Don't you think people would have noticed that the woman they met at the party wasn't the same woman when Jenna came by? We may be a small town but we aren't small-minded."

Riley opened her mouth to say something— what could she really say though that would quell his rising frustration?—when a shout from the hallway drew their attention. The door opened behind them. Jasmine "Jazz" Santiago, Caleb's partner and best friend, gave him a look he couldn't quite place.

"Uh, Jenna? I think someone is looking for you."

Riley didn't correct her as she jumped up and padded by them and out the door. Desmond followed, ready to make the woman admit she'd lied about her identity, when he saw the point of confusion Jazz had latched on to.

"Oh my God," a woman yelled at the sight of Riley. She was at the end of the hallway, a toddler on her hip.

Riley's entire demeanor changed. She let out a cry that instantly turned to tears. Both women ran through the distance between them until they collided in an embrace in the middle of the hallway.

"I knew it," the other woman cried out. "I knew something was wrong. I *felt* it!"

She buried her head in Riley's dark red curls, her own dark red curls matching perfectly.

All at once Desmond realized why the switch had been brilliant.

"They're twins."

Chapter Five

The lights in the kitchen were warm and inviting.

Riley was so tired she felt like languishing on the floor beneath them if that meant she could get some peace. No matter how brief.

Jenna, on the other hand, was not in the mood to let Riley get off that easily. Since the embrace at the hospital two hours earlier, she hadn't left Riley's side. Not even when she'd had to go to the restroom after downing a full bottle of water.

"Next time I get chased down by a madman that no one seems to know and look like I've been put in a blender, we'll see how you handle it," she'd said when Riley had complained.

Not that Riley was surprised. In fact, she wasn't even upset. After what her sister had been through in the last year, she knew Jenna was even more determined to protect what was left of her life. And Jenna was fiercely rooted in the belief that her twin was under that purview.

Now, looking wistfully where Jenna was standing in the kitchen, with both hands on her hips, Riley knew she was about to receive an earful.

"Do you know that I had to run past the hospital guard *and* go around yelling before they could finally calm me down enough to direct me," she said, voice low but still throbbing with anger. Hartley had been asleep since they'd been given the green light to leave by the doctor and the sheriff. Riley had expected to be kept longer once she'd pulled the sheriff aside and admitted she'd given him the wrong name but neither he nor Desmond had berated her—at least not for a second time—or pulled out the cuffs and read her her rights. Instead Riley had been told to go to the sheriff's department first thing in the morning so they could sort everything out.

"I said I was sorry already," Riley tried. "I was going to call you when I got released. I didn't want you to worry."

"Worry? *Worry?*" Jenna placed her hand against her chest. "There I was just making your favorite cookies and I *felt* it, Riley. Right here in my chest. I was so sure that something happened to you that, when you didn't answer your phone, I drove out to the ranch, fully prepared to hunt you down. But I never got there, did I, Riley? Why is that?"

This part Riley had been briefed on earlier. Still, she repeated the answer.

"Because you got stopped at the roadblock... Where you saw the Jeep flipped over on the side of the road."

Jenna nodded with angry enthusiasm.

"When no one could tell me if you were alright after *being taken by ambulance* to the hospital, I had to drive there with a three-year-old and honest-to-God fear in my soul all because you didn't want to worry me by calling."

At the last part Jenna's voice broke. Like Riley she'd nearly sobbed when they'd first seen each other. Now her eyes were as swollen as Riley's. Still, they rimmèd with tears.

"Next time—though there better not *be* a next time—you call, Riley. Plain and simple. You. Call."

Riley nodded.

"I promise, Jen, I will."

Seemingly satisfied, Jenna gave her sister one more long

embrace before shaking herself and moving to the pantry. She pulled out a festive container and set it down on the countertop.

"Now it's time we finally had some snickerdoodles then."

Riley's exhaustion was replaced by acute hunger for the cookies. Jenna had only eaten one by the time Riley had consumed three.

IT WAS ALMOST three in the morning when Riley finally settled into bed. Jenna's house was small yet cozy, including the two bedrooms. Hartley slept on a bed in Jenna's room while Riley was tucked against a full-size mattress that almost took up the entire room. It was a far cry from the massive house Jenna had resided in with her ex-husband over a year ago but Riley couldn't help but love the small home much more.

Its walls were filled with memories; its space filled with knickknacks, decorations and furniture all carrying sentimental value and function to Jenna's and Hartley's lives. It wasn't cold. It wasn't void of feeling. It wasn't a prison.

Jenna had downgraded in space, sure, but she'd more than upgraded in warmth.

Riley lay on her back and stared at the ceiling fan she'd helped Jenna install after it had been Riley's turn to downgrade and move in. They'd fought after Jenna had dropped a screw and then Riley had dropped the screwdriver. Hartley, ever curious, had cried from his gated play area because he couldn't grab either item and put it in his mouth. It had been a disastrous half-hour ordeal and yet there the fan was. They had made it work. Now it was a part of the house's story. A memory that was ingrained in its fabric.

An ache of sentimentality cracked open in Riley's chest. Loneliness and loss reverberated through those cracks. She rolled onto her side, wincing at the shot's injection site, and let out a long, body-sagging breath against the pillow.

Riley thought about Davies, about Jenna, about the jobs she and her sister had both loved and had to give up, about the malicious Brett and then about the prepossessing Desmond Nash.

Claiming to know Desmond was foolish. However, seeing the disappointment and then hearing the anger at her lie?

That had been somewhat painful.

Less than a year ago life had been simpler.

Now it was proving to hurt more often than not.

"WHAT'S THE SAYING? All press is good press?"

Caleb took off his blazer and flung it over the diningroom chair. His detective's badge was still hanging around his neck. Declan had opted to go to the department instead of calling it a night like the rest of them. It *was* almost four in the morning. The sheriff was dedicated to a fault.

"*Any* press is good press 'as long as they spell my name right,'" Desmond corrected. He scrubbed his hand down his face.

Caleb chuckled.

"Well, as much as we're in the paper I'm sure they'll get your name right." Caleb was trying to lighten the mood, something he'd been attempting more since he'd met his wife, Nina. Her optimism, coupled with their mother's fierce belief that you should try any and everything to remain as stress-free as possible, had turned many scowls and silence from the man into teasing jokes and grins.

It was a good look for Caleb but not one Desmond particularly cared for at the moment.

"A bonus to opening Second Wind here in Overlook was to give the residents something positive to associate with our names," he said. "Not just another insane story about some crazy person seeking vengeance or someone with a penchant for senseless violence."

Caleb sighed. He pulled a chair out and fell into it. Desmond dropped into the one opposite. They both took a second to glance at the chair at the head of the table. Sometimes when it was just the two of them together, the urge to look for Madi turned into them physically doing it even when they knew exactly where she was. Their mother called the phenomenon just another piece of their triplet connection.

"As senseless as what happened was, it didn't happen to any of us Nashes," Caleb started. "And just because Ms. Stone was coming from your party doesn't mean it was your fault that she was attacked. Hell, Des, there's no telling what would have happened had you not been there to help. Yeah, the press might bring up all the madness we've been through in the last few years and yeah, maybe even recap—well, *that*, but all they're going to say about you is that you helped make an unfortunate situation a lot better. You might get a little more popular over the next week or two but construction on Second Wind will continue, you'll go back to work and eventually it'll just be another story recirculating in the gossip mill. Okay?"

Desmond nodded. He knew his brother was right. The gala had been open to the public. There had been no screening of the guests and no way for them to know that Brett had intended to do what he had. Or, apparently, who Brett even was. Once Desmond was able to see the man in the light, he confirmed to Declan that he'd never seen the man. In fact, none of the Nashes had recognized him or the name.

"Don't worry. We'll get to the bottom of who he is and why this Brett attacked Riley when we talk to him later today," Caleb added on, sensing his brother's concern. "Men like him like talking. All we have to do is wait and listen."

"It's times like these I wouldn't mind being in law enforcement," Desmond admitted. He smirked, actively trying to loosen the tension in his shoulders. "Can't you and Declan bend the rules and let me in on an interrogation?"

Caleb chuckled.

"I'd like to be a fly on the wall for that request. Maybe if we weren't fraternal we could just switch."

Desmond had a feeling his brother had been waiting to loop back to the fact that Riley and Jenna were twins since he'd found out at the hospital. There was a slight childlike wonder in his eyes. None of the Nash triplets had ever met a set of identical twins. Under different circumstances it would have been more intriguing to Desmond, he was sure.

"It was like seeing someone staring into a mirror," he had to admit. "Madi would have flipped. Hell, it had me speechless for a second. I still can't believe they tried to pull that crap."

Like someone had flipped a switch, the mood changed in the little dining room. Caleb slid into his detective's face, as Desmond had called it through the years. He was on a case. He was looking for clues. He was coming to conclusions.

He was staring at Desmond.

"Two hours," Caleb finally said. Desmond felt his brow rise in question.

"Two hours?"

"That's how long Riley's lie lasted. Only two hours. Remember that the next time you see her. Maybe remind that serious face of yours to calm down." Caleb pushed the chair back and stood. He had spent a good amount of his career hiding the exhaustion that sometimes went with a long day or night but now Desmond saw the drag of it pulling down his shoulders. If he didn't live on the ranch too, no more than five minutes down the road, Desmond would have told him to stay. As it stood, Desmond pulled himself up and walked his brother to the door. Caleb slowed down to make up for his limp.

"I'm fine," Desmond said before Caleb could ask about his leg. "Nothing some pain meds and a few hours of sleep won't fix."

"Good. Just don't let Ma see you doing that pained face tomorrow. We had to move heaven and earth to keep her from leaving the ranch tonight. Madi said she thought she was going to have to get Julian to tackle her at one point to keep her from rushing to the hospital."

"For a woman who preaches doing everything in her power to be stress-free, she sure soaks it up when it's out there."

"Well, when you have kids as awesome as us, can you blame her for being worried?"

Desmond snorted.

"Calling yourself awesome doesn't make it so," he said.

"Agree to disagree, Des. Agree. To. Disagree."

Caleb clapped him on the shoulder and then bounded down the porch steps toward his truck. The main house stood a hundred or so yards away, lights off. The Nash children had grown up in that house and now their mother lived there alone.

Long before Desmond had agreed to bring Second Wind to Overlook—or even had Second Wind as a thought in his head—he'd built his house close to the main one on purpose. He didn't want to live in his childhood home but he also didn't want to leave his mother by herself. Even though he'd barely spent time in Overlook, he felt comforted by the fact that all she had to do was look out her window and see the house there. Now that he was living there full-time, Desmond saw how it could be tricky being so close to his mother. While he had made peace with the fact that he'd have his limp for the remainder of his life, he had a sneaking suspicion his mother still had a hard time seeing it from time to time.

Desmond took a deep breath. The chill that had spread

across Overlook filled his lungs. He hoped in the next few hours it would stay. He was no stranger to sweat-inducing heat and humidity—you wouldn't hear *him* complaining about it—but he had to admit he enjoyed cooler weather. In fact, before the gala had started, he'd found himself staring at the mountains in the distance and hoping for snow.

Now the gala felt like days ago, not hours.

Desmond moved back into the house and straight for the shower. He tried to clear his head as hot water beat against his back and aching leg.

Yet, his thoughts wandered to tangles of dark red hair. *Two hours.*

That's how long the lie had lasted.

Desmond knew his frustration was an overreaction, but there wasn't anything he could do about it now.

He got out of the shower, dried off, slipped on a pair of boxers and fell into bed.

It wasn't until he was dozing off that the reason for him being on Winding Road in the first place when he saw Riley and Brett made noise in his thoughts.

After Caleb had also tried to push off telling him what the graffiti on Second Wind's construction site had said, Desmond had sneaked away to see it for himself.

It had ruined his night with one look. If it hadn't been for the excitement that followed, Desmond had no doubt he would have focused on that for the remainder of the party.

Now the overtly stylized sentence he'd seen spray painted floated behind dozing eyes.

"Can't even win a simple game of hide-and-seek."

Chapter Six

Two weeks went by and the media didn't let a day pass without some mention of what had happened after the Second Wind gala.

Brett had been identified as Brett Calder, a man no one seemed to know personally in town. A newspaper article stated that he had a history of domestic violence and ties to an up-and-coming criminal group out of the city of Kilwin. As far as the attack on Riley Stone, it was one of opportunity. There was no rhyme or reason past that, according to his own admission of guilt. He had seen her leave, alone, and followed.

Desmond Nash, famed local businessman, had been in the right place at the right time. Another story in the form of a social media post for an online publication questioned why Desmond was out on the road during his party in the first place and wondered at his motives, as well as his involvement. A poorly Photoshopped picture was posted in the comments and showed a younger Desmond in a group picture with a younger Brett. The writer called it a conspiracy. That comment was eventually deleted, along with the account that had posted it.

A few other county newspapers and TV stations picked up the story but not for the sheer audacity of Brett Calder's attack. Instead it was blatantly obvious that everyone's interest revolved around Desmond's involvement. Some stories didn't just stop with him. They reported on and recapped earlier news stories about the attacks on Caleb and his wife two years ago and Madeline's wrongly accused involvement in a homicide the year before. Two stories even included the infamous Nash triplet abduction, the greatest unsolved mystery in Overlook's history.

Riley had known that Desmond and his family had lived through trauma; he was very open about that and his intentions of helping others like him through Second Wind, but she didn't know the gritty details that went along with it. She had felt a flare of shame as she'd read a social media post that listed bullet points of facts.

The eight-year-old triplets had sneaked out to a local park.

They'd been playing a game of hide-and-seek when a man with a gun had grabbed Madeline Nash.

Trying to help her, Caleb Nash had been shot in the shoulder and Desmond Nash had had his leg broken by their attacker.

Using the unconscious Madeline as incentive to do as he said, the man took all three to an undisclosed cabin in the woods where the children were kept in the basement for three days.

They finally managed to escape by pretending that Desmond had stopped breathing and overpowering their abductor by working together when he came to check on the boy.

From there they ran through the woods until they found help. By the time authorities made it back to the cabin, their abductor was gone.

To this day no one had any information on the man or why he had done what he did, despite the triplets' father and then detective, Michael Nash, working the case hard until the day he died of a heart attack years later.

The story pulled at Riley's heartstrings, but it also made

her angry. The family had already been through way more than most. People were just dredging up the old stories for shock value and clicks. A thought that was admonished by an opinion editorial in the local newspaper, the *Overlook Explorer*.

The op-ed was written by the current news editor, Delores Dearborn. In it she reminded the community that the Nash family did a lot for the town. She highlighted the sheriff's career as well as Caleb's time as a deputy and detective, pointed out that Dorothy Nash, their mother, had been an upstanding and valued resident of Overlook longer than most had been alive, reminded them of Madeline Nash's continued involvement in the community and wrapped the piece up with the bold statement that the Nash family had helped shape the town of Overlook just as much as the founding families if not more.

"Without the Nash family and their beloved ranch, who would we even be as a town? Not the Overlook I've come to know and love, that's for sure."

Delores had ended the article with a call to action. Give the Nash family the respect and privacy they deserve. Look to the future, instead, with the same excitement and vigor they've been using to dredge up the past.

It had been a wonderful and inspiring read. One that had resonated with Jenna also after they'd finally bought a copy. She put the newspaper down on the jungle gym's platform between them and blew out a long breath.

"I guess what they say is true," she said. "'Be kind because everyone is fighting their own battle.'"

It was a beautiful Saturday morning in Overlook. Sun shining, sixty degrees and they were visiting a kid-friendly park just off Main Street that Riley was excited to explore with her nephew. She had her hair pulled back in a low ponytail, was wearing a purposefully oversize T-shirt and had donned her sister's spandex running pants since half of Riley's clothes were still in boxes in the garage.

Jenna, on the other hand, was wearing a no-nonsense business outfit, complete with a slick black portfolio in one hand. She kept glancing in the direction of Main Street and Claire's Café.

"Just go," Riley finally said. "Claire took this meeting already knowing about the switch. She was a single mom for years. She said she understood why we did it."

Jenna looked unsure.

"What if she just wants to ask me about what happened to you? Or just wants to get mad at me in person for attempting to lie to everyone?"

Hartley let out a trill of laughter as he slapped one of the colorful spinners in the wall of the jungle gym set. Riley couldn't help but smile.

"Listen, I have my phone. If she does anything crazy or mean just send an SOS text and me and the munchkin will come running. Okay? Now *go*."

Jenna nodded, resolute, and reached up to kiss her son on the cheek.

"Don't let him go down the slide by himself," she said as she hurried to the sidewalk. "We don't want a repeat of him jumping off like last time!"

Riley waved her twin off and refocused on the tiny daredevil in question. Hartley was, thankfully, the spitting image of Jenna and not his father. A mop of red curls topped a matching pale complexion and smattering of freckles. The only differing trait was a set of bright green eyes. They followed Riley as she climbed up to the platform and settled down next to him. Together they hit the spinners and built-in music chimes.

Several minutes, and rides down the attached slide, went by without a text from Jenna. Riley hoped she could pull off her freelance career in Overlook, starting with Claire.

As for her own career goals? Riley was still thinking about that. After her divorce many of her life plans had come to a screeching halt. She hadn't been able to rewrite them all yet.

"Hi!"

Hartley's high-pitched greeting flipped Riley's attention from setting herself up at the top of the slide again to someone standing a few feet from the stairs.

"Hi there."

The voice was deep, and for the briefest of moments, Riley hoped it belonged to Desmond Nash. Since he'd helped her, she'd had a hard time getting him out of her thoughts. It wasn't every day a cowboy businessman ran into the darkness to save you.

Yet, as her eyes traced the man's face, Riley didn't recognize him at all.

Stocky, on the shorter side and wearing business casual, his blue eyes swept over her and Hartley as he smiled.

Riley's instincts shot her hand out and looped her finger in the back of Hartley's shorts. She felt the strain as the always-curious toddler tried to toddle in the direction of the new person.

"Hi," Riley said from her spot sitting at the top of the jungle gym. Her legs were already on the slide but Hartley was still in roaming mode. The playground set they were on was meant for small children. It was only a three-or four-foot drop. It put her at the perfect height to have an even eye line with the man. It also made her instantly nervous with how close he was.

Riley knew not every smiling man was a Brett Calder, but that didn't stop the deep mistrust that had rooted within her.

It didn't help that the most precious human she knew was between them.

"I, uh, heard about what happened to your sister," he continued, taking a small step forward. "I was at the Second Wind party and we talked for a bit. It's crazy what happened to her, right?"

Red flags shot up all around Riley. He thought he was talking to Jenna. He was also lying.

She didn't remember talking to him at all.

"It was," she hedged, pulling Hartley closer. The park was a block from Main Street but there were several pedestrians walking across the sidewalk from the communal parking lot to the main strip. Plus, a few other parkgoers lounging around the benches and fountain in the center. Surely the man wouldn't do anything out in the open.

Calm down, Riley. This is a small town. He could be just a friendly townie. Maybe you did *talk to him. You talked to so many people before you left!*

The man was unaware of Riley's inner monologue. He pressed on.

"I actually work for the local newspaper and heard that maybe the more interesting story is you."

Riley couldn't help the eyebrow raise that followed that.

"You want to interview me?"

He shrugged.

"Why not? I heard you're a freelance designer—that's interesting. I heard you used to be part of a pretty successful company based in Kilwin—that's also interesting. I *also* heard you used to be married to the CFO before you left so fast one night you can probably still see the dust in the air."

The man grinned.

He was talking about Jenna.

Riley felt sick.

She didn't try to look inconspicuous as she moved backward and got to her feet. She pulled Hartley up with her.

"You've heard a lot," she said, voice swinging low into an angry thrum. Hartley started to squirm against her hip. Riley didn't let him down. "What did you say your name was?"

"I didn't."

He was still grinning.

Riley felt the weight of her cell phone in her back pocket. She was about to pull it out and call for help, potential misunderstandings be damned.

Maybe he saw she was on the verge of doing just that. He held up his hands in defense.

"Listen, I don't want any trouble. I just want to help get *your* side of the story out there, Ms. Stone. You know, what happened to your sister… And what happened between you and Ryan Alcaster."

If Riley could have spit fire, the man and the name he said with such nonchalance would have gone up in flames.

"Listen here," she started, instead. "You—"

"Geordi?" Another deep voice joined the area around them. This time it was someone other than Riley who whipped their head around at being addressed, and also, this time Riley recognized the newcomer.

Desmond was dressed down in a dark blue button up, a pair of jeans that looked like they were made just for him, a black Stetson and a pair of matching cowboy boots. Dark hair was flipping out beneath the rim on his hat and blue eyes that looked a whole lot more like the sky now that she could see them in the daytime were narrowed in on the man whose name was apparently Geordi. A blond-haired woman with a long braid over her shoulder, a scar on her left cheekbone and a sleeping baby in a sling across her chest stood next to Desmond. Her expression was impassive as she too was staring holes into the man.

"Well if it isn't the man of the hour," Geordi said with a notable lack of enthusiasm. He looked to the woman. "And the last Nash to get her week or two of fame."

"And if it isn't the ambulance-chasing has-been who

took a perfectly good profession and decided to turn into a stereotypical scumbag instead. What brings you to town?"

Desmond said it with a smile but there was obviously no love there. Geordi looked ten shades of angry.

"Despite what you might believe, you don't own this town," he spit back. "Not only can I be here but I can talk to anyone I damn well want to."

"But does Ms. Stone want to talk to *you* is the question."

"I don't," Riley was quick to say. "In fact, I'd like to leave now."

Geordi let out a frustrated growl. Desmond didn't back down. He didn't break eye contact as he walked to the jungle gym's stairs and held out his hand. It was a power move if Riley ever did see one.

A power move that gave her the perfect way to get out of the reporter's vicinity.

She placed one hand inside the cowboy's and walked down the steps, careful to keep Hartley on her hip. He'd gone quiet, no doubt watching the growing group like a tennis enthusiast at Wimbledon.

"Then why don't you join us for coffee at Claire's? We were heading there just now."

Riley wasn't about to tell him that her sister *Jenna* was there in a meeting already. She also wasn't going to go to the car and leave Jenna either.

She definitely wasn't going to stay with Geordi.

"That sounds like a plan."

Desmond let go of her hand and, without prompting, went low and scooped up Jenna's "survival kit" for Hartley. It was a large messenger bag with a floral print across its length.

Desmond slung it over his shoulder like a man on a mission.

Then he tipped his hat to Geordi.

"You bother her again and I'll call the sheriff on you,"

he said, all cool. "If you really believe we Nashes run this town then imagine the trouble we could cause if we really wanted to."

DESMOND WAS SPITTING MAD.

Geordi Green was scourge of the earth, in his humble opinion. A man who could barely be called a journalist let alone a decent human.

"Geordi runs an online tabloid out of his house near here," Madi explained when the three of them—five of them if you counted his niece, Addison, and the boy, one asleep the other watchful—were walking away from the man. "His plan of attack is to wait out the direct aftermath of when something big happens and then put a spin on it once everything has blown over. You know the 'calm before the storm'? Declan says Geordi is the 'crap after the storm.'"

"He's a pot stirrer," Desmond added.

"A big ol' crap pot stirrer," Madi finished.

Dark, worried eyes glanced back over their shoulder at the reporter. Desmond felt the need to defend her still pulsing through him. He slowed a beat and angled his body so he was between her and Geordi. Madi gave him a look but quickened her pace so they both were ahead of him.

Desmond realized the women hadn't met. He swallowed his bristling and remedied that.

"This is my sister Madi Mercer and my niece, Addison," he started. "Madi, this is Riley Stone."

Riley couldn't hide her look of surprise.

"You know I'm not Jenna?"

Desmond raised his eyebrow. Were they trying to switch *again*?

"Was I not supposed to?" Suspicion started to rise in Desmond's chest again. He didn't understand the Stone twins if so.

Riley shook her head. She used her free hand to point to Main Street a few yards away.

"No, I'm babysitting while Jenna is in a meeting with Claire." She actually laughed. "I'm honestly just surprised. I can't even count on one hand how many people can tell us apart, not even my—" The rest of the sentence died on her tongue. A look of almost panic flashed across her expression. She hurried to change whatever she was about to say. "Most people just assume whoever has Hartley is Jenna."

Desmond didn't see how. After he'd met the real Jenna at the hospital, he'd noticed several differences between them. The first and most noticeable being how she carried herself.

Jenna looked like she was always in a moment of exhale, weighted and mentally sagging. The entire world on her shoulders. When he found out she was a single parent, Desmond assumed that's where the worry must have been coming from. He'd seen it on his own mother after their father had passed away, even though the children had all been grown.

Riley, on the other hand, held herself like she was in a perpetual inhale. She stood taller and at the ready. To the point of almost being defensive. He'd seen that same stance clear as day when talking to Geordi. She might have had her nephew with her, but to Desmond, he'd known which sister she was with ease.

Although, if he had been unsure, the second she looked at him, he would have known.

Desmond knew it wasn't rational but after looking into the dark depths of Riley's eyes in the woods, he *knew* them.

It was a realization that made him uncomfortable.

Not only had she lied to him, even if it had been only for two hours, with everything going on Desmond didn't have the time to deal with anything other than Second Wind.

Especially not when people like Geordi Green were still circling.

Second Wind was about creating new beginnings for people who had survived being put through the wringer.

It was Desmond's greatest goal in life.

He didn't have room for anything else.

Not even a siren.

Chapter Seven

Geordi watched Desmond the Great and just another lamb who had fallen for his good-guy schtick walk away. The Nash daughter's presence wasn't surprising. The Nash clan had a habit of being together at almost all times. They did live together on the ranch like some weird commune.

Geordi didn't understand or appreciate the family's obsession with each other.

Just like he didn't understand his client's focus on the Stone twins.

He waited for Desmond and company to turn out of view before deciding to retreat to his car. There, he was and wasn't surprised to see a woman wearing an honest-to-God trench coat and sunglasses. How she thought that was being inconspicuous and her platinum-dyed and straight-as-a-board, down-to-her-hips hair wasn't an attention getter, he had no idea.

She lifted her designer frames and showed him something he assumed were smoky eyes. Geordi tried to keep up with what was "in," considering the only way to keep the tabloid alive was to be connected with the online world.

And, when that didn't work, take paying gigs like this one.

"That seemed to be a disaster," she greeted, eyes roaming to the sidewalk the group had just left. "You were supposed to talk to Jenna, not scare her into the arms of Mr. Dolittle."

Geordi felt his nostrils flare. Just as he felt the urge to strike out at the woman for talking to him like an errant child.

"It isn't my fault the Nash family moves across this town like a plague," he snarled out instead. "You can't throw a rock without hitting one of them and now that they're starting to reproduce? Forget about having peace and quiet in this town."

The woman didn't seem to understand the problem. She slid her sunglasses back up the bridge of her nose.

"I came to you looking for solutions, not problems," she simply stated. "If I had known you were so hung up on pretty boy and his famjam, I would have gone to someone else. A better reporter, for starters."

If it hadn't been midmorning on a Saturday near a park no less, Geordi would have given the woman a piece of his mind. A very loud piece.

"I can go to her house," he said through clenched teeth. It wasn't like finding it would be hard. There weren't many newcomers to Overlook. All he had to do was look at houses that had recently sold or been rented. Or just find Craig Tilly, the local Realtor, and buy him a drink.

The woman shook her head.

"The spotlight is already on the Stones. We don't want to get caught in it. Which is why it would have been so nice if you'd convinced her to come for an interview. I guess you lack charm and skills."

Geordi growled.

"Listen here, you little—"

The woman moved her coat. She pulled a small pistol out but didn't aim it at him. It was meant to be seen.

It was meant to threaten.

It did.

Geordi shut up.

The woman smiled but when she spoke her words were sharp.

"You made a promise. You agreed to a deal. But, more importantly, you took my money," she said. "Now it's up to you to figure out how to deliver what I've asked for. I don't care how you do it, just get it done or keeping that pathetic little blog up and running will be the least of your sleazy little worries. Understand?"

Every fiber of Geordi's being was telling him to walk away. To just leave. To maybe tell the woman off but from a safer distance.

But then he remembered all of that cash.

It would solve the entirety of his problems.

"Don't worry your pretty little head," he said. "I'll get her to talk to me."

"And when you do?"

"I'll make sure you're there for it."

The woman nodded, apparently satisfied. She turned on her heel but looked over her shoulder at him before she walked away.

"And, Mr. Green? You tell anyone about our little arrangement and I'll burn you and your life to the ground."

Geordi hated to admit it but he fully believed her.

Somehow Desmond's morning had taken an unexpected turn.

He'd gone from giving in to his sister's request to put down his work and join her for coffee to sitting opposite a sea of red curls. Jenna and her son, Hartley, were in their own shared mom world with Madi and Addison while Claire moved between them to customers. It left Desmond and Riley sequestered to their non-children-filled lives at the end of the table.

Desmond took a long pull from his coffee. Riley picked

at the sleeve on her cup. Those eyes, dark chocolate, met his after several minutes of pretending to be in the neighboring conversation before going right back into the fray.

It felt like she was avoiding him.

Desmond didn't like it.

"The coffee's good here, isn't it?"

If his brothers had been there they would have immediately gotten gruff with Desmond at his lame opener. The town of Overlook had dubbed him the charming Nash and here he was floundering about coffee.

Desmond blamed it on the sudden spike in anger he'd had at the sight of Geordi. His normal easygoing facade had taken a few hits recently and that sniveling pot stirrer had felt like a cherry on top.

He was off-balance and trying to reclaim his charisma.

But, Riley didn't make it easy.

The woman nodded, eyes meeting and settling in his gaze. They looked far away, lost in thought. A look he was used to seeing in the mirror. Then she took in a deep breath as if to shake herself out of it.

Maybe she hadn't been avoiding him after all.

"It is. Though, to be honest," Desmond's attention wobbled as she leaned in a little and lowered her voice, "I'm not a big coffee drinker—and yes, I know how insane that sounds—but that's how it's always been. Until now. I think there might be some kind of narcotic in here. I already want another cup and I'm not even halfway finished with this one."

Desmond chuckled.

"Welcome to Claire's," he said. "I grew up on black coffee on the ranch but as soon as she opened her doors, she opened my eyes to these sugar monstrosities." He tapped his drink. "One second my eyes are drooping, the next I'm buzzing around, ready for anything."

"It's more of a hit or miss for me. I'm either energized

and raring to go or I'm riding a sugar high all the way to a forced nap." Riley shrugged. "There's no pretty in-between for me."

Desmond saw the conversational bridge ahead unfurling. He knew what to say to get to the other side, just as he knew what to say to avoid it.

You just admitted to yourself you have no room for anything else in your life, his inner voice—angel or demon, he didn't rightly know which was speaking—goaded. *Smile, be nice, leave.*

Yet—

"Have you tried any of the other local eateries?" He thumbed back toward the wall behind him. "Like the Red Oak?"

"The Red Oak?" She shook her head. "I haven't been there."

Desmond felt a genuine smile split his face.

"Boy, you're missing out on that one. I spent the last few years traveling the country and *still* haven't found a restaurant that does it as good as the Oak. It's been around for almost my entire life. I swear it's one of the best things to come out of Overlook."

Leave it there, his inner voice warned.

But Desmond decided not to listen.

"I was actually going to go there tonight. Would you like to join me?"

One dinner wouldn't hurt anything, Desmond reasoned. It wouldn't *mean* anything. Just two friendly acquaintances sharing an old and newfound love for great food.

Right?

Then again, there was something about Riley Stone. Something that made him feel different.

Maybe it wasn't a good idea after all.

No sooner had Desmond's reasoning slipped by, than it was replaced by a startling smile in answer.

"That sounds nice. Sure."

Reasoning or not, Riley was ten kinds of beautiful, a fact he couldn't much deny anymore.

And she was smiling right at him.

"IS THIS A DATE?"

That question had punctuated the second half of Desmond's Saturday with annoying precision. Madi, who did *not* live on the ranch anymore, had come back to the Nash family ranch with stubborn persistence and there she had stayed, up until Desmond was getting into his truck.

"*Is* this a date?" she started, hurrying alongside him. Their mother stood on the porch—another woman who had copied the question and thrown it at Desmond at every chance she had gotten—holding Addison while Julian had agreed to man their bed-and-breakfast so Madi could keep up her verbal assaults. Apparently Desmond was known for being charming but not known for using that charm to go on dates. Not that he was counting dinner with Riley as a date, he'd decided. It was just two people who had been tangled up in each other's lives recently sharing a friendly meal. That was it. "Because *if it is*, I just want to remind you of a few things before you go."

Desmond sighed. If he wasn't so annoyed, he would have taken pleasure in seeing his breath mist out in front of him. February had a habit of unpredictable weather. They'd gone from warm to humid to chill to now, a high chance of rain and a low of thirty-eight. He'd had to break out his leather jacket. It was thick, insulated and had once belonged to his father.

He burrowed his hands into the worn pockets and waited for his sister to catch up. He leaned against the truck door and looked at her expectantly as she started grinning across from him.

"It's not a date," he reminded her. "But say what you want to so you, Ma and the little one don't freeze on my account."

Madi dropped her grin. She got down to business.

"I was going to say *if this is* a date, try not to look like that." She put her thumb between his eyebrows. It was ice-cold. He swatted her away, startled.

"Like what, Crazy Lady?"

"Like you're not there," she stressed. "Be *present*. Leave work on the way, way, way back burner and don't worry about the construction site or reporters, Geordi Green included." She grabbed the opening of his jacket and pulled the sides closer together, a maternal move that softened his annoyance with her. "You can help people live their lives while still living your own. Have *fun*. Even if this isn't a date, that doesn't mean you can't enjoy it. Got it, cowboy?"

Desmond snorted.

"I got it, cowgirl. Thanks."

Madi nodded, satisfied. She let him get into the truck before she issued one last comment.

"And Des? Ma and I have decided to not tell those other two Nashes about this nondate until tomorrow." She smirked. "Enjoy the freedom."

Desmond didn't say so but he did appreciate that gesture.

Winding Road led him to the county road that took him across town to one of the more rural Overlook neighborhoods called Willows Way. Ranch-style houses were planted on large lots with at least a half acre or so between each. While there were an insane amount of trees taking over most of the town, Willows Way had very few. Some of the residents had compensated by creating massive gardens, statue scenes and one even had soccer goals planted in the yard.

Desmond hadn't been to Willows Way in years. In fact, he hadn't been to the opposite side of Overlook at all in some time. Actually, he hadn't been on a social call in general in a while either.

It made him weirdly antsy.

Was he nervous?

Why should he be?

Desmond swore as he cut the engine in the driveway of the all brick house at 207 Willows Way.

"Madi got to me," he told no one.

The home was smaller than the other houses on the road but there was a charm to it. Yet when movement from inside caught his eye, a surge of adrenaline rocketed through him. Desmond's muscles tensed, a dull ache in his leg throbbed and he was seconds away from jumping out of the truck and running inside to rescue anyone who needed it.

But then he felt like an idiot. It took him a few beats of being completely still to realize he had overreacted. The movement belonged to a woman peering out the window then moving and making the curtains sway.

Maybe he was a little more on edge about this nondate—and in general——than he'd admitted.

Desmond took one long breath and told his body to calm down.

Sometimes life could be simple.

There was no reason to believe anything else was going to get messy.

When his cell phone started to ring, Desmond decided he'd listen to Madi's advice. He'd ignore the call. Enjoy his dinner and company. He'd *be present*. He could call whoever it was back. No problem.

But curiosity was a persistent creature. Once he saw the caller ID Desmond couldn't help but click Accept.

Why was one of the town lawyers calling him?

He answered the phone with one hand on the door handle.

"Desmond, here."

"Hey, Desmond, it's Marty McLinnon."

"Hey, Marty, what can I do you for?"

There was rustling on the other side of the phone. Marty was moving around.

"Well, I was at home when I got an alert that the cameras at my law office across the street from your construction site were going off. Since what happened the other week I pointed one of my cameras in that direction and *that's* the one that picked up something. I looked into the live feed and there sure was some movement so I drove on out here and parked in the back and—" There was movement again. The man was breathing a bit harder than normal. "Yep, there's someone in the building. I can see them on the second floor. You got anyone that's supposed to be up there?"

Desmond shook his head even though the man couldn't see him. His adrenaline spiked again. This time with a vengeance.

"Not on a Saturday night, no."

"That's what I thought." Marty started to lower his voice. "Hey, Desmond, my husband is calling. Probably freaking out. I need to get it. Want me to call the cops after?"

"I'll call Declan—don't worry. Just don't go over there, okay? Could be some punk teens being rebellious, could be worse."

"I got you. I'll stay put."

"Thanks, Marty."

The call ended. Desmond got out of the truck, phone to his ear and called Declan on reflex.

"Marty McLinnon is across from Second Wind right now. He says there's someone on the second floor," he jumped in.

Declan was quick to answer. Though there was some heat in his voice.

"Call Caleb. I'm—I'm in a situation right now. Call me if anything else happens."

The phone call ended without another word.

Desmond did as he was told.

Caleb didn't answer, which was unusual. When Jazz's phone went straight to voice mail, the hair on the back of Desmond's neck rose. Something must have been going on with the department. Something pressing.

He hoped his family was okay.

In the meantime, Desmond decided not to call anyone else.

Not until he was on-site. The drive wasn't too far from where he was now. He could join Marty and try to take a picture of the culprit, if he or she *was* a culprit. Plus, if Marty's camera caught the person already, they could use that to ID them if they were gone by the time he showed up. Plus, the department wasn't too far away from Second Wind's construction site anyways.

Desmond was about to run up to the Stone sisters' door and cancel their plans when the front door opened.

He found those dark eyes, framed by crimson fire, and knew then, with surprising ferocity, that he didn't want to cancel at all. Not on Riley.

Not even when his gut was twisting to get a move on and protect his baby, Second Wind.

No. Desmond knew right at that moment that he didn't want to leave without her.

Chapter Eight

What Desmond Nash would never know was just how insane the Stone household became leading up to the moment he arrived at the front door.

"He's here," Jenna had yelled clear across the house. She'd had her nose basically pressed against the living-room window for twenty minutes in anticipation of the man's arrival. Riley had been taken aback by Desmond's casual invite to dinner; Jenna had lost her damn mind.

"Have you seen him?" Jenna had exclaimed when they'd gotten in the car after Claire's. "He's not even my type and my knees went a bit gooey when he *shook my hand*. I mean I saw him at the hospital the other day, sure, but without the adrenaline and sisterly worry I really got to see him, you know? He's like *a cowboy* and he loves his family... I mean, wow-ee!"

Riley wasn't going to disagree.

"So, let me be the first to say, I totally get why you said yes," Jenna had continued. "But, I *do* have to ask, is it a date?"

That had been a question that both women had gone over the rest of the day. Riley didn't think it was, Jenna wanted it to be. The uncertainty ate at Jenna until it had manifested in Riley mere minutes before he was supposed to arrive.

After Jenna had heralded his arrival, chaos had consumed the house.

"What's he wearing?" Riley had yelled back. Jenna's bed was covered in ten different outfits all of varying levels of heat. From completely casual jeans and a button up to a little black dress with heels that tied up and across the ankle.

Jenna had gone silent.

"JENNA?"

"He's still in the truck! I can't see what he's wearing!"

Riley had felt like an idiot as she waited. Mostly because she was standing in her black bra-and-panty set staring at a pile of clothes.

"He's getting out," Jenna had finally yelled.

Riley's muscles had tensed up. Her adrenaline had hit a high. She had waited with bated breath until…

"Dressy casual! Outfit number three!" Footsteps had thundered down the hallway as Jenna flew into the room. She had panted while she repeated herself. "Dressy. Casual."

Riley had dressed faster than she ever had in her entire life. Outfit number three was a Stone sister combo. Jenna's black skinny jeans and suede boots, Riley's navy sheer blouse and faux leather bomber jacket.

"Date or no date, you look hot! Now, teeth."

Jenna had performed the lipstick check before running behind Riley and fluffing her hair. It was down and crazy, as per usual.

Now after opening the front door because Riley couldn't take it anymore, Jenna crouched down behind the oak door, out of sight. She looked like a crazy person.

"Have fun and wear protection," she hissed.

Riley's cheeks turned into flames.

There was a special kind of chaos that came with being a sister.

"Hey there," Riley greeted, lamely. She already felt off

her game around Desmond but Jenna had really thrown her off, especially since Riley knew she was behind the door, listening. It pushed her to almost jump across the door frame, closing that same door shut as she did so.

Desmond watched the move but didn't offer a comment.

Or the greeting Riley had expected.

"Do you mind if we make a quick pit stop?"

Riley, still very much wanting to create distance between them and her eavesdropping sister, was already walking toward him.

"That sounds fine to me!"

Desmond was stepping fast. He paused only long enough to open the door for her. He was in his seat in record time.

"Is something wrong?" she couldn't help but ask. The urgency was clear, she just didn't know what for.

Desmond, who was absolutely owning a dark red button-down, dark jeans and a worn leather jacket that actually matched hers, made a noise in response.

A weird noise.

One that had her turning in her seat with her eyebrow rising high. She saw Desmond glance at her out of his periphery. He turned the engine over. His hand went to the gear shift but he stopped from putting it in Reverse.

He sighed.

Then there were baby blues staring at her.

"I just got a call that someone is lurking around Second Wind's construction site. I think it might be the person who vandalized a wall there the night of the gala. The department seems to have their hands full so I thought I'd go check it out before I call in the rest of cavalry. We can reschedule if you want. It's really no problem."

Riley slapped her seat belt into the clasp with vigor.

"Come on! Let's go before he gets away!"

Desmond's eyes widened in surprise but he got to reversing without making any more fuss.

"I didn't know the construction site was vandalized before," she admitted. It was a bizarre desire to want to be a part of seeing if someone was messing with Second Wind but there Riley was, feeling it.

"Yeah, it was one of the few pieces of news the media around here didn't find and publish. Honestly, I'm okay with that."

"Wait, is that the reason you were on Winding Road when Brett—well, when *that* happened?"

He nodded.

"I slipped away to check it out for myself after my brothers told me. Second Wind, it—it means a lot to me so I wanted to see it in person. I saw the wreck on my way back to the party."

"I'm sorry it happened, the vandalism, but I have to say I'm extremely lucky it did." Riley lightened her tone. "Maybe count the first strike as a necessary evil so you could convert another person to your obsession with this Red Oak place? Is that an okay silver lining?"

A small smile tugged up on the corner of Desmond's lips.

"I suppose so because it really *is* a great place. Their steak?" He brought the tips of his fingers to his mouth and kissed them dramatically. "*Perfecto.* Unless…" A look of acute worry immediately blanketed his expression.

Riley realized, belatedly, she was just staring at the man like he was a riveting action movie playing on a TV.

He didn't seem to care when he whipped his head around to look her in the eye.

"Unless you're vegan? Or a vegetarian?"

Riley laughed.

"Neither."

Desmond let out an exhale of relief.

"I mean, they have salads and other options but the steak

and chicken? As Madi says sometimes when something is really good, 'God bless.'"

The urgency, the tension the cowboy had been carrying seemed to lessen. Riley wanted to capitalize on that. She turned her gaze out the windshield, watching the dark world around them flash by. In the woods it had been terrifying. Here, with Desmond in the truck, it was actually comforting.

"I know everyone assumes multiples *have* to be close but it's nice to see you seem to genuinely be close with your siblings," she said. "I also have to admit, I've never met a set of triplets before. It's kind of exciting."

Desmond let out a howl of laughter. Riley jumped in surprise. It only seemed to balloon that same laughter.

"The other day Caleb and I talked about how wild it was to meet a set of identical twins." He turned, pulling her attention from the road outside. "Like I told him, it's like looking in a mirror with the two of you. What was that like growing up? We're fraternal and Madi still felt like she had to dye her hair blond to feel like an individual."

It was a question Riley and Jenna had been asked a lot growing up. One, she suspected, she'd always get asked. It was also the most she thought Desmond had spoken to her in one breath.

"We went through a phase where we tried to look different. Coincidentally it was the same time I realized that, yes, mohawks are a daring hairstyle but not everyone was meant to rock them." Desmond snorted. They turned out of the neighborhood and bounced along an even darker road. "Other than that I can't say we've ever really disliked being identical twins. Then again, I think I got incredibly lucky with who ended up being mine." A warmth blossomed in Riley's chest. It was followed by a low flame of anger. Old but always hot. She knew she sounded different when she continued. "Jenna is one of those people who has the rare capability to love unconditionally *even* when it's not deserved. She's good people through and through. I think that's what's made being her twin so easy. I don't just like being her sister, I'm proud to be."

The sudden rush of enthusiasm on Desmond's part diminished. Riley felt her cheeks heat. She'd overshared.

"Feel free not to answer but that love that's not deserved, does it have to do with Hartley's father?"

Yep. She'd overshared.

Still, she answered. Though she did so carefully.

"Yes. At first he seemed like the perfect guy. But then… He wasn't." Riley couldn't help her hand from fisting in her lap. Guilt, heavy and hollowing pushed through the fire in her chest. "She stayed with him longer than she should have, so worried leaving would hurt Hartley. Worried that somehow it was her fault too. It took a lot for her to realize that the only good option was to go." She unfurled her fist and took a small breath. "Then she came here, fell in love with the town and rented the first house she saw. At first I think it was a temporary plan but now I think she's in for the long haul."

"Overlook can have that effect on people. How do you like it? Declan said you said you lived in Atlanta before coming here? That's definitely a far cry from small-town Tennessee."

She nodded.

"It is," she admitted. "But it's not bad. Just different. I used to work as an office manager for a company that was in the heart of downtown. The commute was…less than desirable. I don't miss that."

"But you do miss it? The city, I mean."

Riley had thought about that a lot since she'd arrived with all of her belongings on Jenna's doorstep.

"I miss the rhythm. The hustle and bustle. Even though there were so many people doing so many things, I grew

used to it. Here, well, I don't think I've really left the house
enough to learn the rhythm."

She caught the small smile tugging at the corner of his
lips again.

"You ever had a faucet with a slow leak?" he asked. "One
that just goes *drip...drip...drip...* I'd say that's about our
speed in good ol' Overlook."

Riley wanted to point out that in the short time she'd
been there she'd been chased by a man into the woods
with a bat and then approached by a scoundrel reporter
who had done such a good job at digging, he'd hit the one
deep wound she and her sister shared. Instead she laughed.

"A leak is better than a flood, I suppose."

A small silence stretched between them. Riley didn't
know how to fill it. But she knew she wanted to do just
that. She wanted to learn more about the man next to her.

Sure, Desmond Nash was a good-looking guy. He was
the poster boy for strapping young cowboys who could use
their jawlines to slice butter. Yet, there was more to the man
than looks. Tragedy had shaped him as far as Riley could
surmise from the countless news stories. He'd taken that
pain and made it into a tool. One that had created a foundation that was now setting up shop in the same town he'd
experienced that tragedy.

There was a weight to Desmond.

Riley couldn't explain it past that. She'd felt it looking
into his eyes that night in the woods, she'd felt it seeing
his anger at her lie in the hospital and she'd felt it now sitting next to him.

Desmond Nash was a question she wanted to answer and
an answer she wanted to question. All at once.

SECOND WIND'S CONSTRUCTION SITE was five minutes from
downtown Overlook. Placed on a large lot bordered by
pines, it was one of five businesses along the aptly named

Business Boulevard. A back road led to the law offices across the street and the florist farther down. Desmond took it slow and with the truck's lights off until they were parked next to Marty McLinnon's Honda at the law offices.

"I don't think anyone is in there," Riley said, face an inch from the passenger's-side window. She unbuckled her seat belt without looking. "Do you think this Marty guy is inside of the offices?"

Desmond undid his own seat belt. A trickle of excitement ran down his spine, spiked by the excitement he heard in her voice.

"Let's find out."

They moved from the truck to the back door of the office building. It was locked. Desmond knocked but no response. He pulled out his phone and called Marty back.

After a moment Riley touched his arm. She turned her head toward the corner of the building.

"Do you hear that?"

Desmond lowered the phone. It took him a moment to hear a song playing somewhere out in the night. It was faint.

"It sounds so far away," Riley whispered. They followed the length of the building to the corner. Like they were in an episode of *Scooby-Doo*, they leaned over and peeked around the brick. It gave them a clear view of the other side of the road.

To Second Wind.

To where the ringing was coming from.

Right before it stopped.

Marty's voice mail started to play.

"Call back to make sure that's his phone we're hearing." The excitement Desmond had heard in Riley's voice earlier was ebbing. "You told him not to go over there, right?"

Desmond called the number again.

"Yeah, but Marty's stubborn as nails. It's what makes him a good lawyer." The call went through. The music started playing in the distance again. "Me telling him to not go over there might have just convinced him to do the opposite."

"Would he confront whoever it was lurking?"

"Same answer."

Riley turned around. It made him realize how close they were. The smell of lavender filled his senses.

"What do you want to do?"

Dark, entrancing, mesmerizing.

Riley Stone didn't realize the power she could conjure with just one even stare.

It inspired a cocktail of emotions within him. The most potent? Bravado.

"I'm going to go see who's been messing with my site."

A faint smile tugged at Riley's lips. She nodded.

"After you."

Desmond opened his mouth to complain; Riley held up her hand. It was mere inches from his chest.

"I'm going with you. Here." She opened the purse she'd been wearing across her chest. What she pulled out made Desmond chuckle. He saw his breath mist out in front of him.

"Pepper spray?"

"You bet your boots, cowboy. Now let's get going."

Desmond tipped his hat.

"Yes, ma'am."

Business Boulevard was lit by tall and relatively new streetlamps that stood every hundred yards or so. The construction site had four separate lights that bathed each corner in enough light meant to dissuade any theft or vandalism.

A lot of good that had done.

Desmond led the way from the streetlamp's circle of illumination and past a parked Bobcat at the front of the site.

"If anyone is on the second or third floors, I can't see

them," Riley whispered at his side. She was so close again her hair was brushing against his arm and back.

Distracting.

But not as much as the unease growing in his stomach.

Second Wind was mostly just a skeleton of beams and partially constructed walls. There were tarps and stacks of building materials and slight mayhem everywhere. A set of stairs that had been constructed but weren't finished. It still got workers to the upper two floors. The start of the steps was housed in the section of the first floor that was tucked out of sight from the front of the building.

In front of them now, on an expanse of constructed exterior wall, was where the graffiti had been before.

Can't even win a simple game of hide-and-seek.

Those words had been painted over, the only part of the wall that was light gray.

There was no movement near it or them.

Without a word Desmond called Marty again.

This time it went straight to voice mail.

Desmond and Riley shared a look.

His gut started yelling.

He should have listened.

Instead they wordlessly went through the opening and into the first floor. Riley pulled out her phone and switched it to flashlight mode. The new light made shadows skitter over the concrete.

"Empty."

They fanned out across the expanse. Desmond shook his head.

Where was Marty?

Where was the person he'd seen?

Was this some kind of tasteless prank?

Another jab at Desmond to create a new surge of press?

"Desmond?"

He turned around, pulling up his call log as he did so,

ready to call the sheriff's department, but paused when he saw Riley's expression.

Wide eyes. Wide, worried eyes. She was pointing to the stairs in the corner.

"Is that…?"

Desmond looked to where she was pointing. No one was there but something was on the ground. With soft steps he made his way over, his gut yelling even louder.

Riley's light ran across the blood just as Desmond realized what it was.

"Call 9-1-1."

Riley didn't listen. Instead she angled her phone up the dark tunnel that ran up the stairs.

"It leads up there," she whispered. "Marty might be hurt."

Desmond caught her hand, the one holding the pepper spray.

It wasn't enough to calm his fraying nerves.

"We don't know—"

Something large dropped from the second floor to the dirt across from them, just outside of the first-floor concrete. Riley yelled out in surprise. He tightened his grip around her hand.

The something grunted.

Desmond couldn't believe his eyes.

That something was a man.

And it wasn't Marty McLinnon.

Chapter Nine

Desmond took off running. Riley would have been on his heels but she heard something he didn't.

It was a shuffling sound.

And it was coming from the top of the stairs.

Desmond and the man, who she was assuming wasn't his buddy Marty, had kicked up dust and were booking it toward the road. Riley wasn't about to yell for him to come back. She wasn't about to wait for him either.

She ran a thumb under the strap of her purse across her chest to the main part of the bag, securing it while tightening her grip around the pepper spray. The light from her cell phone in the other hand made the blood look glossy.

Riley was careful not to step on it as she took the stairs up two at a time.

The second floor had three walls. Where the fourth was going to be was open and showed the law offices across the street. The closest streetlamp did a better job of illuminating this floor than the one below it.

Along with the man standing in the middle of the space.

Riley was stunned with how well dressed he was. So well dressed, in fact, that it was the first detail she registered. A dark gray suit, three-piece, and shoes that absolutely shone. His hair was dirty blond and combed against his scalp. He had his hands in his pockets like he was waiting for a client to arrive. He even looked at Riley like she was the one who'd come in for the meeting with him.

One that she had been late for.

His tone bit like he was chiding her, yet his words were nothing but alarming.

"Marty McLinnon, husband to one and father to four, is on the third floor of this construction site and battling for his life." He nodded toward the wall to her left. "If there was a window right there you'd see a section of a support beam attached to a chain. That beam is getting lower and lower because it's either dragging an unconscious Mr. Mc-Linnon to the edge of the building or slowly pulling his legs out of joint. I'm not sure which is happening but I'm pretty sure if you don't get up there right now and start cutting through that chain he's going to be in a bad way."

Riley waited for the man to laugh, to say *just kidding*, and then say, "Hey! I'm Marty McLinnon. Did you see that crazy man jump to the ground floor?"

But he didn't.

Instead he bent down, picked something up off the floor and held it out to her.

It was a power tool.

No.

It was a handheld electric saw. Riley knew because she'd seen her dad use a similar one to do drywall work at their home in Georgia.

"You'll need to plug it in but this should cut through the chain," he added. "Drop the pepper spray and your phone and I'll give it to you. If not, I'll throw it off the building and we can hear it break. Just like we'll hear Mr. McLin-non break if you don't decide soon."

He shook the saw.

Riley didn't know the man. *Nothing* about him was familiar. The light and shadows were playing tricks on her eyes. One second he looked younger than her, in the next he had the nonchalance of a wiser, much older man.

However, what she *was* sure of?

This wasn't a joke to him.

Riley dropped her phone and pepper spray. Their *thud*s against the concrete echoed around the unfinished space.

"Who are you?" she had to ask.

The man shook his head. Then he nodded to the stairs.

"That blood had to come from someone and it didn't come from me. The longer you're on this floor, the shorter Mr. McLinnon's life span becomes."

Riley felt like she was having an out-of-body experience. Yet, she ran over to him and took the saw, careful to grab the cord off of the ground.

"Ticktock, Ms. Stone."

DESMOND'S LEG WAS HURTING but the man he was chasing also seemed to be favoring one leg over the other. The jump from the second story had no doubt been less than pleasant.

"Stop," Desmond yelled again.

The man didn't.

They streaked past Business Boulevard in the direction of the law office's parking lot. The man in black had enough of a lead that, when he tripped over the curb, he was able to get back up and start running again. Though he had slowed considerably.

"Stop, dammit!"

Again, the man didn't listen.

He turned so he was running along the back road. That surprised Desmond. If he had been trying to lose someone, he would go into the trees. Yet the man stayed on the road.

It made up Desmond's mind.

He spun around and pulled out his car keys. Hurrying back to his truck, he threw himself inside the cab and turned the engine.

He couldn't follow the man into the trees but if he stayed on the road that was something Desmond could work with.

The tires squealed as the truck reversed. Before popping the gear into Drive he hit Declan's number on his recent-calls list and put it on speaker. It started ringing. Desmond pressed down the gas.

"Des, can I call—"

"We found blood at the construction site and then a man dressed in all black jumped from the second story and took off," Desmond jumped in. "I'm chasing him now in my truck because he's sticking to the back road."

The man glanced over his shoulder. His eyes widened in the headlights' beam. He angled off the road and into the grass. Still he didn't run into the trees.

"Does he have a weapon?" Declan had become completely focused. His tone was curt.

"Not that I can tell. But we haven't seen Marty anywhere and, Dec, I never called in the troops."

Declan swore.

"Hold on," he said in the next breath. He started talking to someone.

Desmond was coming up on the man in black. He was continuing to slow down.

"I'm about to get this guy," he told his older brother.

The truck took to the grass and dirt and the small slope down like a champ. Desmond sped up and turned the wheel, kicking up dirt as he went, and then hit the brakes hard.

The man in black stopped just as abruptly and turned. Desmond realized then that the man had every intention of finally running to the trees, a place he didn't have the clearance to drive his truck between, but then he tripped again.

This time he didn't get back up.

Desmond was out of the truck in a flash.

The man pulled himself up into a sitting position. His head was bent over. He was panting.

Desmond had a lot of questions.

He started with the most pressing.

"Where's Marty McLinnon?"

The man didn't get a chance to react.

They both turned as a scream echoed out across the night air.

It was Riley.

And she was yelling for him.

THE CHAIN TORE at her hands.

"No!"

Riley pulled with all her might. She was standing between the unobstructed edge of the third floor and the limp body of a man who was sliding to his potential death. The motion had been slow when she'd first gotten to his side, but as she'd looked around for an outlet, he'd made a noise.

That noise had heralded a truly terrifying sight. One that made her drop the saw and run. Marty's body had hit something slick covering that section of the floor. Whether it was blood, oil or water, Riley didn't have the time to find out.

It had sped up his movement, whatever it was.

Now Riley was trying and failing to pull the section of support beam up. A foolish attempt. She barely got her hands beneath the chain to pull in the first place.

Something hit the back of her foot.

It was Marty's boot.

Riley let out a strangled gasp, surprised he'd already made it to where she was.

A ball of ice exploded in her gut, filling her veins.

There wasn't enough room between them and the edge. Riley couldn't pull the beam up. She didn't have enough time to find an outlet and cut it. Not with how fast he was sliding now.

She'd already called for Desmond but he wasn't there.

Was she about to watch this poor man go over the edge?

"No no no no no."

Riley abandoned the chain and spun around to focus on a Hail Mary plan. It took a few seconds and was in no way a good idea but Riley didn't care.

She unbuckled her belt and flung it off in two seconds flat. Moving catty-cornered to a steel beam already erected, she threw the belt around the metal and buckled it back. Marty's body kept sliding. She let him until his arm was level with her.

Riley sat her butt down and put a death grip on her belt. Then she grabbed Marty McLinnon's arm.

The tension came shortly after. Riley's stomach nearly turned as she felt the weight trying its best to pull Marty away. If he had been awake, she had no doubt the pain would have been awful.

"Come on, come on," she chanted, having no idea who she was chanting to.

That's when she heard the vehicle approaching. Tires skidded to a stop somewhere near the front of the building. Then Riley heard a sound that temporarily pushed the cold from her veins.

"Riley?"

It was Desmond.

"Up here," she yelled. "Third floor! *Hurry!*"

The pull from the beam was getting worse. Riley tried to stay where she was but the pull was too strong. She was starting to slide herself.

"No!"

Marty's arm lifted above his head and she had to move her grip to his wrist. Her nails bit painfully into the palm of her hand as her hold on the belt tightened with the strain.

Footsteps thundered up the stairs. Riley knew there wasn't time to explain everything. She craned her neck around to see the bewildered expression of the most handsome man she'd ever known and hoped he knew how to handle an electric saw.

"Find an outlet," she yelled in greeting. She could hear the pain in her voice as it started to feel like she was being pulled apart. She couldn't imagine how Marty felt. "There's the saw!"

Desmond, bless him, was quick on the uptake.

He grabbed the saw off of the ground and ran purposefully toward them, stopping to plug it in.

A horrible, twisting worry occurred to Riley then.

What if the cord wasn't long enough to reach the chain?

"It'll reach," Desmond said, answering her thought without realizing it. He slid across the space between it and the chain. Riley squeezed her eyes shut but didn't quell her cry of pain.

A small part of her had hoped the chain was long enough that the beam would hit the ground soon and stop the pull. Yet, it just wasn't happening.

The sound of the saw was a beautiful one. The noise of it eating through the chain was magical.

However, it was a slow process.

By the time he'd cut through the top part of the link, Riley was struggling. Blood was coming out of the hand holding the belt just as blood was coming out of Marty's hand as her grip was maxed out on him.

She felt like a rubber band about to break; her entire body was angled toward the edge.

If she let go, Marty would only have a foot before he was falling through the air.

"Hurry," she yelled. "I can't hold on much longer!"

Desmond didn't respond. It wasn't like he could say anything to help.

Riley squeezed her eyes shut again. A few more seconds passed until, in the darkness behind her lids, she realized another horrifying thought.

The beam was too heavy.

She was about to let go.

"I can't—"

Before she could finish her sentence, Marty McLinnon's hand slid out of hers.

Riley's eyes flashed open, horrified she was about to watch a man fall to his death.

What she saw instead was Desmond as he let out a body-sagging exhale, a severed chain between them.

Marty had finally stopped moving.

Two baby blues found their way to her. He had questions, which was okay because she had answers. But when he dropped the saw and hurried over to her, all Riley could do was express the immense relief she was feeling.

"I'm so sorry I left—" Desmond started, but the moment he was within arm's reach, Riley pulled him down to her.

He hit his knees with a grunt. She fully realized it probably hurt but then she pushed herself up and against him and did exactly what she thought needed to be done.

Their lips crashed together with a smack that echoed. Riley threw her arms around the man's neck like he was a lifeline and she was on the brink.

The kiss was hard but it unfurled something inside her that she hadn't realized had been there in the first place. Her unexpected weight against him sent them backward to the concrete she'd now despise forever. Her arms around his neck kept his head from connecting with that same floor.

Riley ended the kiss as quickly as she had initiated it.

Then she was lying on top of the man and staring into his eyes.

"Thank you," she said, breathless.

Thank you for not letting a man die because I couldn't hold on.

Thank you for not questioning me when I needed you to do something.

Thank you for coming back.

Riley dropped her head against his chest, realizing how tired she was. For the second time since she'd met the man, he held her in silence for a much-needed second or two.

Then she remembered why she was there in the first place.

"There was a man in a suit here," she hurried, rolling off him without an ounce of grace. "He gave me the saw when I dropped my phone and spray. He told me Marty was about to die."

Desmond's brow knitted together. He pulled his phone from his pocket. He had Declan on speaker phone.

"We're almost there," the sheriff yelled out. "EMT should be right on our tails."

Desmond reached over to check Marty's pulse. He nodded to Riley.

"Marty is alive," he yelled to the phone. "I'm—*We're* going to go get the other man to make sure he doesn't escape."

Desmond pulled Riley to her feet and kept hold of her hand. Wordlessly they got into his truck near the open first floor of the construction site and then drove across the street. Riley was about to ask where they were going as they headed toward the back road they'd come in on when she saw a figure on the side of the road.

"I hog-tied him with some rope I had from the barn," he explained when they stopped. The headlights showed the man in all black lying on his stomach on the grass, his arms, wrists and ankles tied up behind him. "I wasn't sure it would hold since I did it so quick."

He started to get out as the man ahead of them turned toward the truck.

Riley sucked in a breath.

Desmond stalled next to his opened door.

"What is it?" he asked, voice already drowning in concern.

Riley didn't speak for a moment.

There's no way...

"Riley?"

A warm hand touched hers. Another grabbed her chin. Desmond gently turned her head.

Riley looked into those crystal blue eyes, so blue she felt like she could swim in them, and said something she never thought she'd utter in Overlook.

"That's my ex-husband."

Chapter Ten

Hitting something seemed too dramatic. The walls of Declan's office in Wildman County's sheriff's department hadn't done anything to Desmond. It seemed unfair to take out his anger and frustration there.

Yelling also didn't seem the best course of action.

Declan and the uniforms who had shown up at the construction site now knew as much as he did. Cussing at them didn't get anyone anywhere. Plus, it was rude.

And not what the most charming Nash was expected to do.

What everyone probably expected of him was to be a cool cucumber. Ready to go with an easy smile and a tip of the hat.

But that wasn't him.

Not right now.

Riley was sitting next to him in an old wingback chair that made her seem impossibly small. She had bandages across each of her palms and they were resting on the tops of her thighs. When she caught him staring, her smile was weak.

Since the revelation that the man in black was her ex-husband, they hadn't gotten a chance to be alone together. Definitely not talk in private. Now, after Declan had told them to wait in his office, was the perfect time to tackle whatever the hell was going on together.

Yet for all Desmond's fame of being the smooth one of the Nash bunch, he was finding that with Riley his words often were raw. He didn't have a prepared speech or thought to share.

He was at a loss and it manifested in nearly palpable hesitation.

One that Riley broke, despite Desmond's intentions to do it first.

"Can we rain check dinner at the Red Oak?"

Desmond offered a weak smile in return.

"I'd be okay with that."

Riley nodded.

"Good. Good."

Silence pushed between them again.

Desmond glanced down at her lips. The same ones that had crushed his at the construction site.

It wasn't the time, the place or the situation to be thinking about them. Yet, there he was. Wishing he could have a do-over. He hadn't kissed back because, honestly, he'd been too surprised.

Now he wasn't.

Now he wanted to.

Now wasn't the time.

The door opened and Declan walked in. His hat had been off since they'd arrived at the department. That usually meant business.

"Marty's husband and kids are at the hospital with Detective Santiago," he said, going to his chair and taking a seat. "He's hurt, but unless something changes, he'll be fine. Eventually. Before you arrived it appears he was knocked out pretty hard. There's a nasty cut on his scalp, explaining all that blood."

"What about his legs?" Riley asked.

Declan looked unsure of what to say. Desmond spoke up.

"Better off than if he'd fallen unconscious three stories, I can tell you that."

Riley gave him a look riddled with guilt. He wanted to wipe it away.

"I know Marty," he added. "Whatever injuries he takes from this he'll gladly accept over the alternative. You saved his life."

Declan nodded his agreement.

Riley visibly let a long breath out.

Then it was back to business.

"As for the man in the suit, we have a BOLO out on him based on your description. Caleb is also at the law offices looking at their security footage with one of the other partners." It was Declan's turn to let out a sigh. "Which brings us to the one man out of the three who can tell us what in the heck was going on out there."

Riley stiffened. Desmond, in response, did too.

"Davies," she said, anger threading clear through the two syllables.

Her ex-husband.

Desmond felt the heat of jealousy push against his gut. He tried to remember that it was her ex, but still, the thought of another man with her put fire in him.

Not the time, he scolded himself, again.

"That's his last name, right?" Declan asked.

She nodded

"He hates the name Evan so everyone calls him by his last name. It was the reason why I didn't take his name when we married. He said it felt like I was stealing a part of his identity."

Desmond snorted.

He'd be proud as hell for Riley to wear his name if she wanted it.

Declan shot him a look and stood up.

"I don't normally do this but Marty is a well-established member of Overlook and, well, we're coming up with a lot more questions than I'm comfortable with," he said. "I'd appreciate if you could come observe the interrogation. You know this Davies better than any of us so you might be able to pick up on something we won't be able to."

Riley stood. Hesitation lined her body.

"He won't be able to see me, right?"

"Right. You'll be behind a two-way mirror. We won't even let him know you're in the building." Declan opened the door and waved a deputy over. "Can you take Ms. Stone to the viewing room? We'll be there in a minute."

The deputy did as she was told and escorted Riley out of the room. Desmond stood but didn't try to go after her. His brother was looking at him with an expression he couldn't read, a rarity between the Nash siblings.

"What is it?"

Declan shut the door behind him. Then he was all big brother.

"I'm not one for victim blaming so don't you go putting that on me after I say this," he started. "But I want to be a friendly reminder that she might be nice, funny and quick on her feet but the fact remains that you don't know Riley or her sister. None of us do. Not really."

Desmond felt his defenses flare.

"What are you trying to say, Dec? Do you think she's behind this?"

"No, what I'm saying is that there's something weird going on here. Brett Calder attacks her at random, you save her and then less than a month later you get her away from Geordi Green. Then, on the night you two decide to go out, *her* ex-husband is a part of some bizarre scene at *your* foundation's construction site." Declan made two fists. He shook one. "You—" He shook the other. "And her—" He put those two fists against each other. "Keep colliding together. And I don't know why or how it keeps happening. Or who might be helping make it happen."

Desmond readied to combat whatever his brother was trying to say when Declan's expression softened. He placed one of his large hands on Desmond's shoulder and squeezed.

"All I'm saying is you can let that heart of yours do what it wants, just make sure that head sticks around too. Okay?"

Desmond nodded, holding back the staggering need to puff his chest out and fight for Riley's innocence.

"Okay," he said, instead.

"JENNA MET RYAN ALCASTER right out of college."

Riley was standing across from the two-way window and trying not to look at a man she, quite frankly, despised.

Declan and Desmond had come in but had given her space. Desmond was leaning against the wall next to the door, facing her, while Declan was in a chair with a notepad next to the window.

He looked up from his writing, brow raised.

"I thought we were talking about Evan Davies?"

Riley sighed. She wished she could melt into the floor and forget every ounce of the story she was about to tell.

"We are but I can't tell you about my ex-husband without talking about hers." Riley glanced at Desmond, then she let the look fall to the floor. A consequence of how much she disliked all of what she was about to say. Still, there were much worse things than telling a story.

She could have lived through Jenna's side.

"Ryan Alcaster is the CFO of Macklin Tech, a company out of Atlanta that deals in technology revolving around memory cards and external hard drives. A business model that's a dime a dozen, if you ask me, but since I've known of it Macklin seems to have been doing really well. So, whatever it is they're doing, it's working." She cleared her throat. "Anyway, right before Jenna and Ryan met, I met Davies.

When we first started dating, we were both struggling to find jobs within our fields. We were considering leaving Atlanta to save some money but then Ryan got Davies a job interview at Macklin. He and Ryan had become fast friends. Ryan honestly became like a mentor too. It was a friendship that connected to their careers. Davies was hired at Macklin within the year, and just as I was about to start my online marketing freelance business, he convinced me to take an office manager job there too." Riley shrugged. "Not where I wanted my career to go but bills don't care all about that. Plus, I really thought we were lucky. We got married and then became the married couple in the office. Sure, the commute was bad but at least I had a partner in it."

Desmond shifted his weight to his other leg. Pen scratched across paper as Declan kept up with his notes. The sound of the AC kicking on created a constant background noise. Riley continued, not meeting either of their gazes.

"It wasn't until Jenna had Hartley that Macklin Tech opened a second location in Kilwin," she continued. "Nothing on the scale of the Atlanta office but strategically placed to work on a different region of the South. At least that's what I was told. What it meant for Jenna was that she had to move with Ryan to Kilwin while Davies was promoted and we stayed in Atlanta. Again, not ideal, but Jenna and I kept in touch. We video chatted daily, spoke on the phone when we had the time and still managed to feel close… But then things changed."

Riley rubbed her thumb across the knuckle of her index finger. She was actively trying not to make a fist.

"Jenna stopped wanting to video chat and then the phone calls stopped a little while after that. It was like pulling teeth to get ahold of her. I started to worry but Davies convinced me it was just Jenna getting used to being a mom and living in a new city. He convinced me to give her space.

So, I did. But then one day she showed up at my door. She was acting weird and I couldn't place it until I saw the bruise on her back."

"Ryan was abusing her," Desmond said. His voice had gone cold.

It matched how Riley felt at remembering.

She nodded.

"She brushed it off in the end. Worried that it was her fault and then citing our parents as a reason for why she had to stay."

"Your parents?"

Riley finally met Desmond's blue eyes.

"We had a really good childhood and our parents often said that was because of their healthy marriage and respect for each other. It gave us stability."

"And she thought if she left Ryan that it would hurt Hartley," he guessed.

Again Riley nodded.

"She went back home and I tried to convince her for weeks to leave. When she finally told me to stop or she would get a new number, I backed off and that night I sat Davies down." That cold, hollow feeling was replaced by red-hot resentment and disbelief, even now. Riley turned to face the man she'd made an oath to stay with until death did them part. How foolish she'd been. "I guess I should have realized that me not telling him up until then was because a part of me didn't trust him. But I didn't know what to do anymore so I told him. I was *so* worried about how he would react. I was shaking. Ryan was his friend, his mentor, the reason in part for his success. Outing Ryan endangered everything Davies had worked for. But do you know what happened when I told him?"

Riley directed this to Desmond. She couldn't stand to look at the man of the story anymore.

Desmond's face was impassive.

He knew it was a rhetorical question.

Still, she paused for effect. She wanted—*needed*—someone else to feel an ounce of the impact of what had happened next.

"I didn't see any surprise in his eyes. It was that moment, that *exact* moment that I stopped loving Evan Davies."

Desmond waited a moment before he spoke. Riley didn't realize how worked up she'd become. Her breathing was faster. Harder. Angrier.

Somehow she knew Desmond felt it too. He might not have lived it but he understood the heat. The life-altering moment. The thing that cannot ever be undone.

The end of something.

Something that should have been much more.

"He knew," Desmond said, words soft. "He knew Ryan was abusing Jenna."

Riley nodded. Everything in her felt clenched.

"He told me that even though she was my twin, my sister, that that didn't give me the right to meddle in her marriage. Their problems were *their* problems. I would have filed for divorce the next day had I not gotten a call from the hospital in Kilwin. Apparently when Jenna moved there she changed her emergency contacts to me only. I flew out that night and got a hotel. The next morning I took my bruised and broken sister to the house of her abuser and helped her get everything we could before Ryan got home."

"And what did Ryan do about that?" Declan's voice was angry.

"He had a lawyer, a man who talked really fast and had a lot of expensive suits. He made a deal with Jenna. Ryan would let her keep all of her belongings and have custody of Hartley as long as she kept her mouth shut about the abuse. If not, he'd destroy her during their divorce. Take Hartley and leave her with nothing." Both men growled in displeasure. "She agreed. That's when she came to Overlook. She could afford the move and it was quiet. I stayed in Atlanta to get all of my ducks in a row and came out here once my divorce was finalized."

Riley pointed to the two-way window. Davies continued to stare at his cup, unaware of the emotional roller coaster three people were going through that he had helped cause in the other room.

"Davies tried to get ahold of me several times after that but I changed my number. No one other than my parents even knows I'm living with Jenna. *He* shouldn't be here."

Desmond pushed off the wall. He walked over to Riley and stood so close that their arms touched. He stared through the window with palpable anger.

"Then let's find out why he is," he said. "So we can get him the hell out."

Chapter Eleven

Evan Davies was taller than Desmond. Obviously using the gym on a regular basis, he had a lean but strong build. His Facebook profile picture showed a carefree-looking man too. Messy hair but groomed beard trimmed short, his expression midlaugh and dark eyes with crinkles at the sides.

Engaging.

Harmless.

He could hold his own in a tussle.

That was the impression Desmond would have drawn of the man under different circumstances.

Yet, as it was in Davies's case, looks had most definitely been deceiving.

"I'm not talking without a lawyer."

Davies had been singing that song since Declan walked into the room. Singing it without meeting his gaze once. He paid devout attention to the drink he'd been given and the cuffs holding him to the table. Those lines at the sides of his eyes that were earned by laughter had all smoothed out. That smile from his picture had sunk low. Any power his physique offered had been lost in the curve of his hunched-over stance.

Desmond wasn't a fan.

Every aspect of the tight-lipped man spoke of cowardice and guilt.

At least, that's how Desmond felt as he watched Declan try to get Davies to rescind his request for a lawyer or just give them any clue as to what was going on.

No dice.

He kept his head down and what he knew to himself.

It was infuriating.

It had a mixed effect in the viewing room.

Riley had gone just as tight-lipped. Desmond kept muttering beneath his breath, unable to keep his anger at bay. This man knew and possibly had a hand in what had happened to Marty, a good man who had only been trying to help Desmond. Based on that fact alone, Desmond was upset. Add to it the fact that he was Riley's ex-husband and just so happened to be in the same town where she was currently living?

Was he stalking her?

And, if so, why was he at Second Wind? He couldn't have known they'd show up, right?

It was driving Desmond crazy that he couldn't get any answers.

If not for him, at least for Riley.

Declan gave up after it was clear Davies wasn't going to say a word more. He kept his composure until he was in the viewing room. There he swore before he addressed them.

"I'm sorry I couldn't get anything. Though I'm not surprised after what we now know about him. He's good at keeping his mouth shut." Riley didn't tear her eyes away from the two-way mirror but Desmond watched her expression at Declan's words. Her jaw tightened. "We'll keep working this whole thing to see if we can't find our own bread crumbs that can lead us somewhere that makes sense, but as for that jerk in there? We're waiting out his lawyer who's supposed to be here in the morning."

"What happens until then?" It was the first time Riley had spoken since the big reveal of her past. Desmond couldn't claim to know her as well as the man she so clearly despised in the room across from them but he could tell something was off with her.

Not surprising, considering.

She sounded different.

"He'll go into one of our cells downstairs," Declan answered. "We have enough to hold him for now." Riley nodded, curt. "As for you two, you're free to go. I just need to talk to Des about something really quickly."

"Would it be okay if I wait outside?" she asked, looking up at Desmond. "I could use some air."

"Yeah, sure." He gave his brother a questioning look while passing Riley his keys. "I don't think she needs to be alone right now," he told Declan once Riley was out of earshot.

"I know, but I didn't want to say this in front of her."

Declan moved them to the wall, away from the closest deputy's desk.

"This doesn't leave the room," he prefaced. "You understand?"

It was the sheriff talking.

Desmond nodded.

"Understood."

Declan didn't whisper but he didn't have his normal volume either.

"Brett Calder is dead."

"What?" Desmond felt his eyebrows go sky-high. "How? I thought he was locked up?"

"He was," Declan confirmed. "And that's where he was killed, by an inmate. A fight in the yard is what I've been told. When you called earlier, I was talking to the warden."

"The warden? Of Jones Correctional?" Desmond asked, doing fast math in his head. "Isn't that an hour away?" There was no way Declan had gone out there considering his response time to Desmond's second call from the construction site.

"He came here."

"To tell you Brett Calder was killed," Desmond deadpanned. That didn't seem like normal protocol.

"It wasn't as much that he was killed as who he was killed by and what they found after."

"Okay…"

Declan sighed.

"A man with a scorpion tattoo killed him, and while trying to save him, the doctor on call found the same scorpion tattoo on Brett."

Desmond understood why he was being told the news in private now.

Scorpion tattoos meant…

"Brett was a Fixer?"

Fixer wasn't the official title of the up-and-coming criminal organization that was based out of Kilwin, but it was the easiest description of what the men and women with the scorpion tattoos did. They were contractors, hired by gangs and less-than-desirables to do the too-difficult jobs or the ones that were just too messy to risk. And, when all else failed, they seemed to be the best at fixing whatever their clients had done wrong.

The Nash family knew of their existence thanks to two Fixers who had targeted Madi the year before at the behest of one very angry man.

"My best guess is that he was a new recruit," Declan said. "And not a good one at that. But I do think that the man who killed him was sent into that place to do just that. I think the Fixers took a hit out on him because of how public his attack on Riley was. Not to mention he was caught, not something that group looks kindly upon."

"The man Riley spoke to at the construction site, the one in the nice suit, you think he's one of them?"

The Fixers were also known for their business ensembles. Madi had been attacked by well-dressed men.

"I'm not ruling it out, but Riley saw his face and he let her leave. He also didn't take or destroy her phone after she dropped it." Declan shrugged. "As morbid as it is to say, that concerns me. If he is a Fixer, I don't know what the current job they're running is but it can't be good."

Desmond knew his brother didn't mean he was concerned because Riley was okay. He was concerned because none of their pieces were matching up. They took a moment to scowl at one another, both lost in their own thoughts. Desmond found another question.

"Why did the warden come to you? Couldn't he have just called and told you?"

Declan's expression softened.

"He's an old friend of Dad's. He knew that Brett had pushed the family back into the spotlight and correctly assumed his death would probably do it again, especially with the mention of the Fixers. He wanted to give me a heads-up in person."

Desmond couldn't help but smile a little.

"Dad's been gone for years and still he finds ways to help us out."

Declan didn't smile but he did agree.

The conversation ended with promises to talk more in the morning after Davies's lawyer came in. Declan gave Desmond a quick embrace, no doubt softened by the mention of their father, and disappeared into his office.

The night air hit Desmond's body as he pushed outside into the cold. He was surprised to see Riley leaning against the passenger's-side door instead of sitting inside the truck. He liked walking out into the cold but he didn't know if he would have been lounging in it. Riley turned her head toward him as he moved into the parking lot. She made no move to open the door. Desmond redirected from the driver's side and stopped in front of her.

He could smell lavender. He could also see she was chewing on saying something. Her brow was creased and her eyes had a cut to them. Desmond couldn't tell what emotion she was dancing on.

"You okay?"

Riley nodded. Then she shook her head. Dark, enchanting eyes found his. When she spoke, Desmond felt like it was the only sound for miles.

"I was happy, married and had a plan for the future. Then I blinked. Suddenly I was angry, divorced and just trying to hold on to some semblance of what my normal was. Then I blinked again and I was here, in Overlook. Happier, and then, the moment I started to think about making new plans, I became a victim. Then I was someone who was saved. But, I know I was lucky. It could have been so much worse and I promise I'm not upset about any of that. It was a speed bump on an already bumpy road so it wasn't that big of a deal. But then? I blinked." She shrugged. Her words were raw. "My ex-husband is in there because of God knows what he did. He shouldn't be here. This is my new life. My new normal. He's not supposed to be in that. And, Desmond, he's a smart man. Resourceful and cunning when needed. What was he doing at the construction site? Who was the man in the suit? How am I going to tell Jenna any of this without bringing up all the bad stuff that happened? And did Davies do that to Marty? How was I married to him? What does that say about me?"

Her words had quickened, her chest rising with an emotional cadence. Desmond acted on instinct. Riley's cheek was smooth and cold against the palm of his hand. The space between them all but disappeared. He tilted her head up. Those beautiful eyes were glossed over with pain, fear, confusion.

He knew the group well.

"It says that you're living your life the way it should be lived," he said with a genuine, if not small, smile. "It means you fell in love, you trusted, you took a chance, you survived, and now you have the luxury of questioning what the future may bring. Life was never meant to be easy, just as it is never promised that it would always be hard. We'll figure out what's going on. Together. I promise, okay?"

Riley's voice was soft but she nodded.

"Okay."

"Okay," he repeated.

Desmond dropped his hand, but he didn't step back.

Instead he glanced at the painted red lips of Riley Stone.

He didn't have time for a lot of things, but a kiss? He could make time for that.

However, those same lips he was imaging against his turned up into a smile. She was trying not to laugh. It earned a skeptical grin from him.

"What?"

"I was just thinking, you asked how I was and I didn't really give a solid answer," she said. "What I *should* have said was *hungry*. I'm guessing the Red Oak isn't open after midnight, huh?"

Desmond laughed. He finally put space between them again.

"No, it's definitely closed." He held up his index finger. "But. If you're up for it, I know someone who makes the *best* PB&Js this side of the Mississippi."

Riley's eyebrow arced up, dangerously close to playful. It made Desmond regret their bodies no longer touching. To his surprise she nodded before he explained.

"I'm in."

DECLAN, CALEB AND his wife, Desmond's mother and Desmond all lived full-time on the ranch at the end of Winding

Road. Yet as they had driven down the paved road through the ranch, Riley hadn't been able to tell.

Everything was quiet. Peaceful.

Now, sitting across from Desmond at his dining-room table, that feeling of contentment had come inside with them.

"You weren't kidding about the best peanut-butter-and-jelly sandwiches," she said after finishing hers off. Desmond was working on his second one already. He shrugged.

"What can I say? I am a man of specific talents." He flashed her what Riley could only describe as a "winning" smile. It brightened the man; it brightened the room. It made *her* feel bright.

"You know, you have the strangest way of making me feel better," she blurted out. Instantly she felt heat in her cheeks. She hurried on. "*What I mean* is I get why everyone roots for you. You help people and seem to genuinely enjoy it."

Desmond waved off the compliment.

"I'm only doing what anyone would in my situation."

Riley scoffed.

"You have money, enough I feel like you could do whatever you wanted. Or, at least, very close to it." She motioned to the house around them. "But here you are. Living a stone's throw away from your mom and in a town you could have left and never come back to. What's more, you didn't have to start Second Wind. But you did. You must enjoy the work or just really enjoy the attention."

Desmond's smile faltered.

It softened Riley.

"And I don't think you Nashes have the luxury here to crave any attention," she added on, gentle.

"No, we get that in spades already."

Riley could have turned the conversational tide. She could have complimented his house—modern rustic, white, black, gray and wood and somehow perfect for the cowboy—or asked about the assortment of books she could see, or listened to an urge that had been simmering since he'd noticeably looked down at her lips outside the sheriff's department and fly across the table and rock his world.

Yet, she stayed the course, her curiosity finally too loud to ignore.

"Why *did* you start Second Wind?"

Chapter Twelve

Desmond put his half-eaten sandwich down. Riley worried she'd overstepped but then his expression turned thoughtful. A clock somewhere in the house ticked off a rhythm. The heat had turned on when they'd first stepped through the front door. Both of their jackets were draped over the couch in the living room.

And now Riley was going to learn another answer about the illustrious Desmond Nash.

"When I was a kid I was given the unique perspective of living through a trauma," he started. "To say it changed me is an understatement. It changed all of us Nashes. Even the town." Riley tried to keep her face impassive but Desmond gave her a knowing look. "I'm assuming you've heard about the real reason everyone knows the Nash name around Overlook?"

"I read about it during the coverage after what happened the night of the gala," she admitted.

Desmond didn't seem at all bothered, or surprised, but Riley still felt shame heating her cheeks.

"The Nash triplet abduction carries a fame all its own around here. The greatest unsolved mystery in Overlook. The tragedy that shook a community to its core. The family who was forever broken when three eight-year-olds sneaked out to the park alone. I've seen and heard several versions of the story, but there's a few things the papers and gossip mill never got quite right." He smiled but it disappeared quickly. "Madi's scream when the man grabbed her with a gun in his hand is the worst sound I've heard to this day. Sometimes I still hear it when my dreams get bad. Caleb once said it was like the trees came alive long enough to scream with her. It's a sound that will always, always haunt us."

Riley wanted to reach out but held off. Desmond was ramping up to a point. She just needed to hang on for the ride and listen.

"They also usually mess up the next part. At least, I've heard several versions of what happened," he continued. "What *really* happened was Madi fought back against the man. She took her tiny fist and hit his throat as hard as she could. Honestly, if she had been older, *bigger*, I think the move would have helped us. But, we were only eight so it just ticked him off. He pistol-whipped Madi, knocked her out cold and then he shot at Caleb and me. The bullet hit Caleb's arm." Riley gasped. That hadn't been in the paper. Desmond touched his biceps. "It was just a graze but at the time all I saw was blood. So much of it. I just—" Up until then his voice had been consistent. He was telling a story in a concise and even way. Now, though, there was an invisible ripple that seemed to move across him.

Tension hardened his shoulders. His jaw tightened. His nostrils flared. He took the smallest of moments to, well, she didn't know what. But Riley let him be. She had already pushed as much as she was going to push.

When Desmond was ready again there was no denying the anger in his words. Deep, boundless anger.

"I lost it. Every part of me snapped. My family was in trouble. I *had* to help. Or at least try." He shifted his leg under the table. The one with the limp. "We jumped on the man's back but it wasn't enough to do much damage. He threw me to the ground and stomped on my leg until it nearly shattered. After that, Caleb was the only one left standing. He made a decision. He wouldn't escape, he wouldn't fight. He'd instead do as the man said to stay with Madi and me. So, that's how we ended up in the basement of Well Water Cabin."

The name bothered him.

It bothered *her* and she wasn't even a part of it.

"The man kept us in the basement apartment for three days. He brought us food, only spoke to threaten us and then disappeared."

"Your leg was broken," Riley had to reiterate. "Did that bother him?"

Desmond shook his head. She could tell he was caught in the memory.

"He didn't seem bothered by any of it, but, then we initiated our plan and he seemed to care about that."

Riley couldn't help but lean a little closer. Her heart hurt for the then children. For that to happen to anyone was terrifying but to be young children too? Riley wouldn't wish that on anyone.

"I was really sick by the third day. We all knew I needed help. And soon. We had to do something or we ran the very real risk of me dying there. So we decided to pretend like I'd stopped breathing since I already looked like death as it was. Caleb and Madi cried and screamed and, I think, forgot that it wasn't actually true. That I was alive. Regardless it was convincing. The man came in, bent over me to check my pulse, and then the triplet power kicked in."

On that he gave a small smile.

"Triplet power?" she had to ask.

"It's what Declan called it. Basically everything after that became a blur for us. We acted as a unit, as a team. We weren't three kids anymore, we were a hive mind. We overpowered the man, managed to lock the door behind us and escaped into the woods and found help. I went to the hospital and Caleb showed everyone where we had been held."

"And no one found the man."

"And no one found the man," he repeated. "And no one found out why he'd done it in the first place or what the endgame had been. My father, a detective at the time, tried. He ran that case into the ground for years. His determination became an obsession. One that built up years and years of stress until it finally made his heart give out."

Riley shook her head, sorrow ringing through her for the man sitting across the table and all that he'd endured.

Desmond surprised her with a chuckle.

"So I guess my answer to your original question of why I started Second Wind is less lengthy." The strain of the story started to fall away. He relaxed into his chair again. "We survived what happened but I realized that was only one part of the battle. To find life again, to *live* life again, was in some ways harder. After I got lucky from investments I'd made during college, I opened a series of nonprofits but realized as well-intentioned as I was, hiring experts and others who had the degrees and training to help was more in my wheelhouse. That's when I had the idea to start a foundation that sought out nonprofits and groups who work with helping people who have lived through trauma and tragedy find new life again. A place that could help others *help others*."

"To find their second wind," Riley realized.

Desmond nodded.

"Not the most clever of names but I'm proud of it."

He was back. Back to the present. Back to a smile. His story was over.

"You *should* be proud," Riley said. She meant it.

Desmond finished off his sandwich and took both of their plates to the kitchen. Riley stood and stretched. She was tired, she knew that, but also there was a restlessness there. One that made the thought of going home leave a bad taste in her mouth.

Maybe it was all the adrenaline that had coursed through her earlier that night, the fear and anguish at what had happened to Marty. Maybe it was the sudden reappearance of Davies and the worry that he'd come to town for her. Maybe it was the memory of kissing Desmond, a knee-jerk reaction that was, admittedly, leaving a long-lasting impression.

Did Riley want to do it again? Now that Davies was back, heralding in every memory of the bad that had happened in the last year, was there any room left in her to want that?

Riley felt her cheeks heat and was aware of a pulse of longing below her waistline, letting her head know that her body certainly wanted to be closer to Desmond.

She spun around on her heel, worried he'd see the no doubt glaring blush against her pale skin, and walked across the hardwood floor to the living room. The house around them was a large two-story but the living area was much more cozy. A deep-cushioned couch sat opposite a flat-screen TV while a bookcase took up most of the wall between the two. Knickknacks, picture frames and other pieces of decor were dispersed among the books, making the room feel even more like a home.

Riley ran her finger across one of the shelves as she danced her gaze between the pictures.

Almost every picture Desmond was in, there was at least one sibling with him. High school and college graduations, birthdays with three kids around one cake, Declan being sworn in as sheriff, a few candids from the dance floor of what looked like two different weddings, a worn picture of Dorothy and Michael Nash smiling and hugging and a group picture of the Nash siblings and their significant others. Riley got hung up on that one a little longer than the rest. Desmond and Declan had no one by their sides.

The last picture was of just Desmond. He was on a beautiful white-and-brown-patched horse, his black Stetson perched atop his head and a wry grin across his lips.

"Winona." Riley jumped; Desmond laughed. "Sorry, I thought you heard me," he said, moving level with her. He motioned to the picture. "That's my horse Winona. I think if you looked up the word *wild* in the dictionary there would be a picture of her there staring at you."

Riley snorted.

"I'd bet Hartley sans a nap would be there too," she added in. "I've found that a sleepy nephew is a terrifying nephew." At that Riley checked the time on her phone. It was almost one in the morning. She'd already updated Jenna about what had happened after giving her official statement at the sheriff's department. She'd also texted Jenna that she was headed to Desmond's house. That text had been met with a series of large-eyes emojis and the teasing reminder to use protection.

There was no way Riley could sneak in without waking both the grumpy beast and the woman who had created him.

Riley shared a look with the man next to her.

This time it was her who was guilty of looking at his lips. She sighed.

"How competitive are you?"

The question caught Riley completely off guard. And that was saying something considering their night.

"Excuse me?"

Desmond swept his arm toward the TV.

"Ma preaches stress-free living but when it comes to *Wheel of Fortune*, not only does she force me to DVR it, she challenges me to solve the puzzle before her." His eyebrow raised, completely playful. "Want to go a round before I take you home?"

Riley didn't think twice.

"Only if you don't mind losing."

DESMOND OPENED HIS eyes slowly.

Something was wrong. He wasn't where he was supposed to be.

The world didn't look the same as it had during the night.

He blinked, confused.

Then he saw white shiplap.

It was his ceiling. He knew because that shiplap had been a big deal to his sister and Mom. They'd seen it on a show and thought it was trendy. He'd caved and, though he'd never admit it to them, enjoyed the look.

But he couldn't piece together why he was seeing it.

Then he saw red.

That's when the haze of sleep lifted.

He was in the living room, on the couch, lying on his back, and he wasn't alone.

Riley was tucked into his side, head on his shoulder and an arm and a leg draped over him. He tilted his chin down to get a better look at their situation. She wasn't just on him; he had his arm around her too. Holding her.

In their sleep.

Desmond replayed the last waking memory he had.

They had watched an episode of *Wheel of Fortune* and made it a competitive affair. Riley had solved two of the four phrases and was raring to beat his two wins during the next episode. Yet, as the commercial break came on, she had quieted. By the time Pat was introducing the contestants she had nodded off against him.

Desmond had fully intended on waking her and taking her home, but looking down at her face, lax in sleep, something in him had softened. Riley had been through a lot just in the last twenty-four hours. He could let her sleep for a few minutes.

So, he'd grabbed the throw blanket next to him, put it around her and tried to guess the Thing or Place that had three *G*s but no *A*s.

Apparently, past that, things hadn't gone according to plan.

The TV had turned itself off because of the lack of activity for, he assumed, hours and the living room was bathed in light from the front windows behind the couch.

Desmond sat still for a moment, perplexed.

Before the night of the gala he didn't have time for distractions. After the run through the woods? He still didn't have the time for distractions.

But now?

The distraction against him was warm and smelled like lavender.

Riley Stone had the intelligence and courage to think on her feet and act with compassion.

Desmond had had his fair share of dates and relationships before he'd come back to Overlook full-time. He'd been attracted to women of all shapes and sizes. Yet, there was something all of them had been missing. Something he couldn't quite put into words.

Lying there, beneath the shiplap, in the sunlight, and with a mass of dark red curls against his chest, Desmond couldn't help but think Riley Stone might just have that *something* he'd been looking for.

He smiled, weirdly calm about the idea, when the woman in question started to stir. Desmond froze but Riley kept moving. Her body shifted farther on top of him. He couldn't stop a grunt at the new position.

The noise must have gotten through to her.

It was Riley's turn to freeze in place.

For a moment no one moved.

Then the red curls shifted. Desmond met a dark, widened gaze with a hopefully impassive expression.

Riley was less quiet about their predicament.

"Oh my God."

Desmond groaned again as Riley did her best impression of an acrobat. She tried to jump off him but went into a sort of roll. Desmond, imaging the coffee table not too far from the couch, scrambled to stop her.

In the end all their actions did was land them both on the floor.

This time it was Desmond on top. He moved his knees on either side of her body to keep his weight off and sat up on his elbows.

Riley, face as red as a cherry, stared up at him without saying a word.

Desmond couldn't help it.

He grinned.

Then, to his undeniable pleasure, Riley burst into laughter.

"JENNA IS NEVER going to believe me," Riley said after she could breathe again.

Desmond grinned. His eyebrow raised so slow it was absolutely devilish. In the daylight he was less of the closed-up businessman and reminded her more of a mischievous teenager. Or maybe that was Riley putting a sneaking-around, trying-not-to-get-caught-by-their-parents vibe to their current situation.

Desmond Nash was literally on top of her.

And she'd be remiss if she didn't acknowledge that she didn't hate it.

"What wouldn't she believe?" His voice didn't help matters. The smooth baritone had become husky.

It was all Riley could do to keep her own from quavering.

"That we fell asleep on the couch watching *Wheel of Fortune*," she said with another bite of laughter. "It sounds like a lie waiting to happen."

Desmond chuckled. Riley felt it against her entire body.

"Or sounds like a pretty poor way to woo a woman."

Riley shrugged against the rug. Her mortification at

waking up on top of the cowboy had turned into fast laughter. Now that urge transformed into a smile and a tease.

"Hey, it *did* get me to sleep with you, didn't it?"

Riley was pretty sure she could heat an entire hot tub with the blush scorching her body, but at the same time, she was leaning into the awkward.

Yet, her little joke didn't seem to land. In fact, the cowboy's expression had gone in the opposite direction of humor. His brow creased, those light blue eyes homed in and his smile vanished.

Then it was like a switch flipped.

The heat of embarrassment was gone. In its place was a different heat. One that she hadn't felt in a long time, marriage included if she was being completely honest.

The kind of heat that made your entire body stand at attention. The kind of heat that made you acutely aware of every breath you took, how high your chest rose along with it and how your body had already made up its mind about what it wanted to do next.

When Desmond's eyes trailed down to her lips, Riley had already been prepared for his kiss for what felt like an eternity.

Chapter Thirteen

If looking at the cowboy was a stimulating event, kissing him was nearly downright debilitating.

Riley had no room between Desmond and the floor to sigh in relief at finally being kissed by him. But she did have the space to moan against his lips as his tongue parted hers.

In the back of her head Riley couldn't help but blanch at the fact that it was morning and she'd just woken up which meant her breath probably wasn't the best. She wasn't charmed out of the realization that Desmond also probably needed a stick of gum or a swig of mouthwash.

Yet, as their kiss deepened, Riley couldn't fault a thing.

She wound her arms around his neck and held on as he maneuvered for a better position. Dropping down onto one elbow, Desmond angled his body so he was on his side and she was pressed against him. It gave her more room to move.

When he grabbed her hip, she pushed toward him.

When that hand went up the back of her shirt, she moved hers to the hem of his.

When his bare skin slid between her shoulder blades, trailing heat and a wonderful tingling sensation, she tugged the man's shirt up to let him know that she wanted more. For both of them.

Desmond broke the kiss but only to listen to her un-asked request. He performed nothing short of a miracle by unbuttoning his shirt one-handed and with speedy precision. Riley started to pull her own shirt up, ready to throw it into oblivion, when a sound that didn't match the mood rocketed through the house around them.

It was the doorbell.

Both of them froze.

Riley took the tiniest of moments to note that Desmond wasn't wearing an undershirt. His button up was opened to reveal the muscled body of a man who might have been strolling through the business world the last several years but was also an active, active man.

Riley was still holding on to the hope that whoever was at the front door would leave before another ring so she could learn the feel of that body when another sound dashed any and all hopes of the show continuing.

It was a laugh.

A very specific laugh.

A *Jenna* laugh.

"Oh my gosh, I think that's my sister," Riley whispered. "How did she even know where to find me? She hasn't been here before."

Desmond, who up until that point had been a cool cucumber, lost his chilled composure.

The doorbell rang again.

He swore.

"Ten bucks she's with my mother."

Riley could have medaled at how quickly she went from pressed against a good-looking man to army crawling to the hallway, out of view from the living-room windows and the front door. She didn't know how Desmond and his opened shirt reacted—it was every man and woman for themselves in her opinion—but the moment she was out of sight, Riley popped up and started smoothing her blouse.

There was no hope for her hair, and she knew that, but she ran her hand across her face like it would wipe away any evidence that she'd just woken up and also just done a whole lot of making out.

"Hey," Desmond whispered. He moved to her side with speed and pulled her through the other entry into the kitchen. "The longer we don't answer, the worse it's going to be."

Riley eyed him up and down and gave a nervous snort.

"Your buttons are messed up on your shirt," she pointed out. "And your lips are as red as red can be."

Desmond turned a critical eye down to his shirt. He attempted to rebutton it with a glance her way. The corner of his lips quirked up.

"Speaking of really red lips."

Riley groaned as the doorbell was replaced by a series of knocks.

"We're busted." There was humor in his defeat but Riley was stubborn. She followed him to the front door, ready to try to test her twin trickery. That thought went straight into the trash the moment Desmond opened the door wide.

Jenna was indeed on the front porch and she wasn't alone. Hartley was on her hip and a woman Riley only recognized from the media was at her side. Jenna's eyes went wide as she took the two of them in. A smile she was losing the struggle to hide split her face. The older woman next to her was a bit more gracious with hers. It was small but definitely there.

"Hey, Ma," Desmond greeted. "What can I do you for?"

Riley felt the flames of embarrassment kick right back up. She was pretty sure she'd done more blushing in one morning than she had in all of her years of life.

Dorothy Nash was in a set of floral-print overalls, work boots, and was sporting a tight braid draped over her shoulder. She looked like she belonged in a gardening edition of *Southern Living* magazine. Friendly, approachable and warm. Yet when she spoke there was nothing but a clever bite to her words.

It was instantly endearing to Riley. Even if it added to the lava-level blush.

"Well, *son*, a few of us have been trying to get ahold of you two and haven't had any luck. So when this wonderful young woman and her strapping young son turned up just after nine, I thought it was a great idea to come and make sure you two were okay. Maybe just interrupt a breakfast y'all forgot to tell anyone about." Her eyes shifted down. Riley followed them and almost died on the spot. Desmond had completely skipped a button on his shirt. "Clearly y'all just lost track of time and forgot to check in."

"We were watching *Wheel of Fortune* and fell asleep," Riley blurted out.

Jenna finally lost it.

"Is that what they're calling it these days?" she teased around her laughter.

"Jenna Mae," Riley screeched, now one hundred percent certain she was about to melt away.

"Riley Lee," she yelled back.

Dorothy chuckled. Desmond sighed. Riley was already moving toward the car.

"You know, I think it's time we leave. So sorry for the—the inconvenience," she said to Dorothy. "Honestly, it was just a little oversight. We'll just go ahead and get out of your hair now." Jenna could *not* stop laughing. Riley couldn't wait to go home and give her a piece of her mind.

"Hey, wait!"

Both women stopped in their tracks. Desmond disappeared into the house only to reappear a few seconds later with Riley's purse and jacket.

"Wow, it was so good you were just going to leave all

of your things," Jenna whispered at her ear. Riley swatted at her.

Desmond wasn't smirking when he walked the distance she had managed to create between them and the front porch but he wasn't frowning either. He seemed amused.

Which somehow made everything worse.

"Yeah, uh, I guess I might need these," Riley said with a laugh that wasn't helping. "Thank you. And thank you for the sandwiches."

Desmond nodded.

"My pleasure."

Jenna made a noise but Riley wasn't having it. She smiled at Hartley, the only innocent one out of them, and took Jenna's elbow.

"Ms. Stone?"

Both Riley and Jenna turned again. This time it was the Nash matriarch who had spoken. She addressed Riley as she continued.

"Tonight is our weekly family dinner. I sure would love it if you three could come." She smiled. The skin next to her eyes crinkled. "It's been a while since we've had new faces around the table."

Riley started to cycle through a few reasons why she didn't want to accept—mostly it was just embarrassment at being caught like a couple of guilty teens—but, once again, Jenna took action.

"We'd *love* to," she called back. "Just tell us a time and we'll be here with bells on!"

Riley found Desmond's gaze. He sighed and rubbed the back of his neck, now annoyed. She worried that her sister had done that, but just as quickly as he looked ready to roll his eyes, he was smirking again.

Riley focused on those lips.

The ones she'd just gotten *very* well acquainted with.

The same set that she couldn't help but hope to touch again.

"Five-thirty. Five if you'd like to see this one here take a ride on his horse."

"Mom," Desmond complained.

She ignored it.

"That sounds *perfect*," Jenna said. "See you then!"

Riley finally got her escape. It wasn't until they were in the car and pointed toward Winding Road that she warned her sister.

"Not a word, Jenna. I mean it."

Jenna, of course, didn't listen.

"This isn't ideal."

It was nearing four in the afternoon and Desmond was about to point out to Caleb that what he'd just said was one hell of an understatement.

What wasn't *ideal* was having your mother show up on your front porch and effectively catching you in the act of getting *close* with someone.

What wasn't *ideal* was having that same mother bebop around your house, peppering you with questions about your intentions, your *feelings* and your future goals in relation to the young woman you so obviously spent that close time with.

What wasn't *ideal* was, after finally getting your nosy mother out of your hair, starting to ask yourself all of those things only to be interrupted by news that was so far from ideal it was laughable.

"Evan Davies being let go less than twenty-four hours after he was arrested is a travesty of justice," Desmond decided. "Way worse than not ideal."

Caleb let out a long breath. He nodded.

"Hey, I'm not thrilled about it either but the department's hands are tied. That lawyer of his was no joke. Once Marty came to and said it was the man in the suit who knocked him out and he hadn't even seen Davies, there wasn't much we could do."

They were standing in the stable between both of their horses. Winona was ready to go on their daily ride while Ax, Caleb's overo, was tired after returning from his. Both men were out of their work clothes and in outfits they'd probably wear every day for the rest of their natural lives. Button-down flannels, Levi's jeans, boots and their Stetsons. There wasn't a stitch of clothes that they were more comfortable in than what was worn as they'd grown up, working the ranch.

"His story made no sense." Desmond thought that was worth repeating. "He came to town to check on Riley after seeing her in the paper. Then just happened to be riding past Second Wind when he saw Marty being jumped? Then when we show up he throws himself from the second story to avoid us?" Desmond growled. "He's lying."

Caleb shrugged.

"I know but that doesn't change what happened. Being weird isn't a crime and we can't prove he did anything other than that."

Desmond felt the urge to cuss someone. Seeing as he was surrounded by horses and his brother, he squashed the urge.

"Listen, we didn't just send him on his merry way," Caleb added. "Declan did his terrifying sheriff voice with a warning that it might be better if Davies just left Overlook. He might have been lying about why he was at Second Wind but you could see clear in his eyes he was going to heed Declan's words."

That didn't make the knot in Desmond's stomach unclench. It also didn't erase the worry that he knew without even hearing her that had been in Riley's tone when Caleb had passed along the information that Davies was free.

Desmond wasn't surprised when Caleb picked up on his thoughts.

"Jazz and her husband followed Davies to the town line without him even knowing. He's gone and do you know who should be here soon?" Caleb reverted to a grin. He answered his own question. "The very same lady you tried to woo with *Wheel of Fortune* and PB&Js."

The serious part of the conversation turned to siblings jabbing at one another. Just as the Stone sisters had on his front porch earlier that day. It was nice to see that the pain of having siblings wasn't a Nash-family-only event.

Caleb left to shower and Desmond took Winona out into the field. Before the abduction he hadn't been a tried-and-true lover of riding like Caleb and Declan. His father had always tried to get him more enthused about it but the words always fell flat. It was like Michael Nash was trying to put an ethereal feeling into mere words. The sentiment never moved Desmond.

Then he'd had surgery on his leg. Worries of partially being paralyzed became worries of permanent nerve damage which in turn became concern that walking would never be the same for him.

Desmond remembered the suffocating feeling of being surrounded by questions, fears and worry. It had sent him on crutches out to the same field. There his father had found him. Unlike his mother, the Nash family patriarch was all blunt, all the time.

He had pointed toward the horses and then laid a heavy truth on his young son's shoulders.

"There's a chance your leg may never be the way it used to be, son. But, that doesn't mean there's not an entire world out there that you can't enjoy," he'd said. "There's never enough time to do every single thing you want to but there's *always* time to do at least one thing. You just need to make that one thing count."

The last part was Michael Nash's mantra. One that he'd told his children countless times. Desmond and Madi had never put much stock in the saying like Caleb had—to them it had just been another memory of their father they repeated to feel close—but in the last few years things had started to change for them.

There was a beauty to their father's words. One that, spoken to him in that moment when he was nine, Desmond now felt deeply as an adult.

"If you can't walk the way you want, then do something else you can," his father had continued, looking out at the horses. "And do it with everything you've got."

That's how Desmond had channeled his frustrations and fears. He'd found an outlet and newfound love for riding. Even now, what felt like a lifetime later, feeling the power of a horse beneath him, feeling the rhythm of hooves against the earth and feeling the rush of wind was second to none.

It always started the same. He was a kid again, running to reclaim a life that had almost been taken. A teen, worried about his father's obsession with their unsolved case. A young adult, mourning his father's death and scared for what it would do to the rest of the family. An adult, trying to help other families from drowning in the wake of tragedy and trauma.

Then, all at once, he was just a kid laughing in the wind. A teen who marveled at how fast he could go. A young adult who felt invincible. An adult who wished the feeling would never end.

And, sometimes, Desmond's mind relaxed enough that he could look back at that same fence he'd stood at when he was nine and see his father.

Smiling because his son finally understood.

Chapter Fourteen

Hartley was in a walking mood.

No sooner had Riley gotten him out of his car seat was he marching toward Mimi's Boutique with a purpose. Riley couldn't help but laugh as she locked the car and hurried to take his hand.

A woman was laughing too when they walked through the front door, setting off the bell over it.

"He must know what he wants," she exclaimed, looking at the one-man marching band with red curls galore.

Riley shrugged.

"I guess so! Usually he's not the best at shopping but today I guess is a good day."

The woman, a few years older and with a few more laugh lines than Riley, stayed behind the counter but motioned to the store.

"And what about his mama? Does she know what she's looking for?"

Hartley made a beeline for the first rack of clothes. Mimi's Boutique, by its name alone, seemed to be just for clothing but Jenna had assured her it was a one-stop shop for a variety of things.

Like fancy tins to put freshly baked chocolate-chip cookies in.

"Actually, his mama has a migraine so I volunteered to

be on aunt duty," Riley felt the need to correct. "But this aunt is wondering where your festive but not-too-festive dessert tins are?"

The woman, who Riley knew wasn't Mimi, placed a bookmark in her current read and came around the counter with the same purpose Hartley was using to browse.

"We have just the thing."

Minutes later, and a quick introduction that led into a chat about the best recipe for rocky-road brownies, and Riley was staring down at a circular tin with a horse-ranch theme to it. A little on the nose but Riley saw it as cute. She just hoped Dorothy Nash wasn't tired of the ranch theme.

"Have fun," the woman, named Patricia, called. "See you later, handsome man!"

Both women laughed as Hartley responded with an excited, "Bye!"

"You're a rock star in your own right, did you know that?" Riley asked him as she went back to the task of buckling him into the car seat.

"I'm a stud," he exclaimed.

That got Riley really giggling.

So much so she didn't hear the man approach her from behind. Yet when she was done and had turned around, there was no way to avoid him.

"Davies."

The first time Riley had met her ex-husband it had been a nice hot summer day. They were at a pool party and boy, had Davies been a sight. Easy on the eyes, quick with a smile and funny. He was sure of himself and confidence in Riley's peers at that age was a rare thing right out of college. It, more so than any of his other traits, drew her to him like a moth to a flame.

He knew what he wanted.

He went for it.

When it didn't happen, he readjusted.

Then went after it again.

There was a poetry to it. An infectious quality. One that had wrapped around her the more time she had spent with him.

Now?

Riley was standing in front of a man she didn't recognize.

He wore a suit, one she'd bought him as a gift for his first big promotion. At the time it had gone hand in hand with his confidence and determination. Now it looked like he'd stolen it from his father in an attempt to seem like an adult. Or, maybe, it was just him. There was a shiftiness to Davies and he looked like sleep had been eluding him for some time.

He was a ghost of his former self and it was taking all Riley could do in that moment not to feel grief over the loss.

Evan Davies had once been a man of potential. Now he was just a man wasting away in a suit.

"Where is she?" he started, no segue or greeting.

"What?"

He lowered his voice. It, like his demeanor, was panicky. "Where is she?"

Riley shook her head. Was he really still trying to find *her* by pestering who he thought was Jenna?

She couldn't believe it.

The nerve.

"I'm not telling you anything other than to leave this town." She angled her body so she was blocking Hartley from view. Her shoulders were squared, anger tensing her muscles.

Davies glanced toward the door of the boutique. Patricia was standing in front of the window staring.

He shifted his eyes back to Riley before averting them.

"There's a lot going on you don't understand," he said, still basically whispering. "It all— It all just keeps happening and I—" He swore. Riley wasn't afraid of Davies. Not when she knew what a coward he really was. Yet, her heartbeat did pick up speed as obvious anger washed over the man. "I'm just trying to do something right. That's—"

The bell over the door to Mimi's Boutique sounded.

"You alright?" Patricia called.

Davies's anger washed away as fast as it had come on.

"I'm sorry," he said. Then he was walking across the street.

Riley turned to Patricia. She had her phone in hand.

"You alright?" she repeated.

Riley heard the sound of a car door shut and the engine come on.

"I am now."

SOME OF THE NASH family were already at the main house when Riley pulled up. She was disappointed that Desmond wasn't among them but she did catch Declan.

"I don't think anything else will come of this but I decided I still needed to give you a heads-up, just in case," she prefaced then she told him about her run-in with Davies. He was less than pleased. Then he went and made some phone calls.

Riley felt bad for putting a scowl on his face.

Dorothy and Madi were in the second wave of Nash family that Riley spoke with. Dorothy was thrilled about the cookies and the tin, while Madi was excited to see Hartley again.

"Addison is inside playing. Maybe we can go in there too?"

It was a cool day but not downright cold. Riley wore a dark blue dress with her suede ankle boots, trying to show off clothing she'd gotten several compliments on before and shoes that made her the perfect height to kiss.

Not that she expected to be doing that but she *did* have

to admit that she'd thought of no one other than a certain cowboy as she was getting ready.

"That sounds like fun! Right?"

Hartley nodded. "Yeah!"

The boy was what Jenna referred to as a true empath. If you were excited, he was excited. If you were sad, he was sad. If you wanted a cookie, he wanted a cookie.

Though Riley wasn't convinced that wasn't just a toddler thing.

The main house was a beautiful construction. Newer than Riley had expected. It was filled with warmth, brightness and walls covered in framed pictures of the family.

"I'm sorry Jenna isn't feeling well," Dorothy said after Hartley had settled into a playpen filled with toys. "She seemed so excited to see the horses."

Riley gave the woman a wry grin.

"Yes. It was the horses she was excited to see."

They shared a look. Dorothy suppressed a laugh. They both knew it was the cowboy Jenna had been ready to drool over while simultaneously slapping Riley in the shoulder with choruses of *You made out with that* and *Do you think he'd take his shirt off if we asked?*

For that reason alone Riley had decided to come to the ranch a little after five. She didn't want to be awkward standing and staring at the fence line waiting for a glimpse of what she could only assume was one heck of a good sight.

Instead of gawking, Riley spent the next few minutes talking to Dorothy and Madi about Hidden Hills, the bed-and-breakfast Madi and Julian ran. Riley found a comfortable groove with the women, despite not knowing them well. There was an ease about them. No pressure to impress, just a cruising conversation you could either ride or watch.

However, neither woman said when Desmond was coming and Riley was getting close to asking when the front door opened and the man himself walked on through.

His hair was wet, his jeans looked painted on and his baby blues went right to her. Riley felt heat move across her body. Very awkward considering her current company.

"Hey! Look!" Hartley grabbed Desmond's attention before he could make it to their group. The boy had his Mr. Puppy, a Great Dane with a cowboy hat sewn between his ears, in his hand. Desmond stopped to inspect it. Then he was talking to the boy with such rapt attention, Riley felt her hormones rise in answer.

"Des is good with kids," Madi said at her side. "Just so you know."

Riley averted her gaze with a smile and tried to get back into the conversation, proving she could concentrate on something other than the man, but failed immediately. She couldn't help but keep an eye on the two as Desmond spent a little time playing with Hartley.

A disappointing thought moved across her chest.

What if Desmond thought she was Jenna?

Geordi had, Davies had, and who was to say he hadn't just gotten lucky that day at the park?

She couldn't blame him if so. Riley and Jenna refused to compromise on the looks they liked just because others confused the two of them. Which meant their hair was nearly the same length and, thanks to a matching metabolism and exercise routine, so was their weight. Their fashion sense went along with it and even their attempts at cat-eye eyeliner were similarly disastrous.

She took a small breath as Hartley lost interest and Desmond finally turned back to her.

He smiled.

Desmond had every right to mistake her for Jenna.

But Riley hoped he wouldn't.

"Where's Jenna?" Desmond greeted, scoping out his family's home but coming up short. Declan was outside on the phone and Caleb and Nina hadn't shown up yet. Maybe she was in the back at the grill with Julian.

Riley stepped away from her conversation with Madi and their mom and let out a noticeable exhale. Her cheeks were flushed. He was about to ask what was wrong when she smiled and answered.

"She was 'taken by a migraine that wouldn't die even with medicine.' That's a direct quote. She fought me on bringing Hartley because she didn't want to inconvenience us but I thought it might be nice to give her a break. Not that I mind hanging out with Hartley."

"I'm sorry about Jenna but I can assure you the kiddo isn't a big deal. Before I created the foundation and was more hands-on with nonprofits I spent a lot of time around kids." He laughed and hoped what he said next wouldn't be construed as weird. "I actually really love kids. I've always wanted a big family one day." Then without a thought left in his head he asked, "What about you? You want any kids?"

Desmond could have sworn it got so quiet in that house that you could hear a pin drop.

Riley's cheeks turned flame red just as Madi and his mother turned to stare at him behind her back. Madi's eyes were as large as saucers. Her smile indicated she was damn near close to laughing.

Once again, Desmond was immensely grateful that his brothers weren't inside yet. First his lame *Wheel of Fortune* idea and now he was only upping his smooth game by asking if the woman he'd made out with that morning wanted a bunch of kids like he did.

And he'd pushed one heck of a spotlight on Riley to boot.

"What I *meant* to say was," he hurriedly tacked on, trying to salvage his foot-in-mouth moment, "do large families bother you? Because, if so, you're about to be really bothered."

The gods took pity on Desmond because, less than a second later, the front door flew open and in walked Caleb and his wife.

"Your favorite child is here, Ma," he yelled in greeting.

His wife, Nina, laughed behind him and pushed him into the house so Declan and she could get through.

Declan rolled his eyes.

"Being the loudest one doesn't a favorite child make," he pointed out.

Then Madi's mountain of a man brought up the rear, shutting the door behind him with a thoughtful look.

"Well, I'm the favorite son-in-law and I think that's pretty cool," he said.

"You've got that right," their mother piped in.

"You're her *only* son-in-law," Madi said. Their mother pushed past her and Desmond and Riley. She patted Julian's stomach.

"It's called son-in-love and he'll always be number one in my book."

"You're only feeding his ego, Ma," Madi said around a snort of laughter.

"Keep giving me grandbabies and I'll feed him whatever he wants," she responded.

That got everyone laughing. Even Riley. The blush from her cheeks had gone away.

"I don't mind this in the least."

THE FAMILY ONLY became more chaotic as they settled around the outdoor dining table on the back porch. The weather was still good enough that the chill was more pleasant than annoying. Riley sat between Desmond and Madi while Hartley floated between Riley's lap and his. Desmond was glad that Hartley seemed to have become taken with him.

Desmond wanted to spend more time with the boy's aunt and had a feeling that included him and Jenna.

A thought that surprised Desmond throughout the dinner.

It wasn't until Madi, Julian and Addison left and then his mother went inside to take a phone call that the conversation took a turn that led him away from any intriguing thoughts of the future.

"I have to say, Riley, I really am sorry about earlier," Declan dove in. His brow was creased and he looked every bit as sorry as Desmond had seen him.

"It's not your fault," she said.

"What's not your fault?" Desmond asked.

Declan shared a look with Riley.

What had he missed?

"I stopped by Mimi's Boutique on the way over here and Davies showed up." Desmond felt his blood pressure skyrocket. Riley touched the top of his hand. "He didn't do anything. Just said a few words and then left. He thought I was Jenna so he didn't stick around and bother me. I told Declan when I got here though, just so law enforcement knew he came back."

Desmond gave his older brother a look. Declan sighed.

"Jazz saw him leave but it wasn't like we were going to ask her to camp out there all day and night. He must've just driven back on in later when she was gone."

"He shouldn't be just coming back on in," Desmond said with heat in his words, even to his own ears.

"If he does it again I can take him in on harassment," he said to both of them. "If I grabbed him now his lawyer and that weird hair of hers would just do their dance again."

"Weird hair?" Riley asked.

Declan nodded.

"It was what I think is called platinum blond, but, good

golly, it was so bright I could barely think when I first saw her."

"It's probably a distraction tactic," Caleb offered.

Declan shrugged.

"Whatever it is, it's attached to a woman who's very well connected and very *well funded* by the looks of the designer tags on everything she was wearing. I had to snap at a few of my deputies who were caught staring at her too long. You'd think they'd never seen a nice-looking lawyer the way they were gawking."

"Was she young?"

The question made sense but the tone in which Riley asked it didn't. Desmond faced her, knowing full well that the crinkle of concentration between his eyebrows that Madi always picked at him about was there.

Something was off with the siren sitting at his shoulder.

"Uh, yeah." Declan heard it too. His eyebrow rose high. "I'd say maybe midtwenties, which is why I assumed she was well connected, with how easily she got him out."

Every part of Riley had gone rigid.

Even Hartley sitting on her lap looked up at her face to try to puzzle out why the change had happened.

"What was the lawyer's name?"

Declan didn't have to think long.

"Maria Wendell."

Riley pushed her chair back but didn't stand. In turn all of the Nash men went on alert.

"Where is she?" Riley said. "That's what Davies kept asking."

Two large, dark and deeply worried eyes found Desmond's.

"What if Brett's attack wasn't just one of opportunity? What if he really did pick me on purpose? Or, really, Jenna," she continued. "She was supposed to be at the gala, not me. Geordi thought *I* was Jenna when we were at the park.

And Davies has always been so bad at telling us apart, I just assumed since he saw Hartley he thought he was talking *to* Jenna today… But I think he actually knew who he was talking to."

Desmond's gut started yelling.

"He was asking where Jenna was," Desmond supplied.

Riley turned her gaze to Declan.

"The last time I saw Maria Wendell was at Macklin Tech right before I left the company," she continued. "Jenna and I have suspected since then that she was having an affair with Ryan." Riley shook her head, a more palpable look passing over her expression.

Terror.

"The man in the suit at Second Wind called you Ms. Stone, not Riley," Declan added.

"Oh, God," Riley said in an almost whisper. She was back looking at Desmond.

His adrenaline shot up as she said the conclusion they had all just come to.

"What if everything that has happened to me hasn't been bad luck or some coincidence? What if it was all just really meant for Jenna?"

Chapter Fifteen

The Nash men took off so fast that Desmond could have believed they broke the sound barrier. He was hauling ass down Winding Road while Declan and Caleb made calls in the front and back seats.

Desmond used the time to focus on the road ahead of him, and not the growing sense of dread that had flipped in his stomach at Riley's last words to him. *Jenna's phone is going straight to voice mail. She never turns it off.*

Those had been the many, but absolutely effective, magic words.

Now they were about to have all of the sheriff's department on Willows Way.

But only after Desmond got them there first.

"We're the closest," Declan said after a few minutes. "There was a wreck out on County Road 11. It's got most of my people there right now."

"Jazz should get there but the way you're driving it'll definitely be after," Caleb added.

Then the inside of the truck became quiet.

They didn't speak again until the house came into view. A light was on inside the house.

"Let's go around the perimeter before we bust up in there," Caleb said, service weapon out. Declan followed suit. They exited the truck, careful to close the doors quietly, and fanned out. Caleb went around the house to the left. Declan went around the house to the right.

Desmond went straight to the front door.

He held his personal gun in one hand and unlocked the door with Riley's keys in the other.

He wasn't going to wait.

Not when Jenna might be in danger.

Jenna was about to be very scared or really thankful.

The house was mostly quiet. Something was making noise deeper within but he couldn't make out what it was. Desmond checked his gun again and took a deep breath. He'd never shot a person but wasn't above doing just that if necessary.

Because, in his gut, he knew Riley was right.

They'd spent too much time counting everything as coincidence and not enough of it stepping back to look at the entire picture. Not that Desmond could tell her exactly what the big picture was but now at least they were counting it as one series of events.

It wasn't just bad luck.

It was a design.

The sound of movement made Desmond stop in the doorway. He raised his gun, trying to place it.

He heard a *tink*. Something fell.

It was coming from the other side of the house, outside.

Desmond spun around, went back outside, and then to the corner. Much like he had with Riley at the law offices, he peeked around the side.

He could have sang in relief.

A mass of red curls could be seen just inside the opened window. The screen from it was on the grass.

Jenna was trying to go through the window.

Desmond slid his gun into the back of his pants and hurried over. Jenna, who was in the process of turning around so she could control the almost-six-foot drop thanks to a raised foundation, had one bare leg out and was working on her backside.

She must have heard him. Her movements became frantic. She was trying to get back inside.

"Jenna," Desmond whispered, reaching out.

She tried to turn to see who it was but only lost her balance. With a strangled screech she slipped backward right out of the window. Desmond was glad he'd put his gun away as he caught the flailing woman like a child.

Her eyes were wide with terror. Even after she recognized him.

"Someone is in the house," she whispered. "I—I heard glass break."

Desmond set her down, angled her behind him and pulled his gun back out. He could see through the opened window that the light they'd seen from the road was in the hallway.

Jenna sucked in a breath as a shadow filled the doorway into the bedroom she'd just fallen out of.

"Move and I'll—"

A shot rang out before Desmond could offer up the threat.

Several things happened at once.

Jenna screamed. So loud and pure that Desmond couldn't help but think of Madi that day in the park. It sent fire into his veins.

He had to protect her.

But there was another heat happening. This one was physical and hurt like hell.

There was also a new sound. Two gunshots.

And it came from Desmond's gun.

The shadow in the doorway crumpled and groaned. The skewed vantage point of them being on the ground versus in the room sent the bullets into his leg.

Desmond readied to make a more critical hit if needed when yelling consumed the house.

Declan and Caleb converged on the man without an ounce of mercy. Desmond didn't lower his gun until he saw the other one kicked across the room.

"Are you okay?" he asked, spinning around to inspect Jenna. Even in the poor light she looked near fainting. "Jenna, *are you okay?*" he repeated. As if he'd physically shaken her awake she moved all at once.

"Am I okay? *Are you?*" she shrieked, hands reaching out to him. "Desmond, you've been shot!"

"What?" yelled Caleb from inside the house.

Declan started talking fast but it wasn't to them.

Desmond looked to where the heat had blossomed on his arm. There was a tear in his flannel at the arm. He *had* been shot after all.

"Well, look at that."

THE TEMPERATURE TURNED COLD like it was sensing their moods.

Riley was staring at the road that led to the main house with a ferocity that still felt as urgent as it had the moment she'd watched the Nash sons take off down it.

Now, even though she knew Jenna was alright, Riley couldn't loosen the worry that had put a vise over her heart. Because it wasn't just her twin she was worried about, it was also Desmond and his family. Every time she got to know them a little better she fell a little more in love with them. Their kindness, compassion and loyalty to one another were heartwarming.

Just what she and Jenna had needed after what happened in the world they'd left behind.

So when that blue Ford appeared on the road that split the ranch, Riley let out a ragged breath. When Jenna *and* Desmond were both inside, she nearly cried.

"Riley!"

"Jenna!"

In true Stone sister fashion they yelled for each other at the same time as Jenna got out. They embraced.

"I'm fine," Jenna assured her. "Desmond showed up just in time."

Riley pulled back to look her sister up and down. The pajama set she'd been wearing last time Riley had seen her had been replaced by pants and a hefty jacket. She also was shouldering a duffel bag. When she saw Riley look at it she gave a small smile of relief.

"Desmond insisted we stay with him tonight," she added. "I've decided we all are going to take him up on that offer. I packed you some clothes too."

Jenna's eyes roamed to the main house behind them. She was looking for her son.

"He's asleep in the living room," Riley said. "Dorothy read him a bedtime story that put him out flat."

Jenna grabbed and squeezed her hand in thanks and walked away.

Riley turned to seek out the second person she'd been worried about. Desmond was slow getting out of his truck but he was smiling.

"I hope you don't mind bunking at my place ton—"

Riley didn't have long, long legs by any means but she somehow ate up the distance between them with surprising speed.

Desmond was warm as she pressed against him. Just like the kiss she gave him.

It was brief.

Riley stepped back and said the one thought on her mind. It was also brief.

"Thank you."

Desmond, bless him, didn't make a big deal about the kiss or the praise. He took his hat off.

"Yes, ma'am."

Headlights turned their attention to a truck coming up the road. The front door to the main house pushed open as Nina, Caleb's wife, ran to her husband when he got out. Riley felt a blush starting to burn in her cheeks as Nina did the same thing she had just done by pressing against Caleb and laying a big one on him.

When they parted Caleb caught their attention and nodded to the house.

Desmond sighed.

"Time to update everyone," he said.

HARTLEY DIDN'T MOVE an inch when the adults sat down and started talking in the living room but Riley, Dorothy and Nina were all having a hard time not reacting in a big way to what they were hearing.

"Do you really think Geordi Green broke into the house to take Jenna?" Riley asked after they said Geordi had busted out the back window. "I know y'all don't like him but surely that's out of character for him."

A muscle in Desmond's jaw twitched.

Caleb handled the answer.

"This would definitely be an escalation for him, that's for sure. Writing garbage about us is one thing, breaking and entering and then—"

Desmond cleared his throat. Jenna tensed.

Caleb shook his head, seemingly changing what he had been about to say.

"Well, I just honestly don't know at this point what's going on with him, but considering what he said to you at the park, we have a direction we'll be going in first thing in the morning."

Riley raised her eyebrow and found her sister's gaze. If it was possible, Jenna tensed more.

"They think it could have something to do with Ryan,

considering Davies and Maria have also shown up in town," Jenna said, dropping into a whisper. "I don't know why he would be after me now but out of everyone here I can say he probably hates me the most."

The question hung heavily in the air around them. Riley took her sister's hand and kept it on top of the couch cushion.

"Regardless of whatever is going on and who's behind it, we'll get to the bottom of it," Caleb added. "As for Geordi, when he's out of surgery, Jazz will be on him faster than a horsefly on Ax's rump."

It was a colorful point. One that made Riley feel better.

"Until then I think it's high time everyone get some rest," Desmond said. Then to Riley and Jenna, "And until we understand what's going on, consider yourselves welcomed guests here on the Nash ranch."

Riley didn't like the situation they were in but she couldn't deny that Desmond's invitation made her feel better.

THE NEXT HALF HOUR was spent saying goodbye to one another—even though no one in the house was actually leaving the ranch grounds—and transitioning to Desmond's home. Dorothy insisted it was fine if the girls wanted to stay with her but Riley already knew where she wanted to be.

And, by this point, everyone seemed to understand that the Stone sisters were a package deal, including one extremely sleepy Hartley.

Desmond carried the little man with one arm protectively wrapped around him. The sight reminded her of their earlier conversation.

Did she want a lot of kids?

Riley smiled into the night air.

She hadn't been about to admit to anyone at dinner that, yes, a big family had always been a goal in her life. She'd just never found the right time to start reaching for that goal with Davies. Though, again, maybe that had been her heart's way of warning her about the man.

But now? Following behind the strapping, messy-haired, drool-worthy cowboy holding one of the few people she loved with her entire being?

Riley found herself wondering what his dark hair and her curls would look like on a child.

"Does he have abs?"

Riley spun her head around so fast it was like she was in *The Exorcist*.

"Come again?"

Jenna kept on like they were talking about the weather.

"I asked if he had abs," she repeated, motioning to Desmond. "He literally caught me in his arms after I fell out of Hartley's bedroom window and it was like hitting a wall. You said you didn't *you know* with him but you did see him shirtless, right?"

Normally, Riley would have swatted away—physically and verbally—the question, but there was an undercurrent to Jenna's words. A small waver that she doubted anyone else would recognize.

Jenna was scared.

And rightly so.

Being attacked at her home was one thing, but the idea that Ryan could be connected to it?

Riley didn't blame her for the fear. Heck, she was feeling it too.

"Remember when we first watched *Magic Mike* and you said that no man really has a body that yummy? That they're probably all computer generated?" Riley whispered instead. Jenna's eyes widened. A whisper of a smile crossed her lips.

"Really? *That* nice?"

Riley nodded, matter-of-factly.

"Abs. For. Days."

Desmond looked over his shoulder as they both devolved into giggles. Bless him again, he didn't ask.

RILEY, JENNA AND HARTLEY opted to stay in the same guest bedroom upstairs. It was down the hall from Desmond's, as was another empty room where Madi had lived before starting the bed-and-breakfast. Still the women hadn't accepted the offer for each of them to have their own room.

Just as Desmond didn't admit that ever since that kiss out by his truck, he'd been thinking about Riley staying in his.

Instead he gave them privacy and showered in his en suite while they used the hall bathroom to get ready for bed. Before saying good-night he promised to keep them updated as soon as he had any information.

Desmond also wanted to make sure he had his own privacy as he undressed and got into the shower. Sure, a certain part of him was really craving some company but his more levelheaded side had reminded himself that he didn't want Riley to know he'd been shot. Just as they had all agreed, even Jenna, at the Stone house, that they would keep that information away from their mother.

He knew it didn't make sense to ask that of Riley's twin—and, honestly, he knew Riley could handle the news—but Desmond couldn't shake the look of worry that had stared back at him at dinner.

He didn't want Riley to go through that needlessly, if he could help it.

Not saying that he believed she would react the same as his mother, but still, Desmond was glad he was able to shower and clean the blood he'd hidden with his jacket.

When he was done, he toweled dry, brushed his teeth and slipped on a pair of boxers. He was contemplating putting a shirt on over his wound, worried about getting blood on his sheets, when a knock sounded on the door.

"Just a sec," he called, trying to spot his robe. It was across the room. He didn't have a chance to traverse the space before the bedroom door opened wide.

Riley Stone, in an oversize T-shirt that cut off at the middle of her thighs and had a picture of French fries on it, stared back at him with anger clear in her eyes.

Desmond realized then that leaving her out of the loop had been a bad, bad idea.

"You were *shot*?"

Chapter Sixteen

Riley said it in a low volume but it came out strong. Then she shut the door behind her and Desmond knew he was really in trouble now.

"Listen, it was only a graze," he tried, putting both his hands up in surrender. The movement made the gash across his bicep hurt. He winced. "I didn't want to go worrying anyone over something that wasn't a big deal."

Riley walked up to him, hands still on her hips.

"Over something that wasn't a big deal? Jenna said not only did you take a bullet that could have been for her, but you also *shot Geordi twice*." She waved her hands around, as if confused as to what thought she wanted to grab on to first. "*All* of those things are big deals. Ones you didn't tell me!"

Desmond lowered his hands and sighed.

"You've been through a lot, is all. I didn't want to add anything unless I had to."

Riley's expression softened. Then her eyes traveled to the gash on his arm. There was a bandage over it but still her look of concern grew.

"That's what I wanted to avoid," he added. "That look."

She snorted.

"I think if someone gets shot, it calls for *some* worry." She lightly touched his arm. "Does it hurt a lot?"

Desmond tried to control his breathing.

And the rest of his body.

Riley's touch was innocent, he knew that, but the desire it stirred within him wasn't.

"Not enough to bother me."

Even to his ears his words came out differently than they had before. It caught Riley's attention. She glanced down at his bare chest and then immediately took a step back. Her cheeks became flushed.

"Wow. I just burst in here, didn't I?" she said around nervous laughter. "I'm so sorry. Jenna just finally told me what happened and I was going to wait for morning to tell you off—not that I was really going to tell you off or anything—but then I couldn't shake it and—"

Desmond crashed his lips into hers. Her words died between their lips. It pushed him closer to the point of no return. He made sure to disengage momentarily from their lip-lock to say something before the start of their next adventure.

"Every time we've kissed you've either been apologizing or thanking me," he said, gravel in his words. "I'm here to tell you now, you don't owe me a thing. You don't have to say sorry or tiptoe around me and what you want. Got it?"

Riley nodded. Her lips were already rosy.

He smirked as he continued.

"But, I'm here to tell you right now what I want and if that lines up with something you're interested in, you let me know." He brought his hand up and ran it across her cheek. Then he looked at her lips and knew the woman in front of him, with wild, wild hair and wearing a shirt with fries on it, had the power to make him do whatever she wanted without question.

"Riley Stone, I'd really like to show you a damn good time. Right now. Here in my bed."

For a second, Desmond thought she might turn him down but then Riley did what she did best.

She pressed her lips against his with purpose.

Desmond supposed that was her way of saying she liked that idea too.

RILEY'S NIGHTSHIRT WAS THROWN so far away she wouldn't be surprised if later she found it in another state.

Desmond's lips moved to her neck and then slid their way right down to her breast. Riley moaned in response.

It encouraged the man.

When he dropped to his knees and slid her sleep shorts off, Riley nearly wept.

But Desmond wasn't quite so direct.

He let out a primal sort of growl and was back to his feet in a flash. Then he gently threw Riley on the bed.

It took all she could muster not to yell, "Take me!"

Instead she watched with bated breath as the man she often called cowboy crawled across the bed and right on top of her.

Unlike their time on the living-room floor there was no awkward innocence or tentative prompting.

Desmond had made it clear he wanted her.

And she wanted to return the favor.

Riley wrapped her legs around his waist and pushed up against his lips like he was the last drink of water in the desert. It surprised the cowboy but in the best way. He reacted by deepening their kiss and using one arm to keep her against him.

Then he flipped them both.

Riley let out a small laugh in surprise. Desmond broke their kiss, eyes hooded and lips swollen. Riley was afraid she'd offended him with the noise but then those same lips pulled up at the corners.

That smile.

That Desmond Nash smile.

It was one in a million.

And more than worked its magic.

Riley relieved Desmond of his boxers while the last vestige of her clothes disappeared too.

When he pushed inside, Riley let him know just how much she enjoyed it. He, in turn, wasn't leaving her wondering. The comforter and sheets twisted. Moans of ecstasy escaped. A rhythm was created, kept and then sped along to a wonderful conclusion.

What had started as a chance meeting at a party had become something so much more, and as Riley lay naked in his arms, breathless and slick with sweat, she couldn't help but feel the shift in her future.

Overlook had been a way station.

A pit stop.

A respite.

A transition that she'd intended to end after she'd made sure Jenna was okay.

Plans for her career, her future family and her happiness weren't ready to be made. Not here. Not in Overlook.

Yet, listening to the still-racing heartbeat of Desmond Nash, Riley found that she was dangerously close to including the cowboy in all of them.

THEY LAY TOGETHER. They laughed together. They showered together. They lay back down together. And they fell asleep together.

It was a lot closer than he'd expected to become with someone in a while.

However, when Desmond woke and found Riley was still there next to him, he was happy it was with her.

A siren who hadn't led him astray.

The lamp on the nightstand bathed the bedroom in low light. It illuminated the relaxed face of the woman at his side. Even though she'd used his body wash, he still could smell the lavender on her. It had a calming effect on him, he realized.

Desmond shifted onto his back. Despite having just woken up he was still dead tired. He hadn't been sleeping that great lately. Not since the night of the gala, if he was being honest with himself.

Not since he'd seen the graffiti at Second Wind's construction site.

If Ryan Alcaster *was* trying to get to Jenna or *get* Jenna, how did the construction site fit into any of it?

Was it a distraction or a pointed jab to ruffle his feathers?

And how did Brett Calder and, possibly, the Fixers fit into any of it?

Desmond closed his eyes again, feeling his body tense in frustration. Madi had once worried about the family's bad luck. Their constant falling in with trouble was pretty damning when it came to the accusation.

But without trouble you wouldn't have gotten to know her, Desmond thought a split second later. *There'd be no Riley in your bed.*

That would be one heck of a shame, if he did say so himself.

Desmond decided to wake up early, make the Stones some breakfast and then dive into a giant cup of coffee and figure out *something* that was going on so they could find some peace. He started to roll over to turn off the lamp when two things happened on top of each other.

A board in the kitchen floor, right under his room, the one Madi used to complain about, yelled out its horrible whine.

And then Desmond realized he hadn't just woken up, he'd *been* woken up.

Instead of turning the lamp off he went for his phone.

There were no new messages or calls. After everything the Nashes had been through in the last few years everyone knew not to just creep around without some kind of warning. Which was why his mother had rung the doorbell the other day and not burst right on in.

The clock on his phone read 4:05 a.m. Nashes were also early risers, came with the territory of helping run a ranch growing up, but that was a little too early for normal.

Surely no one had broken in, he hoped.

Brett was dead, Geordi was in the hospital, but Davies?

Desmond got out of bed in a flash. Riley stirred as he went for his jeans and put them on in record time. He cursed beneath his breath when he realized his gun was still at the department. He had another in the safe but it was downstairs in his office.

"Desmond?"

Riley was sitting up and blinking away sleep. Then her eyes were wide. She'd noticed his worry.

"I think someone is downstairs," he whispered. "Could be nothing, could be something."

Riley vaulted out of bed, impressing Desmond with how quiet the movement was, and started for the door. The fun fries shirt contrasted with her serious expression.

"I have to make sure Jenna and Hartley are okay," she explained, low.

Desmond caught her hand before she could hit the doorknob. For a moment he saw anger flash through her. He understood it just as quick.

No one could stand between him and his family.

Just like no one could stand between her and her sister and nephew.

So Desmond wasn't even going to try.

"Let me go out first. If I don't yell up to you as soon as I go down the stairs, call Caleb. His house is down the road." He tucked his phone in her hand. "Don't come downstairs."

He held her gaze until she nodded.

Then he kissed her, opened the door, and they went their separate ways. Riley to the guest bedroom down the hall and Desmond to the stairs. He made a fist, angry he hadn't thought to keep a weapon in his room, and descended.

Since there were people staying in his house who weren't familiar with it, Desmond had left a light on over the sink in the kitchen and a lamp on in the living room. It didn't do much for the small hallway between or the rest of the first floor but it was enough to see that his family wasn't in his house.

But someone else definitely was.

Desmond pushed back up against the wall next to the bottom step of the stairs. Around the corner from him was someone he didn't recognize.

But given the shock of platinum-blond hair, Desmond assumed it was the fancy lawyer he'd heard about from his brothers.

Maria Wendell.

In his living room at four in the morning.

Desmond took a quick breath and crouched. He eased his head around the corner again.

She was looking toward the front door, as if her being there was normal. She even had her fingers threaded together and against her stomach.

The odd stance showcased the lack of weapon in them.

Something wasn't right.

Why was she there?

Movement across from him in the kitchen changed everything. Desmond didn't even have the chance to move.

A man walked out into the hallway, gun raised.

He was wearing a three-piece suit.

"If you lunge at me, I'll still be able to get at least one shot off," he said, voice cool and calm. "Considering how close we are, that shot will probably cripple, if not kill, you.

Then how will you help Ms. Stone?" He nodded toward the living room. "Let's go in there."

Desmond swore but followed directions. Making noise to wake him had been on purpose. Just as Maria had been a distraction.

The blonde didn't look at all surprised as Desmond stopped in front of her. He angled his body so he could see them both.

"I can't believe that worked," Maria said to the man in the suit. She looked Desmond up and down. "And you were right, no gun."

The man shrugged.

"He gave it to his brother after he shot Geordi and his safe is downstairs."

"Who are you?" Desmond bit at him.

The man ignored him. He kept the gun steady and addressed Maria.

"One of them is probably calling the Nash who lives the closest. You have less than a minute to get her. I suggest you go do that now."

Maria pulled a small pistol from the pocket of her coat.

"*Fine.* Just make sure he doesn't touch me or I *will* shoot him. *Comprende?*"

The man in the suit adopted a look of quick anger.

"You kill him, or anyone in this house, and I will be the only, and the last, problem you ever have. *Comprende?*"

Desmond didn't understand the directive but Maria's gusto was doused by it.

"What do you even want with her?" Desmond asked, trying to stall.

Maria snorted.

"You think just asking me a question is going to get me talking?" She glanced at the man in the suit. "If I can't kill you then I'm certainly not going to talk to you."

Desmond didn't hate the fact that he was about to ruin

her day. The moment she was next to him Desmond threw his shoulder into her as hard as he could, two guns in the room be damned.

He expected a gunshot to go off but the only sound that followed the hit was Maria's short-lived screech as her legs smacked the coffee table and she flailed over. The pistol hit the wood first and then slid as the table toppled with her weight.

Desmond lurched for the weapon but the man in the suit surprised him with a swift kick to the side. It was Desmond who stumbled now. He caught his balance before falling all the way to the floor and then spun on his heel.

Only to be staring into the barrel of a gun.

Maria was cussing up a storm but the man in the suit was still as unruffled as they came.

He looked Desmond right in the eye when he spoke.

"She's not allowed to kill her. Not yet."

Desmond tried to avoid the knockout hit but the man in the suit was too fast. The world turned black before he even landed on the floor.

DESMOND STARED UP at the ceiling and saw white shiplap.

His house.

Living room.

Pain.

It weighed down his body, his head, while at the same time burning him.

Fragments of memories remained scattered around him, even when the yelling started.

"Desmond?"

Caleb's face, full of worry, and his gun both came into view. He ran to Desmond and crouched in front of him.

"God, that's so much blood," he said, touching a spot on Desmond's head that made him suck in a breath. "What happened?"

The question was magnetized. It brought those scattered fragments of memories together and formed one terrifying reality.

Desmond pushed up, stumbled to the side as his head spun at the movement, but kept moving forward.

"Maria and the man in the suit came for Jenna," he hurried. "He knocked me out."

Desmond hated the words.

Hated them almost as much as he hated the man who had done it.

"Riley? Jenna?" he yelled around the hatred flowing through him. He took the stairs two at a time. Caleb was on his heels and had his hand on his back.

No one answered his call. But that didn't stop Desmond from yelling out. He continued to do it all the way into the guest bedroom. Even at the sight of an empty room, he still called out for them.

For her.

"Desmond!"

A woman's voice floated from somewhere else in the house.

"My room," he realized, turning.

Together they rushed into the bedroom and were met with a weird sight.

"Was your dresser in front of the closet before?" Caleb asked after flipping the light on. The dresser had always stood next to the door, not in front of it.

Desmond shook his head.

"No, it wasn't."

Someone started banging against the closet door it was covering. Wordlessly Caleb pushed it out of the way. The second the door was clear, Desmond flung it open.

A sea of wild red curls encased a tear-stained face. Dark eyes rimmed with water looked back at him. The fun shirt with fries on the front contrasted with her look of anguish.

"Oh, Desmond," she said, voice breaking. "She made me."

Movement at the back of the closet showed a scared Hartley. He hurried up to them and grabbed his mom's hand.

Desmond turned to his brother and hated what he said more than anything else in the world.

"They took Riley."

Chapter Seventeen

Hours went by.

Hours.

Desmond absolutely felt them.

So had every Nash alive. Not only had Maria and the man in the suit taken Riley, they'd done so from their home. No one had seen them come onto the ranch and no one had seen them leave. Not even Caleb who had jumped in his truck and hightailed it over after Riley had called.

Riley.

Desmond knew it was useless to try to move his thoughts away from how worried he was. How angry he felt. How helpless he'd become since.

She heard them talking and said we needed to hide, Jenna had tearfully explained. *Then she—she said if it was Ryan that we—we needed to change because he knew about that stupid fries shirt. I told her no but then she pointed to Hartley and I—I did it. I switched clothes.* She'd held Hartley tight to her chest and barely was able to keep from all out sobbing. *Then— Then she told me to be quiet for Hartley and—and she pushed me and shut the door. I couldn't open it. Then I heard you.*

Desmond didn't know Jenna as well as he knew her sister but he had put his arms around her and Hartley, hoping to help her somehow.

We're going to get her back, he had promised. *We're going to get her back.*

Now, hours later, Desmond was at the sheriff's department, waiting for their only lead to pan out. Judging by Caleb's expression after he came out of the interrogation room, panning out wasn't happening.

"Davies is barking for a lawyer again," he greeted.

"A lawyer? You mean the same one who *took Riley*?" Desmond put his hands on his hips. "Please, then, by all means let him get her out here."

They both knew that wasn't going to happen.

Maria Wendell had disappeared completely. Last Desmond heard no one even knew where she had been for at least two weeks.

Ryan Alcaster included.

Declan was in Kilwin talking to him and *his* lawyer. So far that had yielded zero results.

Which left them with Evan Davies. He'd been staying in a hotel outside of Kilwin. Declan had pulled some strings and gotten him sent to the department.

A lot of good that was doing them now.

"I don't think he's lying about not knowing about what happened tonight," Caleb said after a moment. "He seemed genuinely surprised."

"But he does know *something* and he's too much of a coward to say anything."

Caleb nodded in agreement.

"From what we know of him he seems to only have a backbone in the corporate world. Out here, in real life, he looks like he's afraid of his own shadow. Or Ryan Alcaster's or the man in the suit's. Whoever is pulling the strings because you know it's not him."

Desmond grunted his displeasure.

"I've met men like him before. I vowed Second Wind would never employ anyone like that." Desmond ran a hand along his chin. There was already stubble there. He paused as a thought occurred to him. He lowered his voice. "I've met men like him before. I know how he thinks."

Caleb's eyebrow rose in question. It fell just as fast as he figured out the answer.

"You want to talk to him," he spelled out.

"I want to find Riley, and if Davies won't talk to law enforcement, maybe he'll talk to a CEO."

CALEB SHUT THE DOOR behind him. He was going to keep watch because he was a good brother, but mostly, because he knew Riley meant something different to Desmond.

Even without saying anything, it was simply understood.

And they were running out of time to save her.

Now they were breaking the rules and Desmond wasn't going to leave that room until he got the answers he wanted.

"I don't know anything," Davies said, sitting up straight. "And I'm not going to talk to any of you until I have a lawyer in front of me."

Desmond knew two things going into the interrogation room. For one, he knew he looked like a good ol' country boy. Jeans, flannel, boots and his Stetson. He knew those jeans were worn, the flannel was rumpled, his boots had dried mud on them and his cowboy hat sometimes gave outsiders the impression that, for some reason, he wasn't as smart as them.

What he also knew, and what Davies was about to find out, was that Desmond wasn't leaving that room until he had a way to find Riley.

So, he removed his cowboy hat, set it down on the metal table between them and took the seat his brother had been sitting in minutes before.

Davies eyed him with defiance.

That defiance wasn't going to fly with Desmond.

"I'm going to go ahead and stop you right there," Desmond began, threading his hands together on the tabletop. He made sure to keep his voice even. "I'm not law enforcement, never have been. Which means, legally, I don't have to provide you with anything. Least of all a lawyer. So singing that I-want-a-lawyer song isn't going to make me do anything other than get really annoyed."

"If you're not law enforcement you're not supposed to be in here," Davies tried. There was more bite in his voice than Desmond liked. He waved his hand to dismiss the thought.

"Listen, I get it—you want to be alone right now and I respect that. I surely wouldn't want to be in here either." Desmond motioned to the room around them. "These walls? Once you're inside them they mean something different to everyone you meet." He leaned back a touch in his chair, careful to keep his body language light and easy. "Some will think it's exciting you were in here, some even sexy, but others? They'll think you did something wrong. Something bad. Worst of all? Two times in less than forty-eight hours makes you look guilty as sin."

"I didn't *do* anything," Davies said, voice raised.

Desmond shrugged.

"Exactly. You didn't do *anything*. When you were asked what you knew about Ryan Alcaster's, Maria Wendell's and the man in the suit's involvement in the attack and abduction of your ex-wife, you didn't say or do *anything*." Desmond cocked his head to the side and pointed at the man opposite him. "And *that* is what everyone is going to know at the end of this."

Davies was unable to hide his flinch. Desmond guessed the man already had gone over that thought in his head.

And he hadn't liked it.

Desmond leaned forward. He knew he could break the man and he was ready to bring it home.

"Do you know that my dad was a detective?" he started. "A really *good* one too. When my siblings and I were

younger we were so intrigued about all aspects of his job.
But, for me, I was mostly curious about how he was able
to make these people who had found themselves in such
unflattering positions talk. How he could, as a highly respected and well-known law-enforcement person, get these
hardened criminals to tell him what he needed to know. So,
one day I asked him."

Desmond readjusted his casual lean so that he was sitting up tall.

"What he told me really stuck with me. He said, *You
know, Des, every person on this green earth wants to talk,
to tell their story. It's in our nature. And, just like everyone
wants to talk, everyone has at least the one person they
want to talk to. The only challenge is becoming that one
person.*" He once again motioned to the room around them.
"And this is where he did it. Day in and day out, case after
case, he became someone the other person needed before
they said a word."

Desmond thumbed back to the door that led to the hallway.

"My brothers, that detective and the sheriff, they took
my father's job and the lessons that went along with it and
became the law themselves. But me? When I realized I
could help people just by talking? Well, I turned that les-
son into a smile." To put emphasis on his point he brought
up the corners of his lips with ease. "I became known as
the charming one because I figured out the secret. From
investors, volunteers and potential donors to boardroom
meetings and legal teams to my mother's book club, they
all wanted the same thing those hardened criminals and
wrongly accused wanted. To talk. All I had to do was become a good listener."

Desmond dropped his sweet act. He leaned in again, his
elbows on the table.

"So I could sit here as long as they're allowed to hold

you and go through the motions all in the hope you'd finally tell yours." He jabbed one of his index fingers down on the tabletop. Davies was staring at him, unable to look away.

Good.

"Or you can finally do the right thing and just tell me what you know. If you ever loved Riley at all, you owe her that."

A silence settled between them. Davies didn't blink. The heat kicked on somewhere else in the building. Shoes scuffed against tile floor nearby.

Then, all at once, Evan Davies let out a sigh of defeat, his entire body dragging down. There was a hunch to his shoulders when he finally spoke.

"I honest to God don't know where she is and I don't know how Maria Wendell or the man in the suit are involved. I also don't know if Ryan Alcaster is really behind any of it…"

"But?"

Davies let out another long, disheartened breath.

"But I do know the motive, if he is."

"And that is?" Desmond was on the edge of his seat. The door opened. Caleb came in and shut it behind him.

Apparently he had been in the viewing room.

Davies looked between them, but thankfully, didn't have to be talked into continuing to say what he was about to say.

He was just as defeated as he answered.

"Ryan didn't actually get all his money and success by building from the ground up. When he joined Macklin Tech he already was living off his father's money. *Sam* Alcaster inherited a fortune from his uncle when he realized he himself wouldn't have kids. Sam was extremely proud that he could pass that wealth, plus the money he'd added to it over the course of his life, to his son. That had always been the plan." Davies looked uncomfortable. He shifted in his seat. "A few weeks after the divorce, Ryan showed up in the Atlanta office visibly upset. Maria was in-house and saw it too. We were his friends so we followed him into a conference room to see what was wrong. He shut the door and locked it. I should have known right then that he was trouble."

"You should have known it after you found out he was beating his wife."

Desmond didn't mean for the jab to slip out—not that he regretted it, they just didn't have the time for it—and Davies flinched.

"What was wrong with him?" Caleb interjected, keeping the new information moving.

"Apparently his father had done some digging into the divorce," Davies continued. "He didn't understand why Jenna was given full custody and cut every part of her life with Ryan off."

"Let me guess," Desmond jumped in. "He found out what his son had been doing."

Davies nodded.

"He had hired a private investigator. One who found records, video and pictures of when Jenna was hospitalized. He put it together after that and then he changed his will."

Money. It was about money.

Desmond should have known.

"Ryan isn't getting a penny?"

Davies shook his head.

"Sam is leaving every cent of his fortune to Hartley… Which can only be accessed and used by Hartley's legal guardian if he receives it before the age of twenty-two."

For a moment no one spoke.

Desmond shared a look with his brother. Neither liked what they had just heard.

"So Ryan wants custody of Hartley to secure his original inheritance," Caleb said.

"But the only reason Jenna didn't expose Ryan in the

first place was because she'd been given full custody of Hartley without a fight," Desmond recapped. "There's no way she would have been quiet if he'd tried to get full custody again. She'd out him and everything he'd done."

A sickening thought blossomed in Desmond's head. He saw it reflected in Davies's expression.

"Unless something happened to Jenna," he realized. "Brett Calder, the Fixer. Geordi and Maria. He's not getting his hands dirty, he's dirtying everyone else's."

"He never said he was going to do anything but he very clearly realized the only way to get his inheritance was through Hartley," Davies said. "I assumed he was spending so much time with Maria because she was helping him, I don't know, build a case or something. But then I heard about a news story of famous small-town triplets saving a twin just outside of Kilwin. When I saw that it was Riley and that Jenna was also in town, I worried Ryan had come up with a more malicious plan."

Desmond was getting hot.

Angry.

"Why didn't you warn her then? Why not warn law enforcement? Why were you at the construction site instead?"

"Because of me," Davies said, confusing both Nashes. He blew out a frustrated breath and explained. "I didn't say anything to anyone about Ryan beating his wife. I sacrificed my marriage to keep that secret, all because I believed my job was that important." Davies looked to Desmond. "You said it yourself in so many words—being charming can be a tool but it can also be a weapon. Do you know how many friends Ryan has? How many 'me's he's mentored and helped through the years? He's not a man you take on head-to-head. You have to catch him in the act. So I tried to." Another long sigh. He was so hunched over by now that Desmond had to angle his gaze down. "I said I found a way to get him what he wanted and asked him to meet me at a place where we could make that happen. I chose the construction site because of how much the media around here seems to love you Nashes. I figured the response time would be quicker and the coverage greater if anything went south with me trying to record his confession without him realizing it. But when I got there I was met by the man in the suit. He said he had been sent there to talk to me. He never specifically said Ryan, but, well, I guess that's the only person who knew I was going there."

"Then Marty showed up."

Davies shook his head with vigor, sitting up a little taller than before.

"I never saw Marty. He must have been on the third floor already. I swear," he hurried. "When I heard you downstairs I panicked and ran."

"And the next day Maria Wendell was your lawyer," Caleb said, disgust clear in his tone.

"You have to understand, Maria has been a friend for the last several months. Calling her didn't seem that crazy at the time." He shook his head. "I didn't know she was involved in Ryan's plans."

Desmond rubbed his chin again. In the late hours of the night Riley had done the same motion and laughed.

The memory made him feel warm and hollowed out at the same time.

He fixed Davies with a stare he hoped hurt.

"You know Ryan, better than anyone we've talked to," he said. "And now you're going to tell *us* everything."

Desmond didn't ask if he understood.

Because, *not* understanding wasn't an option.

Desmond had to find her.

There was no other option.

Chapter Eighteen

The AC unit made a tired, wheezing sound as the heat cut on.

It reminded Riley of a prop plane that had been flying without any problems, only to lose its engine while at a cruising altitude. Then, by some miracle, the propeller would kick back into gear.

The unit beneath the window would strain, sputter and then stop altogether. When Riley believed it had finally died—finally giving in to its inevitable mechanical death—it would cut on with some *clank*s and then slide into the wheeze. Where it would keep that pace for at least half an hour before doing the entire loud dance all over again.

It was driving Riley insane.

Along with rope that had been thoroughly wrapped around her and the chair she was sitting on. Maria might have been slight in frame and have supermodel good looks but Riley had spent the last several hours seeing the demon beneath the makeup and expensive clothes. Not to mention a surprising proficiency at tying knots. Ones that didn't come undone no matter how much you moved.

Maria let out a loud huff just as the AC chugged back to life again. Riley didn't bother turning to look over her shoulder at the woman. She was used to her routine too by now. The blonde was sitting on one of the two beds with her heels kicked off and a cell phone in front of her face.

And apparently not getting the call that she wanted.

This time Maria's sigh was punctuated by noise that fell somewhere between a grunt and a scream. It wasn't loud enough to escape the hotel-room walls but it did make Riley's muscles tense in anticipation.

She'd had every intention in the world, when she switched with Jenna, to try to get Maria and the man in the suit as far away from the ranch as possible and, only then, to try to fight her way out. She'd heard Desmond, Maria and the man in the suit talking in the living room at his house.

For whatever reason, Maria wasn't allowed to kill any of them.

But Riley wasn't betting on that verbal agreement to hold. She had gotten into the car with them and immediately started to make a game plan for when they stopped again.

Yet, the moment they'd pulled up to a roadside motel on the outskirts of Kilwin, the man in the suit had turned in his seat to face her. He had said something that made Riley's stomach go cold.

Good luck.

Those two words had taken away Riley's hope of escaping. When he left the car right after and then Maria swung around with her pistol aimed, that hope further deteriorated.

I've made a career out of getting results, she had said. *So here are the results I'm going to see and incur based on what you do now.* The motel was a long two-story building that was shaped like a warped *L*. She motioned toward the office. A woman and a preteen were sitting at a white iron patio table next to the door. A book was open in front of the girl and the woman seemed to be enjoying a mug of something. *That woman there is Abela. She's the day manager and a single mother to Dina, sitting across from her. They know and like me so I could walk right up to them and shoot Abela in the face before either would think to be worried.*

Riley had gasped. Maria had held up her other hand to silence her.

Or you could come quietly into my room where we'll sit and wait for me to get a call.

Riley had glanced from Abela and Dina to the busy road they'd just come off. Maria hadn't missed it.

Listen. Don't underestimate me just because I'm not wearing a suit, she said with a snap of her fingers. *If you say anything or if you run, I won't try to shut you up and I won't try to chase you.* She'd pointed back at the mom and daughter. *I* will *walk across the parking lot and shoot Abela in the face right in front of her daughter.*

You're disgusting, Riley had seethed.

Maria had smiled.

I'm a woman of my word and I've given you two options and the results of picking either. Now, once I put this gun in my pocket, will you follow me calmly to my room or are you ready to be the reason a sweet girl is about to become an orphan?

Riley had seen it then. The intention. The promise.

She had believed Maria.

So she'd abandoned her plans of escape.

Let's go.

Now hours had gone by, and that call Maria had been waiting for still hadn't come. As for conversation while they had waited? Riley would have had better luck with the old AC unit.

Not having a talk with Maria wasn't breaking Riley's heart, though. The blonde hadn't just proven to be malicious; she was also impatient. Riley didn't want to exacerbate her nasty tendencies by digging into that impatience.

Plus, Riley wanted to give Desmond as much time as possible to find her.

Because Riley knew he would try his damnedest.

"What is *taking* so long?"

Maria kicked her feet against the bed like she was Hartley after being denied fruit gummy snacks. Riley looked over her shoulder, unable to hide her growing annoyance with the woman.

"Don't look at me like that," Maria snapped, stilling herself.

"Like what?" Riley couldn't help but say. "Like I'm tied to a chair, being held captive and not happy about it? Are you saying I should smile instead?"

Maria was fast. She was off the bed and standing in front of Riley wearing a pair of very expensive shoes.

"Don't look at me like you don't know why you're in this situation in the first place." She bent over, hands on the arms of the chair. Riley refused to flinch. "If you hadn't lied in the first place, this never would have happened. You did this. Not him."

Up until then Riley had been working under the assumption that Ryan was behind everything. It was the best theory that she had, but one that wasn't proven on account of Maria's lack of communication. Now there was no room left to interpret another mastermind.

"Ryan."

"A man who deserved, and got, way better than you." Maria was smirking. Riley hated the sight.

"A man who beats his wife deserves to rot in jail," she bit out.

The slap against her cheek happened so fast that Riley didn't have time to react. Pain radiated across the side of her face. Maria's composure had cracked again, the malicious side of her personality pushing through with growing aggression.

"That man did everything for you, and how did you repay him? Lie at every turn," she said. "We both know he didn't lay a hand on you."

"I was hospitalized," Riley exclaimed, keeping in line with the lie that she was her sister. "I have pictures and witnesses!"

"Having a sister lie to corroborate your story doesn't equal any evidence. It just means she's a filthy liar like you are."

Riley could feel the heat of anger burning through her. Ryan was still tainting every part of their lives.

"It wasn't a lie, but I'm assuming, you'll find that out at some point." Riley lowered her voice. "He was nice in the beginning with me too."

The second slap Riley *did* see coming. She was able to brace before Maria's hand connected with the already-stinging cheek. Still, Riley continued. She was finally getting somewhere with the woman.

"I'm going to go out on a limb here and take that as a confirmation that you're with Ryan now. But, if you're so happy and sure of him being a good man, then why am I here? Why have you been after me?"

Maria took a step back, standing to her full height, and pulled her arms over her chest. She'd ditched her laughable trench coat on the bed and was sporting an expensive blouse-and-pencil-skirt set. Not that Riley ever wanted to attack or kidnap someone but she had to believe if she did, she would wear something a little less corporate while doing it.

"Because even though your lies didn't fool everyone, they did get to Sam. But once that's cleared up we can finally get on with our lives again."

Riley's eyebrow shot up despite trying to remain impassive. Sam Alcaster? Hartley's grandfather? From what Riley knew from Jenna, Sam had genuinely seemed to be a good, caring man. He'd even called the house to talk to Hartley on the phone from time to time, even when Hartley was too young to make any sense.

Then again, Ryan had seemed to be a genuinely nice man too at one point.

"What do you mean, once it's cleared up?" Riley asked. "Whatever you do to me won't take away from the fact that the authorities know who you are by now. They know you took me. The only chance you have at getting on with the rest of your life will be if you let me go and turn yourself in."

Maria was unfazed.

In fact, she smiled.

"You couldn't even begin to guess at my future."

The bed started to vibrate. Both women looked at Maria's phone dancing on the comforter.

Riley couldn't see the caller ID but when Maria scooped it up, she smiled wide.

Ryan.

"Hey, babe." She answered the phone with hearts in her eyes and sex in her voice. There was no question in Riley's mind that Ryan had absolutely hooked Maria.

And that it would spell the end for the woman.

Maybe sooner rather than later too. Maria's face fell two seconds into the conversation. She turned and headed to the bathroom.

"It's not my... But I had to... But I..."

Riley strained to hear more but Maria shut the bathroom door.

The urge to try to escape pulsed through her veins like blood. If Maria didn't have the pistol on her, she would have tried. All Riley could think about now, though, was the mother-daughter pair living their lives a few rooms down from them.

Again, Riley believed Maria would absolutely take out her anger at Riley escaping on them.

She wasn't willing to risk that.

For a phone call Maria had waited hours to receive, it was surprisingly brief. Only a minute or two went by before she huffed out of the bathroom with an expression that said she was close to throwing another tantrum.

"Not what you wanted to hear?" Riley asked, readying to apply pressure to the idea that Ryan was *not* a good man again. "I told you. Ryan has a short fuse. He—"

"He's waiting for us," Maria interrupted. Riley had misread that look of anger the woman had been wearing. She simply seemed annoyed now at the prospect of doing more work.

Riley's stomach tightened, nerves waking up again.

In the quiet of the hotel room, when Maria was minding her own business, it was easier to pretend everything was normal. Or, at least, everything wasn't life-and-death.

Maria pulled her pistol out.

"I'm going to untie you and then the same rules apply," she said. "Cute kid and single mom get their lives destroyed or you walk calmly to the car and get in. And before you start wondering what stops you from causing all hell when we're on the road, I just want you to know that I'm going to have backup again." A grin split her contoured face. "And this individual is highly motivated."

Maria stopped talking after that. She didn't untie Riley and Riley didn't feel like talking anymore either. Minutes that felt like hours went by until the sound of a car door shutting made both women turn their heads toward the curtain over the window.

Only one of them ran to it and peered out.

"Finally," Maria breathed.

She leaned against the wall next to the door until someone knocked.

Riley's heartbeat thundered in her chest.

If this wasn't Ryan, who was it?

The man in the suit again?

How was he highly motivated?

"It's about time something happened," Maria greeted after she let the man in. "I'll let you get her untied while I do a refresh on my makeup. Heaven knows this hotel air isn't doing it any favors."

Maria took her purse and disappeared into the bathroom, not bothering to even look at the woman she'd tied up.

Which was good, because Riley was having a hard time keeping her composure.

Evan Davies looked as guilty as sin as he crouched down in front of her. He didn't even flinch at the sight of her tied up.

"What are you doing here?" Riley bit out.

He eyed the first knot he'd been ordered to untie, refusing to meet her stare.

"I'm supposed to take you to meet Ryan."

If Riley's legs had been free she would have kicked him with every ounce of power she had.

"I can't believe this," she seethed. "I can't believe you'd—"

Davies moved in closer and dropped his voice into a whisper. Finally he met her gaze.

"We think Ryan wants to kill Jenna so he can get custody of Hartley and then his inheritance." Riley felt her eyes widen. He kept on. "Ryan has played everything smart enough that nothing will stick to him when this is all over." Davies glanced at the bathroom door. "Which is why Desmond wants to set a trap." At the mention of her cowboy's name, Riley couldn't help but feel relief. It must have shown. Davies's face softened. "If you don't want to we can get you out now, no problem, but if you do want to then you need to play along."

"I'm only in here because Maria has been threatening to kill the owner if I don't cooperate," Riley hurried. "I don't care about me—I just don't want anyone to get hurt."

"Don't worry—we'll have Maria covered. She won't hurt anyone if we do this."

Don't worry was a piece of advice that was hard to take when tied up in a motel room and given by a man who Riley absolutely did not trust anymore.

And maybe Davies realized that too.

"You don't believe in me—I get that," he said quickly. "But I *do* think you believe in him."

"You could be lying," she pointed out.

"Which is why I'm supposed to tell you that after this he said you two could enjoy PB&Js and watch *Wheel of Fortune*."

The sound of the toilet flushing followed by the sink turning on were the only noises that filled the room for a few moments.

Then Riley made a decision.

She didn't trust the man in front of her but she did trust Desmond.

"Okay," she said. "Let's get the bastard."

Chapter Nineteen

Riley hadn't been privy to Desmond's plan but now, less than an hour later, she knew without a doubt that every part of it had gone sideways. The rain had thoroughly soaked their clothes. Which was good, considering it had also washed away most of the blood. Still, the pain was there. It blanketed their bodies and made navigating through the trees even more difficult.

Riley clutched her side; Jenna ran with a heavy limp.

Both were panting from effort; neither was slowing down.

They couldn't. Not when he was still free.

"Ca-Caleb said it's around—around here?" Jenna huffed out.

They had made it to a stream. The trees overhead had thinned letting the rainstorm that had started at the absolutely worst time hit them with ease. Riley shielded her eyes and looked as far down the stream to the left as she could.

"Yeah. Two hundred yards or—or so."

Jenna grunted. She reached out for Riley's hand and they splashed through the water and onto the bank opposite. Then they were running along the tree line.

Riley's body hurt but it was her heart that had taken the biggest blow. The only reason she was as focused as she was on finding the vacation cabin had to do with the woman who was holding her hand.

If Ryan caught Jenna, he would kill her.

That had been made abundantly clear at the barn.

The gunfire and yelling still rang through her head.

Riley didn't know if she'd ever sleep again if that was the nightmare that might appear.

"There," Jenna yelled out. She tugged Riley so hard along with her that the pain in her side from falling temporarily redirected to her arm.

That's when Riley saw the rental, deeper within the trees.

It's a vacation rental. No one is there now, Caleb had hurriedly told them behind their cover. *Break in, hide and try your phones. Cell service there is spotty, though, so if there's no landline then regroup and head out when you think it's safe. Now go!*

The cabin was probably a sanctuary to those who rented it. Set between a mountain and the county road that led to town, and covered by trees, it was a large yet secluded escape. Which would have been nice had they been vacationing. As they ran up the stairs to the wraparound porch, the serenity was eerie.

Jenna went up to the back door. Riley took her hand and pulled her to, and then past, the front door. She went to one of the windows on the opposite side of the stream and out of view from the drive.

"If we're going to break in, let's do it somewhere kind of hidden."

Riley grabbed a bear figurine hanging out on the porch railing and readied to throw it through the glass.

Jenna grabbed her arm to stop her. Wordlessly she pressed her palms against the window and pushed up. The window didn't budge. It was locked. Riley raised her eyebrow at her sister. Jenna motioned to the window and stepped back.

"As you were."

The bear statue shattered the glass on the first throw. Jenna picked up one of the small wooden patio tables along the porch and used its legs to clear the rest of the bottom portion's glass away.

"Be careful," she warned as Riley ducked and went through.

Glass crunched under her shoes.

While she would never think of Maria in any good terms, she was thankful the woman had forced her to change before they'd walked into the motel room, even if it was into one of Maria's work outfits. Apparently walking around in slippers and Jenna's pajamas had been too suspicious even by her standards.

Now Riley was in a drenched blouse, pair of slacks and flats that were too small and bit at her toes.

Not that she was concerned about that minor annoyance at the moment.

"Try your phone," Riley said as soon as Jenna was inside. The room they'd come into was large, vaulted and furnished to the nines. Jenna pulled her phone out and dialed while Riley stepped back onto the glass to grab the curtains. She pulled them over the window hoping that it wouldn't make the broken window as noticeable from the outside.

"I have no bars here," Jenna said after a moment.

"Keep trying and look for a landline!"

Riley clutched at her side as the pain reminded her she'd been hurt and hurried to the back door. It was off a small hall at the rear of the kitchen, attached to the living area. She peeked out the window through the top half of the door. The rain had died way down and the sun was already starting to show again.

Riley hoped it stayed that way.

She was glad to see no one coming through the trees after them.

"I'm going upstairs to see if that helps," Jenna called. "There's no landline down here."

"Hurry!"

Riley didn't know where the stairs were but she heard Jenna pound up them.

Then she was alone.

Riley leaned against the door and fought the urge to squeeze her eyes closed and cry.

This was all a nightmare. Every second since Desmond had warned her someone was in his house. Sure, there had been hope within that nightmare. Hope that they'd catch Ryan so he wouldn't be able to weasel his way out of everything. Hope that he'd finally pay for what he'd done and spend the rest of his life behind bars.

That hope had only grown when Davies had taken them to the barn out on someone's—she still had no idea who that person was, though—property and there had been Desmond.

Even with Desmond on his knees, face bloodied and bruised and a gun pointed at him, Riley had felt that hope well in her chest at being near him.

Then that hope had turned hot. She'd been scared that Davies had lied.

That's when she'd realized who it was pointing the gun at him.

Julian Mercer had been dressed in a suit meant to impress and had looked absolutely terrifying.

Maria hadn't flinched in the slightest at the sight of him.

I have to admit, I'm more impressed with the men in suits for their sense of style rather than their cunning, she'd noted before they'd gotten out.

That's when Riley had really believed their plan might work. Maria had taken one look at the intimidating appearance of Desmond's brother-in-law and had assumed he was on her side, just as the man in the suit had been at Desmond's house earlier.

Just as she had trusted Davies wasn't lying to her.

But then...

Then Ryan had shown up.

And then everything had gone wrong.

Riley's vision started to blur. Jenna's footfalls coming down the stairs made her straighten again but there was no fooling her sister. Jenna's eyes softened, even as she gave the bad news.

"Caleb's right. I can't get any call out but I hit Send on texts to Dorothy's and Madi's phones. If we hit a pocket of service hopefully they'll go through. I never found a landline."

"Dorothy and Madi know you're here?"

Jenna looked guilty as all get-out.

"No. No one knew," she admitted. "I nearly gave Desmond a heart attack when I popped up in his back seat once we left the ranch."

Riley opened her mouth to scold her sister when Jenna moved directly in front of her.

It was the first time they'd had any chance to have a conversation since Maria and the man in the suit had come for her.

"I understand why you switched places with me. And now I need you to understand why I had to go out to that barn." She put her hand flat over her heart. They hadn't had a moment to talk about the plan or the barn they'd all found themselves at before everything wrong had happened. "Twin or not, you and Hartley are my heart. There's no me without you two. So there was no force on this earth that would keep me from trying to help take down the man who is trying to take you both. I love you, Riley Lee, but you're just plain stupid if you think I was going to sit this one out."

"What about Hartley?"

Jenna didn't waver in her resolve.

"He's with Madi. I may have let myself down when it came to my relationship with Ryan but I wasn't about to do the same for Hartley. When Desmond and Davies told me what he was most likely after, I convinced Madi to let me record a video on her phone just in case. I detailed everything Ryan ever did to me, how he'd never shown real love to Hartley and how in the event of my death and your death that his home would be with Mom and Dad. Madi swore if anything happened to us that the entire Nash family would make sure that wish was held up." She smiled. It was small. "And, I'll be honest, I believe that they would fight for us even though we're not technically family."

"Did you call Mom and Dad?" Riley asked, even though she knew the answer already.

Jenna shook her head.

"They'd be on the first flight out. If everything went sideways I didn't want them getting caught in the cross fire."

"Smart," Riley had to agree. "Especially since everything *did* go sideways."

Riley's vision started to blur again as tears rimmed her eyes. This time Jenna put her arms around her.

"He could still be okay," she tried to assure. "They all could still be alright."

But Riley heard the uncertainty in her statement.

Just as she heard the footsteps on the porch outside.

Riley turned to the window, hoping that just thinking about Desmond had conjured him.

Her heart broke all over again.

It wasn't Desmond. It wasn't Julian. It wasn't Caleb.

It wasn't even Davies or Maria.

It was Ryan Alcaster.

And he still had his gun.

"MADI IS GOING to be so pissed."

Caleb had lost too much blood. He was pale and it had nothing to do with how soaked they were from the rain or their jaunt in the river. Julian must have thought the same. He shared a worried look with Desmond after they had helped him from the water and into the trees.

The barn was in the distance, mocking them.

No one had followed them.

Then again, there had been little left to interpret after Ryan and the men with him had unloaded a barrage of bullets in their direction.

They all should have been dead.

They all *would* have been had they not been faster into the water.

Then again, not all of them had been fast enough.

Julian was bleeding heavily from the split in his head thanks to the fight he'd gotten into with one of the men who had come with Ryan. The crimson was a shock against Julian's tan skin and one of the reasons Desmond hadn't noticed that his own graze from earlier had opened and had bled through his shirt.

Neither wound could compare to Caleb's.

"Why is Madi going to be pissed?" Desmond asked, crouching next to his brother. Julian followed suit. He didn't ask for permission as he ripped open Caleb's pant leg.

"Because now she's the only Nash sibling who hasn't been shot."

Desmond hated seeing the bullet wound in Caleb's leg just as much as he'd hated hearing him yell out before they had jumped off the raised bank overhang and made it into the water. Julian, a former marine, was all analytical as he inspected it. His voice was nothing but calm when he spoke.

"And we're going to let her stay mad because that's never going to happen." He motioned to Desmond. "Give me your belt. I need to make a tourniquet or he's going to bleed out."

Desmond ripped his belt off and handed it over feeling the terrible weight of helplessness press against him. Caleb watched the move. Then he looked to the river.

"Remember when I fished Declan and Nina out of that river?" His voice was strained.

"It's about the only two things you can say you caught in there," Desmond replied, trying to smile. "Because you sure never caught any fish."

Caleb chuckled. Then he winced.

Julian adjusted the belt around his thigh.

"Hold him down."

Desmond didn't have to be told twice.

His brother let out a terrible cry of pain as Julian twisted the belt tight.

"He might pass out but that's okay," Julian warned.

"I'm still here, big guy," Caleb said.

Julian kept quiet as he kept turning. Desmond had his arm wrapped around Caleb's chest. Before he finished Desmond felt his body go limp.

"It's the pain," Julian answered his unspoken fear. "He's lost a lot of blood but this should help him remain stable for a bit. He needs medical attention now."

Julian pulled his phone out. It was wet.

"Let's see if this is actually waterproof like they claim."

Desmond patted his brother on the chest and slipped out from under him. He pointed to the trees behind them as Julian dialed.

"County 11 is a half mile that way. If you can walk him there it'll save the ambulance a lot of time getting back here."

Julian nodded, nonplussed at the idea of carrying a full-grown, unconscious man a half mile through the woods while soaking wet, hurt and in the rain. Then again, he was their very own gentle giant.

"You're going to the rental Caleb told the women about?" he asked, already putting the phone between his ear and shoulder and positioning himself to pick up Caleb.

"Yeah, and I'm not waiting for backup to get here." Julian snorted.

"If it was Madi, I wouldn't let some jerk like me tell me not to go." He gave Desmond a deep nod. "If you get the chance, take them out one by one. Stealth is strength's enemy when used right."

Whoever he called answered the phone and that was that. Julian threw Caleb over his shoulder like a rag doll and took off at a jog.

Desmond didn't waste any of his time either. He ran back to the river and followed it. The overhang of raised grass and dirt gave him cover until he was near the barn. He climbed up, slipping on the dirt turned to mud in the rain, and was met with the sight of bullet holes, abandoned vehicles and bodies.

If Desmond hadn't been part of the distraction that had allowed Riley and Jenna to disappear into the woods, he would have had ice in his stomach.

Instead, he walked past a man in slacks and a blazer who he didn't recognize lying motionless on the ground, Maria with her eyes open and staring up at the sky and Davies across from her.

Desmond only paused by the first man long enough to grab the gun at his feet.

The SUV Ryan and the three men had driven up in was still parked next to the road while they were nowhere to be found.

Which meant they must have followed Riley and Jenna into the woods.

Desmond took off running, limp be damned.

Chapter Twenty

Riley was so terrified and mad and frustrated, she didn't know which emotion to jump in and soak up. Instead she took a little of each.

"We should have grabbed one of the guns," she said at Jenna's ear as they hurried up the stairs that were tucked away at the opposite side of the living room. There was a loft lounge area that opened up to the front of the house and a hallway that branched off in both directions from it.

"I *did* have one but after Ryan shot Maria I just—" Jenna didn't finish the thought. While neither had been a fan of the woman, it had been absolutely horrible to watch the bullet hit her in the chest. And, perhaps even worse, the betrayal and pain that had crossed her face as she realized the man she loved had been the one to do it.

Not only had he pulled the trigger, he'd smiled.

It was an awful end for anyone.

Riley knew it would haunt her and Jenna for a long time to come.

That is, if the same madman didn't find them first.

"We need to hide," Riley said, choosing the hallway to the left.

"Hard to do when we're trailing water and mud," Jenna whispered.

Riley looked back the way they'd come.

She was right.

The rain had been light when Ryan had pulled up. After he'd shot Maria and his friends had surprised them the bottom had dropped out.

It had created more chaos that only made seeing what happened to the rest of their friends harder.

The gunshots, the yelling, the splintering of wood.

Then nothing but the rain.

Just as fast as it had come over them, it had started to ebb.

Now it was still managing to make everything worse. The runner along the hardwood floors on the second-floor landing had collected the water still coming off their hair, clothes and shoes. Hiding was going to be impossible.

"They're going to know exactly where we go."

"*If* they come inside."

"This is the only place for miles," Riley hissed back. "Of course they're going to come in."

A small puddle of water was already pooling around them as they spoke. Riley decided on a bad idea.

"Strip down," she hurried, already ripping open Maria's blouse and stepping out of her shoes. "They might find us but we're not going to make it easy."

Riley didn't know if Jenna would have agreed with the plan had a terrifying sound not floated up to them from the first floor.

Shattering glass.

Jenna's eyes widened.

Then her shirt was off in a flash.

STEALTH.

Not something any of the people Desmond was following had used.

From the bank of the stream all the way to the wraparound porch of the vacation rental, there were muddy footprints. It was a blessing and a concern all at the same time.

Following the men to stop them was made easier, sure, but based on two sets of smaller prints he saw every few feet, the women's footprints had been easy to follow too.

Desmond checked that the safety was off on the gun in his hand. He made sure it was loaded too. He'd never wanted to shoot anyone in his life and yet he'd already shot Geordi Green and, he believed, the man at the clearing. Caleb had shot one of the men who was with Ryan too.

At least, he hoped it was one of the bad guys because, mixed in with the mud, was a decent amount of blood.

He wasn't built like a house like Julian but if it was Riley or Jenna who was hurt, he was going to throw them over his shoulder and walk them to safety too.

No one was going to stop him.

Desmond slowed as he made it to the corner of the back side of the house. No footsteps were visible across the stones that led to the front.

Stealth was strength's enemy.

Solid advice from Julian.

Advice Desmond was going to take.

He kept low and hurried along the side of the raised porch. The rain had stopped. He strained to hear any movement inside.

Someone was talking. A man.

Desmond stopped, crouching next to the stairs that led to the front door, and firmly ignored the pain radiating up his leg. If he had to, he'd crawl his way to end this.

He slowed his breathing, felt the weight of the gun in his hand and peered around the wooden railing. The front door was open, the window at its side broken. Desmond could see movement through it.

At least one of the gunmen from earlier was inside the house.

Desmond readied himself, muscles and pain thrumming in anticipation, when a figure walked around the other side of the house.

It was the man in the suit who had taken Riley that morning from his house. Even soaked, his clothes were immaculate. It made the gun he had aimed at Desmond even more intimidating.

He pressed his finger to his lips.

Desmond was about to get to shooting bad guys earlier than intended when the man moved his hand to a stop motion. Then lowered his gun.

"We need to talk," he said, loud enough for Desmond to hear but not enough that the men inside came out.

Desmond pulled his gun up and aimed. He didn't shoot.

Part of him was ready to pull the trigger. The same part that had been hit hard enough to lose consciousness. The same part that had failed so that Riley could be taken from *his* house.

The other part wasn't as quick to jump the literal gun.

That part was reading the body language of the man and remembering how he'd kept Maria from shooting him or Riley.

That part was also quite aware that the man wasn't calm and collected as he had been in the house.

He was angry.

And it wasn't at Desmond.

"Slowly," he warned as the man kept low and made his way over. He stopped on the other side of the stairs. He made no move for his gun once there.

"Ryan Alcaster is in there with two of my guys," the man stated. Desmond hadn't read the man wrong. There was anger in his words.

"Anyone else?" Desmond ventured, fishing to see if he knew about the women.

"A set of twins who have a lot more spunk than I gave either credit for."

Desmond felt his jaw harden. His trigger finger was itching.

"Sounds like getting you out of the picture makes things a little easier for me then."

The man eyed the gun and then got down to business.

"I'm here to help even the playing field, not add to it."

Desmond snorted, glanced at the door and shook his head.

"I don't believe you."

That annoyed the man.

"Ryan Alcaster broke the terms of our agreement," he said with a growl. "The person I work for doesn't take that lightly."

"So what does that mean for him and the Stone sisters?" Desmond motioned between them. "You're just going to let me go in there and shoot your own people?"

The sun was back in the sky, uncovered by the clouds. It bathed the front half of the house next to them in light. It also gave Desmond the clearest view of the man he'd seen so far.

Tall, well built and custom tailored. His hair was on the longer side of short and well kept. There was no stubble above his lip or against his jaw. A youthfulness rang from his quick and fluid movements but there was an aged wariness that circled his eyes. They were dark gray, much like the cloud that had moved on with the storm.

Desmond didn't recognize him at all.

Not a hint. Not a whisper.

But then he saw the scar on his hand.

Suddenly Desmond was eight again.

The man who had taken them had had that same scar. An *X* on the skin between the knuckles of his thumb and index finger and his wrist. Such a small but memorable detail. One of the only details the triplets had remembered that had made their abductor stand out.

Caleb, especially, had been affected by that scar. He'd admitted to Desmond that it had taken him years until he stopped looking for that scar on every man he met.

Now here Desmond was seeing it for the first time since he was a terrified and hurt kid living a nightmare.

Yet the man with the same scar wasn't the same man.

But he sure enough recognized the connection Desmond had just made. He glanced at his hand and then used it to point to the house.

"The man you managed to shoot out near the barn was an idiot, but my other two men in there are not. They're good shots, which is why I'm assuming you and Mr. Mercer are still in good shape. Those two knew not to shoot you," he said. A flash of anger moved across his face, tensing a muscle in his forehead. "Ryan is the one who hit Caleb and that's exactly what broke the rules." He jabbed his index finger in the air again toward the house. "You can sit here and ask me questions. Then shoot me and try to go in there and put two highly trained men down and hope you can deal with the egotistical maniac before he kills your girl-friend and her sister *or* I can walk in there right now and make my men leave with me. But, either way, we're both running out of time. I know the cavalry is on their way and Ryan has been in that house for at least two minutes."

He dropped his hand to his side again. Desmond watched as the scar shaped like an *X* went with it.

"So what will it be, Desmond? Me or the redheads?"

The Nash triplet abduction had consumed every part of the Nash family's lives since that interrupted game of hide-and-seek all those years ago. He'd given Riley his version of what had happened and how it had affected him but he hadn't told her everything.

He hadn't told her how it had cracked a marriage that should have withstood decades.

He hadn't told her how it had taken a good, honest man and made him lose faith in the world around him, seeing ghosts where there were none and creating his own personal demons that eventually saw to the end of him.

He hadn't told her how it had convinced Declan he was somehow responsible and in turn put him in a profession that held nothing but responsibility to everyone but himself, making a happy boy ready for the future into a man who toed the line between justice and obsession as their father had.

He hadn't told her how it had created a rage within Madi. One that had burned so hot that an invisible ring of fire had kept anyone and everyone away from her for years, driving her slowly into self-imposed isolation.

He hadn't told her that, while Caleb had tried his best to live a happier life, he'd subconsciously marched right into his father's old one, hell-bent on finding the answer to every mystery no matter the cost.

He hadn't told her that the real reason he had gone into business in the beginning was to make enough money so that he could buy the world. Buy *their* world. The one in which the story of the Nash family abduction was common knowledge. The one that they'd all never really left. And, only then, have every tool imaginable to find out the truth of what happened.

Because, one thing the Nash triplets and Declan hadn't told anyone was that they were all still waiting for the second shoe to drop.

They were all still those scared children, at least in part, and probably always would be. At least, until they found the man who took them.

The man with the scar on his hand.

He hadn't told Riley any of this but, in that moment, staring at the first clue they'd had in over a decade, Desmond realized he'd already planned to tell her one day.

In the future. In *their* future.

So, there wasn't an option. Not really. Not for Desmond.

He looked the man in the suit in the eyes and had never been more sure in his decision than he was now.

"I choose the redheads."

There was surprise in the man's expression but he didn't waste any more time talking. He stood, kept his gun down and walked up the stairs. Desmond followed, a firm grip on his own weapon. They walked right through the open front door like they were ready to start their vacation.

A man wearing a black blazer spun to face them. Desmond worried he'd made a mistake at the sight of his gun. Yet the second his eyes settled on the man in the suit, he lowered it.

Another man, dressed nicely as well, walked from the back of the room with widened eyes.

"We're leaving," the man in the suit said to both of them. His voice carried despite his lowered tone. Desmond glanced around to see if Ryan was there.

He wasn't.

He also wasn't in the loft space on the second floor.

It made his gut twist.

"He wasn't supposed to shoot anyone," the man said, coming closer. He looked like a scared child tattling on another child to avoid getting into trouble. "We told him not to but he hit one of them."

The man in the suit nodded.

"Which is why we're leaving. Now."

The lackey kept his eyes widened but didn't complain. He was out the front door in a flash. As the one in the blazer went to follow, Desmond stopped him.

"Where are the women?"

The man looked at his boss who gave a quick nod.

"Hiding somewhere in here. Alcaster has been cussing going through the rooms."

Desmond didn't dare feel relief. Not until he could see Riley. *Touch* her. Know she was safe.

The man followed his friend out. His boss hung back a second.

"We both know that the only way to stop a man like Alcaster from coming back is to kill him."

Then he left too.

Chapter Twenty-One

Their plan had been simple.

Two of the bedrooms upstairs were connected by a Jack-and-Jill bathroom. When Ryan and his unmerry men came into the first bedroom Riley and Jenna would be listening at the bathroom and then fall back to the other bedroom and slip out into the hallway and leave.

If the men split up and searched the bedrooms at the same time, they'd use the bathroom to hide.

If the men decided to search the bathroom at the same time, effectively cutting off their options for escape, while they were hiding in it?

Well, they were screwed.

A simple plan with a simple conclusion.

But, it wasn't like Riley or Jenna had many options. Once they'd stripped down to their underwear—with Riley thanking every god that might exist that she'd put her panties and bra back on after she'd showered with Desmond, scared that his mother would somehow show up again—and thrown the clothes and shoes out of view in the corner of the loft, they'd barely had the time to slip into the first bedroom.

Considering the jump from the second story to the ground was too high, there were no roof overhangs, and no weapons, makeshift or otherwise, unless you counted pillows with embroidered sunsets and a myriad of white linen towels, they weren't escaping or fighting their way out. At least not with any good odds in their favor. So, they'd taken to their simple yet extremely easy-to-foil plan with vigor.

Which was why they were presently in the room farthest from the loft, Riley with her ear to the bathroom door and Jenna with her ear to the hallway door. For what felt like hours neither did so much as breathe.

Then Jenna started to point wildly at her door.

She hurriedly went to Riley and together, as quietly as they could, they slipped into the bathroom.

Riley's heart was in her throat and she closed the door behind them. Unlike the bedroom doors, these locked. That didn't mean anything when it came to bullets but it would slow them down. Riley twisted the lock and they hurried through the next door.

Then they were standing in the other bedroom.

When Ryan started laughing from just inside the bedroom door, gun aimed at them, they didn't even have time to scream.

"Move and I shoot one of you," Ryan announced around his smile. "I don't care which at this point so may that keep the other one of you from doing anything dumb for fear of me taking out your beloved twin."

Riley was prepared to angle herself in front of Jenna when Jenna instead pushed against her shoulder. It was a subtle move that meant she didn't want Riley to do exactly what she was going to do.

Ryan motioned to the door they'd just come through and laughed again.

"By the way, that little attempt at a trick to get past me was what you used to do with Hartley when you played hide-and-seek." He surprised Riley by addressing Jenna without hesitation. That shock must have shown. He glanced down at Riley's thigh. "And may I take a moment to say thank you for your impulsiveness. It makes telling you two apart much easier."

Riley had never in her life been so mad at herself for getting a tattoo. She didn't have time to bask in that anger for too long.

Ryan was a talkative man. He was used to walking into a room and commanding it. Just as he had thought he should be able to command a wife. Even now, in such an intense situation that was so far from a boardroom or cocktail party, he was raring to capture their attention.

To be entertaining.

To talk.

To hear his own voice.

Riley couldn't believe she'd ever thought any nice thing about the man. She'd once called him handsome with his thick, dark hair, sharp facial features and jade-green eyes. She'd once been impressed with his unwavering confidence and smarts. She'd once been enamored at how wonderfully he'd treated her sister.

Now every opinion had twisted into the *thing* that stood no more than a few feet from them.

"I have to say, the last few weeks have been a bit of a headache. Who knew either of you had it in you to be so much of an obstacle. I certainly didn't." He shook his head. "Do you know how much I've had to pay just to make it all look like Maria went insane? A lot of money. More than either one of you is worth, I can tell you that."

"You wanted to kill me and blame it on your mistress?"

Jenna's voice bit as she asked the question. Ryan's smile moved into a smirk.

"Oh no, my darling Jenna, that was plan C." He looked at Riley. "Thanks to this one switching places with you *and* Brett's idiocy, I had to make a new contract with my nicely dressed friends. But then, when you weren't busy messing everything up, your poor, lovesick ex-husband had to try to sabotage me." He snorted. "Davies was a good guy but he's never had the strength to know his place about the likes of you. Even after you abandoned him he still ran after you like some whipped little pup. Disgusting, if you ask me."

"So you manipulated Maria to go right where you wanted her to be," Riley guessed.

He nodded.

"Maria had many assets I'll be sad to lose but one I appreciated the most was her willingness to listen to what I had to say without question." He cut his eyes to Jenna. "A trait we both know you never possessed."

Riley grabbed Jenna's arm. It was more to keep her from springing forward and wiping the smugness from the man they both once thought they knew. Just as it was also to keep Riley from doing the same. If they attacked him when he was so close, there was no doubt in her mind that he'd shoot at least one of them.

And Riley couldn't be sure it wouldn't be Jenna. Just as she was sure Jenna knew the bullet might hit Riley.

It was the perfect way to keep them both in line.

"So what was the plan? Your girlfriend goes crazy, terrorizes your ex-wife and kills a bunch of people?" Riley asked.

"That was the idea. Until that pathetic puppy Davies decided to team up with the most annoying family in the world."

"But then you shot him and Maria."

Riley replayed the scene in her head again. It still made her stomach knot.

Ryan had gotten out to talk to Maria, Julian and Desmond who was playing the part of captive. The plan, as far as Riley could tell, had been to catch the man in the act of issuing the deaths of Jenna and Desmond in front of Julian, Davies and Caleb, who was lurking behind the cars.

But then Ryan had shocked them all by shooting the two people who had been and pretended to be on his side.

If Jenna hadn't have sprung out and pulled Riley aside in time, he would have ended her too.

"There were too many players in the game," Ryan replied. "So I shelled out some more money to get more of a team willing to play for me and started to clean shop. My girlfriend killing my ex and your ex killing you *and* your new lover? Honestly, that would have been perfect. But this story is still writing itself. Between Maria and Davies? I can just switch their roles. Either way it's all about exes killing exes. And who doesn't like a story about that?"

He looked around the room.

"It doesn't matter where the end of it happens. I'm untouchable. And I'll be even more so when my son is back in my custody."

Riley tightened her grip on Jenna.

"You're insane if you think you'll ever get him," she roared, maternal glory coming to the forefront. "Once again your hubris has fooled you into thinking that you're a god when you're not even a man."

Rage, the kind he used to hide behind closed doors, flashed across Ryan's face. His hand tightened on the gun.

"Listen here you little—"

"Move and I'll shoot."

Riley's very own cowboy moved into the room behind Ryan with gun raised and face made of stone.

Riley dropped her hold on Jenna's arm only for Jenna to grab her hand. She squeezed it as Desmond issued his command again.

Ryan's anger at Jenna smoothed away.

It was alarming.

"I'm assuming by Riley's reaction that Desmond Nash is behind me?"

Desmond didn't take his eyes off the back of Ryan's head.

"All you need to know is I'll have no problem shooting you if it means saving them." His baritone was thrumming with authority. The sound wrapped around Riley like an invisible safety blanket.

Ryan started to smirk. His gun was still raised. Now it was pointed at Riley.

"If you shoot me this close to them, I'm afraid your bullet would find a second, unwanted target. The women would need to move. *But* the second they do I'll shoot and then *you'll* shoot and that will probably just kill whichever twin I didn't. You see, it's all just a mess that starts and ends with you trying to save them."

Ryan was right. They were too close. It was too much of a risk. Desmond finally met her eye. The smallest pinch of warmth spread at the fact he looked at her and stayed looking at her. Riley believed then that the world could be ending around them and Desmond would still be able to know which sister she was.

"That silence you hear? That's the sound of an impasse," Ryan added.

Desmond tilted his head to the left. Jenna squeezed her hand. Whether it was a bond created because they were twins, best friends, or just two half-naked women in a bad situation trying to make it out alive, Riley knew exactly what the Stone sisters were about to do.

She gave the smallest of nods to Desmond.

It did not go unnoticed.

"It looks like I've found the sister I'm—" Ryan started.

Desmond didn't let him finish.

Riley lunged to the left as Jenna lunged in sync to the right.

However, the gunshot that sounded afterward was followed by glass shattering and not by Ryan in pain.

RILEY SCRAMBLED INTO the open bathroom and spun around to see Jenna throw herself over the bed. Another gunshot went off and exploded into the wall next to the newly broken window.

The sound of a scuffle ensued.

Riley backpedaled and turned toward the other door. She unlocked it and hightailed it through the adjoining bedroom and back out into the hall.

Just in time to see Desmond and Ryan tumble into the hallway.

"Run," Desmond yelled out as he grabbed Ryan's arm.

Riley's stomach turned to ice as she realized he still had his gun but Desmond didn't. When Ryan saw her he kicked out of Desmond's grip like a bucking bronco.

One second went by where Ryan was completely free.

It was all the time he needed to take aim at Riley and pull the trigger.

Riley closed her eyes on reflex, waiting for the pain.

She thought about her sister and parents and Hartley. About the Nash family, Marty McLinnon, and she even thought about Davies.

The last person who flashed in her mind's eye, however, was the most detailed of all.

Desmond Nash in his cowboy hat, giving her that charming smile that made her stomach flutter.

Riley waited for her end but, after a moment, felt nothing but the chill of being half-naked and wet.

She opened her eyes, confused.

"No!"

Desmond dropped to the floor with a sickening *thud*.

"No!"

Riley lost every sense of self-preservation she had and ran right at her former brother-in-law. When he raised his gun again at her, she didn't even flinch.

When he pulled the trigger and the sound of an empty chamber sang through the hallway, she didn't slow down either.

When Jenna came out in the hallway behind Riley with

Desmond's gun in her hand and shot over her sister's shoulder, Riley didn't miss a beat.

Ryan yelled out in shock and ducked into the first bedroom he'd surprised them in earlier. Riley made it to Desmond's side and crouched, tears already in her eyes.

She rolled him over, forgetting about the world around them.

Baby blues stared up at her. His expression was pained but he was alive.

"Pistol in—in my ankle holster," he hurried, wheezing in the middle. "Get—get him."

Getting Ryan had, up until that point, been about saving her sister and her nephew. Now it was for Desmond too.

Rejuvenated by his request, Riley found his ankle holster and took the small pistol out of it. She turned around and met Jenna's wide eyes.

They didn't need to say anything out loud.

Moving in sync once again they ran into the bedrooms that were next to them and then right up to the opened bathroom doors.

Ryan Alcaster was caught between them, standing next to the tub without any options left.

He looked from one sister with a gun pointing at him to the other sister with a gun pointing at him.

His face, his confidence, his ego came crashing down.

When Jenna spoke she did so with a wonderful amount of sass.

"What's wrong, dear? Are you seeing double?"

The real Ryan, the nasty, manipulative and abusive Ryan, opened his mouth to say something. Then he decided against it. Lost for words.

"You know, I was really hoping *someone* would say something clever and twin-related."

Desmond's weight pressed around her as he leaned between her and the door frame. He took the gun from her hand as she examined his chest.

The bullet had torn through his shirt yet there was no blood.

"What?" was all she could manage to ask.

Desmond smiled.

"We might not have included Declan in our plan just in case everything went wrong but that didn't mean we walked in unprepared." Riley took a closer look at his shirt. There was something black against his chest.

"You're wearing a bulletproof vest," Jenna exclaimed.

He gave her a scolding look.

"We all were and *you would have been wearing one too* had we known you were coming."

Riley couldn't help but throw her arms around the man. He didn't drop the gun but he did groan.

"I'm pretty sure some ribs are broken so watch out."

Riley immediately let go.

"You took another bullet for us," Riley realized.

Desmond's face softened.

"And I would have done it without the vest in a heartbeat too."

Ryan made an annoyed noise.

Desmond was back to angry.

"And you are going to go away for a very, very long time," he said.

Ryan actually laughed. It wasn't as powerful as when he had the upper hand.

"People like me don't go away," he said. "Not when money talks a more convincing game."

This time Desmond was the one to laugh.

"You know, my brother and I talked about that. About you and your money and your seemingly unending influence over people ready to do your bidding. Riley, can you reach into my pocket and pull out my cell phone?"

Riley obliged, confused.

Until she saw what was on the screen.

"So before we left for the barn all of us cleared our phones and started to hit Record the second you pulled up. And the best part about the app we used? It doesn't need service or internet to keep working. Riley, is it still going?"

"Yes. It is."

Jenna made a noise. Tears were falling down her cheeks.

They had him.

They had Ryan.

And he knew it.

He didn't say another word.

Desmond, however, had to get in one last jab.

"You gotta love technology, huh?"

Epilogue

"Desmond?"

The house was quiet. Riley stared at the bed, her stomach knotted.

"Desmond?" she tried again, raising her voice.

This time his baritone made its way up the stairs to her.

"I don't know what she's wearing yet! She hasn't gotten out of the car!"

Riley shook her head and focused on the different outfits spread out on the cowboy's bed. The first outfit was casual but put-together, jeans and a button-down. The last outfit was a finely pressed, stylish blouse and pencil skirt. There were three cowgirl hats in different colors sitting on the pillows, courtesy of the Nash downstairs.

Riley tapped her bare foot against the rug. The AC she'd been praising for the last month was now making her cold. Then again, she *was* standing in her underwear beneath a vent.

It was now June in Overlook and summer had more than made its way to town. In the five months between Ryan being arrested and now, a lot had changed.

And a lot hadn't.

Like that flutter that danced in her stomach when Desmond smiled, even when she just heard it in his voice from the other room.

"Outfit number two," he yelled after another moment. "Outfit number two!"

Riley heard this as the man ran up the stairs and into his bedroom. Or what would be theirs starting next week after they finished moving the last of her stuff in. Bless the man, he was good at so many things, but when it came to moving her book collection and winter clothes he'd gotten right near grumpy. It probably hadn't helped that Jenna had stopped him countless times to open the box he was carrying and steal out an item or two.

"She's wearing dark jeans and a frilly top," Desmond said almost out of breath. He motioned to his shirt. "You know, kind of like that one you wore last week when we went to the Red Oak with Marty and his husband."

Riley nodded, touched Desmond always remembered the details, and shimmied into a pair of nice jeans and one of Jenna's red blouses that *she'd* managed to steal when Jenna was stealing from her.

"Was she wearing flats or—"

"Cowboy boots."

Riley ran to the closet and pulled out a pair Madi had gifted to her for her birthday. Jenna had gotten a matching pair and she and Riley, in the privacy of Jenna's room, had put them on and danced around in them while yelling "Yeehaw." Their mother, who had flown in with their dad to celebrate the twins' birthday, had insisted on buying her own pair too. Hartley, naturally, already had a pair.

"Okay, how do I look?" Riley asked, spinning around when she was done.

She was met with *that* smile. One that often preceded both of them having a very good time.

"You said I can't call you perfect because it doesn't exist but I just can't find another word." He closed the distance between them and dipped her down for a brief but powerful kiss. She laughed against him and then struggled to regain her composure.

"But does it say, *Hire me to manage your social media and website because I've got great ideas, the know-how, and work with my brilliant designer sister*?"

Desmond laughed. The doorbell rang.

"Claire already hired you, babe," he pointed out. "And she asked to come here just to talk about some ideas. You don't need to worry."

Riley let out a long breath.

"I know but, well, sometimes I can't help it."

Desmond swung low again and kissed her. Then he was headed for the door in a rush.

"If you really want to impress her, wear the gray Stetson," he called over his shoulder. "You know, the one that makes me *wild*!"

Riley couldn't help but laugh at that. She waited a beat, looked at her reflection over the dresser with an encouraging nod to herself and followed the same steps the man she loved had just taken.

But only after she grabbed the cowgirl hat.

THE BREEZE WAS NICE and so was the company.

Desmond sat atop Winona as she walked back toward the stables in the distance. Declan, on his horse Rocky, matched their pace next to them.

They'd ridden the ranch's fence perimeter together in companionable silence but now it felt like time to talk. While both men enjoyed riding as a solo adventure most of the time, there was just something to be said about enjoying it with family.

"I saw Claire pull up to the house earlier," Declan started in. "Ma said she's Riley's newest client?"

Desmond nodded, proud.

"Yep. Her third so far in Overlook, actually. Apparently

our small town is great at word of mouth but not so great at marketing on the internet. After the work she and Jenna have done with Second Wind, it's been a no-brainer for people to hire them."

"I'm glad they're doing what they love too. It sure makes a difference. I ran into Jenna at the store earlier and she practically was lighting the place up with how much she was smiling."

Desmond nodded in agreement.

Jenna had completely broken down in relief when Declan and his deputies had arrived at the vacation rental after both women had stopped Ryan from fleeing. The recording, plus eyewitnesses of what had happened at the barn, had been enough to send Ryan to prison for life. There was no way he'd ever get out and there was no way he'd ever get Hartley.

That fact, plus being surrounded by people who genuinely cared for and respected her, had finally allowed her to start healing from Ryan's abuse.

In turn, an invisible weight had seemed to lift from Riley too. It was helped by her finally getting some closure she said she hadn't realized she'd needed from Davies. While Ryan had killed Maria, Davies had survived his wounds. Riley had stayed with him at the hospital until his sister had arrived. Before then he'd finally apologized for his silence about Ryan and Jenna. He'd even told what he knew of the abuse on the stand at the trial against Ryan. It had been another nail in the businessman's coffin.

After that, life in Overlook had gone back to as normal as it ever got. Caleb started physical therapy and had improved to almost new. Nina and he had made it no secret how thankful they were for what Julian had done to save him, and when they announced that Nina was pregnant with a baby boy, they also announced that the boy's middle name would match the man who had saved his father.

Julian, the mountain of the man he was, had teared up at the honor. Madi had all but cried.

Between the barn incident and now, Desmond had spent his time making sure the red-haired siren had known he had fallen for her hook, line and sinker. Riley moving in was only the beginning.

What she didn't know, but her father did, was that Desmond was already planning on popping the question.

He intended on talking to Jenna about it later that night after dinner. Because, if there was one thing he knew about the sisters with absolute certainty, it was that you didn't get one without the other.

Desmond actually loved that about them because it was exactly how he felt when it came to his family.

As for his big brother, riding next to him with the obvious weight of the world on his shoulders, Desmond was a little worried. Everyone was getting their happy endings while Declan was only getting more and more into his work.

Even now, with the sun shining and the breeze blowing, there was something he was holding on to that Desmond couldn't see.

So, he asked.

"You know, I think you've looked worried since the day we got Ryan Alcaster. What's wrong? We got the bad guy."

Declan didn't bother denying the accusation.

"We got Ryan, Maria and *a* man in a suit. But we didn't get *the* man, did we?"

It was true. The man Desmond had shot outside the barn had succumbed to his injuries, and with his death whatever secrets he had were also gone. They'd never been able to ID him. The man with the scar on his hand had also disappeared. There had been no trace of him at all.

Declan had said he wasn't actively looking anymore.

Desmond suspected that was a lie.

His older brother let out a long sigh.

"It's just that every time we think we're getting back to normal around here something *bizarre* happens. How much bad luck can we have before it stops being bad luck and becomes a pattern?"

"We also deal with danger in our everyday careers, even by proxy, more than most," Desmond pointed out. "You and Caleb *are* in law enforcement after all."

Declan conceded but with a slight caveat.

"And I could stomach that, and even chalk up the man in the suit not wanting to kill any of the Nashes because of the spotlight it could be on them as a group, if it wasn't for the man at the bar."

Desmond had to think on that.

Declan explained before he could figure it out.

"When we caught who had targeted Nina and Caleb, they said a man at the bar gave them the idea to do it. When Madi was targeted, the idea was also from a man in a bar." Desmond felt the tightness of realization and worry zip through him.

"And Ryan Alcaster said at his trial that a stranger in a bar gave him the idea to use his girlfriend to get back at his ex-wife," he finished.

Declan nodded, brow creased in a thought he didn't particular like.

"One mention of a man in a bar I can let roll off my shoulders. Two mentions of a man in a bar is a coincidence that makes me pause, but three?"

"What are you thinking?"

"I'm thinking it feels like someone is pulling a set of strings we can't see," he said. "Like someone is three steps away from taking out our king while we're just now figuring out we're even pieces on a game board." He rolled his shoulders back and patted Rocky. They were almost to the stables. "Caleb first, Madi second and now you."

Neither man voiced it, but if there was a pattern, it meant that Declan could be next. A thought that darkened the mood even further.

"It *could* be nothing," Desmond tried. "I think it's easy for this family to feel targeted, to feel attacked. It could very well be the professions and life choices we've made because of the abduction. They've put us all in danger at one time or another. You could be borrowing trouble that's not ours."

Declan nodded; again it was a slow one. One filled to the brim with questions that Desmond knew his big brother would still try to answer. But, for now, he seemed to brush off the concern. He tried on a smile. It didn't reach his eyes but it was something.

"I think I might just need a break," he admitted. "I'm starting to lose myself in the job. Even I can see that. I'm starting to copy Dad's habits, the not-good kind. It might be time for a vacation. If only to recharge."

"I think that would be a great idea."

Movement pulled their attention over to the fence next to the stable. Someone was standing on it and smiling back at him. Just like his father once had.

This time it was a different kind of love Desmond felt. One that burrowed into his bones, into his heart and into his soul. His future wife. The mother of their future children. The woman he was ready to spend the rest of his life with.

A mass of dark red curls flew around Riley's head as she waved.

Desmond waved back, unable to not smile.

"I guess their meeting went okay," he said. "Which means I'm on the hook to take her out to Red Oak for a celebratory drink or two tonight."

Not that he minded at all.

Desmond turned back to his brother. Declan was smiling.

"You know another way to help keep the stress off?" Desmond couldn't help but ask. "Finally find someone who keeps that scowl off your face. At the very least I think it's safe to say that, if you have to borrow trouble, having someone by your side sure does help keep you sane."

Declan snorted.

"I might take a short break from work but I don't think I have time for all of that."

Desmond threw his head back in laughter, really feeling it in his heart. He reached over between their horses and managed to clap his brother on the shoulder.

When Desmond spoke again, he might have been staring at Declan, but all he could see was his very own siren.

"When you find the right one, you'll make the time."

He tipped his cowboy hat to his brother and felt the thrill of riding take over as he and Winona started to gallop.

He could already hear Riley laughing before he ever got to the fence.

* * * * *

COMING SOON!

We really hope you enjoyed reading this book.
If you're looking for more romance, be sure to
head to the shops when new books are
available on

Thursday 6th August

LET'S TALK
Romance

For exclusive extracts, competitions
and special offers, find us online:

- f facebook.com/millsandboon
- 🐦 @MillsandBoon
- 📷 @MillsandBoonUK

Get in touch on 01413 063232

For all the latest titles coming soon, visit
millsandboon.co.uk/nextmonth

MILLS & BOON

MODERN

Power and Passion

Prepare to be swept off your feet by sophisticated, sexy and seductive heroes, in some of the world's most glamourous and romantic locations, where power and passion collide.

Sensual love stories featuring smart, sassy heroines you'd want as a best friend, and compelling intense heroes who are worthy of them.

MILLS & BOON
True Love
Romance from the Heart

Celebrate true love with tender stories of
heartfelt romance, from the rush of falling
in love to the joy a new baby can bring,
and a focus on the emotional
heart of a relationship.